EXTREME COURAGE

X-TREME LOVE SERIES
BOOK 6

KAY MANIS

To those who battle the demons within. May you find peace.

～

Where there is no struggle, there is no strength.
- Oprah Winfrey

～

CHAPTER 1
GENEVA

EVERYONE STOOD AROUND THE CAKE, our voices singing out the familiar song, "Happy Birthday to You," only the words to this rendition were a little different. Dana's idea.

"Happy gotcha day to you," we sang. "Happy gotcha day to you…happy gotcha day dear Lucas, Levi and Lilly…happy gotcha day to you."

The adoption of Dana and Peter's children had been finalized the day before. The couple planned what they called a "Gotcha Day" party. Better than a birthday party because, as Dana explained to the kids, she and Peter *chose* them.

I scanned the room that was filled with all the people I loved in life. Dana and Peter's faces were beaming with pride as they held the kids in their arms and helped them blow out all twenty-one candles, their combined ages.

Peter's sister Tori glided up next to me. She'd graduated college in California and had received her first field assignment as an environmental studies analyst, but the job didn't start for a few more months. I knew she wanted to stay in Austin to be closer to her family so I'd invited her to move in with me. Although most of the time she spent the night with Dana, Peter and the kids in their new home.

"What's shaking, bean pole?" She nudged my hip.

I glanced down at my body, laughing out loud. "I would hardly call *this* body a bean pole. Especially now." I touched my stomach.

"I'm not talking to you." She bent at the waist so that her face was level with my now distended belly. "I'm talking to my little nugget in here." She rubbed on my stomach. "Oh my God." Tori jumped back.

I laughed at her reaction.

"He just kicked me!"

"I know." I smiled, rubbing the spot where her hand had been. "He already likes tall blondes."

Tori snorted. "That is just the coolest thing."

"What is?" Hindley asked, stepping beside me and handing me a glass of punch.

"Oh, thank you. I'm always so thirsty." I took the cup and downed half its contents in one gulp.

"Yeah, me, too," Hindley said. "Rory got so freaked out, thinking I was dehydrated again the other day, that he rushed me to the doctor. With no appointment." She rolled her eyes and huffed.

Tori and I couldn't hold in our laughter. I'd always known Rory was protective over Hindley, but when it came to his daughters, even the unborn one, he was fiercely defensive.

"I was so embarrassed." Hindley shook her head.

"Ah, it's kind of sweet, though, Hindley," Tori said. "At least you know he's super worried about you."

"It's borderline crazy actually," Hindley said.

"Does that really surprise you?" I asked.

She shook her head.

"Just enjoy it." I smiled, trying to suppress my natural tendency to be jealous of her. "It's nice to have someone care about what happens to you and your baby." My hand involuntarily rubbed my stomach. One of my greatest fears was fast approaching—becoming a single mom. Well, becoming a mom at all had completely freaked me.

"Has she told you yet?" Dana asked, joining our circle of friends. She leaned in and looked from right to left as if she were the quarterback taking us into a secret huddle.

"Told who what?" Hindley asked.

"Have you told them who the father is?" Dana's arctic blue eyes stared at me. Most times, Dana's frankness was refreshing given the sea of fake friends I'd once had. Today, it was a nightmare.

They all assumed it was Berk, my week-long affair in Hawaii five months ago. I'd never confirmed it. I hadn't denied it either. They were smart girls, though, they knew. But I didn't want to admit my mistake to them—or him. He was in love with another woman and I did *not* need that kind of drama in my life. I could and would do this on my own.

"No," Tori sighed.

"What's the big deal anyway?" I asked.

"Just admit it's him," Dana said.

"Leave her alone, Dana. If she doesn't want to say then that's her decision," Hindley said. "It's not like we're in the 1950s and she has to get married or something."

"Yeah," Tori piped in, "it's totally kosher to be pregnant and unwed and not committed nowadays."

Tori and Hindley were trying to make me feel better and support my decision to have this baby on my own, but their words were reminders that I was just that—on my own. And it scared the ever-loving shit out of me. I had no experience, and no business being anyone's mother, especially on my own.

"Hey," Hindley brushed my arm, "you're gonna be fine, Geneva. I promise."

Tears burned my eyes, but I refused to lose control of my emotions. Oh, who the fuck was I kidding. I was pregnant, of course

I had no control over my emotions, my eating habits, or my bathroom needs.

I'd changed a lot over the years, but this mushy-feely shit was still all new to me, and I hated losing control in front of anyone. Even if it was in front of three women who'd come to mean the world to me.

"I need to go pee," I blurted out.

I pushed through the girls and bumped through the crowd of people gathered for the party as I made my way through Dana and Peter's new house. Everyone we all loved was in attendance—Leif and his parents, my parents, Peter's mom and her new husband, along with several of Peter's brothers. I had support, I knew that. But in the end, it would just be me and my little peanut.

"Geneva, isn't that the guy you were with in Hawaii?" Leif called from behind me.

My heart seized at the mention of Hawaii. I gazed over my shoulder and saw him pointing to the wide screen TV where all the men were now huddled. My breath caught and I gasped at the face that appeared on the screen.

Berk Rigby. My seven-day Hawaiian fling.

He looked different. His long hair that had once hung to his shoulders was now clipped short, almost like he was in the military. His caramel-colored eyes were recognizable, but they were narrowed in a menacing glare as he stood atop some type of mountain.

"What the—" I whispered.

Every eye turned to me. I'd hoped my statement was quieter, but apparently it wasn't.

"What's he doing?" I asked, rooted in place despite my bladder's urging.

"It's the winter X Games," Rory explained. "I knew that guy looked familiar in Hawaii, but I had no idea he was Berk Rigby. *The* Berk Rigby."

"That's insane that it was him and we didn't even snap," Leif said.

"Why?" I asked, moving closer to the television.

"You don't know his story?" Peter looked over his shoulder at me.

"It's just awful," Leif's father, Jack, commented.

"What happened?" Before I realized it, I'd made my way to the sofa and was sitting on the arm, staring at Berk, my mouth gaping. He was still just as beautiful as I'd remembered.

"He lost his family—his wife and daughter—in a tragic accident," Rory said.

"Daughter?" I shouted.

"You didn't know he had a daughter?" All the men jerked their heads toward me and spoke in unison.

I covered my mouth with my hand and shook my head. I knew Berk had been married but a daughter? He'd never told me.

"Yeah, it was a horrible accident. Apparently, their deaths destroyed him," Rory said.

"Well, they *say* it was an accident," Leif added.

The television show flashed pictures of a woman and a small girl. I assumed they were Berk's wife and daughter. My breath caught at the sight of his wife. She looked a lot like the woman Berk had been talking to when I'd left Hawaii.

"*I love you, Berk,*" the woman had said just outside his home. She looked so much like Berk's late wife, they had to be related. Of course, she loved him. They were family. Shit! What had I done?

"Turn it up." I pointed to the television.

"…and some of you may remember the story. Berk's three-year-old daughter drowned in the lake near their home three years ago,*" the commentator said.

"Oh my God," I gasped.

"Jeez," Hindley whispered behind me, her arm now draped over my shoulder.

I couldn't bear to look at Hindley, or any of them. If I did, I'd lose all control. Instead, I focused my attention on the program.

"One month later, police found Berk's wife Jaime drowned in the same lake," the commentator continued.

My breathing grew shallow as my heart slammed hard against my chest.

"Although Jaime Rigby's death was officially ruled an accident, there has been speculation," the announcer said. "Berk escaped to his home in Hawaii for several years, but now he's back here in Aspen at this year's winter X Games, skiing better than ever." The commentator's voice sounded so upbeat, as if the story he'd just revealed hadn't destroyed a man's life.

"I wonder what brought him back, Steve?" another commentator asked.

I thought I might vomit. I glanced up at Hindley, tears now pooling in my eyes. I didn't have to say a word.

She wrapped her hand around mine and tugged me down the hallway, shoving me into the bathroom and slamming the door shut.

"Oh my God, Geneva. It *is* Berk, isn't it? Berk's the father of your baby?"

Tears streamed down my face as I worked to quiet the sobs now threatening. All I could do was nod my head.

"Oh, Geneva." She wrapped me in her arms, and this time I took the comfort she was willing to provide.

"What the fuck!" Dana busted through the door.

I didn't have the energy to even acknowledge her. I was in shock. I couldn't believe the tragedy of Berk's life—losing his daughter, then his wife. How could anyone survive that?

"Oh my God, Geneva, Berk's the dad, isn't he?" Tori asked, scooting into the bathroom and closing the door.

I stood still, heaving sobs wracking my body as Hindley held me. More hands began to caress my back and hair. It felt strange, but so needed.

"Do you think they know?" I choked out.

"Know what?" Dana asked.

I pulled back from Hindley's hold, staring at all three girls, whose own eyes were now brimming with tears.

Tori handed me a wad of toilet paper and I wiped my nose as she leaned in and dragged her thumb under my eyes, wiping away the makeup that I was sure was running down my face.

"Do you think everyone out there knows that Berk is the father?" I nodded toward the door. "Did I totally lose it out there?"

"They're men," Dana said. "They're dumbasses, totally clueless."

We all laughed. Leave it to Dana to illicit a giggle from me at my lowest point.

"But they're gonna want to know why the fuck we're all huddled in the bathroom together," she added.

"We'll tell them you got sick, Geneva," Tori said. "We'll just say we had to help you."

I smiled at Tori's flawless face. She could seriously be an angel. Her long, platinum blonde hair was like fine silk, and her blue eyes popped against her fair skin.

"So, what are you going to do now?" Hindley asked.

I slid down on top of the toilet with a thud, all thoughts of needing to pee gone. "I have no fuckin' clue." I stared blankly at the wall, my mind a whirlwind of thoughts and emotions.

"I'm assuming he doesn't know?" Dana asked.

I shook my head.

"Oh, fuck," she sighed. "Did you know he had a daughter?"

I shook my head again.

"Shit," Hindley said under her breath.

"I think you should tell him," Tori said.

My head snapped up, and my eyes caught hers. She was completely serious.

"I can't tell him."

"Why not?" Dana asked.

"Yeah, why not?" Hindley sat down beside me on the edge of the tub.

"Um, yeah. I don't talk to him for like five months, and then suddenly I just happen to pop in and say 'Hi, I'm pregnant…oh, and it's yours.'"

"What's wrong with that?" Tori asked.

My head fell into my hands as I shook it back and forth. "I can't, you guys." My words were muffled through my hands. "He's obviously suffered so much loss. I had no idea. Did you guys?" I lifted my head as I panned their faces. All three shook their heads.

"That's awful," Hindley sighed. "I can't imagine what he's gone through. Did you know any of this while we were in Hawaii? I mean, I'm guessing not, because you're in complete shock like the rest of us right now."

"I asked him if he had a child and he said no so I believed him. I knew he'd been married before. He told me his wife had died, but not under mysterious circumstances."

"I know I sure as fuck would want to die if anything happened to one of my kids," Dana said.

I smiled at my friend. Just the mention that she was a mom now had me near tears again.

With Dana's complete hysterectomy ten years ago due to ovarian cancer, she'd lived the last decade thinking she'd never have kids. Until she met the love of her life. Peter had given her a reason to live. Now she had not one, but three bright, gorgeous children who were all hers. Dana, a mom. The thought made me laugh out loud.

"What's so funny?" Dana asked.

"Nothing." I smiled at her, shaking my head.

"Well, I still say he needs to know," Tori said. "He's already lost one child. Knowing he has another might help him heal." Tori's plan sounded good, in theory.

"Or it could send him off the deep end," I said.

Hindley took my hand. "Either way, he deserves to know, Gen."

I drew in a deep breath, trying to steady my heartbeat, but it was no use. "What if he wants to take the baby from me? What if he files for custody?" I started to hyperventilate as panic welled up inside me.

"Calm the fuck down." Dana knelt beside me. "First of all, he'd have to go through us three bitches just to get to you. Then he'd have to go through you to get to the baby."

I smiled down at her. Despite my deplorable behavior over all the years I'd known her and Hindley, both had chosen to forgive me and give me a second chance to be the kind of friend I'd never had in my life. This type of protectiveness from a female was new to me. I'd never realized how much I'd lost until I opened myself up to receive another person's love and respect.

"When should I tell him?" I barely recognized my own timid voice.

"The sooner the better," Hindley answered.

Silence filled the room as I stared at all three of them. "You mean like *now*, sooner?"

"Yep." Tori nodded.

"What, go to Colorado, to the X Games?"

All three remained silent.

I jumped up from the toilet. "You guys, it's the *X Games*. I don't want to screw that up for him."

"So, wait until after his final run, then go tell him." Tori explained it as if it were elementary math.

I clutched my belly when my baby kicked deep within me. *Our* baby. It seemed as if even little peanut wanted to meet his father.

"I'll go with you." Tori obviously sensed my apprehension.

"Me, too," Hindley piped in.

"Me, three." Dana smiled up at me.

I loved these girls. I'd done nothing in my life to deserve them,

but I was blessed to have them, and I would never take their friendship, or their love, for granted.

"That's sweet of you guys to offer, but I think this is something I
need to do on my own."

"No, you don't." Tori moved closer, sliding her arm around my
shoulders. "You need support."

"Well, at least let Tori go," Hindley said. "Rory would probably
have a shit-fit if I traveled right now." She ran a hand over her
midsection, smiling lovingly down at her rotund belly. She gazed
back up and immediately we all four burst into laughter.

"Hey!" someone shouted on the other side of the door.

We all jumped.

"What's going on in there?" Rory asked.

"Speak of the devil." Hindley giggled. "We're fine!" she
shouted above our heads.

"Then open the door so I can see for myself."

"Go away, Rory Gregor!" she yelled. She leaned in closer, whispering to the three of us. "Watch this." A mischievous grin spread
wide across her face.

"Goddammit, Hindley, I'm not kidding. Open this fucking door
so I can see you or I'm gonna break the fucker off the hinges."

We all looked at one another and burst into laughter again.

Obviously incensed by our response, Rory beat on the door
harder. "Hindley," he growled.

"Rory." She laughed, reaching for the door handle and swinging
it open.

The look on Rory's face was priceless. It was a combination of
fear, anxiety, and sexual desire. Hindley was so lucky to have Rory,
someone to protect her and her children fiercely.

I wanted that. But more than for myself, I knew my baby *needed*
that. Berk may never look at me as if the sun rose and set around me
the way Rory did Hindley, but he was fierce and strong. He would
protect our son. *But first, he has to know he has a son.*

"Let's go, Tori," I said.

All three girls turned to face me, their faces washed with relief.

"Really?" Tori squeezed me.

"Well, thank fuck!" I stood and Dana grabbed me around my belly, squeezing me so tight I thought she might actually push the baby out of me.

"Good God, Dana, I can't breathe."

She laughed and both she and Tori released me.

Hindley came to stand in front of me, taking both my hands in hers. Her brown eyes stared lovingly into mine. "It's the right thing to do, Gen. It will suck and it will be hard, but he deserves to know."

"Who deserves to know what?" Rory asked.

Oh, God, I'd completely forgotten he was in the bathroom with us.

"None of your business," Hindley scolded. She placed her hand on his chest. "You've seen I'm fine, that we're all in one piece, so go." She shoved him toward the door.

He grabbed her wrist and slid it off his chest with ease, tugging her flush into his body. "Ease up, little momma." He smiled down at her.

Hindley's eyes went gooey and Rory's went dark as a fall storm.

"Oh, shit," Dana sighed, "here it comes."

We all knew what she meant. A full-on make-out session between the two of them was about to ensue. Tori, Dana and I scooted around the couple as we slipped through the door.

"Please don't have sex in my new bathroom," Dana said. "I'd like Peter and me to christen every room, not you and One-Nighter." Dana poked Hindley in the arm, but she was oblivious, lost in Rory's gaze.

Dana closed the door behind us and we all giggled.

I was jealous. I could admit it. But it wasn't the vindictive kind of rage that once consumed me. This time, I was happy for my stepsister. Happy that she had overcome all the obstacles, many that I'd intentionally placed in front of her, to cruelly watch her fall.

I wasn't sure how Berk would react to me. I'd left Hawaii without a word to him, consumed by jealousy that perhaps wasn't valid.

I couldn't imagine the pain and the anguish he'd been through in the last three years—losing not only his child, but his wife, too—and then having to relive it every time he competed. No wonder he'd escaped to Hawaii.

Why hadn't he told me that he'd been a professional athlete, though? Then I remembered our vow—no past, no future, only the present. How apropos would that be, three extreme sports athletes in one family.

I understood Berk's need for anonymity. I sought it as well. I didn't want my past on public display for just anyone to see. He knew nothing about my past either. That was the way we'd planned it. But even in Hawaii I'd been drawn to him on a deeper level, wanting to know more about him.

I couldn't think of having a relationship with Berk. As much as I'd like to see where one may lead, I was no longer under the romantic illusion brought on by Walt Disney when I was six.

I would go to Colorado. I would tell Berk I was pregnant with his son. It was the least I could do. But I wouldn't expect anything from him. At least, that was what I told myself. Inside, though, all I could see was the movie reel playing over and over in my head, the three of us—me, Berk, and our son—walking on the beach, chasing the sunset. I didn't deserve a happily ever after, but God help me, I wanted one.

CHAPTER 2

GENEVA

"HOLY SHIT, it's freezing out here." Tori tugged her jacket tighter under her chin.

My metabolism was ramped up with pregnancy, which meant my core temperature was like a raging inferno. The brisk winter air of Aspen, Colorado, actually felt good to me.

"Oh, I forgot, you've got your own little homemade heater inside you." Tori rubbed my belly. "You're probably loving this nipple-hardening weather. I swear to God, it's so cold out here you could freeze the balls off a penguin."

"What?" I furrowed my brow as I stared at her.

Her teeth were chattering. "It's an expression about the cold."

"But you're from Utah. It gets cold there, too."

"Yeah, but still. This crap is so cold it would freeze the nipples off of Jack Frost's momma."

"You're insane." I laughed, thankful that I'd brought Tori with me. "This is his last snowboard run, then I promise we'll go inside." I'd never seen a snowboard competition before. Never had a reason to. Until now.

"I'm just giving you a hard time, Geneva. It's fine. We can stay out here as long as you need."

Her willingness to go through this by my side, her reassuring smile and warm eyes, gave me the strength I needed to do what had to be done.

"This is it, folks, the finals of the men's superpipe! A voice boomed over the loud speaker.

I surveyed the area. It was packed with X Games fans, out in masses to cheer on their favorite athletes. I was only looking for one.

"Berk Rigby is making his last few adjustments before his final run of the night. He's had one hell of a showing at this year's X Games," the announcer said. "Coming back from what seemed like insurmountable odds, we have to give it to Berk. He's shredding bigger and better than ever. It's great to have him back in the sport of snowboarding again."

My heart sank. This was Berk's life. Snowboarding was what he did well, apparently. Even if he decided to be a part of our baby's life, he'd more than likely want to stay in Colorado—or some other equally as cold environment—so he could train. I couldn't move away from my family and friends. Not now that I actually had genuine relationships for the first time since my mother had died.

A blast of freezing cold air battered my face, unexpectedly chilling me to the bone. I yanked my coat tighter and secured my pink hat on top of my head. "Maybe this is a mistake." I leaned in close to Tori, trying to speak above the noise of the crowd.

"What?" she asked, never taking her eyes off the giant snow-board run.

I gazed above me at the huge *superpipe*, as the sportscasters had called it. The lights illuminating the course were over thirty feet tall, and blinding. They looked like the ones used to light up the baseball parks and football stadiums for night games.

The pipe appeared to be nothing more than the bottom half of a frozen tunnel made of packed snow. The course was massive in width and length, and so steep I wondered how the skiers ever stopped themselves at the end. The snow-covered platform that ran along the side of the course was packed solid with fans from the starting point all the way down to the finish line.

Before I could make an excuse for leaving, Berk's face appeared on the giant screen at the base of the course.

He wore a green and black helmet with several logos stamped across the front and side. Underneath, I knew all his thick, black hair had been cut off and part of me was sad about that. His goggles were wrapped around the top and the camera focused on his eyes. They were intense, completely captivating, and the same brilliant whiskey-colored brown that I remembered.

My stomach fluttered with nervous anticipation. *Maybe it's the baby.* No, definitely not the baby.

His eyes rolled heavenward and his lips moved ever so slightly as if he were speaking to someone, or something. My heart clenched, wondering if he was offering up words to his deceased wife and daughter.

I couldn't do this. It was too much. Berk had already suffered enough loss.

Doesn't he deserve a second chance?

"You're not going anywhere, Geneva." Tori captured my arm, bringing me back to the present. "You're not leaving Colorado until Berk knows the truth. He deserves to know." Her face wasn't condescending or stern, but loving and kind, her bright blue eyes filled with concern for me.

"You're right."

Suddenly the crowd erupted in deafening cheers.

I gazed up and saw Berk hit the first jump. He soared so high I thought he'd fly right out of the pipe. The pole next to him lit up, indicating the height of his jump.

"Holy smokes, Berk's on fire tonight. Did you see that frontside 1080 double cork?" The announcer's voice echoed through the mountains.

I had no idea what the hell he was talking about. All these terms were foreign to me. My breath was held captive as I watched Berk fly high into the air, twisting and turning, flipping upside down. Part of me was excited, watching him float effortlessly down the mountain, captivated by his talent. But the other half was scared shitless. What if he fell? What if he injured himself? What if he died?

Within seconds of his run, everything in my periphery disappeared. The only thing I could focus on was the man I knew intimately, who was snowboarding his way down the steep mountain. With every jump he took, my heart followed, my stomach a mass of nerves.

I knew nothing about snowboarding, but watching Berk fly down the mountain was like watching perfection. It was effortless for him. This was his passion. Even if he wanted to be a part of his baby's life, I knew he'd never leave Colorado. And I couldn't do long-distance co-parenting.

I backed away into the crowd, hoping to make a quiet exit, but Tori grabbed me around the waist.

"No, Geneva. You're going to do this."

My eyes focused on Berk's body soaring through the air, skiing from side to side in the huge pipe. Before I could take another breath, he was at the end of the course, cutting his board sideways and spraying the crowd with a cloud of snow. I could barely see him above the crowd now, but thankfully he was tall.

I held my breath when he removed his helmet. Just as I'd seen on the television at home, his short hair accentuated his native island bone structure. Cutting my eyes to the big screen, it was illuminated with Berk Rigby. The baby kicked several times as if recognizing his father.

Berk's face was passive, unyielding as he waited at the bottom for his scores.

"That was a near perfect run for Berk Rigby, folks!" The

announcer's voice boomed over the bottom of the mountain. "Let's see if the judges agree."

Every spectator's eyes were glued to the scoreboard, but mine were solidly fixed on Berk. I saw the tiniest lift of his lips in a smile. He knew he'd nailed his run. And without knowing anything about this sport, I knew it, too.

"Berk needs a ninety-four point six or higher to pull into first place and squeak by Paxton Laine from Finland. Will he do it?"

The crowd erupted into cheers and chants as the final score was posted bright—ninety-five point seven.

"Berk has done it! He's pushed past Paxton Laine to win the gold, folks. Berk Rigby is officially back."

I couldn't help but smile as my gloved hands clapped together in a muffled tone.

"Oh my God, that was amazing!" Tori shouted in my ear above the noise of the crowd. "I've never seen anything like it."

I had to admit, Berk's run looked like perfection. *He* looked like perfection. I studied his face, now washed with a semi smile that still didn't reach his eyes. I wondered what was holding him back, why he wasn't totally ecstatic over the news that he'd won gold.

Suddenly, a woman with long, jet-black hair jumped into his arms, her hands wrapping around his neck. He caught her mid-air and his face finally lit up with joy.

Shit!

"We need to go." I spoke in Tori's ear.

"Why?"

"I just need to get out of here. This was wrong. I should never have come." I turned to leave but looked over my shoulder one last time. From the huge expanse of space between us, Berk's eyes connected with mine. He shoved the girl away, nearly knocking her to the ground. He launched himself toward the fencing that held the spectators back.

"Now!" I shouted to Tori as I grabbed her wrist and dragged her along behind me.

Berk Rigby had a new life, a new passion and obviously a new love. I was not about to stand here and watch it all unfold in front of me.

I'd never admitted it to anyone, not even to myself, but somewhere in Hawaii I was pretty sure I'd fallen in love with Berk. This was all too much for me. I'd never make him choose. His past life had been haunted by tragedy. He deserved a better life. I wouldn't be an obligation to him—to anyone. Not any more.

Nothing is more wretched than the mind of a man conscious of guilt.
- Plautus

CHAPTER 3

BERK

THE COOL RUSH of the mountain air brushed over the exposed skin of my neck as I stood on top of the mountain at the starting area. I wrapped my gloved hand around the zipper of my jacket, yanking it up until it was tight around my chin.

I knew my next downhill run would be incredibly cold. The slopes in Aspen were unusually brisk this year at the X Games. We'd been warned earlier that the course was getting icier by the minute.

Ice.

Don't go there, man. Not now.

I drew in a deep breath to calm my racing heart then blew it out into the cold night air, watching as the heated vapors materialized into a rising cloud. I repeated the action three more times, but still my pulse raced.

"You all right, man?" Benji asked, slapping me on the back.

I nodded once, knowing if I spoke I might pussy out and not take the run. It was bad enough that the fucking camera was right there in front of my face, and the huge screen at the bottom of the course was flashing my story all over the place.

Great. Now everyone knew about my wife and daughter and their tragic deaths. Like they didn't already?

Come on, concentrate, man. Get your head in this.

"You'll do fine. This is your final run, man," Benji said. "You know what you need to do for the gold. But screw all that, dude. Go down the pipe for yourself, Berk, no one else. For once, have fun."

Benji Thompson was my coach and a good friend. He'd been with me through my darkest days after I'd lost Alana and Jaime, allowing me time off to lick my wounds when he realized the sport I'd been in love with for the last decade couldn't help ease my pain.

When I'd called him from Hawaii almost five months ago and told him I'd be coming back to Colorado to ski again, he'd been so excited, I thought he was going to deafen me with cheers of excitement.

He'd immediately put me on a brutal workout regimen, and we'd entered every competition known to man just to get to where I was standing today. The X Games.

As much as I didn't want to admit it, I really had Geneva to thank for me being on top of this mountain in Aspen, competing again. She'd lit a fire inside my long dormant furnace, but not in a good way. Her sudden departure from Kauai had left me reeling. I couldn't figure out why she'd disappeared without so much as a "Fuck you very much."

Her friends assured me I'd never get any answers from them and made it quite clear they were pissed as shit at me. I guessed Geneva was, too, although I had no idea why. I'd badgered her friends relentlessly the evening I'd discovered her missing, especially her friend Tori, but they'd refused to talk to me. The more they shut me out, the madder I got.

"It's for the best," the pixie bride had told me the morning her family left the resort.

I couldn't believe I'd talked about Jaime, shared details of her with Geneva, things I hadn't told anyone since Jaime's death. I didn't talk about them, wouldn't talk about them, to *anyone*. But Geneva wasn't just *some* woman, and that was what hurt most of all. I thought I'd come to mean something more to her. She had come to mean a lot to me. But obviously I'd been just a vacation fuck for her, an island tryst, and that stung most of all.

According to Geneva, this was her MO, though, so I shouldn't be surprised. She'd hinted of her days as a wild child. Even though she'd said she'd changed, it was probably all a lie. I mean hell, the woman had been reading a BDSM book for God's sake. And she'd had no problems when I suggested we role play.

Don't even act like you didn't want that, too.

The problem was, I'd fallen for Geneva. I'd envisioned a future with her. It pissed the fuck out of me that she'd just blown me off, leaving without even a note to say good-bye. After her friends told me she was gone for good, I'd searched my entire house for just one word from her but found nothing.

When I'd left Colorado for the sanctity of Hawaii after Jaime and Alana died, I'd had no plans of returning to the mainland. Ever. But Geneva had stirred feelings inside me, given me a picture of what life *might* be like if I came home. As quickly as she'd flashed me the picture of hope, she'd destroyed it by leaving without so much as a good-bye or explanation.

I couldn't hate her, though, as much as I wanted to. She'd actually made me feel again. Even though those emotions were anger and betrayal, at least I was feeling *something* again.

"You ready, big guy?" Yellow Jacket asked. He was tonight's rider caller at the top of the mountain and lined up all the snowboarders, prepping them for their start, coordinating with the judges and cameras below. They varied from event to event and were named for the bright yellow jackets they all wore.

We're with you, baby.

A familiar voice sounded in my mind. Jaime.

You'll do fine. Just remember, it's about the ride, not the compe-

tition. Enjoy it! I love you. We'll see you at the bottom for your medal.

Jaime's words rang through my head. It was the same sentiment she always sent me off with before the start of any competition.

I'd cut my mind off to her voice for the last three years, but even before the wheels touched down on the runway in Denver when I returned, so did Jaime's voice. At first it scared me, but over the last few months of training, I'd learned to embrace it, appreciate it and let it motivate me. Sometimes the guilt was too much. Hearing her voice reminded me of what my anger had cost me.

I lifted my head to the dark night sky and saw both my girls, their faces alight with anticipation and excitement for me. I didn't deserve their love. I'd failed them. "I'm sorry." I said out loud.

"What?" Yellow Jacket hollered, covering the microphone of his headset with his hand.

Shaking my head and ignoring him, I adjusted the chinstrap on my helmet one last time before securing my goggles and staring down at the course before me.

"I'm ready." Without waiting, I hopped down to the drop-in mound with my snowboard, balancing myself on the berm of packed snow as I mentally prepared for my run.

The crowd below was at record capacity, or so they'd said. I closed my eyes, breathing in the cold Colorado air as memories floated through my mind—the first time I'd ever snapped on a board, the first time I'd literally ran into Jaime on the course, the day Alana was born and her angelic face had captured my heart for all time. The glow of three lone candles on her cake as we sang her "Happy Birthday." These were the memories I didn't deserve to have.

"Rigby!" someone shouted behind me. I knew it was Yellow Jacket. He was reminding me that this was televised and they were on time constraints. Well, fuck TV, fuck the X Games, and fuck everyone else. I was going to take my time on this run. It was about me. I was back. Just like Jaime reminded me at the top of the hill, this was about the ride, not about the show.

Turning my board parallel with the pipe, my adrenaline surged. I slid down the opening, building up speed as I dropped into the superpipe. I squatted low on my board to build the force I'd need to reach the height of my first trick.

As the edge of my board hit the lip of the pipe and my body flew effortlessly in the air, my eyes caught the starry heavens for a brief moment. Jaime's and Alana's faces shone above me, casting their heavenly light along the track to guide me. I didn't deserve their love and devotion, but I'd be a fool to say I didn't want it. Actually, I *needed* it tonight.

I'd lied to myself earlier saying this run was for me. It was really for Jaime and for my sweet Alana. I loved them both so much that each breath I'd taken since their deaths burned every inch of my lungs and threatened to end my own existence. I had to move on, though. Another woman from my past had made me acutely aware of that. I had to let my guilt over their deaths go if I ever wanted to have a real life again.

As Jaime and Alana's faces disappeared into the dark, night sky, and the blue lines of the pipe came into focus, reminding me of the depths of the flat bottom of the course, my mind returned to the present. I prepared my board and my body for the landing of a lifetime. If I could hit this one, I knew I had a chance of finally living again.

CHAPTER 4

BERK

"OH MY GOD!" Jackie screamed above the noise of the crowd. Her voice used to irritate me. It sounded so much like Jaime's. But they were sisters, so of course it would.

I held on to the edge of the plastic fencing, awaiting my scores at the bottom of the slope.

"Berk, that was amazing!" My mother wrapped her delicate arms around my neck and squeezed me with all her might.

Her long black hair blew in my face but I was glad to be hidden from the cameras. Tears burned the back of my eyes. My mother understood what this run meant to me—a new beginning, a fresh start, the first step on the long road to recovery and forgiveness.

I gathered my mother in a strong embrace, listening to her words of praise and adoration. Gazing over her shoulder, I saw my family and friends just beyond the fencing. They all knew what a monumental run this had been for me. Suddenly I was thankful for my return to Colorado and the sport I loved so much.

I knew you could do it, baby. I'm so proud of you. Ski for you, Berk. Just for you. Alana and I love you so much and we'll always be with you. Don't ever doubt that. Live in peace now, my love. Do that, for us.

I wanted to believe that my wife and daughter loved me, but how could they? The images of Jaime and Alana's faces on the Trinitron throughout the competition, the telling and retelling of their story, kept my wounds gaping for the world to see, and to judge.

The way social media had fixated on their deaths instead of their lives left me in constant turmoil. Not to mention, the television crews who'd been hounding me all week for interviews. Thankfully, my sister Palla acted as a semi-manager for me and had kept them all at bay.

"Berk." My mother shook me. "You won. You won the gold medal."

Pulling my goggles down and pushing up on my helmet I felt the cold air whip around my head. Maybe cutting off my long hair when I'd arrived back in Colorado *hadn't* been such a good idea after all. But I'd needed a fresh start.

I'd won? I glanced up at the scoreboard. I'd won.

My mother leaned in to hug me. "I'm so proud of you, *ku'uipo*," she said, using the traditional Hawaiian term of endearment.

I smiled, really smiled, for the first time in over three years.

Casting my gaze over her shoulder and peering into the growing crowd, my eyes adjusted to the blinding lights surrounding me. Suddenly, I saw familiar eyes locked on mine. *No fucking way*. It couldn't be. Could it?

I saw the hint of blonde hair escaping under her pink stocking cap, the powder blue scarf encircling her neck brought out the familiar blue of her eyes. I was captured, mesmerized, paralyzed, just as much as she was.

Her eyes were narrowed, her perfectly manicured brows wrinkled in confusion as she stared at me. There was no doubt it was Geneva. I'd tried to forget her over the past few months, focusing instead on my training, but I'd fooled myself into thinking her face would never haunt my dreams.

I cast my mother aside with more force than I'd intended. "I'm sorry, Mom." I stepped toward the orange barricade, fully intending to jump over it.

"Berk, what is it?" she asked, looking beyond me into the crowd.

"Berk." Palla shook my arm. "The sportscasters." She nodded to a camera crew in front of me with an X Games correspondent shoving a mic in my face.

I owed ESPN something. An interview, a word…but all I wanted to do was capture the woman who'd eluded me five months ago in my island home and ask her why the fuck she'd left without a word.

Pushing past the reporter, I made my way to the plastic barrier to peer over the crowd. Hands slapped against me as fans congratulated me. Normally I would have shared in their jubilation, but now I was frantic to find her. In a split second, I'd lost her. I couldn't see her anywhere, but I knew I wasn't going to give up. There was no way I was letting Geneva Barton run away from me again. Not without an explanation first.

"Berk, where are you going?" Jackie yelled, tugging me back.

I yanked my arm from her grip. I was determined to find Geneva. As I pushed my way through the crowd, their words of congratulations were muffled by my racing thoughts. What would I say to Geneva when I caught her?

I looked toward the edge of the crowd and saw a familiar pink hat. The blonde hair blowing in the breeze was definitely hers. I'd recognize it anywhere. It was longer now, and a bit darker, probably thanks to the lack of sun during the winter. Before I could bat an eye, she rounded the corner of the huge judges' booth and disappeared from sight.

"Shit!" I said under my breath.

"Berk!" Jackie yelled.

"What do you want, Jackie!" I turned to face her. God, she was pissing the fuck out of me lately. She'd become so needy and possessive over the last few months since I'd been back in Colorado. At first, I knew she was just trying to help me acclimate to my surroundings and get my bearings. But now, her stifling hold on me, her need to control my every move, was getting to be too much.

Her eyes were wide in disappointment at my outburst and part of me felt bad. She was Jaime's sister, a link to my late wife and daughter. She deserved more respect.

"I'm sorry," I sighed, making my way back to her as the crowd parted.

"It's okay." She gave me a half-hearted smile that I knew meant it wasn't really okay, but she accepted it. "The TV crew wants to get an interview with you."

The last thing I wanted to do was have these guys asking me dumbass questions about my wife and daughter. No one could ever just let me ski. They had to dig deeper, find that edge, gouge the wound that would bleed and make a story sell in order to get higher ratings. They didn't give two fucks what I'd been through, how much I'd lost.

"It's okay," Palla said, pushing past Jackie to stand next to me. "I shut them down, told them you'd only be doing interviews later." And that was why I loved my sister. She wasn't always the brightest bulb on the tree, but when I needed her the most, she was always there, casting a guiding light for me to follow.

"Thanks, Palla." I wrapped my arms around her shoulder and squeezed her tight.

"Oh, by the way." Palla smiled, jumping up and down. "You won the gold!"

Palla's words echoed in my mind, but they didn't register. I was still scanning the crowd for the infamous pink hat.

"Where were you going anyway?" she asked.

"Just thought I saw someone I knew." I trudged toward the

entrance of the lodge located next to the slope. If it really was Geneva, she wouldn't get far in this crowd.

"I'll come with you," Jackie offered.

I stopped mid-stride. "Uh, no, that's all right. I'll try to catch up with them later." There was no way I wanted to involve Jackie and Palla in my obsessive quest to find Geneva. I was pissed as fuck at her for leaving me without a word in Hawaii, but it didn't mean I didn't still think about her from time to time. *Time to time? Yeah, right. Try every day.*

When I'd first returned to Colorado, I'd thought about calling Geneva. I had her cell phone number. She'd given it to me that first night we'd spent together. She'd written it on a napkin that had slipped away in the island breeze during the night. It was one of many miscommunications we'd had while she was in Kauai.

Maybe her quick departure had been just that. Another cluster fuck of mishaps and misunderstandings.

I'd promised myself I wouldn't call her, that whatever had made her leave without saying good-bye in Hawaii must be important .enough that she didn't want to bother me with it. Putting Geneva out of my mind had been easier while I was training for the X Games. But now that the competition was nearly over, I knew my mind would wander back to the passionate memories we shared.

Geneva had been the first girl to stir my heart since Jaime. I couldn't discount that. But her abrupt departure left a sour taste in my mouth. Why the hell was she here now?

"Berk," Jackie tugged on my arm, "I think they want you over by the announcer's booth."

Staring at the lodge before me, I scanned the perimeter one last time. My shoulders sunk in disappointment when I didn't see her anywhere. Geneva would remain a figment of my imagination, a fleeting moment to hold on to, much like Jaime and Alana. Unless I could find her. Again.

CHAPTER 5

BERK

THE RESTAURANT WAS FILLED to capacity as we walked through the door. It had taken me forever just to make it inside. The fans had rallied around me since my return and they all wanted to wish me well. For that, I was grateful.

It was the press that irritated me. They were relentless in their pursuit for interviews, especially since I'd just won the gold medal. It seemed my comeback was in full swing and they wanted the *inside* scoop, whatever the hell that was.

The victory felt hollow, though. Winning the gold had been a dream for both Jaime and me. Not being able to share it with her was devastating.

Jaime was an Olympic down-hill skier and trained just as hard as I did. That was what drew me to her, her strong work ethic and dedication to the sport she loved. I laughed silently. Actually, it had been a collision at the bottom of the mountain that first drew me to her.

I could still picture Jaime splayed out on the snow, her auburn hair spread out like an eagle's wing against the powdery snow, those bright hazel-green eyes wide with fear. They were the same eyes that our daughter shared, but Alana's hair was darker, almost jet-black like mine.

"Berk, they have our table."

I startled from my thoughts. Turning toward the voice, I saw familiar hazel eyes staring up at me expectantly. I wished like hell Jackie would just leave me alone. She looked too much like Jaime, sounded too much like her...reminded me too much of what I'd lost. Jackie meant well, though. I knew her heart was in the right place. That was what had kept me from totally casting her aside when she'd come to see me in Hawaii.

The hostess led our party into the restaurant and I stepped back to allow my parents, Jackie, my brother Rhen and sister Palla to follow.

Jackie pulled me back. "I know this may be the wrong time to bring it up, but I just wanted to say, Jaime would be so proud of you. Winning the gold was her only dream for you."

Without another word, she left me standing alone, feeling like shit for wishing she were gone. Jackie was my only link to my wife and daughter.

I hadn't talked to their parents since the funeral, fearing they blamed me for everything. As much as Jackie tried to tell me otherwise, I just knew. How could they ever forgive the man who hadn't taken care of their daughter in her darkest hour of need? I had been a father once, too. I knew I would never forgive someone who didn't take the utmost care of Alana, no matter what the cost to his own well-being.

With heavy steps, I followed after my family, making my way toward our table. I needed to stop acting like such a jerk to Jackie. She meant well. All I wanted to do was forget my past, but Jackie wouldn't let me. Maybe that was why I pushed her away. She was right, though. Jaime would have been proud of me. But it was my fault my family wasn't here celebrating with me tonight.

I rounded the corner and stood behind Jackie's chair, pulling it out. She glanced over her shoulder at me, her eyes holding no disdain or judgment. Maybe her parents really did feel the same way.

"Thank you," she said, her smile as bright as the lights on the course.

"You're welcome." I returned the sentiment with as much enthusiasm as I could, even though everything felt off without Jaime and Alana by my side. The only other person I remotely cared about being here had walked away from me in Hawaii without so much as a "Good-bye" or a "Fuck you."

I pulled out my own chair, about to take my place next to Jackie, when my chest seized in pain, like someone had seared me with a hot knife. My eyes focused on the pink stocking cap from earlier. Fuck! Geneva was here, just a short distance away from me.

I pushed my chair to the side, stalking toward her. Her back was facing me as she pulled off her shimmering silver coat, oblivious to my presence. She turned to the side and my heart stopped. I nearly choked on my tongue when I saw her protruding midsection. Holy shit! She was pregnant.

What the fuck?

Geneva lifted her head and when she did, her gaze caught mine. She bolted straight up and gasped, her hand slapping her chest as her eyes went wide.

"Berk," she whispered.

"Geneva." I seethed.

"I, um, I…" she stammered.

"What the fuck is going on here?" I clenched my fists.

"Well, I…"

"Are you fucking pregnant? And who the fuck is the father?" My voice was growing louder by the second, but I didn't give a shit. I was pissed. Had she been seeing someone in the states while fucking me in Hawaii?

"You need to back the hell up, dude." The fair-haired woman

sitting with her jumped to her feet, scooting around the table to separate Geneva and me.

I recognized her. It was Geneva's friend Tori, the one who wouldn't offer me one shred of information about why Geneva had disappeared without saying good-bye.

"It's all right, Tori." Geneva nudged her aside. "This is why we came, remember?"

Why we came? What the fuck did that mean?

Tori nodded once, but her eyes were blazing as she scanned me from top to bottom. I swear I heard her snarl.

"What do you mean, this is why you came here?" I asked. My eyes darted between the two women.

"Berk," Geneva said quietly, "is there somewhere we can go to talk?"

"Hell no, I'm not going anywhere until you tell me why the hell you were fucking me in Hawaii when you obviously were screwing someone else back at home."

"Berk!"

My mother's voice cut me to the quick. I glanced beside me and saw her small hand locked around my arm, jerking on me for attention.

"For your information, the only person I've been *screwing* in the past two years is you, you asshole," Geneva said. Her eyes narrowed and her expression bristled in anger.

"How the hell do I know that?" I asked. "In Hawaii, you all but admitted to me you were a slut."

Everyone gasped. The restaurant went silent.

Oh, shit.

Geneva's body caved in on itself as if she'd been struck with an arrow and was coiling around its deadly shaft.

My body burned with remorse from head to toe, a sensation I was all too familiar with. I was a classic at fucking with people's minds and making them feel like shit.

She straightened and squared her shoulders. "You can believe whatever the hell you want to believe, Berk." Her blue eyes burned through mine before turning toward her friend. "Let's go. I told you this was a mistake." She reached down, gathering her coat and pink hat. "But for the record, you *are* the father. Don't worry, though. Your name won't be anywhere on his birth certificate."

"His?" I whispered, leaning in toward her.

Her eyes went wide as she scooted around me, her legs bumping into the table. She hadn't meant to disclose *that* information.

She was carrying a boy. My boy. My son.

~

We must accept finite disappointment, but never lose infinite hope.
- Martin Luther King, Jr.

~

CHAPTER 6

GENEVA

MY HANDS TREMBLED and my teeth clenched as I stared up at this man I no longer recognized. He was hateful, mean and vindictive. Not the man I'd fallen for in Hawaii. It was hard to believe I was carrying a part of him inside me.

I loved my son more than anything, but at that moment, I didn't want to be anywhere near his father. Not after he'd insulted me and called me a slut in an upscale restaurant filled to capacity.

I clutched my coat in my hand, not even worrying about putting it on as I pushed past him.

"Wait." He reached out for me.

Tori stepped between us. "You put one fucking finger on her and I will scream so loud, even God himself will hear me and bring down His wrath on your sorry ass."

As if sensing Tori would do just that, Berk stepped to the side and allowed me to pass.

Every eye in the restaurant was staring at me. Even the employees had halted their motion. I walked toward the exit and noticed one table filled with people of Hawaiian descent. All but one. She stood out among the group and I recognized her instantly.

She was the woman I'd seen in the lobby at his family's resort. The one Berk was speaking to the night I left Hawaii.

As I passed the table, I looked over my shoulder and saw Berk following me. "You know it's really funny how you claim I'm a slut, seeing as you were in love with someone else while we were together in Hawaii, Berk," I whispered as I narrowly escaped his reach.

"What the hell are you talking about, Geneva?"

"Your girlfriend there." I nodded toward the woman with auburn hair and gorgeous green eyes. She was strikingly beautiful. "She came to get you in Hawaii. I heard you. She professed her love for you." I had no idea why I was explaining *anything* to this asshole. I wasn't one hundred percent sure this woman was related to his late wife. Maybe they actually *were* seeing each other.

Berk's eyes went wide with surprise and defeat.

I'd wounded him. Good. He deserved it.

I stalked past their table and I saw the girl staring at me, her eyes wide and mouth slightly ajar. She didn't seem jealous, just sorrowful, her expression filled with regret.

"Wait," she called out, reaching for my arm.

"He's all yours now," I said as I slid past her. "Forget I ever existed." I didn't dare glance back at Berk for fear of losing it completely. My body was already full of raging hormones as it was. But being called a slut in the middle of a crowded restaurant was more than I could handle.

"Let's get the hell out of here." Tori took the coat from my hands and wrapped it around me.

"Geneva, wait!" a woman shouted.

Tori and I both glanced behind me. It was the woman who'd been standing next to Berk as he berated me at our table. She was now in the foyer of the restaurant, hurrying toward me.

"I'm Kalani Rigby, Berk's mother. May I speak to you for just a moment?"

"Get me the fuck out of here," I whispered to Tori.

"Stop!" Tori turned to the woman. "Don't come near her. I mean it. She's been through enough shit already without your asshole of a son accusing her of being a slut."

"I know, I know." She moved closer. "I'm so sorry, I don't know what's wrong with my boy. He didn't mean it. I know that."

"It doesn't matter." Tori continued to speak for me. "Berk had his chance. Geneva's done what she came here to do. He can forget she ever existed, because I guarantee you, we sure as hell will forget him."

Without another word, Tori pushed on the front door and ushered me outside. With the wave of a hand, she hailed a taxi that pulled to the curb within seconds. She flung open the back door and pushed me into the cab, climbing in beside me.

Just as the door closed with a bang, I saw Berk and his entire table rushing out of the restaurant, spilling onto the snowy sidewalk. Cameras attacked him, snapping photos, their flashes blinding him as he held up his hand to shield his eyes. Pushing past them, he ran after the cab but we gained speed and soon he disappeared from our view.

"It's over," Tori said as she pulled me down into her lap. "You don't need him, Geneva."

I clutched her waist and hid my face in her jacket as tears ran freely down my face. My chest heaved with sobs I didn't want. Try as I might, I couldn't will them away.

The stupid little girl in me, the naive one that hadn't yet lost her own mother, had still thought there was a chance for Berk and me. That maybe we'd find our romance novel ending. But never in all the years of my father reading *Cinderella* to me at night had I ever remembered Prince Charming calling Cinderella a slut.

Tori stroked my hair lovingly and shushed me. "You've got me, Gen. You've got all of us. It will be okay, I promise."

Giving in to the darkness that surrounded me, I closed my eyes and drifted away. *It's okay, Peanut*, I thought to myself as I rubbed my belly. We've got each other. And that's all we need.

CHAPTER 7

GENEVA

STARING at the lesson plans scattered across my dining room table, I cursed myself for still thinking about Berk and the way he'd attacked me in Colorado. It had been three weeks and still I was letting that asshole get to me. I had to concentrate on my lessons.

I was about to start a new course of study on, of all things, childcare. I worked at a facility for adults with cognitive learning issues and developmental delays. Even though none of them would ever be parents in their own right, it hadn't stopped them from wanting to learn everything about childrearing when they'd discovered I was pregnant.

They'd bombarded me with so many questions, I didn't know how to respond. The staff and I agreed it would be better to go with the truth, not sugar coat things or dumb it down for them. They were after all adults. And they were worried about me.

Many of the girls in the facility wanted to know the ins and outs of pregnancy, which I shared with them. But most wanted to know how to take care of a baby once it was born. To be honest, I had no idea, and the thought scared the crap out of me. I mean, I knew the basics—feed a baby, change its diaper, burp him. Maybe not in that order, but at least I knew the routine.

What had me in knots was the mothering aspect. How could I possibly nurture a child and love it unconditionally when I couldn't even do that for myself? And more importantly, how the hell was I going to teach that lesson to other adults if I had no concept of it?

A soft knock on the door interrupted my thoughts. I smiled realizing who it was. Only my father knocked. He said doorbells were impersonal. Of course, he lived in a 6,000 square foot house so using a doorbell wasn't an option. In my three-bedroom duplex, it wasn't a problem.

I waddled to the door, thankful my father had agreed to do this interview. My students needed a sense of what it was like as a male caretaker. Since my own baby daddy was missing, I thought my father would be the next best thing.

"Hi, Daddy!" I squealed. I was about to throw myself into his arms like a little girl when I noticed a box in his hands.

Shifting it to one arm, he took the other and pulled me in for an embrace that nearly brought tears to my eyes. My father knew me well. He understood how tough this pregnancy had been on me, emotionally.

While I hadn't shared the particulars of my visit to Colorado, instinct told me he'd gathered enough information from those closest to me to figure out that the father of my baby wasn't going to be around for the long haul. Probably sensing that it would upset me, he'd never asked me directly, and for that I was thankful.

"What's in the box?" I ushered him in then closed the door.

"Caroline is cleaning out yours and Hindley's old rooms."

"Why?" I pushed away the papers on the table, clearing a spot for him to set the box.

"She's turning my house into a daycare center, I swear."

I laughed. "So, you don't want your grandchildren staying with you?"

Once my stepmother had found out Hindley was pregnant with her first child, Caroline Hagen-Barton had gone on redecorating overload. Now that she had Dana's three children *and* two more grandbabies on the way, she was out of control.

My dad rolled his eyes. "Of course, I want my grandchildren with me as much as you, Dana, and Hindley will let them. But my God, Caroline is knocking out walls now."

"What?" My hand went to my chest in shock as my other rubbed on my ever-growing belly.

"I gave up asking weeks ago. Something about a flowing play-room with space for psycho-social stimulation, or some crap like that."

I giggled. "Maybe I should have asked Caroline over instead of you."

"Why *did* you ask me over, princess?" He leaned against the box as he secured a hand on his hip.

"What's in the box?"

"Typical woman, change the subject." He smiled. "Your old room is one of the areas being demolished and turned into a Baby Einstein workroom." He chuckled at his own joke, and I couldn't help but smile.

I loved my father so much. Tears stung my eyes thinking that Peanut would never have this, a bond with his own father.

"What's wrong, Geneva?" he asked, scooting next to me and slipping his arm around my shoulders.

"Nothing, Daddy." I tried to shrug out of his hold but he held me close.

Smelling his familiar cologne and the soft texture of his polo shirt took me back to all the times he'd offered his shoulder to cry on. Something inside me snapped. I lost all semblance of control and collapsed in his arms, sobbing like a baby.

"Geneva," he cooed, wrapping me in his embrace as he led me over to the couch. "Sweetheart, what's going on?" He gently set us down on the couch and I curled up into a tight ball in the comfort of his arms.

"Oh, Daddy," I hiccupped through my tears. "I'm going to screw this all up. I know it. I'm going to screw Peanut up more than I've screwed up my own life." My words were barely discernable between my stuttering sobs.

"Geneva Marie, what on *earth* are you talking about, sweetheart?" He pushed against my shoulders to lean me back. His soft blue eyes scanned my face, which I was sure was blotchy red and stained with tears.

"I have to teach my class a lesson on parenthood." I gulped in air, trying to get my words out. "I have no idea what I'm doing, Daddy. I have no idea how I'm going to raise this baby by myself."

My father's face wrinkled in confusion. "Geneva, you're going to be an amazing mother."

"How do you know, Daddy? I've screwed up so much in my own life. And I've hurt Hindley and Rory, and Stan. I've hurt and embarrassed so many people. I'm a complete fuck-up." New tears rolled down my cheeks as I fought to catch my next breath.

"Geneva, we all make mistakes. I've made my share for sure. But I did it. I raised you on my own. Well, for a while, until I met Caroline."

"You're different, Daddy."

"How?"

"You've always had a kind heart."

"Geneva, you have, too. Yours just got lost for a while. Part of that was my fault."

I pushed completely out of his hold, wiping at the tears with the back of my hand. "Daddy, don't ever think that. What I did, what I became, that had nothing to do with you."

"Didn't it?" His eyes were glassy now and I feared I'd wounded him.

"Oh, Daddy, no." I flung myself into his lap, my arms wrapping tight around his neck. "You were the best father. And you chose an amazing woman to be my stepmother. I'm just sorry I screwed it up so much."

"But she wasn't your *real* mother, Geneva."

"Daddy, you couldn't help it that my mother died."

"Neither could you."

I leaned back and looked into his loving face. And there it was. The words I'd always needed to hear but never had.

"Why do you feel so responsible for her death, Geneva?"

I didn't know how to answer. I was afraid if I shared what was in my heart, he'd hate me and leave me, like my mother had.

"Geneva, talk to me. Maybe this is what's holding you back from feeling like you're capable of doing this mother thing by yourself. Although, you know you'll never be alone. Caroline would hunt you down to find PB&J here." He touched my belly and smiled.

I laughed silently at his nickname for my son. When we'd discovered my baby was a boy, my father begged me to name him Paul Barton, Jr. When I refused, he changed his request to PB&J. I loved my father, but it still wasn't happening.

"And I would hunt you down, too, sweetheart," my father continued. "I'm not going anywhere."

"That's what I thought about Mom, too."

"What do you mean?"

I shook my head, not wanting to admit to my father, or anyone, how I'd caused my mother's death.

"Geneva." My father grasped my shoulders and drew me close. "Do you think you're responsible for your mother's death?"

I couldn't answer. My voice was suddenly gone. Instead, I nodded.

My father drew me into his chest, wrapping his strong arms around me. "Oh, sweetheart, how could you possibly think that?" He stroked my back as tears once again erupted and spilled down my cheeks. "Geneva, you were only seven years old."

"I was almost eight," I answered, as if that were a legitimate age to accept responsibility for my mother's death. "I prayed, Daddy. I prayed every night. I begged God. I told him I'd give up every Christmas and birthday wish I had if he would just let her stay."

"Geneva, that's not how it works, sweetheart."

"I cried, Daddy."

He put me at arm's length as he scanned my face, a look of confusion marring his handsome features. "Of course, you cried, Geneva. We all did. She was your mother."

"No, you don't understand." I shook my head. "I knew if she saw me cry, she would cry, too. I knew that would take away all her energy and make it harder for her to fight the cancer. So, I'd go into my room to pray. And to cry." My breath caught as I tried to hold back my sobs, my hands shaking with fear.

My father tucked a wayward strand of hair from my face then his thumbs wiped away the trail of tears on my cheeks. "Geneva, do you honestly think you killed your mother?"

I nodded. "Oh, Daddy. It was just before my eighth birthday, and all I wanted was for Mommy to get better and be able to make my cake like she always did. That's what I asked for. I didn't ask for her to get better. I asked for a cake. A stupid, fucking cake."

"Oh, sweet girl," my father cooed, rocking me in his lap. "You have to know that this is all twisted around in your mind, right?"

I nodded. "The sane part of my brain does, the one that's finally grown up."

"But somewhere deep down, that little girl still lives, huddled up in a corner, crying, believing she killed her mother?" he asked.

I couldn't speak. My voice escaped me. All I could do was nod.

We sat in silence, my father rocking me as if I were that seven-year-old girl, just like he had for weeks after my mother died. I would hear him at night in his own room after she died, sobbing and crying out with his own grief, but he'd never let me see it. I loved him for that. But the grown woman in me wished that I had seen his grief, seen his sorrow, seen his road to recovery from my mother's death.

I sat back on my heels, staring at my father who now had tears streaming down his face.

"Not only did I feel like I killed Mom, I felt like I'd pushed you away, too."

He wiped away his tears and took my hands in his. "What are you talking about?"

"I never saw you cry, Daddy. I thought I was weak and selfish. I didn't know how it all worked in the grown-up world. Then you met Caroline and it felt like you moved on without me."

"Oh, God, sweetie." He tugged me back to his chest, his hands caressing my hair. "Why didn't you tell me this before, Geneva?"

I shrugged.

"Losing your mother crushed me." He rubbed my back. "But I had to be strong. For you."

"I know that now, Daddy. But back then…" I trailed off, unable to explain my reasoning.

"When I met Caroline, do you know what my first thought was?"

I shook my head against his chest.

"You, Geneva. I thought of you."

I sat up, staring straight into his guilt-ridden face. Shit! This was not what I'd intended. I didn't want him to feel bad for my misconceptions. "What do you mean, Daddy?"

"When I first saw Caroline I fell for her, instantly. Not only did I see a partner for me, but I saw a mother in her, for you. I didn't mean to find her, Geneva. I never meant to replace your mother, but I have to be honest. I was so thankful I found her because I knew you needed her more than me."

"Daddy, I never faulted you for finding Caroline, for falling in love with her. You know I love her just as much. I'm just so sorry I let my jealousy take over my life. As much as I loved her, I hated Hindley."

"Why?"

I hiccupped a sob and covered my mouth. "Because she took you. I lost you, too, when Hindley came into your life."

My father's eyes roamed over my face, lost in grief and remorse. He stayed silent, his expression telling me how sorry he was and how wrong I was in my assumption that I'd lost him.

"I know, Daddy, that's not what really happened, but I was young. I was immature. And more than anything, I wanted Hindley to hurt half as much as I did. It was wrong. I get that. But that's what it was." I shrugged my shoulders, having no other way to explain my emotions.

"Oh, Geneva, I'm so sorry, baby girl." He tenderly rubbed my back. "I never left you. Your mom never left you."

I gazed up at his face, my eyes narrowed in confusion.

"Hold on." He pushed me aside and rose from the sofa, walking toward the table and grabbing the box he'd brought in earlier. He made his way back then leaned over the coffee table, setting the box down in front of me.

"What is it, Daddy?" I scooted to the edge of the couch, peering over the edge of the cardboard box. My breath caught and my heart seized in pain. Letters. My mother's letters. Unopened.

"She wrote them all for you, Geneva. Why didn't you read them?"

My father's words were void of any judgment or disappointment. Instead, he was offering me love, and a way out of my misery. He was giving me my mother. My mind drifted back.

On my eighth birthday my father had given me a beautiful box wrapped in white and tied securely with a bright pink bow, my mother's favorite color. Inside had been two things—a star pendant necklace covered in diamonds that had been my mother's, and a pink envelope with my name gracefully written across it in my mother's distinct handwriting. Underneath my name it read, "Happy 8th Birthday Geneva."

At the time it had all been too much. We'd just buried my mother two days before my eighth birthday and I was confused. Maybe she was still alive and waiting for me in my bedroom. Maybe this had all been a cruel, sick joke? Not wanting to find out, I'd hidden the letter under my mattress.

Each year, my father would present me with the same gift on my birthday, a box wrapped in white paper and tied with a beautiful pink bow. As each year passed, I dreaded that gift more and more. It was the nail in my mother's coffin, assuring me that she was gone, forever. Even though her letters were meant to keep her near, I shoved them all under my mattress and never read one of them.

On my twenty-second birthday they'd stopped coming. And every year since then, I'd mourned a little more. Even though I'd never read the letters my mother had written, expecting a new one each year had comforted me. I missed receiving the boxes that contained a little piece of my mother inside.

"Here, sweetie." My father's words brought me back to the present.

I gazed up and saw a box wrapped in white and tied with a beautiful pink bow.

"She hasn't written since I turned twenty-one. It's not my birthday, Daddy."

"Your mother didn't just write you on your birthday, baby girl." He reached out and gently caressed my cheek with the back of his hand. "She also wrote to you on special occasions in your life."

"What's this one?" I wrapped my trembling hand around the box and brought it closer as if my own mother was wrapped inside.

"It's for when you have your own baby, Geneva."

Tears welled in my eyes and my chin quivered with regret.

"You think you don't know how to love a child like a mother should, Geneva. But I think in these letters you will find *your* mother. She's the one who can show you how to love Peanut. She's the best example I can think of to show you how to love yourself again. How to forgive yourself. That's really what you need, sweetheart. You need to forgive yourself."

"Oh, Daddy," I cried, flinging myself into his arms. "Thank you so much. I'm so sorry."

"For what, baby girl?" He kissed my head.

"For everything."

"Me, too, Geneva. I'm sorry, too."

"What do you have to be sorry for, Daddy?"

"For not making sure you knew exactly how much you meant to me, how much you *do* mean to me. How much I love you. How much your mother loved you. And how not even death or a new marriage could separate you from my love."

"If I'm half the mom that you are a dad, I will consider Peanut a very lucky boy."

"Well, PB&J is going to be lucky anyway to have me as a grandpa." He patted his chest.

I laughed and swiped at my tears as I sat back and placed the gift on my lap. "So, I guess begging you to stop calling my son by a famous sandwich is still not going to work?"

He shook his head with a glimmer of mischief in his eyes. I loved my dad so much. If Peanut couldn't have a dad, at least he would have an amazing grandfather.

"Now I'm hungry." I smiled as I stood and reached out for my father. "Why don't we go make a PB&J sandwich, for your namesake?"

He slid his large hand in mine as he pushed off the couch. "So that's a yes to naming my grandson Paul Barton, Jr.?"

"Fix me lunch first and then we'll talk."

"Anything for my baby girl." My father reached down and placed a small kiss on my forehead. "Anything for you, and for Peanut."

CHAPTER 8

GENEVA

I STOOD in the middle of my guest bedroom, which was now converted into a nursery, staring up at the new light fixture, praying this time it would turn on.

"Tah dah!" Stanley exclaimed as the light illuminated the room.

Stanley Winston, III, or "Third" as Hindley affectionately called him, was my ex-husband. Even though I'd totally fucked him over with my attempts to destroy Hindley several years ago, he'd found a way to forgive my atrocious behavior. Along the way we'd found an odd sort of friendship with one another.

I loved Stan, but not in the way he needed me to as a wife. I'd been more drawn to his money than to him, in the beginning, and that shame still haunted me.

Not now, Gen.

"I can't believe you did it, Stan." I rushed toward him, throwing my arms around his neck. "I've tried so many times—"

"Geneva, please tell me you were *not* messing around with electrical wiring." He held me away from him, staring down at me, his dark brown eyes filled with concern, not hostility. Stan was not a mean, vindictive person. He was genuinely concerned for me.

I stood, casting my gaze down to my belly. I flinched as Peanut kicked me. It seemed that even my son was upset with me for trying to be a Do-It-Yourselfer.

Stan placed a finger under my chin and raised my head so I had no choice but to look at him. "Gen, you have to be careful. It's not just you any more. I know you're a stubborn, prideful woman," he chuckled, "but you've got this little guy to think of, too." He placed his hand on my stomach. "Oh my God, was that him kicking?" His eyes went wide with excitement.

I nodded. Part of my heart broke a little, wishing it were Berk here feeling his son move. But his hateful words from Colorado rang through my head.

"I like the nursery," Stan said, scooting away from me, sensing I needed a change of topic.

I surveyed the room. I'd decided on a circus theme, since the only name I had for my son so far was Peanut. Most would have called me crazy, but given my degree in interior design, I'd made the room work.

The ceiling was draped with yards of red and yellow gossamer fabric to form the illusion of being under the tent of a circus. I'd painted a mural around all four walls with animals you'd find at the show. My baby's crib was a deep cherry wood and above it was a random quote I'd found on the internet that I thought was fitting.

Life is like a circus...random and full of surprises.

Up until this point, my life *had* been a circus. But I'd done it to myself so I had no one to blame. Hopefully, the only surprises in my future would be good ones.

"I thought maybe it would turn out gaudy," Stan said, "but the chandelier looks really nice." He looked up at the beaded light fixture now hanging in the middle of the room.

"Thanks for helping me hook it up, Stan."

"You know you can always count on me, Geneva." His forgiveness had become something I needed, and today was no different.

I'd destroyed a lot of people in my life, people I loved. None of them deserved it—especially Stan.

"Hey," Stan said, wiping away a tear that was sliding down my cheek. "What's going on?"

"Pregnancy hormones." I laughed, letting my head fall onto his chest. I was so tired.

Thankfully, the doorbell chimed, saving me from further explanation. How could I tell Stan how terrified I was of being a mom, fearing I would screw up this baby more than I'd messed up my own life? I lifted my head.

"It's probably the pizza." He smiled down affectionately at me.

God, why had I fucked up my marriage to him? Stan had been a saint to me, he'd adored me. All he'd really wanted was a family, more than his next breath. Not only had I robbed him of that, I'd betrayed him, broken sacred promises—

Stop! Just stop. You can't talk like this anymore.

"Let me go get it. You fold the clothes." He nodded to the closet that was crammed full of baby clothes, thanks to Caroline.

I laughed. "My stepmother has gone a little overboard."

Stan chuckled as he left me alone in the nursery.

"Well, Peanut, looks like it's just me and you." He kicked my side and I smiled. "Okay, that's not true. We have Grammy and Grampy." I laughed at the ridiculous names my dad and stepmother had decided on when Hindley's daughter was born. "And we have your Aunt Hindley and Uncle Rory. Although Uncle Rory has a mouth worse than your Aunt Dana and me combined."

The thought of Rory having to censor his potty mouth for his own daughter Abbi made me laugh out loud.

"So, what do you think, little man?" I rubbed on my belly as I turned around, pointing at all the little things. "Do you like your new room?"

I stopped mid-conversation with my unborn son when I heard voices growing louder in the entryway. Was Stan arguing with the pizza delivery guy? I'd given him a coupon. Maybe the bratty teenager was refusing to take it.

Waddling down the hall, I froze as soon as my eyes focused on the beast in the doorway. It wasn't the pizza delivery boy. It was Berk.

Oh, shit.

"What the hell are you doing here, Berk?" I surprised myself by keeping my voice steady despite the trembling in my body. My eyes narrowed and my hands fisted in anger.

His caramel-colored eyes scrutinized Stan, scanning his body up and down as if surveying him for consumption.

Stan wasn't small, but he wasn't as large as Berk. Hell, no one was bigger than this mythical God. No one I'd ever been with before anyway.

Berk held up an envelope and shook it out in front of me. "This!" he exclaimed.

"I have no idea what you're talking about." Actually, I did. I knew *exactly* what it was, but I wasn't going to acknowledge that.

Berk lunged as if he were going to enter my house, his eyes menacing as his fist white-knuckled the letter.

"You need to back up." Stan held up his hand. "No one is coming in here without an invitation from Geneva." Stan gazed at me over his shoulder. He saw my answer. Turning all his attention back to Berk, he squared his shoulders as if readying for a fight.

I had fucked over Stan years ago because of my need to destroy Hindley—so much so that he'd left me, which I totally deserved. But he was defending me, even though I didn't deserve any kind gesture he gave me.

Berk's threatening glare went from Stan over to me.

It was obvious he thought Stan and I were involved. Good. Maybe that would make him leave. I didn't want to offer any explanation to him. He didn't deserve it. He'd called me horrible names in front of his family and a packed restaurant of strangers. If he thought Stan and I were in a relationship then maybe this whole thing would be easier for him to accept.

"What do you want, Berk?" I put one hand on my hip as I supported my belly with my other.

Berk's eyes immediately shot to my stomach. Slowly his gaze returned to my face and his beauty stole my breath. Even though he had treated me like trash, the lustful woman inside me was still drawn to him on a primal level. *Damn pregnancy hormones.*

"What the hell is this, Geneva?" he asked again, leaning forward, waving the envelope in the air.

"No way, man." Stan threw up a palm at Berk's chest. "Is this the douche bag, Gen?" Stan glanced over at me.

I'd told Stan the entire story of my trip to Colorado, of how Berk had denied he was the father. Stan had told me not to worry, that he wasn't going anywhere and if I needed his help, despite our past, he would always be there for me and Peanut.

I didn't deserve Stan, but damn it all if I didn't lean on him more than I probably should. Now was one of those times. I had no intentions of having this conversation with Berk. If he wanted to talk, he could do it through my attorney.

"It looks like a letter." I raised one brow as I cocked my head, praying my sarcasm was evident.

"It's a fucking Petition to Terminate Parental Rights." He lowered his chin, glaring down at me, his cold eyes piercing through me. I swear I almost saw smoke coming out of his ears.

For a split second I feared him. Then my mind raced with the memories of how he'd attacked me, belittled me, insulted me, and suddenly my resolve was strengthened.

"Then I guess that's what it is." I shrugged one shoulder as if the entire scene meant nothing, even though my insides were about to explode from fear. I was anxious for Peanut's future. I truly wanted him to have a father figure, but not one who would demean his mother. I didn't want Peanut involved in a custody battle. And since Berk had already questioned his paternity, I thought it best to absolve him of all claims to our baby.

"Look, man, you need to leave," Stan said, taking a step forward. "Any communication you want to have with Geneva should be done through our attorney." I loved how Stanley said *our* attorney. He wasn't going to back down to this brute of a man.

Part of me liked that Stan had joined me in solidarity, but I realized I would have to be clearer with him as to his role with me and Peanut. I loved Stan, I always would, but I didn't want him to misunderstand the kind of love I had for him. For now, though, I steeled my shoulders and joined Stan in his posture of defiance against Berk's attempts to enter my home.

The silence was deafening. We were in a standoff of wills. Sensing we were at a stalemate, Stan stepped back to close the door.

Berk stopped the motion with his giant hand. "Why are you doing this, Geneva?" His eyes softened, but my resistance did not.

"What do you mean, *why am I doing this*?" I shook my head, baffled by his question. "You're the one who accused me of being a slut in public and said you weren't the father of my baby. I'm just making it legal."

"Did someone order a pizza?" a young boy called from behind Berk.

Stan scooted around Berk as he dug in his pocket for his wallet and fished out two twenty-dollar bills. "Thanks, guy." He took the cardboard boxes.

The smell of pepperoni and fresh baked bread wafted across my nose. Then the scent of Canadian bacon and olives assaulted me. My stomach growled and all three of us stared at my belly.

Stan turned and handed me the pizzas. "Go into the kitchen, Geneva." His words were demanding yet gentle. It was a side of

Stan I'd never seen before. He was protecting me and my unborn child.

I stood silent, staring up at Stan, his eyes foreign to me. Why had I fucked him over so bad? He was one of the kindest men on the planet. Guilt wrapped around my heart like a vise.

I shifted my gaze and stared at Berk, whose intimidating glare was squarely set on Stan. Since he was much larger than Stan, given the chance, he could probably knock him down with one punch.

Stan wasn't fazed in the least. "You need to leave." His words were calm but definitive.

"This isn't over, Geneva." Berk's voice wavered but there was no denying he wasn't done with me. Not yet.

I steadied my body and squared my shoulders, lifting my chin in defiance. "It was over a long time ago, Berk," I said.

Without waiting for a response, Stan slammed the door in his face.

I dropped the pizza boxes on the floor, following after them.

Stan grabbed me just before I collapsed.

Burying my face in his shoulder, I cried. I muffled my sobs for fear that Berk was still standing just beyond the door.

"I've got you, Gen." Stan soothed me with his words as his hands lovingly stroked my back.

Peanut kicked.

Stan pushed back but still kept me solidly in his grasp. "I think someone is hungry." He smiled down at me as he released me and picked up the boxes of pizza. His eyes locked on mine. "Whether it truly is over with you and Berk, or if Peanut's custody is just beginning, I'll be here for you, Geneva. Any way I can be."

Just thinking of Berk fighting me for custody had my stomach twisted in knots. Peanut kicked again, and I clutched my midsection, trying to calm him. He was just as worried as I was. I'd lost my mom a long time ago. There was no way in hell I would lose my son, too.

CHAPTER 9

GENEVA

I GAZED up at the clock on the wall in my living room. It was a quarter past two in the morning. I couldn't sleep. Berk's presence today had rattled me, scared the shit out of me.

What if he really *did* fight for custody of our son? I was a fuck-up. My past would surely come up in court. He would learn about how I'd drugged my brother-in-law and tried to force myself on Rory. How the police tried to bring charges against me. Yeah, that would bode really well for me winning full custody of my son.

Thankfully, I'd served an ass-ton of community service and the charges had never been filed. But still, if Berk dug hard enough, he'd find shit on me, a lot of it. What kind of mother would I make?

I rubbed my belly when Peanut kicked. I hoped it was his way of reassuring me that I would be all right, that we both would.

I nudged the box on my coffee table with my feet so I could prop them up. Then I remembered that my mother's letters were inside.

With a shaky hand, I reached in and found the wrapped gift box my father had given me earlier. Did I want to read it? Did I want to hear my mother's voice? Yes, I did. I needed reassurance that I could do this on my own. That I could be the kind of mother my son deserved. That if it came to a fight for his custody, I could stand tall and not waiver.

I slowly pulled on the pink ribbon and watched as it uncurled into my lap. With trembling hands, I tore at the white paper, revealing a box. Lifting its lid, my breath caught as I saw a familiar pink envelope lying inside. I caressed it as if it were actually my mother. Her familiar handwriting on the outside was like a salve to my injured soul.

"To The Mommy-to-Be, My Sweet Geneva"

This letter was meant to be read while I was still pregnant, not after the baby was born like my father had said. I hadn't even pulled out the envelope and already tears streamed down my face.

"Mommy," I whispered.

I tore at the seam of the envelope then pulled out the white paper. Gently unfolding the letter, I let out a heavy sigh and leaned back on my couch. I could hear my mother's voice so clearly as I read her letter, as if she were sitting right beside me.

My Dearest Geneva,

Oh, my goodness, words cannot express how happy I am that you are going to become a mother soon. My only regret is that I'm not there to squeeze you and hold you and tell you how tremendously happy I am for you, my baby girl.

I paused, my eyes already blinded by tears. Reaching for the blanket beside me, I wiped my face dry and took in another steadying breath.

I remember when I found out I was pregnant with you. It was an amazing day. I already knew in my heart you were growing inside me, but your father insisted I take a test. Even when it came up positive, he still didn't believe me. He demanded we go to the doctor.

When the phone rang later that afternoon, your father was in the garage, doing God knows what.

I laughed at my mother's words. My father was forever

tinkering around in the garage. He said it was his Man Cave, and Caroline was always happy to leave him alone when he was there.

As soon as the phone rang, your father ran inside the house, sliding on the hardwood floors as he came to a stop in front of the phone. He just stared at it with a blank face, as if it were a ghost.

I reached over and snatched it out of the cradle. I didn't even need to ask, I knew it was the doctor, and I knew exactly what the answer would be. As the nurse told me the test was positive, I nodded my head to your dad and watched as tears flowed down his face.

Geneva, I can't express to you how much your father loves you. His supply of love for you is limitless. I'd be lying if I said sometimes I wasn't jealous of the close relationship you two have. I was never close with my father. I'm so glad you have him in your life. I'm grateful that I married a man who loves my baby girl more than he loves his own life. I hope you have found that in your husband as well.

A fresh wave of tears hit me full on. I'd been fortunate to have a father, for my mom to have a husband. Peanut and I wouldn't be so lucky.

Even if you're going this alone, please know one thing, Geneva. You have the biggest heart of anyone I know. If there is one person in this world who is capable of caring for another human being, for passing on your passion and your zest for life, it is you.

I remember watching you as a child. At night you would prepare all your stuffed animals for bed, much the way that Daddy and I did you. It would take you forever, and oftentimes it delayed your own bedtime. But I let you, because that was your nature. You'd have to read to them and check on them. Make sure there was nothing they wanted before you kissed each one good night and snuggled them in with their blankets.

And then the way you helped Daddy care for me in the end was beyond amazing. I don't know any girl who has been braver or stronger than you, Genny girl. Not only did you give me your heart and soul as you cared for me, you gave it to your father as well, knowing somewhere in your young heart that he couldn't do it all alone.

One thing I will tell you is that men are not good at dealing with physical or emotional pain. When it comes to death or illness, especially with the ones they love, men lose it. They don't know how to cope, how to deal with it all, so they usually hide.

You were the shining star for your father, Geneva. I'm sure you still are his constant source of light and love. That is why I passed on my necklace to you. To always remind you how bright your love shines through. And it will for your baby, too.

I clutched the letter to my chest and curled into a ball as the sobbing rumbled from deep within my chest and erupted into heaving moans. My body sagged as I rocked back and forth, my sadness and anguish assaulting me. How could my mother have known all those years ago that these were the words I needed to hear most of all?

There was only one explanation. She was a mother. It was instinctual for her to know my needs, even in life beyond her own death.

I spread my fingers wide on my stomach, gently caressing Peanut. I wrapped us in a warm blanket, tucking us in, much like I'd done when I was younger with my stuffed animals. I smiled at the memories. I did have it in me. The loving protector inside of me had just gotten lost over the years.

"I can do this," I said aloud. "*We* can do this, Peanut."

I didn't remember that strong, brave girl that I used to be—the one who my father and mother leaned on. But if I'd been that girl once before, surely, I could be her again. For myself and for my son.

With the new day comes new strength and new thoughts.
- Eleanor Roosevelt

CHAPTER 10

BERK

WELL, way to go, fuckwad.

I stalked back to the car, knowing I'd fucked up royally by trying to confront Geneva in person. Rhen tried to warn me, but I'd been so infuriated when I'd been hand delivered the letter in Colorado, requesting termination of my parental rights, I knew I had to see her face-to-face.

I'd secretly prayed she was telling the truth in that restaurant in Colorado, that I really was the father, even though my actions and words said otherwise. But since I hadn't heard from her after she'd skipped out on me in Hawaii—and the fact that she'd assured me she was on the pill—how the hell was I supposed to believe the baby was mine?

I let out a deep sigh as I opened the passenger side door of the car and flopped down in the seat.

"Well, how'd it go, Romeo?" Rhen asked.

I shook my head.

"Judging from the scene at the door, I'd say you're a little late. Who the hell was that guy? Her husband?"

"I have no fucking clue, man. He used the word *our*, so I'm assuming they're involved."

"Oh, shit, maybe he's the dad."

"Maybe," I sighed. "But why would she serve me with this?" I waved the envelope in the air. I scrubbed my face with my hand. "Let's just get the fuck out of here."

Rhen started the car and slowly pulled away from Geneva's house.

I turned to look over my shoulder, wondering if that would be the last time I'd ever see her. My gut said no, but my heart said I'd fucked up. Bad.

"So, what are you gonna do now?" Rhen pulled onto the freeway as I rolled down the window, allowing the cool air to wash over my heated face.

"Fuck if I know."

When I'd been served with Geneva's legal papers, I'd thought it was a joke. I still wasn't one hundred percent convinced that this kid was mine. I didn't want a child. I never wanted children again. Ever.

I stared at the envelope in my hand with my name typed across the front. If I could trust Geneva, I had no choice but to believe her baby was mine. She didn't seem like a liar. And judging from her distended belly, there was no denying she was pregnant.

It was odd that she waited until *after* I won the gold medal to tell me, though. The term "Gold Digger" came to mind.

I wasn't sure how to calculate the progression of her pregnancy, but if this truly was my baby, then that would mean she'd gotten pregnant during her stay in Hawaii, long before I'd started my comeback. But still, I couldn't shake the feeling that maybe she just wanted me for my status now.

It wasn't like she had a palatial home. Hell, it was a fucking duplex. I wasn't judging, but it definitely didn't bode well in her favor as far as my quest to prove she'd only told me she was carrying my baby so she could secure money.

"Where to now, Casanova?" Rhen hit me in the chest with a closed fist.

I sunk in on myself from the blow, sputtering out a cough.

He laughed hysterically.

"Why the fuck do you think hitting me in the chest as hard as you can is funny?"

"Are you serious? Look at you, you dumb fuck. You're hilarious."

"I guess take us back to your friend's house."

Rhen offered to make the trip from Colorado to Austin with me. His band was performing in a music festival here later this month. His friend Ryan, the drummer, moved to Austin to make connections a few months before. My time spent on Ryan's sofa would be short lived.

Rhen and Ryan had band members and other friends coming into town from all over the country for this week-long music festival. They would invade Ryan's home and soon there would be no room for me. What the fuck was I gonna do then?

"So, are you gonna stay?"

"I've gotta stay and figure out what the fuck is going on. If this is my son, I'm not walking away." My mind wandered back to Jaime, what all I'd put her through in the weeks after our daughter's death. "Maybe I should leave, though."

"What the hell is that supposed to mean?" Rhen turned the corner into his friend's neighborhood. Surprisingly, it wasn't far from Geneva's.

"I don't know, Rhen, my mind is so fucked up right now."

"Do you think it's your kid?"

I nodded.

"I'll talk to Ryan and see if he can find you a place to stay after his friends get to town. You need to sort this out, Berk. If you don't, you'll always wonder. And I know you're not going to sign that petition to relinquish your rights." He nodded toward the paperwork in my lap.

"Never." I shook my head. As much as I didn't want a child, I'd never walk away from one if I knew it was mine. My gut told me Geneva wasn't a liar, but was she a gold digger looking to cash in on child support?

It didn't matter. If her son was mine, I wouldn't leave him. Or her. Even though my mind told me I should leave to protect them both from myself.

∼

"You know stalking is illegal in like…every state, right?" Rhen tapped on the steering wheel as my eyes darted across the vast campus of Geneva's work.

"What the hell am I supposed to do? She won't talk to me. She won't return my calls."

"Uh, I think her note spoke volumes." He chuckled, nodding to the crumpled letter in my hand.

My gaze fell to my lap, visions of me snatching the note from her door when she once again refused to answer my repeated banging. It had been day number three of my stalking quest. I had balled the paper into a crumpled mess once I read it.

Any and all communication with my client can be done through me.
Sincerely,
Luis Marquez, Attorney at Law

Well, fuck Mr. Marquez. Geneva was going to talk to me, face-to-face, whether she liked it or not.

"Hey, man," Rhen said, "I saw a huge sign when we drove in to this place. It said this is private property. Your ass could get in serious trouble, Berk."

My eyes darted around the campus, trying to figure out which building Geneva was in. I didn't want to accost her at work, but her ability to anticipate my arrival at her home and bail before I could reach her left me no choice.

I wasn't going to sign this paperwork without talking to her first. Honestly, I would never sign it, but discussing the petition face-to-face would allow me a chance to apologize for my horrific behavior in Colorado.

"Berk?"

Rhen's voice jarred me from my musings. "Yeah?"

"Isn't that her?" He pointed to his left, just beyond his driver's side window.

My breath caught when I saw her walking across the campus toward the parking lot. Her blonde hair was just a shade darker than it was in Hawaii and hung several inches longer. I remembered Jaime's hair had darkened during pregnancy. Geneva's protruding midsection was put on full display with her snug tank top and billowy skirt that wafted across her bare legs. Something inside me stirred. She still affected me. I knew she would. I had to talk to her.

"Earth to Berk. Are you gonna let her get away, shit-for-brains?"

"Should I?"

"Oh my God, you sound like a pansy ass little school girl on the playground. Should I ask Timmy if he likes me?" he squeaked in a high-pitched tone.

"Fuck you, Rhen."

"Nope. I'm not into dudes. Or family members." He chuckled at his own humor.

My eyes panned over to my brother, the mischief shining in his eyes. He was one of my best friends. When I'd lost Jaime and Alana, he'd been my rock.

"You need to talk to her, Berk. You don't need me to tell you that. Go." He shoved on my shoulder.

"What should I say...how should I start?" God, I even sounded pathetic to myself.

"Just get the fuck out of the car and go talk to your baby momma." He reached across me and opened the car door. "Go, you little pussy."

I chuckled as he cocked his leg and placed his heel securely at my hip, pushing with all his might. Rhen was a big guy, but not nearly as big as me. Try as he might, he'd never be able to budge my huge frame. Saving him the embarrassment, I slipped out of the car on my own. I leaned down to face him. "Wish me luck." I chuckled in anxious amusement.

"I'll wait here in case the cops come."

His roaring laughter was the last thing I heard before I slammed the door. The sad part was, I may need him. Geneva legally had the right to have me hauled off the premises.

I scanned the parking lot and saw she had plopped her belongings on the hood of her car and was digging through her huge purse. Taking advantage of her distractedness, I jogged toward her, being mindful that I truly was trespassing. But no one else was close by.

"Geneva," I called out.

Her head darted up, her blue eyes wide with surprise. She stared at me, reaching for her purse as she studied me. Instead of grabbing hold of her bag, she knocked it over. It slid off her hood and plummeted to the ground, the contents spilling all over the pavement.

"Shit!" She fell to her knees and haphazardly grabbed her belongings, shoving them into her mammoth purse.

I raced to her side and fell to the ground, digging under her car to gather all the items that had spilled out.

"Don't!" she shouted.

I drew back as if she was threatening me with a gun.

"What are you doing here, Berk?" Her words were just as flat as her gaze. Ice blue eyes that were colder than the darkest of Colorado nights stared back at me.

"I need to talk to you, Geneva. You owe me that."

She laughed, sitting back on her heels. "That's classic. You call me a whore and you say I owe *you* something."

"I'm sorry for that, Geneva. That's what I want to talk about. I want a chance to explain it to you."

"You can talk to my lawyer." She pushed up off the pavement, trying to stand but wobbled on her unsteady feet.

I bolted up and leaned over, slipping my hands around her shoulders to steady her. I was surprised when she didn't push me away. Instead, her eyes met mine.

The late afternoon sun created a prism of a hundred different shades of blue as she stared back at me.

Shaking her head as if finally coming back to the present, she shrugged out of my hold. "You can apologize through my attorney." She spoke sharply, her words meant to cut me. Her body betrayed her though as her eyes roamed over my body. Her pink tongue licked at her dry lips. She still felt *something* for me. It was a start.

Just beyond the front tire I noticed a paperback book. Leaning down, I scooped it up and surveyed the front cover. It was the same book we'd been reading in Hawaii.

"Still haven't finished?" I chuckled, remembering our mishaps of trying to recreate the BDSM scenes on our own.

"Give me that." She snatched at the book.

I clutched it to my chest. "Oh, no." I smirked. Maybe this book would be my saving grace. At least maybe it would buy me enough time to apologize. I fanned through the pages and found certain pages were dog-eared. Stopping on one, I looked down and read the passage out loud.

West's fingers skim the border of CC's red corset, his thumbs flicking her exposed nipples.

Heat and desire skirts across her skin as CC's folds grow damp—

"Give me the fucking book, Berk," she hissed through gritted teeth as she lunged for me. Her jaw was clenched so tight I feared she may actually break a tooth. Her blue eyes scanned the parking lot, trying to ensure no one overheard me.

"Only if you'll have dinner with me."

"Hell no!"

"Fine. I guess I'll just drop this book off at the front office and let them know what their staff is reading on their off time."

She literally laughed in my face. "Please. Where do you think I found out about that book? The president's secretary is a freak in the sack." Her head fell back as she roared with laughter from her own admission. The movement exposed her delicate neck.

Images of me licking and sucking that neck suddenly had my dick as hard as the pavement I was standing on. Shit!

She wiped at her eyes, the moisture from her antics causing tears to form.

I stared at her.

"What?" she asked, fanning her flushed face.

"You're beautiful, Geneva." I didn't mean to sound so cheesy right off the bat. I just wanted to talk. But seeing her laughing, *really* laughing, stole my breath.

She rolled her eyes and snatched the book from my hand. "Whatever, Berk."

I stroked her bare shoulder, my hand running down to her wrist. "I mean it, Geneva. I know I was a total dick in Aspen and I don't deserve a chance to make this right. But I'm going to try. And yes, you're still just as beautiful."

Her eyes fell down to where my hand still held her wrist. She seemed paralyzed by my touch. At least she wasn't screaming and running away from me.

"Have dinner with me. Without your attorney." I smiled.

She lifted her lids, her gaze rolling up to meet mine, her eyes still filled with a questioning look. She couldn't trust me.

My pulsating dick assured me that I couldn't trust myself either. This was about the baby, though. Our baby. Our son.

"Please," I whispered, stepping closer.

A light breeze dusted over her shoulder, taking her blonde hair with it as her scent washed over me. Shit! *Baby, Berk. Dinner, Berk.* I reminded myself.

"Please, Geneva," I pleaded. I was desperate and didn't care how pathetic or whiny I sounded. I needed a chance, a second chance to make this right.

Her chest heaved with a deep breath and her head fell back, exposing her face to the bright sky. Her swelling breasts finally released with an exhale as she righted her head and her lids fluttered open.

"Fine," she sighed.

Yes!

"I'll pick you up at seven?"

"That's fine." Her words were a whisper. It seemed like she was in a daze.

"Geneva." I squeezed her wrist that was still securely in my hand.

She gazed up at me.

I saw the fear and the hurt in her eyes, anguish that I had caused her. Taking one step closer, I released her wrist and brought my hand up to her flawless face, stroking her cheek. "I'm so sorry, Geneva. Sorrier than you'll ever know. My behavior was reprehensible. I have no excuse. But I do have a story that will maybe explain some of my behavior."

Her eyes penetrated to my soul as she stared through me.

My mind raced, wondering if she would in fact meet me or if she would leave another note from her attorney. "Seven?" I'd meant it as a statement, but given the fact she had control in everything, it came out like a question.

She blew out another heavy breath. "Fine, I guess."

I leaned down and brushed my lips against her cheek. Her skin was just as soft as I remembered. My heart filled with hope when I realized she didn't pull away. Knowing not to wear out my welcome, I quickly drew away and turned to leave.

"Berk."

I turned and found her staring back at me, lost in a trance. A trance I'd put her in.

"How did you get here?" she asked.

"Magic." I winked and jogged toward the front of the facility where Rhen was waiting for me. "Magic," I repeated under my breath, knowing full well I'd need magic and luck to rectify this situation with Geneva. But her reaction to my touch was promising. Like magic.

CHAPTER 11

BERK

I stood on the porch of Geneva's home, my palms sweating like a pimply-faced high school kid picking up his date for prom. Why the hell was I so damned nervous?

I reached out to press the doorbell, surprised that my finger was actually trembling.

Be cool, man. She'll understand. But would she?

I depressed the buzzer and waited patiently. And waited…and waited. Fuck, was she standing me up? I reached out and pushed it again. And waited…and waited. I was shaking now, but not from nervousness. Suddenly, a loud bang sounded from within the house.

"Geneva!" I yelled as I pounded on the door. A riotous clattering from inside had the hair on my arms raised in alert. "Geneva!" I banged on the door before twisting at the knob, surprised when it opened. What the fuck?

"Geneva!" I yelled again as I stepped through the door into her home.

"In here!" Her voice echoed from deep within her house.

"Where?"

"In the kitchen!"

I followed her voice and stopped just short of the threshold into her kitchen. The room was soaked with water and Geneva was on her hands and knees mopping up pooling water.

"Geneva, you shouldn't be down working like that when you're pregnant."

Her eyes snapped to mine as she blew at the hair now covering her face that had escaped her ponytail. "I don't have a maid, and Prince Charming left the building a long time ago." She sounded amused and perturbed all at the same time.

I pulled off my shoes and socks and rolled up my jeans. "Here, get up."

I tugged at her arms, securing my hands around her shoulders as I gently lifted her up. "Be careful and don't slip." I led her out of the kitchen to drier ground before releasing my hold on her. "What in the hell happened?"

"There's a leak somewhere in there." Her eyes darted around the kitchen.

"Obviously."

Her eyes narrowed and her lips twisted as she threw a wet dish-cloth at my head.

I ducked just in time. It hit the cabinet behind me with a wet thud. "Do you want my help or not?" I raised one brow and cocked my head.

"Just figure it out, Berk," she cried, flailing her arms like a two-year-old having a tantrum. "Rory is going to kill me if I screw up this kitchen again."

"Who's Rory?" I asked with suspicion.

"Water! Leak! Fix it, Berk!" She waved her hand across the kitchen. "Find it."

My eyes narrowed.

"Please," she whispered.

Hearing her soft pleas, my heart melted like it had many times while she'd been in Hawaii.

"It's probably the water line into your ice maker." I tugged on the refrigerator, jarring it from the wall just enough for me to peer behind it. Water was jetting out of a busted tube. I snaked my hand behind the appliance and twisted the main water line off. Instantly, the water stopped flowing, but the floor was still a mess.

"Oh, God," Geneva moaned.

Geneva knelt at the threshold, several large towels in her hand as she wiped at the mess. "Rory is going to be pissed."

"Who's Rory?" I asked again. "And why is he going to be pissed?"

"He's my brother-in-law. The duplex belongs to him and my stepsister."

Rory Gregor, the skateboarder. Of course. He was family. Something in me sagged in relief.

"There's not that much water." I tried to soothe her.

She was frantically rubbing at the floor, and I feared she might go into labor from the exertion.

"Geneva, stop. I'll get it."

"You can't. It's not your mess." There was a tinge of sorrow in her voice, even regret, and I didn't understand why.

"We'll clean it up together. Look." I pointed to the area close to me. "There's not much to wipe up."

"Oh, God, it looks horrible." Her chin quivered as tears pooled in her eyes.

Fucking pregnancy hormones. They could turn the simplest problem into an all-out war zone for a chick. The damage really wasn't that bad in the big scheme of things. I'd seen way worse at my own home.

"We just need a few more towels and some fans. Do you have that?" I looked up and saw tears rolling down her face. "Geneva." I called her name softly, not surprised when she didn't answer. "Geneva," I said a little louder.

Her blue eyes scanned the scene in front of her before they

locked on mine. Even in the midst of her mini meltdown, she still took my breath away.

"Go get a few more towels and any other rags you may have. Where's your mop?"

She shrugged.

"You don't have one?"

She shook her head, tears welling up again.

Oh, fuck me.

"Do you have any fans?" I asked.

She nodded.

"Where?"

"In my closet. I'll get some more things to mop it up, and then I'll get the fan."

"There you go." I smiled at her, hoping my expression would assure her there was no imminent danger. "Now you've got a plan. Disaster averted."

A small smile broke through the tension in her face.

"Go." I motioned with my hand.

"Thank you, Berk. I don't know what I would have done without you." There was a look of apprehension in her face, as if she wanted to say more but didn't.

"You're welcome, Geneva."

Without another word, she disappeared, leaving me in a puddle of water.

Hope sprang up in my chest. What had started out as a disaster to the evening might actually end up being my one and only chance to redeem myself.

"Your pants are soaked," Geneva said, looking down at my jeans which were stuck to my legs. "Why don't you take them off and let me throw them in the dryer."

"Already trying to get me out of my clothes." I waggled my brows and gave her a playful smirk.

"You wish." She flung one of the wet towels at me. "I'll get one of my robes. Come on, follow me."

She led me down a short hallway with two doors on either side. Peering to the left I looked through the doorway and saw your typical guest bedroom. Although the bed was unmade and the room looked as if someone had personalized it.

Shit. What if someone lived with her? A guy? I had to ask. "Do you have a roommate?"

"Peter's sister Tori has moved in with me for a short time. She's an environmentalist and is waiting for her assignment to begin later this summer."

"Who's Peter?"

"Oh, sorry. Peter and his wife Dana were the couple who were married in Hawaii."

She looked over her shoulder at me, and I could see I was losing her. The mere mention of our past was taking her to a place I didn't want either of us to go.

"Ah, yes, Dana. The feisty girl with the curly black hair, I remember her." How could I forget her? She'd practically strangled me when I'd asked her why Geneva had left Hawaii so abruptly. She'd growled at me, as if I should have known.

Geneva stopped in the middle of the hallway and turned to face me. "Why do you say it like that?"

I didn't want to relive that scenario from Hawaii—the morning after the night Geneva hadn't shown up at my house. When I'd found out Geneva had abruptly returned to the mainland without even saying good-bye, I'd gone into a rage and Dynamite Dana had laid into me as if *I* had done something wrong. When I'd tried to get more information out of her, she'd become tight-lipped.

"I just remember her from the week. She's hard to forget." I shrugged one shoulder.

"Yes, she is." Geneva chuckled under her breath.

Turning my gaze, I peered into the second guest bedroom and I lost my next breath. A tight band wrapped around my chest, constricting my inhalations. It was a nursery. Our baby's nursery.

"Come on." Geneva grabbed my wrist and yanked on me, pulling me away from the doorway. She obviously didn't want me to venture into his room.

Visions of Alana's nursery flashed in front of my eyes. Jaime had decorated the room in varying shades of pink with stuffed animals everywhere.

My heart ached from the memories of my former family. Maybe if Geneva understood a little of my past, she'd be able to forgive me for my behavior in Colorado. But since I'd already fucked up one family, perhaps it would be better to sign the papers and walk away before I fucked up another.

"Berk." Geneva's light voice broke through my thoughts. Her hand released me as she shoved a robe in my face. We were standing in her small bathroom.

How the hell had I gotten here without even realizing it?

"Take off your jeans and bring them out to me. I'll throw them in the dryer."

I nodded once, still lost in memories of my past that were slowly consuming my present.

"Are you all right?"

"Yeah." I nodded several times, trying to clear my thoughts. "I'm fine."

"Are you hungry?"

My eyes met hers and saw there was genuine concern etched on her face.

"I kind of ruined going out to dinner." She smiled. "But I could order takeout and have it delivered. Do you like Chinese?"

Before I could answer she continued.

"This little guy loves sweet and sour shrimp." She rubbed on her belly. "Which is really strange because before I couldn't stand seafood. Although my dad teases me and says shrimp isn't seafood. But still, they're slimy and icky and…" She shook her head, her face scrunched up in disgust like she'd eaten a lemon. "It seems like Peanut is a fan, so I have sweet and sour shrimp at least once a week." She chuckled at the thought.

"Peanut?" I asked.

"Oh, yeah, sorry. That's my nickname for the little guy. It's a long story." She stared down at her belly as her hand gently grazed over it.

"Maybe you could tell me over dinner?"

"What do you want to eat?"

"Sweet and sour shrimp sounds good." And it did. "It's actually one of my favorites. I love seafood."

Her eyes went wide as if something in my statement shocked her. Then I realized what I'd disclosed. Maybe *Peanut* took after me in his preference for seafood.

"Just throw your jeans in the dryer when you're done while I call in our order." She turned on her heels and left the bathroom without another glance. We'd jumped over a hurdle, but it didn't feel like a victory.

Removing my jeans, I slipped on the robe and tightened the belt around me. I studied myself in the mirror. The damn thing hit me above the knee and barely fastened around me. I looked ridiculous. Maybe my vulnerability would help set the stage for the story I needed to tell.

I walked down the hall and pulled open two folding doors, finding a washer and dryer inside. I tossed my jeans in the dryer and surveyed the instrument panel. Selecting a setting, I pushed the button and my jeans began to tumble inside.

As I walked down the hall, I saw the door to the baby's room was slightly ajar. I didn't have a right to venture in, but that didn't stop me. I gently pushed the door open all the way and rubbed my hand on the wall, searching for a light switch. As soon as the over-head lamp illuminated the room, I drew in a sharp breath. I'd never seen a room quite like this one. The décor was indescribable, the theme as unique as Geneva.

The red and yellow draped fabric above my head latched on to an old-style chandelier and gave the room a tent-like feeling. There was a mural running across the walls, filled with all sorts of animals —elephants, monkeys, giraffes and more. They all galloped around the room. Stuffed animals adorned nearly every piece of furniture. Geneva had created a make-believe wild kingdom come to life.

My eyes panned over to the crib. It was a dark wood, very modern in style. Above the bed was a quote.

Life is like a circus...random and full of surprises.

"It's a circus," I whispered as my hands skimmed across the dark wood railing of the crib. My son's crib.

"Do you like it?" Geneva's voice startled me.

I turned to face her. "I'm sorry, I know I shouldn't have come in."

"It's all right." She smiled at me, a lightness returning to her face that I hadn't seen since she'd been in Hawaii. "I figured, my life is a circus, so why not Peanut's, too."

"Peanut." I laughed.

"Peanuts are sold at circuses so it seemed fitting."

I surveyed the room, taking in each nuance. Someone had found a way to incorporate the experience of being in a circus without being gaudy. "Who did this?"

"Me." Her statement was given as an afterthought.

"You did all of this?"

"Yeah." She walked around the room, straightening the stuffed animals that didn't need adjusting. Anyone could tell she was nervous. "My degree is in interior design."

"But I thought you were a teacher."

"I am. I went back and got my teacher certificate after—" Her eyes cut to mine.

She'd almost revealed a part of her past, a part she obviously wanted to forget. I understood that kind of censorship.

"We better get back to the living room so I can hear the doorbell." She pushed past me and flipped the light switch off, leaving me standing in the dark, in the middle of my son's nursery.

It seemed fitting. I'd lost one child already, and if I didn't make this right with Geneva, I may lose another, even though I wasn't really convinced I wanted one.

My hand skimmed across the wood railing of the crib and I remembered all the sleepless nights with Alana—up at 3:00 a.m. for diaper changes and bottles, worrying when a fever set in, teething. Did I want all that again? Visions of her tiny hand reaching out to stroke my face as she uttered her first words "Dah Dah" ran through my head. A burning lump gnawed at the back of my throat, and I swallowed down the memories.

I'd had absolutely no desire to have another child after we lost Alana, but it seemed life had thrown me another curve ball. There was no denying that I wanted my son. We'd have to talk about the name, though. I wasn't a fan of *Peanut*, nickname or not, but it wasn't my call to make right now.

Geneva had been doing this pregnancy thing on her own, and it pissed me off that she hadn't reached out to me. Given my reaction in Colorado, I could see why she wouldn't. No one wants to be accused of being a slut when they're pregnant. Especially in a packed restaurant.

"Berk!" Geneva's voice rang down the hallway.

"Coming!" I shouted back. I walked toward the doorway but turned back to gaze over the room one last time. "Peanut," I whispered, trying on the name for size. "I think you're gonna love your room, son."

CHAPTER 12

BERK

"God, I love sweet and sour shrimp." Geneva pushed her plate away from the table as she scooted her chair back and rubbed on her belly. "Yep, right on cue." She laughed.

"What?"

"I told you, Peanut loves shrimp, too. He's kicking away."

My eyes shot wide. I didn't deserve it, but I wanted to feel him, feel the life inside her. A life we'd created. "May I?" My eyes darted from her eyes down to her midsection and then back again.

She nodded her head several times as her lips curved into a smile.

I dragged my chair closer to hers and leaned down, laying my hand on her belly. It only took a few seconds before I felt the movement inside. My heart leapt with joy as I connected with my son for the first time. A joy I hadn't experienced since before Alana and Jaime died. I couldn't keep the silly-assed grin from my face.

I gazed up at Geneva. A massive smile spread across her face, her eyes glowing with the same kind of joy.

"That's Peanut." Her words were soft and affectionate. She already sounded like a loving mother, doting on her son.

I leaned in closer, my lips nearly touching her stomach. "Hey,

Peanut. It's your dad." I spoke with as much confidence as I felt. He kicked several times.

"Holy hell." Geneva startled as she pulled away.

"What?"

"He's never moved like *that* before. It was like he did a somersault."

"Well, he is going to live under a circus tent so…" I chuckled, relieved to see Geneva laughing with me. Suddenly the room went silent as Geneva and I stared at one another. "May I talk to you, about my life before Hawaii and why I said the things I did in Colorado?"

She stared at me, her face void of any emotion.

"I know there's no excuse for my behavior, for the things I said and accused you of. For that I'm truly sorry, Geneva. No matter what the circumstances, no one should be talked to or treated that way." My eyes darted between hers and still she remained quiet.

Finally, she nodded once. "Let me throw away the containers then we can talk."

"Let me get them," I said, scooping up the boxes and utensils then making my way to the kitchen. I was happy to see all the water was now gone and the fan was doing a good job of drying the area.

"Berk," Geneva spoke behind me.

I glanced over my shoulder as I cleaned off the forks. I cut off the water and dried my hands, turning around to face her fully.

"What you did, the things you said in Colorado, really did hurt me. I won't lie."

Oh, fuck. She wasn't going to listen to me. She wasn't even going to give me a chance to explain.

"But I've done way shittier things in my past, and thankfully my family and friends have given me the chance to make amends over the past few years. I owe you that."

Amends? What the hell had she done? I knew she wasn't an

innocent. She'd admitted that in Hawaii. But amends? That sounded bad. Who the fuck was I to judge, though?

"Come on." I took her hand in mine and intertwined our fingers as I led her out of the kitchen and into the living room. "Sit," I said, extending my hand toward the couch as if this was my home.

She sat at the end of the sofa as far away from me as she could. Tucking her legs underneath her, her hands instinctively rested on her belly.

I sat at the opposite end. The space between us was probably a good idea.

"How much about my past do you know? About my wife and daughter, I mean?"

"I just saw the story when you were competing at X Games. They flashed your face and they had a little of your back story."

"What did they say?"

Geneva sat silently, her fingers fiddling with the cushion sitting on her lap.

"It's okay, Geneva. I mean, yeah, it's hard as shit, but I need to tell you about them." Well, not everything. If she found out what a jackass I had been, still was, she may decide to cut me out of our son's life before he was even born.

Her eyes lifted and locked on mine. There was sorrow and pity within them.

I didn't want that. I didn't deserve that.

"They said that your wife and daughter drowned in an accident." Her words flew out quickly, as if it pained her to speak.

"That's all?" Surely it wasn't. My story had been national news for months after Jaime and Alana died. Moving to Hawaii had isolated me from those reports, but I hadn't been able to escape Jaime and Alana's haunting screams at night.

"Berk." Geneva's voice was suddenly closer.

I opened my eyes, unaware I'd closed them, and found she'd scooted closer to me on the sofa.

Her hand rested on my knee. Surprisingly enough, it gave me courage.

"Jaime loved to ice skate," I spoke softly. My eyes looked anywhere but into Geneva's. "There was a small lake by our house in Colorado. It never iced over thick enough to skate on until at least January, but this particular winter had been brutally cold. Jaime thought the ice would be thick enough to skate on in December. I disagreed. Jaime was pretty stubborn, though." I laughed out loud, remembering the countless times we'd fought. Some good, some not so good.

Geneva scooted closer, her hand now gripping my knee.

"Alana, our daughter, was three. Jaime had been teaching her to ice skate since the year before. This year Alana was so excited to get back on the ice that she pestered us, starting in September with the first snow fall. Try as I might, I couldn't explain to her that the water had to freeze, a lot, for her to skate."

I finally braved a glance at Geneva. Her face was passive, void of any judgment or remorse. She was intently listening with no objective other than to let me finish.

I drew in a deep breath and released a heavy sigh. Remembering the deaths of my wife and daughter were gut-wrenching. This was the most I'd shared with anyone, including my own family. I'd screwed up with Geneva, though, and I had to make amends. My story, the story of how I lost my family, seemed like a good start. Then Geneva could decide for herself just how much she wanted me in our son's life.

"By December, Alana's requests to skate were driving Jaime and me crazy, our entire family actually." I chuckled, remembering how Alana would beg both sets of grandparents, aunts and uncles, anyone who would listen, to take her skating. "Even Jaime was starting to whine, claiming the weather had surely iced over the lake enough for them to skate. I didn't want them to go until the local authorities could test it by drilling."

I sat back, my head rolling up to the ceiling, remembering the monstrous fight Jaime and I'd had the night before Alana died. Tears burned the back of my eyes as guilt rolled over me. I loved Jaime. But I hated her for not listening to me that fateful day. And the days after Alana's death, I'd had no problems voicing my disappointment.

"The day before Alana's accident, the sun was shining brightly. It was a beautiful day, and Alana and I spent most of it outside, hiking and roaming around the forest near our home. Alana loved nature." I smiled as memories of Alana flooded my mind. I swallowed the lump that was lodged in my throat.

Geneva returned my smile, so I continued.

"When I put Alana to bed that night, she was a chatterbox. The only way I could get her to calm down was to promise her that she and Jaime could go ice skating in the next day or two, as long as the authorities said the ice was deep enough. It seemed to appease her so she drifted off to sleep."

My voice cracked and my chin quivered as I remembered my last night with Alana. Her dark hair spilled over her pillow and she clung to her favorite stuffed animal, a grizzly bear we'd purchased at Yellowstone National Park earlier that summer.

"Even when I kissed her goodnight, something twisted in my gut," I continued. "Some kind of sixth sense, warning me, but I didn't think anything of it. I had no idea it would be the last time I ever kissed her goodnight again." My voice broke as emotions choked me.

I pushed my thumbs into my eye sockets to hold back the tears. My breathing came in staccato and my heart fired in rapid succession, adrenaline, guilt and shame coursing through me.

"It's okay, Berk," Geneva spoke as she moved closer, nearly sitting on my lap.

"No, it's not okay, Geneva. You need to know what I did, what I said. I'm a complete dick. It's all my fault."

"No, it's not." She spoke softly and tenderly, offering words of comfort.

Instinct and history warned me that once she learned what I'd done to Jaime, what I'd said in the days after Alana's death, she wouldn't believe that.

I rubbed at my eyes with the heels of my palms, wiping away the moisture that had pooled. Finally, I opened my eyes and stared at Geneva. Hers were filled with tears. Guilt washed over me.

"You don't have to go on," she whispered.

"Yes." I nodded. "Yes, I do. For you, and only you." I wanted her to understand I was revealing a part of my past that I didn't want her to share.

She scooted back on the couch, giving me more room.

I shook out my hands and steadied my breath, knowing the worst part of the story was yet to come. I willed my tears away, trying to erect a wall around my emotions so that I could get through this story. I would wait until later, in the safety of my darkened room, to completely break down.

"I really wanted to let Alana and Jaime skate the next day, but the weather reports the evening before said that due to the warmer temperatures over the past week, there had been a freeze-thaw effect on area lakes and water reservoirs. It made the ice conditions unstable and unsafe to be on unless checked by a licensed government official. Since our lake was on private property, we had to call and schedule the officials to come out and certify it. That process could take a few days if not a week. Alana would be devastated, but there was no way I was going to let her skate on unsafe ice."

I sat up straighter on the couch and cleared my throat, which was now choked with unshed tears.

"I told Jaime that night that there was no way they could go skating this week. She was pissed. Like *really* pissed. Jaime could be that way." I made the statement with little compassion, probably trying to relieve my own guilt. "We had a wicked fight. She said I couldn't tell her what to do, I wasn't her father."

Geneva gasped.

I didn't mean to paint Jaime as a bad person. I was trying to justify my actions, which thinking about it now was probably worse.

"Anyway," I sighed, "the next day, after I finished my morning training run, I came back to the house. My heart stopped when I saw that not only were Jaime's skates missing, but Alana's were, too. I swore and kicked shit around in our mudroom. I couldn't believe Jaime would jeopardize her life, and Alana's, just for a fucking day of ice skating."

My voice rose in tenor and echoed throughout Geneva's small living room.

Fucking Jaime!

Those were the two words I uttered that day and every day after until Jaime's own death. Even now though, after all these years, it was hard not to blame her.

"I swung open the front door, about to run down to the lake, and that's when I saw them."

"Who?" Geneva asked.

Her voice jarred me back to the present. I'd practically forgotten that she was there.

"The police."

She gasped.

"Their red and blue lights reflected against the trees surrounding our house as they made their way up the sidewalk to where I was standing. In that moment I knew. I just knew. It's a sixth sense when you're a parent. No one had to tell me Alana was dead." My head sagged into my hands. The tears I'd worked hard to keep at bay rolled down my face.

"Oh, God, Berk, I'm so sorry." Geneva wrapped her arms around me as best she could as she pulled me close.

I didn't deserve her empathy, but I took it, wrapping my own arms around her waist.

The baby kicked against my abdomen.

I pushed back and looked down at her stomach. My eyes rolled up to meet hers, and I saw unconditional love, but I knew it wouldn't last. "I fucked up, Geneva. Just like I did with you in Colorado."

"No, you didn't, Berk. It was an accident."

"Alana's death was no accident. Jaime took her out to the lake against my will, and against the advice of the weathermen and officials."

"She didn't intentionally mean to hurt your daughter."

"But she *knew* her actions *could*, Geneva. I was furious with Jaime. I was torn to shreds after Alana died. I tried to forgive Jaime, I really did, but it never happened. That's what I'm trying to tell you."

"What?" Geneva's voice cracked, along with my heart.

"I killed Jaime. *I* did!" I pounded my chest with my fist. "My words, my actions, my inability to forgive her—that's what killed Jaime. Her death wasn't an accident."

～

Happiness is not something ready-made. It comes from your own actions.

- Dalai Lama

～

CHAPTER 13

GENEVA

BERK'S EYES were drilled shut and his entire body trembled. His jaw clenched and his fists were knotted so tight, the knuckles on his hands were white.

I was clueless as to what to do next. Should I move in and comfort him in some way? Should I scoot back and prepare for his wrath?

Suddenly, Peanut kicked inside, giving me an answer, and I knew exactly what I had to do.

I scooted over the few inches separating us and took Berk in my arms as best I could. He was a giant of a man, but tonight he looked so small and helpless it broke my heart.

Yes, he had called me mean names and lashed out at me in Colorado. There was time to settle that issue later. But now wasn't that time. Berk needed comforting, he needed reassuring words that absolved him from the guilt he obviously felt over the death of his wife and daughter.

"Berk," I whispered into his neck as I drew him closer and rocked him like a small child.

His chest heaved with unrelenting sobs, and my own heart broke for his misery.

The moist stream of tears hit my own face as I relived my mother's death and the guilt that always suffocated me. Even though my father recently assured me I had nothing to do with it, I still couldn't shake the feeling that my selfish actions had brought about her death. It was so clear that Berk felt the same way. I had to absolve him.

"Berk, honey, please." I rubbed circles on his back as I shushed him. "You didn't cause anyone's death. It was an accident."

"No," he choked through his tears.

"Yes, Berk. It was."

He violently shook his head and fought to free himself from my hold, but in a surprising show of strength, I held on to him. I wouldn't let him run, not while he was holding on to so much guilt and shame.

"Geneva," he moaned, "you don't know. You don't know the things I said to her, the way I treated her. Jaime's death wasn't an accident."

He'd repeated the words so many times that now I was beginning to wonder what the real story was. Should I ask him? Or should I try to convince him otherwise? Unless I knew the entire story, there was really no way for me to know.

I pushed him back from my chest and stared at his downcast eyes. He was gripped with such raw emotion and suffering that my own chest ached for his pain.

"Berk, look at me."

He was slow to open his eyes, but eventually his lids fluttered open. His eyes were rimmed with red and his face flushed from the exertion of his tears. Even though Berk was a grown man, sitting here in front of me with his emotions on display, he looked like a small child. I wondered if our own son would look like him one day.

"Tell me what happened, Berk."

His ragged breathing was coming in tiny spurts and I feared he may hyperventilate.

"Berk." I rubbed up and down his forearm.

His large hand covered mine, stopping my movement.

I stole a peek into his eyes and saw they were dark tonight, the demons that haunted him had taken up residence and, now *they* were in control. He was pained, and it was clear he didn't feel worthy of my sympathy. But he would get it anyway.

Slowly pulling my hand out from under his, I placed my palm on the side of his face, surprised when I felt him lean into my touch.

"Tell me," I whispered.

"I…I…" he stuttered, "I don't know if I can, Geneva."

I sat silently, my hand still molded to his face. I would stay here all night if I had to. My heart told me Berk needed to confess, to purge himself, if he was ever going to have a healthy relationship with our son.

He pulled my hand away from his face.

My heart stopped. This was it. He was shutting me out. Not that he'd ever let me in before.

Instead of releasing my hand, he gave it a gentle kiss on the palm and pressed it against his chest.

I twitched at the surge of electricity that shot through my body. Even Peanut jolted. I'd never felt this connected to anyone, except my unborn child.

I sat in silence, staring into his beautiful face, willing Berk to speak. It wasn't my decision, though, it had to be his, but it didn't mean I couldn't silently beg him to share his darkest secrets. I wasn't sure he'd ever told his story before, and I was almost positive that was what had fueled his outburst with me in Colorado. I certainly understood that type of behavior. I'd unleashed my pent-up fury on lots of people in my life. Thankfully, a few had given me a second chance. I at least owed that much to the father of my baby.

"It had been almost a month since Alana died," Berk spoke

softly. "Both Jaime and I were a mess," Berk spoke softly. "We each had our own way of coping with it. For me, I hit the slopes. For her, she walked. Our house was adjacent to a large, wooded area. The clearing on the other side of the trees was where the lake was."

The way he said "the lake" sent chills up my spine.

"I knew Jaime's guilt was driving her insane. I understood better than anyone. But I couldn't shake my anger at her. I tried so hard." He clutched my hand. "I tried so hard to forgive her. But I couldn't. Jaime *never* should have taken Alana skating that day. If she would have listened to me, obeyed my warning, Alana wouldn't have drowned. I knew that, Jaime knew that, and I never let her forget it."

Oh, shit. What had he done? My eyes went wide with worry.

"Anytime Jaime would start to break down, I couldn't find it in me to comfort her," Berk said quietly. "I know it's awful, especially saying it out loud, but I couldn't." His eyes rolled up to meet mine, asking for forgiveness that he didn't need. At least not from me.

Berk drew in a deep breath, releasing it before continuing. "The night before Jaime died, she was crying on the couch and I just couldn't take it. She said, 'I should have died, it should have been me, not Alana.'"

Berk tried to drop my hand but I wouldn't let him. Instead, I grasped his hand and pulled it toward my chest, clutching him, giving him *my* strength.

His eyes flickered for a moment, and I hoped that he felt my compassion. We sat in silence, his hand in mine, me pleading with my eyes, trying to make him feel safe.

"It's okay, Berk," I whispered.

"I didn't correct her, Geneva," he finally said. "I didn't say 'No, it's not your fault, Jaime, you shouldn't have died either.' I didn't say what a husband should. I should have comforted her and reassured her, but I didn't. I couldn't. The bitter man inside me couldn't disagree with her."

Tears welled in his eyes and his hand trembled in mine.

"She felt every ounce of guilt that my silence sent her. In the end, it was too much for her to bear."

My brows furrowed. "What do you mean? I thought her death was an accident."

"That's what it was ruled on her death certificate."

Oh, shit. Had she committed suicide? "But…" I stuttered.

His eyes darted back and forth between mine like a nervous animal, awaiting its own death by lethal injection.

"What happened, Berk?"

"I came home from a training session and couldn't find her. I assumed she was either sleeping or taking a walk in the woods, so I didn't think much of it." He paused and drew his hand away from mine.

This time I let him go, but kept my own hands clutched in my lap, fearing the rest of his story.

"I stumbled around in the kitchen," he said, "looking for something to eat. That's when I noticed a card on the dining table addressed to me in Jaime's handwriting."

Oh, shit. A suicide note?

"I was in the middle of opening the envelope when someone knocked on the door. I swung it open and saw Jackie standing outside."

"Jackie?"

"Yes, Jaime's sister—the one who was sitting with my family at the restaurant in Colorado."

"The one I saw you with in Hawaii?"

"Yes." His answer was flat, void of any feeling.

His sister-in-law. I felt like a shit for ever thinking they were involved. "So, what happened?" I asked, not sure I really wanted to know.

His chest rattled with unshed tears as he sucked in a heavy breath. His eyes cut to the ceiling. "I wondered why Jackie was at my house. The look on her face was almost identical to the one when we'd received word about Alana's death. It was like someone kicked me in the gut all over again. I looked behind her and saw a squad car with an officer leaning against his door, only this time there were no lights flashing."

Shit.

Berk's expression went blank, as if he was curling into himself for protection, putting up a thick wall so he wouldn't have to feel...anything.

"Berk, I'm so sorry." I scooted in close to him and ran my hand up and down his arm.

"Officially, she drowned in the water. Apparently, she went back to the lake and slipped through the ice as well. They called it an accident. But—" He hiccupped a sob.

I gave him a moment to collect his thoughts, knowing that his admission must be gut-wrenching.

He swallowed hard and somehow found the strength to continue. "But the toxicology reports showed large amounts of benzodiazepine in her system."

I shuddered when I recognized the drug, remembering how awful I'd been and the lengths I'd gone to in order to destroy Hindley and Rory.

"The doctor prescribed the medicine to Jaime shortly after Alana's death, due to her anxiety and inability to sleep. I'm sure if I would have been a better husband, she wouldn't have needed sleeping pills." His head sank to his chest.

"Berk, you don't know that."

"Yes," he whispered, "yes, I do."

"How?"

"Her note."

"What did it say?" The question was out of my mouth before I could stop it and instantly, I regretted asking. "I'm sorry, you don't have to answer that. I'm sure it was private."

He ignored me as he fumbled with his hands, his fingers twisted together. "It just said, 'I'm sorry.'"

How could he pile so much guilt and anguish on himself with just those two words?

"She was apologizing because she knew I blamed her for Alana's death, even though I hadn't spoken the words outright to her. She knew it."

"Berk, that's not true. Maybe she meant she was sorry that she couldn't be strong enough."

"I should have been her strength. I should have carried her. Instead, all I could think of was my *own* grief, my *own* loss, as if she hadn't lost her daughter, too." His shoulders shook as he cried.

Leaning in further, I grasped his strong arms.

He wrapped them around me and fell into my embrace. "I'm no good at this, Geneva." His breath skimmed across the exposed skin of my shoulder.

"No good at what?"

"Being a father, being a husband." He choked on his tears. "Being a man."

I shoved against his shoulders, trying to push him away, but he clung to me as if I were his favorite stuffed animal—the one that guarded a child at night and promised to take all their nightmares away.

"I pushed Jaime over the edge. I tried to protect Alana, but I failed."

Forcibly prying myself out of his grip, I steadied my hands around his shoulders and looked him square in the eyes. "There were a lot of 'I's' in that statement, Berk."

"What do you mean?" His head tilted and his eyes narrowed.

I drew in a steadying breath. How could I explain this to him, explain my own recovery without admitting how fucked up I really was and how much therapy I continued to receive.

"When we find ourselves saying 'I' a lot," I said, "we have to dig deeper and find out why we're so fixated on ourselves, on our own suffering, when there are so many other things to worry about."

Berk jerked back as if affronted. "That's what I'm saying to you, Geneva. I was so fixated on my own loss that I completely failed Jaime as a husband."

"That may be true, Berk, but it doesn't mean you put lethal amounts of drugs in her system or made her go back out to the lake."

His face contorted and I felt as if maybe I'd overstepped my bounds and not explained myself well enough.

"Maybe you could have done more, but you were grieving, too," I said. "There's no right or wrong way to do that. And your anger was justifiable. Blaming yourself for a decision that was ultimately Jaime's to make, though won't help you heal."

His eyes were bloodshot from crying. They scanned mine as he tried to process everything I was saying.

"I couldn't even look at her, Geneva."

"Who?"

"Jaime. They wanted me to identify her body, but I couldn't."

"Why?"

"I told everyone that I didn't want my last image of her to be her dead body. I'd already done that with Alana because Jaime couldn't and it had gutted me."

"But that wasn't the real reason?"

He shook his head. "I was too ashamed of what I'd done."

"You hadn't done anything, Berk." I tried to console him, but he withdrew from my touch.

"I did to her exactly what I did to you in Colorado." His words were so quiet I could barely hear them, as if he was talking to himself.

"What are you talking about?"

"I lashed out at you, called you names, made you feel horrible about yourself. I escaped to Hawaii after Jaime's death to avoid feeling *anything*. But then, when I saw you pregnant in that restaurant, and you told me the baby was mine, all those feelings I'd suppressed came to the surface. I acted out the only way I know how. Selfishly."

His statement made sense, and I really couldn't argue. It was common for people to suppress their grief—Lord knew I had for years after my mother's death—only to have it return in the strangest of ways. For me, it was hatred toward my stepsister. For Berk, it was hatred toward his late wife, and then me.

"I get it, Berk, believe me, I do."

"How? How can you possibly justify my behavior toward you?"

"We're more alike than you know."

His eyes narrowed as he studied me.

A stabbing pain hit me under my rib cage and I doubled over in agony. "Oh, God," I moaned through gritted teeth.

"What? What happened?" The fear in Berk's voice was palpable.

I fell into his lap as I fought to catch my breath. It wasn't unlike Peanut to kick me in the ribs every so often, but this felt different, a lot different. I sat silently for several moments, trying to catch my breath as the pain subsided.

"Geneva," Berk spoke as he rubbed on my back. "What's going on? Are you all right?"

"I'll be fine," I said through gritted teeth. "Just give me a second." I drew in two deep breaths and my body began to relax. I sat up and smiled when Berk pulled me close to him.

His eyes scanned my face. "What happened, Geneva? Are you sick? Is something wrong with the baby?" His voice wavered, the fear so audible.

I was worried myself—I'd never experienced that type of pain before—but I needed to take care of Berk, reassure him that I was all right.

"It's probably just the shrimp coming back to haunt me." I laughed.

"That's not it." His tone was serious, his expression stern. "I saw the look on your face. You're just as worried as I am. I'm taking you to the hospital." He jumped up, pulling me with him.

I yelped. "No, Berk, really. I'm fine. Let's just sit down and I'll take it easy. I have a doctor's appointment tomorrow. I'll let her know what happened and she can check me out." Peanut kicked. "See, there he is, healthy and happy, kicking the crap out of me. That's all it was, his heel in my ribs."

His eyes studied my face.

I wasn't fooling him any more than I was fooling myself.

"How far along are you?"

"Almost twenty-one weeks."

His face washed over with that blank stare people got when they didn't understand gestation.

"Sorry," I laughed quietly, "just over five months."

"When are you due?"

"The first of June."

His eyes scanned my body. "I'm sorry, Geneva."

Oh, God. Was he leaving already? "Why?" My voice cracked.

"I'm sorry I questioned you and talked horribly to you. That I haven't been here all this time." He placed his hand over my belly. "For you. And for *Peanut*." The name came strained out of his mouth.

"You don't like my nickname for our baby?" I giggled. *Our baby*. It sounded nice.

"It's definitely not one of my favorites, no." He smiled. "But I'm in no position to argue with you."

"What does that mean?"

"I haven't been here, to support you. I really have no say in the matter at this point."

"Berk, what are you talking about? You're the baby's father. Of course, you have a say."

His eyes shot wide and his full lips curled up into a smile. One of the first I'd seen all evening.

"Thank you, Geneva."

"For what?"

"For giving me a second chance." His body slumped in what felt like relief. "I just wish I'd had one with Jaime."

Well, hell. What could I say to that? Nothing.

Peanut kicked again.

Berk stared at my stomach, his hand still on the spot where his son had nudged him. A small smile broke across Berk's face.

I was grateful Peanut could give Berk the words of love I couldn't.

CHAPTER 14

GENEVA

"Hi, Geneva," Dr. Rusk said as she entered the examining room.

I squirmed on the table, my paper gown crunching against my skin. I both loved and loathed my prenatal doctor appointments. Listening to Peanut's heartbeat always put a smile on my face. But having to wear these skimpy, flimsy paper gowns and have someone's hand shoved up my vagina wasn't so pleasant.

Today I loathed it even more as I gazed over my belly and saw Berk sitting in the chair at the end of the table. He was going to move before Dr. Rusk stuck her hand up my gown. No way was he getting *that* view of me.

Dr. Rusk's gaze traveled from me over to Berk, her brow furrowed.

"Oh, I'm sorry. Dr. Rusk, this is Berk Rigby."

Berk stood and extended his hand. "Nice to meet you." He looked as nervous as a virgin at a prison rodeo.

Dr. Rusk's gaze returned to me, her head tilting in silent question.

"Berk is the baby's father."

She nodded once and the conversation was over. She thumbed

through my folder. "Well, it says here on the chart you had some unusual pain yesterday."

"Yes," I answered, trying to keep the worry from my voice. Berk had done enough for the both of us.

"Hmmm." She shook her head. "It was under your ribs?"

"Yes."

"And you're sure it wasn't the baby, it felt different?"

"He's never kicked me that hard before."

"It could just be indigestion," she explained.

My shoulders sank in relief.

Berk rose from his chair and came to stand by my side near my head.

"Could it be something else, Dr. Rusk?"

His concern shouldn't have surprised me. He'd gone through a pregnancy before.

"At twenty-one weeks it could be any kind of innocuous problem that has nothing to do with the baby. But just to be safe and to reassure you," she smiled at Berk, "let's do an ultrasound, shall we?"

Berk looked down at me, his eyes alight like a child on Christmas morning.

"That way Dad gets to see his baby boy." Dr. Rusk smiled as she reached across the exam table and pressed a button. "Wendy, will you bring in the ultrasound to room four. Thank you, dear." She turned back to face us. "So, Berk, I know this is Geneva's first child. Is it yours?"

Berk's face went ashen.

My hands clamped around the table, fearing his reaction as my heart beat out of my chest.

"No, ma'am, this isn't my first child."

"Oh." Dr. Rusk nodded once. "For medical purposes, I just need to know the health of your child so I can document it in Geneva's chart. Was his or her birth normal or did the baby experience complications?"

I stared up at Berk.

His lips were pressed in a fine line, his forehead creased.

I released the death grip I had on the exam table and reached out to take his hand in mine, giving him a small squeeze.

He looked down at me and his face softened slightly. His eyes were fixed on mine as he answered. "No, nothing unusual. She was a healthy baby."

"Oh, good," Dr. Rusk said.

I blew out a sigh of relief.

"How old is she now?"

Oh, fuck. Why wouldn't the doctor let this go?

Berk's grip tightened on mine and he remained silent.

I gave him the voice he needed. "She passed away a few years ago, Dr. Rusk," I said.

"Oh, heavens. I'm so sorry." Her brown eyes spoke volumes, the sympathy pooling deep within. "I hate to pry, but for medical purposes again, was it anything genetic that I should know about?"

"No, ma'am. It was an accident." Berk paused as he took a steadying breath.

I wanted to speak for him again, but I knew that was not what he needed. He needed to say the words out loud, as much for the doctor as for himself.

"She drowned," he said quietly. "Accidentally."

The door flew open as a woman dressed in bright pink scrubs entered, pushing an ultrasound machine. Her eyes scanned the room and instantly her head dropped, realizing something wasn't right.

"I'm so sorry, Berk." Dr. Rusk spoke quietly. "Forgive me for the intrusion but I had to ask."

"It's all right," Berk said. "I understand, it's for the baby."

"Speaking of baby," Dr. Rusk smiled as she looked over at the girl in pink scrubs, "let's let Daddy get a first look at his son, shall we." Her jovial attitude pervaded the room and quickly dissipated the somber mood. "I'm sure he's fine, but we'll count fingers and toes just to be safe."

Dr. Rusk spread a blanket across my chest and another over my abdomen before separating my paper gown.

My eyes darted up to Berk, hoping to connect with him but his gaze was fixated on the computer monitor.

I wondered what he'd thought the first time he'd seen his daughter on the ultrasound. Would this visit to the doctor help him or hurt him?

"I know we all say it, but it's true." Dr. Rusk laughed to herself. "This is going to be cold."

I sucked in a breath as she squirted the gel on my protruding belly. I couldn't believe how much my stomach had grown in the last four weeks.

Berk gently squeezed my hand.

I looked up at him as he stood next to my head, thankful he wasn't south of my navel.

His eyes were bright and a small smile tugged at his full lips. He was beautiful. Even though he'd treated me horribly and called me names in Colorado, I understood why and I forgave him. I had to.

He gave me a quick wink and a panty-dropping smile.

Oh, shit. My stomach fluttered—and not from Peanut. My legs clenched with desire. I was in trouble.

"There he is." Dr. Rusk interrupted my sordid thoughts.

I'd completely spaced out and forgotten she was rubbing a wand on my bare belly. I looked up at Berk whose attention was fully on the screen across from us, his mouth lax but curved slightly with the hint of a smile.

"That's my son," he whispered.

"Yep, healthy as a horse." Dr. Rusk pointed to the screen.

"There's ten fingers and ten toes. And a steady, strong heartbeat. Everything looks fine. Would you like a picture, Daddy?"

"Definitely." Berk beamed.

She hit a few buttons on the keyboard and the machine spurted out a piece of paper. "There he is." She held the paper toward Berk.

I already had my own keepsake ultrasound photo when she'd done one at ten weeks. This visit, this picture, was all for Berk.

"I am slightly concerned about your blood pressure, though," Dr. Rusk said as she powered off the machine and gave me tissues to wipe my belly.

"Why?" Berk answered before I could, the concern vibrating from his voice.

"It could be excitement. Are you stressed at work?"

I laughed.

"What?" she asked.

"I'm supposed to be teaching a lesson on childcare and I'm completely clueless."

"There are classes you can take. I can give you some brochures if you'd like."

I nodded.

"They would contain some good contacts for you. Maybe you could have a guest lecturer," she said.

"That sounds good."

Dr. Rusk held out her hand and I grabbed it, pulling myself up to a sitting position.

"I'd like to check your blood pressure one more time before you leave, though."

"Why?" Now I was worried.

"It could be the early signs of preeclampsia."

"That's not good." Berk moved closer to me.

"No, preeclampsia isn't good, but it's manageable, controllable, as long as we know she has it. Right now, it's just cautionary."

"So, you don't know for sure if I have it?" My heartbeat was racing now. Not a good time to take my blood pressure, but I wanted everything to be okay with Peanut.

"No, but I just want to note it on your chart and monitor you. I have brochures here." She reached up on the wall and pulled down pamphlets, handing them to me. "And you can research it on the Internet. Don't worry, though. Even if you do progress, we can take care of you and the baby just fine."

"You're sure?" My tone revealed the panic I felt inside.

Berk gently squeezed my shoulder, and I melted into his hold.

"You're fine, Geneva," Dr. Rusk said. "I'm sure it's nothing. But I don't want to miss *anything*. I'm overly cautious with my patients. That's a good thing. I don't mean to worry you at all."

She pulled the blood pressure cuff from the wall as she secured it around my upper arm and shoved her stethoscope into her ears. "Try to relax and take in some deep breaths."

I sucked in through my mouth, but it was shaky at best.

"It's all right, Geneva. Everything is fine." Berk's words caressed my cheek. "I'm here with you now." His caramel eyes bore through mine and I felt all my anxiety wash away.

The cuff tightened and still my gaze stayed firmly on Berk. Before I realized it, I heard the familiar rip of the Velcro breaking the cuff free from my arm.

"One twenty-five over eighty-five. See, it's already come down." Dr. Rusk patted my leg. "You're just fine. I'll make sure we monitor it on your next visit." She jotted down notes in my chart then looked up at both of us. "Four weeks, all right?"

I nodded my head.

"Berk, it was a pleasure to meet you. I'm sorry about the inquisition, I just need to make sure that your baby has the best prenatal care he can get."

"I understand." Berk took her outstretched hand and shook it. "And I appreciate it."

"Enjoy your photo." She smiled at both of us before leaving the room.

"I'm sorry you had to go through all of that." I stepped off the table as Berk took my arm and helped me.

"Go through what?" Berk asked.

"The doctor asking so many questions."

"It's all right. It's her job. She needs to make sure *Peanut* is going to have the best chance to survive."

"You're still not in love with my nickname." I laughed and motioned for him to turn around while I redressed.

"I don't think I'll ever *love* the name. But I'll tolerate it, for his mother's sake."

I fastened my bra and pulled my dress over my head. "Well, thanks for appeasing me."

He chuckled.

"Are you ready?" I pulled my hair out from my collar.

Berk turned to face me, his eyes full of admiration. "I'm sorry you've had to do this on your own for so long, Geneva."

"It's not your fault." I laughed nervously. "I'm the one who didn't tell you."

"Why didn't you?"

"Can we have this conversation somewhere else besides my gynecologist's office?"

"Are you hungry?"

I looked down at my stomach. "Are you serious? I have your son inside me. I'm always hungry."

He stepped closer to me, pinning me against the wall, his hand gently pushing a stray lock of hair behind my ear. "I like the sound of that."

"The sound of what?" I stuttered, my voice shaky and unsure. His proximity and his touch were doing weird things to me.

"My son inside you."

My legs trembled and my face flushed red. I skirted away from his hold and made a beeline for the door. "Pizza!" I shouted, sounding like I had Tourette's.

"Buffet I'm assuming." Berk chuckled as he placed his hand on my lower back, escorting me out.

The touch of his hand in support of me felt like heaven. I was in trouble. Big time.

CHAPTER 15

GENEVA

"GOD, I *SO* NEEDED THIS GIRLS' Night Out." Dana raised her margarita glass high in the air. "To girls."

"To girls," we all chimed in, raising our own glasses, mine and Hindley's full of sweet, iced tea, Tori's filled with water.

"Don't get me wrong," Dana said, "I love my kids, and my husband. But God, they can drive me fucking crazy some days."

"You love it." I bumped Dana's arm, causing her margarita to splash.

"Hey, watch it, dumbass, you nearly wasted good alcohol." She laughed, the joy of her life radiating from her crystal blue eyes.

"Just admit it." I raised a brow.

"God, I do love it. I never thought I'd have a big family of my own. I mean, it's work, a lot of work, but I love it. I've never felt more alive."

"But…" Hindley trailed off.

"But some days, Momma needs a night off." Dana giggled.

"Here, here to that, sister." Hindley raised her glass in the air, and we clanked our drinks together again.

"I don't have any kids, but I grew up with six brothers and I saw what my mom went through with all of us." Tori shook her head. "No thanks."

"You don't want any kids?" I asked.

"Nuh-uh, no way, no how," she answered.

I wasn't sure why, but her response surprised me.

"Ever?" Hindley asked.

"Nope. Never." She shook her head. "I never want to go through what my mom went through. Hell, I don't even want to get married. I don't know how my mom put up with all my dad's shit for all those years."

"What happened?" Hindley asked.

"Long story. Suffice to say, my dad was a total asshole." Tori let out a heavy breath.

I could see the pain in her blue eyes. My heart ached for the father she never had.

"But I do enjoy a good girls' night out." She waggled her brows.

Dana raised her half empty glass. "To girls' night out!"

"No more toasts, little one." Hindley laughed as she pushed Dana's arm down. "I think you're already feeling no pain, and we're only at dinner."

"Are we gonna go clubbing?" Dana's perfectly groomed eyebrow lifted in anticipation.

"I hardly think we're in any condition to go dancing." Hindley's hand went from her own belly to mine.

"Screw that. Even pregnant chicks need to let loose sometimes," Dana said.

"Actually, I'm starting to get a bad headache." I didn't want to say anything and ruin our first girls' night out in forever, but I couldn't shake this headache of mine.

"Are you okay?" Hindley's concerned voice brought a pang of regret to my heart. I'd hurt her, completely destroyed her once, and yet she still had compassion for me.

"I'll be fine." I smiled, wanting to divert the attention from me.

"Probably just work. And Berk and I—" Oh, shit. I hadn't meant to bring up Berk. Not yet. He and I were still trying to figure things out.

"What!" they all yelled in unison.

"Berk is here? Like here, here?" Dana pointed to the table, her attention drawn away from her drink.

"Well, not *here*, here, as in this restaurant, no."

"Cut the shit, Gen, you know what I'm talking about." Dana's eyes narrowed.

"He's here, in town, in Austin," I confessed.

"Holy shit." Tori reared back and threw her hands in the air, shaking her head. "How is this possible? I live with you and I didn't know."

"You've been spending a lot of time at Dana and Peter's house, with them and the kids. And he's not at the house a lot. We've actually only seen each other a few times."

"Seeing him *once* and not telling us is cause for me to kick your ass." Dana's jaw clenched, and her once bright eyes turned to frozen steel.

Crap.

"What did he say?" Hindley asked.

"Please tell me he apologized for being a total dick in Colorado." Tori's gaze wasn't as menacing as Dana's, but there was still a look of betrayal on her face.

"Look, I'm sorry that I didn't tell you guys. It's only been a few days."

"A few days! What the fuck, Geneva?" Dana exclaimed.

"Keep your voice down." I held up my hand to Dana's face. "He showed up a few days ago because I'd sent him papers to absolve his parental rights." I looked at Hindley and she nodded her head. A former colleague of Hindley's had actually drafted the petition, with Hindley's help.

"I knew you were talking about it when we got back from

Colorado, but I didn't know you had gone through with it." Tori's shoulders slumped and her face went slack. I'd hurt her by not telling her sooner.

Tori and I had grown close since our trip to Hawaii for Dana and Peter's wedding. She was rough and rowdy but had the capacity to be demure and refined when needed, like me. We'd been a natural fit from the start.

"I didn't mean to keep it from you guys. I just didn't know what was going to become of it."

"So, what has *become of it*?" Dana asked, mocking my words, using air quotes. She couldn't hide the care and concern in her face, though. "What did he say?"

"Well, at first, Berk was super pissed," I said. "Stan answered the door when Berk knocked."

"Oh, that's classic." Dana bellowed with laughter as she leaned back in her chair. "I bet that went over like a turd in a punchbowl at prom."

We all fell into a fit of laughter.

"Yeah, I'm sure that didn't help the situation any," I said.

"So," Tori encouraged me.

"So, I told him to sign it and leave me alone."

"Did he?" Hindley asked.

"Obviously not, because she already said they've been talking." Dana stared at Hindley as if she had an octopus on her face.

"All right, we're cutting you off, Miss Sassy Pants." Hindley reached over and dragged Dana's empty margarita glass away.

"Hey," Dana moaned.

"So anyway…" Tori said.

"So anyway," I continued, "he basically stalked me and confronted me at work."

"What the fuck?" Dana's words spewed out.

"Watch it, Dana. We're in public." Hindley's glare reminded Dana to keep her voice down.

"You're such a party pooper, *Mom*." Dana swatted at Hindley playfully, their interaction evidence of years of friendship.

I'd missed out on having a best friend because of my past, because of my mean girl attitude. I had these three now, but I envied the way that Hindley and Dana knew one another. Just with one glance they could speak volumes to each other, no words needed between them.

"Can we *please* find out what the hell happened next?" Tori rolled her eyes in exasperation.

"Another margarita?" The waiter stood over our table, staring at Dana.

"No." Hindley answered for her.

"Yes," Dana countered.

The poor waiter's face scrunched in confusion while his eyes darted back and forth between Hindley and Dana.

"Fine, Mommy," Dana pouted. "I'll have water."

"You'll thank me in the morning when you're not half dead from a hangover while dealing with a house full of kids and a grumpy husband."

"You speak from experience." The waiter's words were more of a statement than a question.

"Unfortunately, yes," Hindley answered.

"One water coming up. Anything else?" The waiter's attention suddenly focused on Tori, and I noticed her blush. Tori *never* blushed.

"Nothing for us," Dana answered. "But you could bring us back your phone number for the little lady here." Dana nodded toward Tori.

Her eyes bulged as she swatted at Dana, but we could all see a hint of thankfulness in her eyes.

"One water, and one phone number coming right up." The waiter winked at Tori.

Her face lit up like the neon "open" sign outside.

Holy hell, the sexual tension between those two was almost as palpable as the one between Berk and me.

"Oh, damn, girl." Dana laughed. "He is super hot."

Hindley and I nodded in agreement.

"You *totally* need to tap that." Dana giggled.

Tori laughed and swatted at her again.

"I'm serious," Dana continued. "We're all either married or pregnant, or both. We're living vicariously through you now, you slut. I want details." Dana squeezed her sister-in-law's arm with tenderness. "I swear I won't tell your brother anything."

"Promises made under duress from alcohol consumption don't count," Hindley said.

"Oh, whatever, Miss Wise Ass Lawyer."

"Better to be a wise ass than a dumbass." Hindley cocked her head and raised a brow.

Dana cackled. "So true. Okay, so back to *this* skank." She pointed at me. "Spill, bitch."

"Well, he found me at work, I have no idea how, and told me he wasn't going to sign without talking to me first. I could tell by his reaction when he'd first showed up at my house that he had no intention of signing the papers if he truly thought the baby was his."

"Of course, it's his. Right?" Dana asked.

"Yes, it's his. I mean, I *was* a skank," I answered. "But not any more. I hadn't been with anyone in a long time when I met Berk in Hawaii. And I haven't been with anyone since. But in his defense, I did tell him I used to be kind of slutty."

"Why the hell would you tell him that?" Dana asked, her lip curled.

"I thought it was a vacation fuck," I answered. "So, who cared, right? I mean, shit, I didn't know I was going to get pregnant."

"How did you anyway?" Hindley asked. "I thought you were on the pill."

"And we gave you a handful of condoms," Dana reminded me.

"You gave me *three*. Which we used up in one night."

"Oh, shit!" Dana exclaimed.

Hindley glared at her.

"Sorry, it's just, being out with my girls is the only time I can cuss like a sailor now. These kids are bankrupting me with their damn Cuss Bucket."

We all laughed at Dana's admission. She was trying so hard to tame her potty mouth. We all had the propensity to spout off expletives, but no one did it better than Dana.

"Anyway, enough about my filthy mouth," Dana said. "How did you get pregnant if you were on the pill?"

"A few weeks before we left for Hawaii I got that awful stomach bug, you remember?"

All three girls nodded.

"That shit was awful, you were puking up your toenails," Hindley said. "You had to go stay with Mom and Dad."

I smiled at Hindley's use of the term 'Dad' for my father. Now she considered him *her* father, too, and that thought warmed not only *my* heart but our dad's as well.

"Yeah, it was nasty all right." I shook my head. "Well, I guess in all of that I either forgot to take the pills or threw them up. So, for several days I didn't have the hormone in my system."

"And that was enough?" Dana asked.

I knew Dana didn't understand it all. She'd had a full hysterectomy at nineteen so she'd never had to worry about contraceptives.

"Yep. Even if you just miss one dose apparently you have a chance." I rolled my eyes as my hand rubbed on my belly. "Peanut here is a fluke." I laughed nervously.

"But a miracle all the same." Hindley placed her hand on top of mine as she stared into my eyes, her sisterly love filling the void inside me. How the hell had I gotten so lucky as to be given a second chance with this amazing woman? I didn't know, and I wasn't going to question it. I just knew I had to give Berk the same.

"Here's to a miracle." Dana held up her empty hand. "Ah, shit. I don't have a glass."

We all laughed at our friend's semi-drunk antics.

"If I have to say, 'So Berk' one more time, I'm gonna snap." Tori's eyes narrowed as her hand splayed on the table.

"Okay, okay. So Berk…" I trailed off, smiling at Tori's disgruntled stare. "I agreed to have dinner with him. He said he wanted to apologize."

"What happened?" Tori bounced in her seat.

"When he came over, there was a household disaster."

"Oh, no." Hindley's face went ashen.

"The hose to the ice maker on the fridge busted."

She gasped.

Hindley still owned the duplex I lived in. She was meticulous about its upkeep, even after she'd moved out and gone to California to live with Rory. When they came into town, Hindley and Rory would stay in the other side of the house. But now they were moving back to Austin permanently and were building a new house. She really didn't need the duplex. She could have sold it and made a good profit, considering our dad was a real estate investor. But I think she held on to it because she didn't have the heart to kick me out.

"It's okay." I reached over and stroked her forearm. "Berk fixed it and cleaned up the mess."

"Why the hell are you so concerned about rental property anyway?" Dana plopped her elbow on the table as her chin flopped down on her open palm, staring at Hindley.

"Rory is just very particular."

"He's a fucking worry wart is what he is," Dana said. "About anything connected to you. You can't go two steps outside his shadow without the dude freaking the fuck out."

We all laughed. It was the truth.

"If you think he's bad about me, you should see him with poor Abbi." She rolled her eyes.

"So anyway!" Tori shouted.

"Okay, okay, back to Gen. No more interruptions." Dana's gaze darted between Hindley and Tori and they both nodded in agreement.

"Well, he fixed the leak and helped me clean up the mess," I said, "but dinner was ruined. Instead of going out, we ordered Chinese and talked."

"About?" Tori cocked her head.

"His wife. And daughter."

"Oh, shit," all three said in unison.

"Yeah, it was pretty bad. He broke down."

"Oh, no," Tori whispered.

"What happened to them?" Hindley's eyes were wide with fear.

"They both drowned."

They all gasped even though they knew how Berk's daughter had died from the newscasters commentating during the X Games.

"Without going into all the details, his wife was basically full of regret and guilt. Apparently, Berk wasn't very forgiving because she'd deliberately taken their daughter ice skating against his wishes. The ice wasn't safe, but she did it anyway."

"Oh, damn. Poor woman." Dana's hand clutched her mouth.

"Well, Berk didn't see it that way. He didn't out-and-out blame her, but he said he wasn't supportive of her in any way."

"So, what happened to her?" Tori asked.

"Apparently she wasn't sleeping well." I looked around the restaurant and leaned in further. "Look, guys, I don't know how much of this I should be saying. I got the impression that some of this isn't public knowledge."

"We get it," Hindley said. "We're not going to say anything. But you don't have to tell us if you're not comfortable."

I knew I could trust my girls. And they would help me navigate these uncharted waters of how to deal with Berk if he was really going to be part of my future.

"The reports said her death was ruled an accident," I said. "Apparently, she slipped through the same patch of ice as her daughter."

"Why the hell would she go back out on the ice?" Tori asked.

I stared at Tori, not wanting to reveal all the details, but silently answering her question.

"Oh, fuck," Dana whispered, leaning in. "She killed herself?"

"That's what Berk thinks. And he blames himself."

"Why?" Hindley's forehead scrunched in confusion.

"Because he wasn't compassionate with his wife after their daughter died. He blamed her."

"Did he say that to her face?" Tori's body stiffened.

"Look, she knew the ice might not be stable but she took her daughter out on the water anyway."

"Are you defending him?" Hindley snarled.

"What if Rory deliberately went against your wishes and put Abbi in harm's way and she died?"

Hindley gasped, and one hand slapped over her mouth as the other dropped to her belly.

"Exactly," I said. "You'd be furious, not loving at all. Right?" I couldn't figure out why I was defending Berk, but I was.

Hindley nodded in confession.

"Look, thank God none of us knows what it's like to lose a child and I pray we never do," I said. "We have *no* idea how we would react, especially if the accident was a result of negligence on the part of our partner."

"True," Dana said.

"Berk was so tied up in knots when he told me the story. He broke down. He's never forgiven himself for either one of their deaths."

"God, that's horrible." Tori shook her head. "I can't even imagine."

"He escaped to Hawaii shortly after they died and said he blocked it all out. When he saw me in Colorado and I told him the baby was his, he said he flipped shit. All the old emotions and feelings flooded him—guilt, shame, remorse—like a nightmare. He took it all out on me."

"Makes sense, I guess," Tori said.

"He apologized and said he believes the baby is his and he wants to start over. He even went to my doctor's appointment." I laughed.

"No way." Hindley reared back in surprise.

"Yes way. The doctor even performed an ultrasound so he could see the baby."

"Did Berk flip shit?" Dana asked.

"He was good. But the doctor asked him a lot of questions about Alana."

"Is Alana his daughter?" Tori asked.

I nodded.

"What a beautiful name." Hindley's face lit up.

"I know, right. I'm pretty sure it's Hawaiian. So anyway," I continued, "the doctor asked Berk how old Alana was, and he had to tell her that she died. She asked how, because she wanted to make sure it was nothing genetic, anything that could put Peanut at risk."

"Oh my God, poor Berk," Hindley said.

"So, what's the deal now? Is he in the picture, for good?" Dana sat back in her chair, crossing her arms over her chest. I loved that she was protective of me.

"I'm not sure. We haven't really talked about it. I think he lives in Colorado full-time now. It scares the shit out of me to think about joint custody, of having to ship my baby off to him for extended periods of time."

"Man, that *would* suck," Tori said.

"Where's he staying?" Hindley raised her brow.

"I don't know. He said his brother brought him to my house."

"His brother lives in Austin?" Dana cocked her head.

"No, he's here for South By."

"The music festival? His brother is a musician?" Tori's eyes lit up. She loved guys in bands.

"They're staying at a hotel then?" Hindley asked.

"No, I think at a friend's house. I'm not sure."

"Invite him to Lucas's party," Dana said. Lucas was Dana's soon-to-be eleven-year-old son.

"What?" I pulled back. "No way."

"Why?" Dana tilted her head, her raven curls spilling over her shoulder.

"Because it will be all family, and you guys will tear him to shreds after the way he treated me."

"Not after that story you just told," Dana answered. "The dude has been through some major shit and is probably totally fucked up. Especially now that you sprung it on him that you're preggers."

"It's not like I did it on purpose." My eyes burned with unshed tears and my head throbbed. My headache was becoming unbearable.

"I'm sorry, sweetie." Dana reached across the table and grabbed my hand. "I totally didn't mean it that way. I just meant, if he's here in town and he's going to be part of this baby's life, then he has to meet all of us eventually. The sooner the better, right?"

She looked at both girls and they nodded.

"So, what do you say?" she asked. "Invite him?" Deep dimples appeared on Dana's face as she smiled at me.

"I'll ask him."

Dana's smile grew and she squeezed my hand before releasing it.

"Are you sure you're okay?" Hindley surveyed me. "You look tired."

"I'm pregnant." I laughed.

"I know, but I mean, you just look worn out."

"I'm sure having her baby daddy back in town and all the drama that's surrounding him has her completely freaked," Tori said.

"Yeah, probably so. Would you guys mind if I cut out early?"

"Nah. I gotta get home soon and fuck the shit out of my husband." Dana giggled as she waggled her brows.

"Dana!" Hindley shouted.

"Whatever. It's not like you and Rory aren't freaks under the sheets." Dana stared at Hindley.

We all burst into laughter. It was true. Rory and Hindley had the propensity to get pretty crazy, not that I asked. But I'd heard some of the stories from Dana. I'd be lying if I said I wasn't jealous.

"Oh, speaking of freaky," Hindley said. "I ordered some furniture and it's being delivered to the duplex. Will you let them in to my side when they show up?"

"Since when is furniture freaky?" Dana raised one brow.

"Why aren't they delivering it to your house?" I asked.

Hindley's face flushed crimson and I knew I did *not* want to know. *Freaks in the sheets.*

"Never mind." I laughed.

Hindley giggled.

"Fucking freaks." Dana shook her head.

"Here's your water." The waiter set a glass in front of Dana. "And one phone number." He slid a napkin toward Tori and whispered something in her ear that made her shiver.

It seemed as if everyone was getting lucky tonight, everyone but me. These pregnancy hormones were making me horny as shit.

"I gotta go." I stood and looked down at these women who had now become my closest friends.

"Vibrator time?" Dana winked as she stared up at me.

The waiter stiffened and his eyes went wide.

"What?" Dana jerked her head back as if offended by the waiter's shock. "Guys can beat off, but a girl can't get her rocks off with motorized machinery?" She glared at the poor waiter.

He was silent, white as a ghost. His mouth was hanging open so wide I feared a flock of birds might fly in and choke him.

"Good luck with that one." I laughed, making my way to the exit, wondering if I should stop by the store for more batteries.

∾

There is no grief like the grief that does not speak.
- Henry Wadsworth Longfellow

∾

CHAPTER 16

BERK

"Are you all right?" Geneva glanced over at me from her vantage point in the driver's seat.

We were on our way to a birthday party where I would be reintroduced to some of her family and friends. I'd briefly met them in Hawaii, but this would be the first *real* interaction with them. I could only imagine what they thought of me after my tirade in Colorado.

"Just nervous," I admitted, casting my gaze out the window.

"I told you, I already explained everything to the girls."

My head jerked toward her. "What did you tell them?" I hated that sympathetic look people got in their eyes when they knew you'd lost a loved one—especially a child.

"Everything that everyone else knows. Why? Was I not supposed to?"

I released a heavy sigh and leaned back in the seat. "No, it's all right. I just get nervous, wondering what questions people will ask me. I usually put up a wall and don't give a shit. But..." I trailed off, not wanting to admit my real fear.

I liked Geneva, a lot, and I didn't want to screw this up. I would be in her life for the rest of mine now that we had a son together.

Creating tension and friction between us, between our friends and family, could be detrimental for all of us.

"It's okay, Berk." Geneva placed her hand on my thigh.

Something in my pants twitched. God, I did not need this kind of reaction to her right now.

Geneva was still as beautiful as when I'd been with her in Hawaii. Carrying my child gave her a glow that made her even more desirable. But we had shit to figure out, a relationship to rebuild. We had to figure out how to muddle through this thing called parenthood before anything else could happen. I couldn't fuck this up with sex. *Well, not now anyway.* I smiled at my deviant thoughts.

"Hey," she called out to me.

My eyes trailed up her arm and over her bare shoulder. She was wearing a cover up over her bikini and her skin was just as golden and sweet as in Hawaii. It was her natural pigment, just like mine.

"You'll be fine. My friends understand what really happened in Colorado. Yeah, they're protective, especially since I have this guy." She patted her belly.

I peered down at my hands now twisted together.

"What's got your mind racing over there?" she asked.

"I'm trying to remember everyone's names."

"Don't worry about it." Her lips curved into a sideways smile that had parts of my anatomy tightening.

"What?" I tried to hide the anxiety in my voice.

"I'm just glad you said yes. Levi thinks you're some kind of God."

"That's Dana's youngest son?"

"Um hmm."

I remembered Levi from Hawaii. He was small and seemed extremely fragile. I also remembered he was deathly afraid of the water.

"Why does he think I'm a god?"

"Because he knows you surf and because you're a lifeguard. And because you snowboard. He's always wanted to ski."

"He remembers me from Hawaii?" I was surprised and a little honored.

"Oh, yes. He couldn't stop talking about you when we first got back. Believe me, it was a nightmare." Her eyes stared straight ahead, fixated on the road.

"I'm sorry about the miscommunication." I stroked her bare thigh. I felt her skin twitch. "I wish you would have asked me who Jackie was instead of leaving."

"I know," she sighed. "I'm sorry, too." She cut her eyes to me. "I promise to ask you next time before I assume stuff. Even if I think it's something I don't want to hear."

"And I promise to tell you the truth, even when I think you don't want to hear it." I chuckled. "That goes for you, too."

"What?"

"I always want you to tell me the truth, no matter what."

"Deal." She stuck out her hand, and I placed my large fingers around her palm, giving it a slow squeeze. Her pouty lips lifted in a smile that lit her eyes on fire.

My dick jumped. Oh, shit!

"What?" She tried to pull her hand away from mine but I held it tight.

"What, what?"

"Something just happened to you. Your face got all scrunched up like you were in pain."

"It was your death grip on my hand," I teased, trying to buy time to get my midsection under control. Regardless, I still couldn't bring myself to release her.

"I need my hand to drive."

We were on a straight stretch of road that didn't require two hands, but I glanced up and saw the same desire glazing over her eyes that did mine. She was just as affected as I was.

The thought should have scared me. Adding sex to the mix would only fuck up this already fucked-up situation even more. Yet knowing all this, I still couldn't bring myself to let her go.

"My father will be there," she announced.

Fuck! My hand instantly dropped hers as all the blood from my dick drained to my extremities.

She giggled. "I didn't mean to scare you."

Didn't mean to scare you? Meeting a chick's dad under the *best* of circumstances could be gut-wrenching.

"I'm not scared," I squeaked out, surprised by my high pitch.

"I thought you said we weren't going to lie."

I peered over at her face and saw one brow arched high, a smirk curling up her delicious lips. God, those lips.

"Meeting a girl's dad can be nerve-wracking," I said.

"And?"

"And…" I paused to steady my voice. "Well, let's see. I knocked you up, then called you a slut when you tried to get me to take responsibility."

"You kind of did." She laughed. "I've talked to him already. He knows the situation. It will be fine, Berk."

She wanted me to believe her, but I didn't. I couldn't. If someone had done *any* of that to Alana, I would destroy the dude.

"We're here." Her tone was light and airy, as if we were about to embark on a fantastic voyage.

Not.

With great trepidation, I swung open the car door and reached for our bags in the back seat, trying to make it around the car in time to help Geneva out. She wasn't large, not yet, but I knew she'd endured this pregnancy under great stress, thanks to me. My only desire now was to take care of her and our son.

"Here, let me carry one of those bags." She reached for one of the straps but I swatted her hand away.

"I've got it, Geneva."

Her shoulders dropped as she exhaled a deep breath, a look of relief washing over her face. She understood my deeper meaning. I was here, and no matter what our past or our future held, I really would take care of her.

"Thanks." The smile she gave me lit me on fire.

How the hell was I supposed to walk into this party now with a semi-boner? I closed the car door behind us.

She took my hand in hers and led us toward a large building with huge glass windows.

"The party is in the Swim House," she announced as she practically skipped toward the building, which housed an indoor swimming pool at the facility where she worked.

I, on the other hand, walked as if a one-hundred-pound lead weight was attached to each ankle.

She looked over her shoulder, her loose hair blowing with the afternoon breeze. She was breathtaking and beautiful.

"You'll be fine, Berk. I promise. Their bark is so much worse than their bite." She giggled and turned back around, tugging on my hand.

Great. Bark. Bite. I was totally fucked.

Geneva led us down a paved pathway toward the large building. Its windows were covered in steam.

She stopped just before we entered the double doors and looked up at me with those big blue eyes that had captivated me from the first day I'd met her. "I just want to apologize up front."

I gulped. "Uh, for what?"

"My friends can be quite…" she trailed off.

"Mean?"

She laughed. "No, I was going to say crude. But sometimes mean, too. They promised me they'd be on their best behavior today. But truly, that means nothing with this bunch."

"Okay." I drew in a deep breath that did nothing to steady my racing heart. "So, there's your stepmom Caroline, and your dad Paul, right?"

She smiled and nodded.

"And your stepsister, Hindley. She's married to Rory Gregor, the skateboarding legend?"

"Yes."

"Okay, I think I've got that. And Peter Fontenot. I know him from X Games. He's the one that married Dana in Hawaii?"

"Berk." She laughed, resting her hand on my arm. "You're going to be fine. I promise. They'll give you shit, I'm sure, but they're all really sweet people once you get to know them."

My head fell back as I stared up at the dark cloud looming overhead. This couldn't be a good sign.

"Come on." She tugged on my hand. "Let's go inside before you bolt."

"Wait, Geneva." I yanked her back.

She fell flush against my body, her protruding belly pressed against my abdomen.

We stared into each other's eyes and suddenly I forgot what I was going to say. I bent lower, our lips just inches apart and watched as her eyes fluttered closed.

"You already knocked her up once. You going for twins now, sailor?" someone yelled behind me.

Geneva and I shot apart as if we'd been electrocuted.

"Dammit, Dana," Geneva seethed as she marched toward the tiny woman with the big mouth and huge dimples. I recognized her —Dana. The bride. She would be my first hurdle.

"Well, come on, Poseidon. Levi can't wait to see you." Dana nodded toward the door she was holding open.

"Everybody!" Dana shouted as we entered the building, her voice echoing through the huge facility. "They're here."

I scanned the building and saw every activity stop at her words as all eyes focused on me. You could have heard a pin drop. My stomach twisted in pain and I seriously thought about running.

"Where's all your hair?" Someone tugged on my shorts. I looked down and saw huge brown eyes staring back at me. It had to be Dana's son, Levi. He was the cutest thing I'd ever seen, this side of Alana. My heart seized with pain and I fought my racing thoughts.

"You okay?" Geneva tugged on my arm.

"Yeah, I'm good." I smiled at her.

I squatted down so that Levi and I were eye level. He had jet-black hair like his mother but anyone could tell their ancestry was not the same.

"Where are your orange shorts?" Levi asked.

I looked up at Dana in question.

"Back in Hawaii, you were wearing your lifeguard trunks," she explained.

I nodded in understanding and turned my attention back to Levi. "Well, I only wear my orange shorts when I'm the lifeguard. Do you know what that is?"

"Yes." He nodded his head, his smile lighting up the room. "Where is your hair?" His face contorted as he searched my head.

My hand rubbed over my cropped hair. I'd wanted a new life, a fresh start when I'd returned from Hawaii. "Um…," I stumbled with my words, unsure of how to explain that to a small boy, "I just decided to cut it off one day."

"I wanted to cut my sister's hair one time, but my mommy said no." Levi looked back at his mom.

Dana raised a single brow in warning as her arms crossed over her chest. She was fierce in any role she played.

Levi leaned into me, his mouth pressed to my ear. "I cut a little bit of it when she was sleeping though, but my mommy doesn't know." He peeked back over his shoulder.

Both of Dana's brows were raised and her hands firmly attached to her hips. "What did you say, Levi?"

His eyes grew wide. Dana was obviously a loving mom, but she kept her kids on a short leash.

"Guy stuff." I winked at Dana.

"Yeah, Mommy. Guy stuff." Levi crossed his hands over his bare chest and squared his shoulders.

A tall man with black hair saddled up next to Levi. "You're gonna get in trouble, little man." He rubbed Levi's head.

"Guy stuff, Daddy. Right?" Levi stared up at him for help and solidarity.

"Hey, I'm Peter Fontenot," the man announced, sticking his hand in my face.

I stood. "Hi, I'm Berk Rigby." I shook his hand. "It's nice to meet you. Formally. I mean, I saw you in Hawaii but..." God, I was already stumbling.

He smiled and instantly I felt like I'd made a friend.

"Welcome to the party. This is my son, Levi." Beams of adoration and love for his son shone from deep within him. It didn't matter if it was from birth or adoption, anyone could see these kids were a part of him, a part of Dana.

Children. The steel band around my heart tightened, and I nearly gasped to catch my next breath. I had to pull my shit together.

"And this is Lucas." Geneva broke through my thoughts. "It's his birthday."

An older boy appeared next to Geneva, and she slipped her arm around his shoulders. He was similar in coloring to his brother, Levi, but you could see the innocence had left him a long time ago.

"Happy Birthday, Lucas," I said. He was at that awkward age, not quite a young man, but not a kid either, and it made me unsure of how to address him.

He stuck his hand out and I hid a smile as I took his smaller hand in mine.

"Thank you," he said quietly.

"Oh, um, we brought you something." I dug through the huge bag Geneva brought until I found the gift inside. It was wrapped in *Star Wars* paper. Geneva told me that was his absolute favorite thing.

"Thanks." He took it and inspected the package as if expecting it to explode.

"I'm sorry about the paper," I said. "I'm more of an original *Star Wars* trilogy kind of fan, not prequel, but this was all they had at the store."

Lucas's mouth fell lax as his eyes darted from me to the gift.

"What?" I asked.

"You like *Star Wars*?"

I scanned the people surrounding us. They were all staring at me as if I were on fire.

"Of course, I do." I smiled. "I love all the *Star Wars* movies. *Return of the Jedi* is the best in my opinion. You just can't beat old school *Star Wars*, you know?"

"Totally." He nodded his head. "My dad likes *The Clone Wars*."

My eyes went wide. "No way," I said. *The Clone Wars* was the animated movie of *Star Wars*. No true, self-respecting fan would actually profess that was their *favorite* movie.

Lucas and I laughed in unison.

"I know, right. See," Lucas turned to Peter, "not cool."

Peter laughed and shrugged his shoulders at me.

Something inside told me I'd passed my first test with Geneva's friends and family.

Dana scooted in next to me. "Looks like you've captured another one of our sons, Poseidon."

"Why do you keep calling me Poseidon?"

Dana wiggled her brows and stared at Geneva.

Geneva shook her head and rolled her eyes. "Do you remember back in Hawaii, I told you I couldn't remember your name?"

I furrowed my brow trying to remember.

"I told you I had a nickname for you, the god of the sea." She jutted her head, her eyes going wider, willing me to remember.

"Oh, yes," I chuckled, "Poseidon."

"There ya go, tiger." Dana hit my arm.

I was surprised the punch actually stung a little.

"Poseidon," she repeated.

"You know I have an actual name though, right?"

"Yep." She slurped on her soda. "I know you do." She gave me a wink and a nod, her icy blue eyes sparkling with mischief.

I felt sorry for Peter. He had his hands full taming that one. But the deep dimples that drilled into Dana's cheeks let me know I'd cleared another hurdle.

"Hey, Berk, I'm Rory Gregor."

I turned to find one of the most famous X Games athletes in history. He was legendary in extreme sports, hell, in all of the sports really.

He extended a hand toward me. I noticed his other was holding a precious little girl with blonde ringlet hair and bright blue eyes so big you could get lost in them.

"Dah-Dah!" the little girl exclaimed as she hit Rory's chest.

A lump swelled in my throat as I suppressed my instinctual reaction to hearing that name, especially from a little girl held in the arms of her father.

Keep it together, man.

"It's really nice to meet you, Rory. I've seen you skate. You're incredible." I grabbed hold of his hand, trying not to gush like a teenage girl. "I'm Berk Rigby."

"Yes, I know," he said. "I've seen you snowboard. You're amazing to watch."

"My dah-dah 'kate," the little girl said, her eyes glowing with pride as she kissed his cheek.

Rory pulled away and smattered her with his own kisses.

Her giggles echoed through the pool house.

The steel band around my chest cinched tighter and I felt light-headed. I could hear Alana's voice, her laughter. I could feel her skin on mine, the way she littered my face with kisses the way this precious girl did to Rory.

"And this," Rory said, interrupting my thoughts, "is Miss Abbi."

God, even their names were similar. *Breathe in. Breathe out.* It was the only way I could keep from collapsing.

"Abbi ehs me." Abbi's face spread wide with a huge grin as she patted her chest with pride. "Momma!" she shouted, all but falling out of Rory's arms into what I assumed actually was her mother's.

This woman was quite recognizable as well—Hindley Gregor, Rory's wife and Geneva's stepsister. Her face had littered magazines with her own tragic story of pain and loss several years ago. She and Rory had done a few public interviews when their heart-breaking story made national news.

Hindley's blonde hair was pulled back tight in a ponytail. Her dark brown eyes and light skin stood in stark contrast to her daughter's. But their warm smiles and loving eyes made it more than obvious she was Abbi's mother.

"This is my sister, Hindley," Geneva announced.

"It's nice to finally meet you, for real," Hindley said. "I mean, we met in Hawaii, on the beach." She smiled, and the warmth in her eyes drew you in. She was genuine, real, no fake pretenses. I liked her instantly.

"You've already met?" Rory asked, his tone slightly possessive.

"Yes." She laughed.

He clutched her around the waist and pulled her in as if she'd float away.

She shook her head, obviously used to his possessive nature. "I was a little less pregnant then." She looked down at her stomach and I saw she was indeed pregnant. Very pregnant.

"How far along are you?" I knew most guys didn't ask questions like that as they had no idea about gestation and pregnancy terms, but I had experienced it all before.

Jaime becoming pregnant had been a surprise. But I had been so excited, I dove in head first, learning all I could about pregnancy, actually reading the *What to Expect When You're Expecting* book cover to cover in three days.

"I'm just a couple of months ahead of Geneva actually, even though I'm twice her size and big as a house."

"You look beautiful, baby." Rory placed his hand on her belly and bent in for a kiss that turned pretty passionate.

"All right already," Geneva interrupted them. "You're holding a small person."

Rory pulled back, but the lust in his eyes didn't diminish. These two had serious chemistry.

"Dah-dah, kiss me now," Abbi demanded, leaning toward Rory.

He scooped her up in his arms and held her high above his head as her giggles bounced off every wall in the room.

My heart filled with sadness as I remembered the joy of holding my own daughter in my arms.

"Berk?" Another deep voice sounded behind me.

The hairs on my neck stood at attention, and a wave of nausea rolled through my stomach.

"Oh, shit," Rory whispered.

I turned on my heel, thinking better of it when I saw the man standing in front of me.

He was older, with dark hair graying at the temples and creases around the edges of his blue eyes—familiar blue eyes that bore through me. This was Geneva's father, and I knew in that moment I was fucked.

"May I have a word with you?"

My entire body broke out in a cold sweat. I felt light-headed as my limbs tingled.

"Um, Berk." Geneva cleared her throat, her eyes going wide. "This is my father, Paul Barton."

"Nice to meet you, sir." My voice cracked. I extended my hand even though it was shaking like a third grader about to get the shit knocked out of him.

"Berk," he repeated, his voice monotone.

"It's a little too late to tell him to keep his banana in his pants now, Paul," Rory said, laughing out loud, along with Hindley and the others.

I stood stark still, my body paralyzed with fear. I had no idea what Rory's comment meant, and I didn't dare ask.

"Yes, Rory, you're absolutely right." Paul surveyed Rory from head to toe, a slight lift to his lips revealing a smirk. "But judging by my adorable grandbaby in your arms and the bump of my daughter's belly, I'd say you didn't do a very good job of keeping the peel on your banana either."

Everyone standing within earshot burst into laughter, including me. Paul's teasing nature lowered my anxiety, only by a fraction.

"Shall we?" Paul motioned toward the exit doors.

"Daddy." Geneva grabbed his arm, her eyes pleading.

He patted her hand several times before gently removing it then bringing it to his lips for a gentle kiss. The man had a tenderness about him. For that I was thankful.

"We'll be back soon, dear." He smiled down at Geneva before casting his gaze over his shoulder at me. "Both in one piece, I promise."

I swallowed the lump in my throat, not so sure I would survive this trip with Paul Barton. Fuck.

"Well, at least *I'll* still be in once piece." He laughed. "It looks as if Berk may pass out and crash to the floor at any minute."

"Daddy," she scolded, her eyes narrowing, but her lips curled slightly in a smile.

"Come on, Berk." Without another word Paul strolled toward the door, unaware that I really was about to pass out at any minute.

"I'm sorry," I said as the doors slammed shut behind us, jogging to catch up with him. He was shorter than me, but his strides were long and purposeful, a man on a mission. He did not squander his time. I hoped this attack on me would be swift.

"Sorry for what?" He looked over at me as I scooted up next to his side, following him along the stone path.

"For the way I treated Geneva in Colorado."

"What did you do in Colorado?" His head tilted slightly as he squinted his eyes.

Paul Barton was an intelligent man. There was no *way* he didn't know what I'd done. He was baiting me, trying to find out my side of the story. I liked him already, but I was scared shitless of him, too, right now.

"Well," I rubbed my hands together, my palms sweating, "I said some pretty nasty things to Geneva, accused her of being a lot of things a man shouldn't."

"Like?"

Oh, shit. There was no way I was going to repeat the scenario, not to her father. Hell, I didn't even remember half the shit I'd said I was so freaked out that night.

"I don't remember a lot of it, but I know I would never want anyone to call my daughter the things I'm sure I called Geneva. I didn't mean to. I was just in shock and I never—"

"It's okay, Berk." Paul stopped my babbling mid-sentence. "That's not why I brought you out here. Sit." His hand motioned toward an Adirondack chair sitting under a large oak tree.

I slid down into the unforgiving wood and watched as Paul took the seat next to me.

"First and foremost, I want to offer my sincere condolences to you on the loss of your wife and daughter."

What? Was he serious? He was offering me condolences. After

his words sunk in, images of Alana and Jaime flashed across my mind. I fell back into the chair, exhaling a large breath. They were the last thing I thought this man would want to discuss. And certainly, the last thing I wanted to discuss with him, or anyone for that matter.

"You can't block them out forever, Berk."

I cut my gaze to his, surprised by his blunt comment.

"How do you know I'm blocking them out?"

"I can see the struggle on your face. You're afraid if you think about them, you won't ever get over them, right?"

Paul was partially right. But it was also the crushing weight of guilt that paralyzed me. That was the reason I never thought about my wife and daughter. The shame of my own involvement in their deaths was too much to bear.

"It's more than that, Mr. Barton."

"Please, call me Paul. I know I came on a little strong in there and I apologize. It was just in fun."

"So, you're not mad at me for how I treated Geneva?"

"I'm not sure what all you did or said, she's never told me, but what I've gathered from everyone else's observations and remarks about you, I can only assume it wasn't nice. And after discovering that you lost your wife and daughter, I'm guessing part of your outburst had to do with unresolved emotions you have surrounding their deaths. Am I right?"

I sat in silence for a moment, staring up at the large oak tree we sat under. New leaves were beginning to form after the harsh winter that had robbed the tree of its foliage.

"It's kind of like you," Paul said.

I looked over at him and found his gaze cast up at the tree as well.

"I'm sorry?" I asked.

"The tree." He nodded toward the limbs overhead. "It lost all its leaves just a few short months ago. But now the warmth of the sun has brought on a new season for Mr. Oak here, a time for new birth, new growth, new life."

I continued to stare at him, his words hitting my heart like an arrow. I was scared, really scared of having this baby with Geneva. What if I fucked it up? Again. What if I caused *Peanut's* death, and Geneva's, too?

"I lost my wife just before Geneva turned eight," Paul said. His gaze left the tree and focused on me.

"I'm so sorry."

"Thank you. It was a hard time for me, but even more so for Geneva. She lost her best friend. And worse than that, she shut herself off from the world. Even from me. That's what hardened her heart and turned her into the calloused young woman she used to be. Don't blame her for that."

I had absolutely no idea what the hell Paul was talking about.

"I think this baby is good for her. And for you," he added. "It's a fresh start, for both of you." He smiled, a loving expression that any good parent would give their child.

Only, I wasn't his child. Apparently, I was his comrade, though, and he was coming to save me from the depths of my despair. He thought he had true empathy for my loss, but he didn't. Fate had allowed him to keep his daughter. Mine had been snatched away from me. And I'm sure he hadn't caused his own wife's death like I had.

"With all due respect, sir, you have your daughter. I don't." My words were colder than I meant. Paul had been kind to me so far, but, as usual, the mention of my daughter hardened my heart.

"That's true." He nodded. "It doesn't mean I didn't lose Geneva, though. I mean, not in the sense that you lost your daughter. I get that. I'm not trying to diminish your loss."

I stared into his eyes and I could see the love he had for his daughter. It was the same affection I had for Alana.

"I missed my wife, terribly. I still do," Paul said. "Sometimes when I'm alone, I can still hear her laughter or smell her perfume." His eyes cut to the ground. It was clear he was overcome with emotion.

"That's the difference between us, Paul."

"I know."

"Know what?" Now I was puzzled.

"I know you won't let yourself experience the loss, the pain, the remorse of losing your family. But I'm telling you, Berk, if you want to move on, if you *really* want to be a father again, you have to."

I jumped to my feet. How dare he tell me how to grieve? He didn't even know me.

He stayed in his seat and stared up at me. "You can run, Berk, from all of us. I get it. It's hard to process all those feelings. Especially when guilt is involved."

"What do you know about my loss?"

He slowly stood from his chair as if not to spook me.

My heart beat out of my chest. It was the first time anyone had confronted me about my family's death. Not even my *own* family dared to talk to me about them.

"I don't know what it's like to lose a child, I'll give you that," he spoke softly. "I, too, put off my grieving for a long time. It wasn't until I met Caroline, my wife now, and Hindley, that I really began to process everything. Caroline wouldn't let me run any more."

"So, you think I'm running?"

"I know you are, son."

"I'm not your son."

Paul took a step back as if I'd punched him in the nuts.

"I apologize, Berk. It wasn't my intent to upset you."

"Then what *is* your intent, sir?" I squared my shoulders, preparing for a lecture.

His eyes went soft as his shoulders slumped.

"I haven't been the best father to my daughter," he confessed.

"It doesn't mean I didn't love her. I just didn't understand how difficult her own loss had been. I didn't protect her, and as a result I lost her. For many years."

His eyes scanned the vast land that surrounded the campus. He drew in a deep breath, holding on to it as his eyes closed. After several moments, his shoulders sunk as he exhaled.

"I won't let her be hurt again, Berk. Not if I can help it," he said quietly.

His words were short and succinct. It was a warning. To me.

"I understand part of your pain, Berk, whether you believe it or not. I won't stand here and act like I know your entire story or can empathize with *everything* you've been through. I wouldn't disrespect you like that."

My own shoulders slumped in despair and remorse. I felt like a prick for confronting the man earlier when his only intent had been to protect his daughter.

"I'm sorry," I said.

"I don't want your apology. What I want is an honest answer to a difficult question."

I stared at him, my lungs burning as I held my own breath.

"If you want to be a father to this baby, then I will welcome you into our family. I'm not asking for a commitment to my daughter, but I am asking for one to her son. To *your* son. If you can't commit to being his father, if you're teetering on whether you want to fulfill this role in his life, then I'm asking you to bow out—now—before relationships are built and bonds formed that could destroy my daughter."

I stepped back, affronted by his words.

"I let Geneva go when she was young," he continued, "thinking that was the best way for her to heal after her mother's death. She pulled away from me and I let her. I refuse to do that again. I will protect her, physically and emotionally, with my life, as I'm sure you would have your daughter."

"I didn't protect my daughter, Paul. That's why I'm standing here without her."

"That's not true, Berk. And if you want to be in your son's life, then you need to figure out a way to forgive yourself and move on. I'm not saying forget her or your wife, but you *have* to forgive yourself."

My breathing came in short spurts, and my vision faded. "What are you saying?" I whispered.

"I'm saying," he moved closer to me, "that whatever you're feeling about your wife and daughter is completely normal and okay. But *feel* them, Berk, feel *something* or you'll never heal. And if you don't, it may cost you another child."

Without another word, he left me standing alone under the large oak tree, my world completely turned on its axis. Tears burned my eyes and I worked to keep them contained, but it was useless.

I'd hid in the shadows for three years, like a coward, unwilling and unable to face the demons that kept me up at night—the ghosts that chased me, leaving me calling after Alana and Jaime at night, their voices begging me for help. Maybe it was me who needed *their* help to heal.

In confronting me, Paul had lanced a festering wound, and now there was no way for me to close. it.

CHAPTER 17

BERK

"BERK?" Geneva's voice broke through the silence.

I remained still, sitting in the chair underneath the oak tree, unable and unwilling to look at her for fear my guilt would blind her.

"Are you all right?" Her hand burned my back as she gently rubbed across my shoulder blades.

I didn't deserve her affections. I didn't deserve anyone's. I stood up and pushed her hand away, not surprised when I turned and saw the frown on her face.

"I'm sorry for whatever it is my father said." Her eyes darted between mine.

"He didn't say anything that wasn't true."

"What *did* he say?" She slid up beside me like we were magnetized.

"He said if I can't commit to this baby then I need to bow out now."

"And what did you say?" Her eyes were wide and I knew she feared I would leave.

"Do you want me to leave, Geneva? Leave you and the baby?"

"No." She placed her hands on my shoulder. "I want you here.

For sure." Just as quickly as she came, she dropped her hands and stepped back. "I mean, if you want to. I don't expect anything from you, as far as a relationship between us, if that's what you mean."

I shook my head. "No, that's not what I meant." I drew in a deep breath, realizing what Paul said was right. I did want to be in my son's life. The pain and guilt from Alana and Jaime's deaths were crushing me, though, and I wasn't sure I could work my way through it.

"What's wrong, Berk?" Geneva's voice was heartbreakingly gentle.

"Have a seat." I motioned toward one of the chairs.

I watched as she slid into the large chair, her protruding belly a constant reminder to me that I couldn't fuck this up.

"Your father said I need to get over the guilt of my family's death."

She sat silent, and for that I was grateful.

"He's the first person to confront me about them, about their deaths I mean. Not even my own family talks about Alana and Jaime. At least not in front of me. At my request," I added.

"I'm so sorry if he hurt you, Berk. I know that wasn't his intent."

"I know," I sighed, shaking my head. "It's just, I don't know how, Geneva. I don't know how to move on. I mean, I want to, but I don't know if I can."

"Have you ever talked about this with anyone, ever?"

I shook my head. "I'm serious when I told you, I forbid my family to even mention their names to me when I left for Hawaii. I cut Alana and Jaime out of my memories for years."

Geneva stared at me with those bright blue eyes, her look not one of condemnation but of genuine sympathy.

"And now?" she asked.

"Now." I drew in a deep breath, gazing up at the oak tree as I let out a heavy sigh. "Now, there's new life." My eyes drifted down to her belly as I moved toward her, kneeling and placing both hands on her abdomen. "I do want this, Geneva." I stared at her stomach, willing *Peanut* to answer me, but he remained still.

I peeked up at her eyes, my breath caught in my throat as I surveyed her flawless face. She was beautiful, surreal and I couldn't imagine her heart ever being hardened like her father had spoken of earlier.

"There are some things I need to tell you, too, Berk." Her face went sullen. "But not here, not today. Okay?"

I nodded once in understanding.

"Maybe at home," she said.

Home. Crap. "Oh, no, I completely forgot."

"What?" she asked.

"Well, I've been kicked out of Rhen's friend's house."

"Rhen's your brother, right?"

"Yes."

"Do you want to stay? Here in Austin, I mean?" There was hopefulness in her voice.

"I may mess this all up, Geneva, I'm not going to lie."

"Me, too," she whispered. "That's why God invented therapists. To fix all our fuck-ups. Especially the ones we pass on to our kids." She laughed, a tinge of sorrow laced in her words. "Do you want to talk to someone, Berk? A therapist?"

Shit, did I? "I don't know, Geneva. But I want to be here, with you and the baby."

"Well, the facility here has some great therapists, and they can recommend more, if you want. I go every other week and it's helped me process a lot. I could go with you, if you want."

"Can I think about it?"

"Of course." She smiled, her hand moving from atop mine up to my face, cupping my cheek.

I leaned into her hand, closing my eyes and relishing her nurturing touch.

"We'll find you a place to stay."

I was surprised she didn't offer up her own house, but thankful at the same time.

"Maybe next door to me, the other side of my duplex. Rory and Hindley don't live there any more. They just use it for their sex-capades."

"Their what?"

She giggled, and for the first time in a long time, I had hope—hope of a future that didn't seem so bleak and bare.

"Come on, I'll explain later." She stood and pulled on my hand.

I stood in front of her, gazing down into her blue eyes, watching as the sun shone on her blonde hair and tanned shoulders.

Her gaze held mine as her arms wrapped around my waist, our stomachs touching one another as she pulled me in and gently laid her cheek against my chest.

"We'll figure it out, Berk. Together."

I slid my arms around her shoulders, relishing her soft, silky skin. Her hold tightened on me and I drew her in even further. We both jumped as the baby kicked. Releasing our hold on one another, we both stared down at her stomach.

Geneva's eyes met mine and her full lips lifted into a smile that lit up my world.

I slid my hands along her cheeks and wrapped my fingers around the base of her neck as my thumbs caressed her skin.

"Together," I whispered as my lips gently pressed against hers. It was a light kiss, meant to display the tenderness I felt but had a hard time articulating.

Her hands covered mine and I pulled away, captivated by the look of adoration in her face. It had been a long time since anyone had cherished me.

"Together." She smiled.

CHAPTER 18

BERK

"So, Berk, please have a seat."

I stared at the green leather sofa and compared it to the matching chair in Dr. Elsher's office, wondering if this was her first test for me. She was the therapist Geneva had recommended.

"Is something wrong?" she asked as she took a seat in her office chair.

Her oak desk was butted up against the wall, leaving herself totally exposed to her patients. She created no barriers between them, and I liked that.

Dr. Elsher leaned back casually, one elbow resting on the dark wooden structure as she thumped the chair handle with her index finger.

"Um, no, nothing's wrong." *Other than the fact you're at a shrink's office, no, nothing is wrong.*

"Are you nervous?" she asked.

"You could say that." I tentatively chose the single-person chair and sunk into the lush leather. I didn't want to leave space around me for anyone else to sit, especially the ghosts of my past.

"Would you like some water?"

"Uh, sure." *Anything to delay the inevitable, right?*

She reached to the side of her desk and opened a small refrigerator, producing a bottle of water. "Here you go." She held the drink out for me.

I grabbed it from her hand, twisting the top and gulping down half the bottle. The water hit my stomach hard and I nearly upchucked.

"So, what brings you in today?" Dr. Elsher smiled, and I noted that her tone was genuine.

"Geneva didn't tell you?"

"She told me a little, but I'm more interested in hearing why *you* chose to come today."

I tilted my head and narrowed my eyes in skepticism.

"You seem surprised," she said.

"Well, yeah. I guess I just assumed Geneva would have told you all about me."

"Why would she have done that?" Her tone wasn't condescending, more inquisitive.

I shrugged.

"Geneva is a professional," she said. "And I assume you trust her."

I nodded once.

"She would never do anything to jeopardize your trust, or her job."

"Jeopardize her job? What does that mean?"

"Geneva is privy to a lot of confidential information here at Whispering Oaks," Dr. Elsher said. "She knows the penalty for divulging any contents within a resident's file."

"But I'm not a resident." I was confused, and I was sure my face revealed as much.

"No, you're not. You're obviously much more than that."

"What makes you say that?"

"Geneva was very concerned. She's never asked me to see

anyone before. I assumed her request marked you as a significant person in her life."

A small smile touched my lips, realizing I might be significant to Geneva. We may share a baby together, that was true, but what Dr. Elsher was saying felt even more reverent.

"So anyway, tell me a little about yourself." She reached down and grabbed another bottle of water from the fridge and popped the cap, taking a small sip.

I sat silent, having no idea where to begin.

"What about your family of origin?" she asked.

"What's that?"

"Your birth family—your mother, father, any brothers and sisters."

"Oh, uh…" I stumbled, wondering what, if anything, this had to do with resolving my guilt and grief.

"Where were you born?" Dr. Elsher sat in silence, her scrutinizing stare already unnerving me.

"Hawaii," I finally answered.

"Oh, what a wonderful place to grow up." She smiled, and my anxiety dulled slightly.

"I didn't grow up there. Well, not my entire life," I corrected.

"How long were you there?"

"Until I was twelve. Then we moved to Colorado."

"How did moving at twelve make you feel?"

I rolled my eyes. Here we went with the psychoanalysis bullshit that I wasn't interested in.

"What's wrong?" she asked, sounding genuinely concerned.

"I'm not here for you to analyze my childhood or find out if I have Freudian mommy issues."

She placed her water bottle on top of her desk and intertwined her fingers, gently laying them on top of her abdomen. Leaning back in her chair she narrowed her eyes. "Then tell me why you *are* here, Berk."

I rubbed my jawline nervously as my palms began to sweat. How much did I want to say? How much *could* I say? Why *was* I here?

"I want to be a good father to my son."

"That seems like a very valid reason for seeking therapy."

My eyes locked on hers, and I saw nothing but sincerity.

"Is there a reason you think you *wouldn't* be a good father, in your present state?" Her fingers thrummed along her knuckles.

"I killed my daughter." I punched the words out, swallowing hard to keep the water from working its way back up my throat.

Dr. Elsher sat impassively, not moving, not blinking, just studying me with no judgment.

"Tell me why you think you killed her."

I tensed in the chair and sat silent, praying that she would take my non-answer as an answer.

Once again, she sat stone still, but her eyes begged me to trudge on.

"I didn't *physically* kill her." The words gutted me. My insides twisted in painful knots. "I just didn't protect her."

"Protect her how?"

"I didn't let her walk out into traffic or anything, if that's what you're thinking."

"What is it you think you did do, or should I ask *not* do, to protect her?"

"I should have stayed home that day. I never should have let her and my wife go ice skating."

"What is your daughter's name?"

My eyes cut to hers. "Her name *was* Alana."

"Did you change it after her death?"

"What?"

"You said her name *was* Alana." She tilted her head.

"Yes. What's wrong with that?"

"It's your use of verb tense."

I stared at her, completely baffled by where she was going with this.

"Her name still *is* Alana, Berk. Just because she's passed doesn't mean it's no longer her name. You're allowed to talk about her."

I sat in silence, dumfounded by her words.

"Tell me about Alana."

I focused my attention on Dr. Elsher, surprised to find her expression expectant, almost giddy, as if I were about to share something special with her that she'd waited years for.

"Berk?"

I didn't move, I couldn't move. I couldn't breathe, afraid I may crumble with my next inhalation.

"May I ask how old she was when she died?" Dr. Elsher asked.

My eyes darted around the room like a caged animal. Talk about Alana? I drew in a deep, steadying breath. This was for my son. I had to move on, and that meant cleaning out the old wounds, for him. For *Peanut.*

"She was three when she drowned." My voice cracked as I whispered the words I rarely said. I was barely able to hear myself above the pounding in my ears.

"I'm so sorry."

I focused on her expression and saw genuine sorrow and sympathy.

"She fell through a patch of ice on a lake near our home." My stomach rolled and cramped.

"Were you with her?" Dr. Elsher tilted her head, still no judgment evident anywhere.

"No. Her mother took her." My voice was ice cold.

"That upsets you, I can tell."

"How can you tell?"

"Well, your tone firstly," she said. "And now, your entire body has gone stiff."

I gazed down and saw my hands white-knuckled around the

arms of the chair. I blew out my breath and released my hold, drawing my hands into my lap.

"Alana's mother was your wife. Is that correct?"

"Yes, we were married."

"How would you describe your marriage?"

"What do you mean?"

"Was it a mutually fulfilling relationship? Did you feel like you received as much emotionally from your wife as she did you? Was it a balanced relationship?"

I fell back in the chair, scraping my fingers through my short hair. Why on earth was she asking *this* question? I didn't want to talk about my marriage. But Dr. Elsher was the specialist, or so the door said. And I obviously needed help.

"We had good times and bad, just like any other couple," I answered.

"Did you love your wife?"

I jerked my head and my eyes locked on hers. "Of course, I did."

"Do you miss your wife?"

"Yes." I stumbled with the word.

"But..." Dr. Elsher leaned forward in her chair, silently asking me to continue.

"But...," I echoed. My heart was heavy, knowing what I had to divulge. "I loved her, but I blamed her for Alana's death."

"What's your wife's name?"

"Her name was Jaime."

"*Is* Jaime," she corrected with a reassuring smile.

"Sure." I shrugged.

"Why do you blame Jaime for Alana's death?"

I hated the way she was using their names. No one *ever* said their names out loud. I only heard them in my nightmares when I screamed out their names as I rushed around in total darkness, trying to reach them. I never could, though, their cries for help were always just a breath away from me.

"I specifically asked Jaime *not* to take Alana ice skating that day."

"Why?"

"The weather forecast had changed, and the ice on the lake was unstable. Jaime understood that better than anyone."

"I see." She leaned back in her chair, drawing in a breath through her nose and holding it.

"See what?"

Dr. Elsher sighed deeply and brought her gaze to me. "I see how you would blame Jaime for Alana's death."

"You do?"

"When someone does something deliberately against our wishes, it is cause for us to be upset. Setting limits and parameters in a relationship is crucial. You and Geneva will have to work on that as her pregnancy progresses, and well into your son's life."

"But, I blamed Jaime."

"Did you tell her? Jaime, I mean? Did you say those words to her directly?"

"Well, no. But my actions showed it."

"How did Jaime die, may I ask?"

Dr. Elsher's words cut me like a knife to the gut. I thought I might vomit on her very clean, very expensive area rug.

She sat in her chair, one leg crossed over the other as she dangled her foot in the air. Her elbow was leaning on the arm of her chair and her fingers rubbed her chin.

She was waiting for me to answer.

"She drowned." My words were flat and emotionless, a trick I'd learned a long time ago to keep the suffocating guilt from devouring me.

"Not by accident?" Her question hit me square on the jaw, like a prized fighter. She needed no explanation. The guilt must have been written all over my face.

"The death certificate says it was an accidental drowning. She died from cardiac arrest brought on by her submersion in icy water."

"But you say otherwise?"

My eyes cut down to the floor, staring at the abstract pattern in the rug below my feet.

"Did she drown in the same lake as your daughter?"

"Yes," I whispered.

"So, her death was also an accident, like your daughter's?"

I sat silently, pissed when tears pooled in my eyes. I shook my head. "No, it wasn't an accident," I choked out.

"What was it?"

I shook my head, not wanting to say the word out loud. My short experience with her told me Dr. Elsher would remain silent the rest of the session until I answered. "Suicide," I whispered. The word slashed my soul like a dull, rusty razorblade.

"What makes you think it was suicide?"

I drew in a deep breath and raised my head, staring into Dr. Elsher's eyes as tears rolled down my face. "Because she left a note. A note for me."

"May I ask what it said? If it's too personal or too long, I certainly understand, Berk."

"It wasn't long, it only contained two words." Two of the hardest words I'd ever had to read. Two words I couldn't even give to myself.

Dr. Elsher sat stark still, awaiting my response.

I'd only disclosed the contents of Jaime's note to one other person. Geneva. "It said, 'I'm sorry.'" My back went straight as I willed myself not to physically and mentally break down.

"And you feel responsible? For Jaime's death, I mean?"

"Of course, I do." I stared at her like she was an alien.

"Anger and guilt are the two most common feelings when a loved one commits suicide, Berk."

Suicide. There was the word I'd tried to avoid for all these years.

"Understanding why Jaime did this takes time," she went on.

"Jaime did it because I didn't help her grieve after Alana's death. Because I was a selfish fuck! Because I basically said she was responsible for our daughter's death." I jumped to my feet, hovering over Dr. Elsher, glaring down at her. "I fucking killed her. I killed my wife *and* my daughter!"

Dr. Elsher remained seated, unfazed by my outburst. "No, you didn't, Berk. And until we can move past that mountain of guilt you've hidden behind for years, you can't properly grieve. If you can't grieve, your wounds will never heal."

"What the fuck do you know about this, *Dr.* Elsher?" My words rang out cold and heartless, laced with sarcasm.

"I know more than I want to," she answered quietly.

Oh, shit. I stared at her, my own demons taunting me with words of guilt and anger.

Dr. Elsher sat up straight and squared her shoulders. "If you leave today and never come back for another session, I want you to remember something, Berk."

My eyes darted between hers, watching as the darkness receded, replaced with love and genuine concern, for me.

"When someone commits to the idea and act of suicide, there is *nothing* we loved ones can do to stop them."

We loved ones? What the fuck?

"We don't have control over another person's actions," she continued. "Unfortunately, you don't have that much power, Berk. If you did, you surely would have stopped your Jaime from ending her own life. The pain your wife experienced after the death of your daughter outweighed the resources she had to alleviate it. At least in *her* mind it did."

Tears burned my eyes as her words punctured my hardened soul.

"The only thing you can control is how you deal with your own pain, going forward. But believe me, Berk," she scooted forward in her chair, "you must deal with it or it will eat you alive. It will rob you of the joy that lies in wait for you as you experience the birth of another child. One who will need you even more."

This so-called doctor had no *clue* what I'd been through. Fuck this shit. I turned on my heels and barreled through her office door, my fists clenched tight and my jaw tighter, vowing never to return again.

The greatest gift of life is friendship, and I have received it.
- Hubert H. Humphrey

CHAPTER 19

GENEVA

I STOOD OUTSIDE, near the entrance to the cafeteria on campus, staring up at the ominous sky. The spring storm clouds had rolled in a few moments before, and I couldn't help but wonder if they were a prediction of Berk's mood.

His first psychotherapy session was today with Camille. I didn't want to pry and had to force myself not to go to the main campus and wait for him outside of her office. Instead, I'd chosen to have dinner with the residents.

It was my night to call bingo in the activity center, and even though I was dog-tired, I couldn't say no. The guys loved the game so much, the staff knew they *had* to keep it on the calendar or risk a mutiny.

Normally, volunteers ran the evening activities, but they'd called in sick at the last minute. I was next on the rotation block, so they'd told me during my last class. I didn't mind calling bingo. I loved spending time with the residents. But tonight, my feet and hands were swollen and my head was killing me. I was so tired, all I wanted to do was collapse into bed.

"Bean-go! Bean-go! Bean-go!" The chanting preceded the residents.

I gazed over my shoulder and saw Dana's twin brother Sam and his two best friends, Greg and Justin, marching on the stone path on their way to dinner.

Dana's brother was born with cerebral palsy after suffering a stroke in utero. Unable to care for her brother full-time after her parents' death at nineteen, she'd enrolled Sam here at Whispering Oaks, where he had thrived.

"You call bingo, Geneva!" Sam shouted as he stumbled along the walkway.

I knew better than to try and help. Sam never liked to be reminded of the physical and mental limitations of his cerebral palsy. He was strong and fierce, just like his twin sister.

One of his best friends, Justin, marched beside him, his gait a little smaller and more cautious.

Justin was thirty-four but was stuck in the mind of an eighteen-year-old due to a head-on car crash when he was a freshman in college. Lucky to be alive, the wreck had left him with multiple broken bones and a traumatic brain injury, which caused mobility issues, memory loss, and cognitive mental set-backs. He was now unable to properly care for himself on his own, but his family wanted him to have a sense of independence, so Whispering Oaks was a perfect spot for him.

Justin had a zest for life that most people never experienced, and his outgoing personality was a bonus for the residents and staff. The only problem was, since he never mentally evolved past the age of eighteen, he flirted with females relentlessly.

"Geneva!" Sam shouted as he ran toward me, the slight paralysis on his left side causing him to move slower.

As much as I wanted to throw my arms around Sam and give him a big hug, the campus policy forbid it. We tried to keep our physical contact with the residents to a minimum, instead teaching them how to properly interact in social settings when they were outside of Whispering Oaks. But these residents were so sweet and kind, it was hard not to love on them.

"Hey, Sam." I smiled as I took him into a one-armed side hug. It was the best I could do on campus.

"Are you calling bingo tonight?" Justin asked.

I peered over Justin's shoulder and saw Greg standing off by himself, rhythmically patting his legs with flattened hands.

Greg had autism which kept him from socially interacting with others. It also delayed his speech development. He was new to Whispering Oaks but immediately Sam and Justin had taken him under their protective wings. Greg had made great strides with the residents but was still mostly non-verbal with the staff and volunteers and preferred to keep his distance from others in social settings.

Greg could play any musical instrument you laid in front of him. It was a perplexing part of the autism spectrum. In some areas, such as language, speech and reading, he was so delayed, but in others, like music, he was a prodigy, a genius. It took a lot to coax him into playing, but when he did everyone would stand in awe, struck speechless—like *he* was most days.

"Yes, I'm calling bingo." I smiled at Greg, trying to make him feel at ease with me. "Are you coming, Greg?"

His eyes darted up to the sky. I knew he didn't like bingo because it was a large social gathering, but if I added any kind of music, he'd always smile.

"Will you sing, Geneva?" Justin asked.

"You sing?" Greg asked.

My eyes went wide. He'd spoken. To me.

"Yes, Geneva sing purrrr-dee." Sam laid his head on my shoulder.

"Thank you, Sam." I smiled at his compliment, but as much as it pained me, I pulled away from his embrace.

"I sing," Greg said quietly.

That was news to me, but I had no doubt he could, given his past performances. "I bet you sound amazing, Greg. Would you sing with me sometime?" I asked.

"Tonight! Tonight! Tonight!" Sam chanted.

"Not tonight, guys. I'm kind of tired." I looked at Greg who'd averted his gaze again. Just as soon as I'd captured his attention, I'd lost it. But now that I knew singing could bring him out, I would plan something.

"How about another Karaoke party?" Justin asked, stealing my idea.

Greg lifted his head, his attention back in the conversation as he scooted closer to our group.

"Next week, I promise, guys," I said.

The glimpse of a smile washed across Greg's face, the expression so slight I would have missed it had I not been staring. But just as quickly as it came, it was gone. Music was Greg's motivator.

I made a mental note to add this information to his file. Who was I kidding, though? I could barely remember to tie my own shoes in the morning because my brain was so fried with these pregnancy hormones.

"Geneva?" a familiar voice called behind me.

"Berk!" Sam shouted as he darted toward him.

"Sam," I said calmly, trying to remind him we were in a social setting in public, not at the pool party where acts of intimacy were different.

Sam stopped abruptly, sticking out his hand toward Berk, but the smile on his face never faltered.

"Hey, Sam." Berk gave him a slight smile and grabbed Sam's hand, shaking it gently, but his body remained rigid. Obviously, his session with Camille had not gone well.

Camille had lost her sixteen-year-old son to suicide almost ten years ago, and I'd hoped her own personal healing story would resonate with Berk. Judging from his clenched fists and tight jaw, I guess it hadn't.

"Dis is my freh-end, Berk." Sam proudly announced to the other residents as he waved his hand up and down Berk's body.

"Hi, Berk." Justin marched toward him, jutting out his hand just as Sam had.

"Who's Berk?" someone whispered in my ear.

I turned, surprised to find Greg so close to me, and talking. His eyes were firmly planted on Berk in a predatory stare, as if trying to decide if he were friend or foe. I looked in Greg's bright green eyes. I'd never noted the color before.

He studied me, staring at me as if I were an open book he was trying to read. His eyes lowered and he looked at my belly, staring at it for a few moments before his gaze returned to my face.

Greg may be non-verbal, but it didn't mean he wasn't communicating. He knew exactly who Berk was and he was letting me know it.

His eyebrows arched high and I understood the question. He already knew the answer but I gave him one single nod in acknowledgement. He returned my gesture before quietly slipping away.

"You play bingo, Berk." Sam led Berk to where we stood, his words a demand, not a question.

Berk cocked his head in confusion.

"Tonight is bingo," I explained. "It's my night to call, after dinner."

"Oh," Berk answered, his face so forlorn I thought I would cry.

"Do you want to come?" I thought maybe interacting with the guys might help him overcome whatever ghosts Camille had stirred up during her session.

"Um, not tonight."

"Ahhh," Sam and Justin said in disappointment.

Berk's eyes caught mine and I saw the sorrow—and his silent

request. He needed to be alone, to process things. I needed to give that to him.

"Well, my car's over there." I nodded toward the parking lot. Berk's brother had dropped him off earlier for his session since Berk didn't have a car. "You can take it if you want. Just stop back by around 8:30 p.m. or 9:00 p.m. to pick me up if you would."

Berk glanced down at his watch. "You're staying that late tonight?"

I looked around at the circle of men now formed around me. Most of them had no concept of time, or the fact that I had been there since 7:30 a.m. this morning. This was my job, though. A job I loved. A job that didn't feel like work.

"It's bingo, Berk," Justin said, as if everyone should know the significance of the weekly ritual.

"I'll be back to pick you up then." He mustered a small smile, but everyone could see it was half-hearted at best. He turned to leave.

I caught his arm. "Are you all right?" I whispered.

He looked down at my hand and immediately I pulled it away. Finally, he lifted his head, his eyes so full of sorrow my own heart ached. He nodded once, and I understood that I needed to let him go.

"I'll be back a little later." He lifted his hand and cupped my jaw, bringing my face level with his. A genuine smile that finally touched his eyes appeared for a nanosecond before Berk's hand fell away and he walked toward the parking lot.

"Is he okay?" Greg asked.

My jaw fell open, surprised at the amount of words Greg had spoken in the last five minutes. It was more than I'd heard him say in the last five *weeks* since he'd been at Whispering Oaks.

"I don't know," I finally replied. And that was the truth.

CHAPTER 20
GENEVA

"Dance, dance, dance!" the residents cheered.

"No way," I said.

"Come on, Geneva, just one song?" Justin pleaded as he sat at the table in the rec room.

"Just one," Tanya added from across the table where we were playing bingo. Tanya had Down's syndrome and was Sam's quasi-girlfriend, even though residents weren't allowed to have romantic relationships. *Yeah, good luck keeping those two apart.* Or at least, keeping Tanya away from Sam.

"You guys, let's finish the last game and then we'll talk," I said.

My headache had diminished some after I ate dinner with the residents, but barely. My fingers were so puffy, I could barely squeeze them around the bingo balls. I'd been on my feet way too long tonight, and I needed to get home and prop them up, hopefully in a tub full of bubbles and hot water.

I glanced up and studied their sad, droopy faces. Part of me felt bad. Usually, I had more energy than this, but tonight I was dog-tired.

I heard the hissing noise of the speakers turning on. I looked over my shoulder.

Greg stood in front of the CD player and shoved a CD into the system and hit some buttons. He turned to face me, a small smile spreading over his face as he held up a single index finger. "One," he mouthed.

How could I say no to this man? He was finally warming up to me. He was interacting with others through music.

For Greg, I would dance.

"One," I mouthed back as I held up my finger.

A smile brighter than the lights overhead lit up his face as he pushed the button on the player.

Any pain I'd felt earlier thanks to Peanut's growth quickly dissipated with that one smile from Greg. I could endure *one* song, couldn't I?

The familiar strum began and I heard the narrator's voice speak. Oh, shit. He'd selected "Tubthumping" by Chumbawamba. There was no *way* I'd survive. These guys were gonna dance, like *really* dance. And they would never let me sit this one out.

I watched Greg standing next to the CD player, his fingers strumming with the beat as the song continued, smiling as he surveyed the room.

Chairs kicked back and fell to the floor as the residents recognized the song. I played it in my classroom anytime someone was having a difficult day. Its lyrics talked about how we all get knocked down in life, but you couldn't stay down. You had to get back up again.

My eyes locked with Greg's and he held up one lone finger. "One. For you." He smiled.

I realized in that moment that Greg felt things others never even noticed. He didn't speak words. He didn't have to. He was far too attuned to me. He knew I'd had a long day and he was trying to make me feel better.

I stood and walked to the center of the room where the other residents were gathered in a circle.

Everyone shouted the familiar words as they twisted low to the floor then jumped high every time the band shouted "up." *Tubthumping* was a song that no one was immune to. You couldn't help but shake your hips and jump up and down to the words that spoke of how nothing should keep you down. You had no choice but to persevere.

We wiggled our hips in between each verse as we sunk low and then jumped high, our words echoing off the walls of the rec center as we sang along. The song never failed to infuse me, and the residents, with energy.

We all laughed as sweat broke out over our foreheads. Latching hands, we made a circle and went round and round as the singer chanted words in between the chorus, then immediately released our hands as the song resumed, shaking down low then jumping high.

I peeked over my shoulder and saw Greg still standing by the CD player, his hand strumming on his hip, keeping perfect time to the song. I nodded toward the group as we circled, silently inviting him to join us.

Greg shook his head.

"Okay," I mouthed. Today he'd made progress and I wouldn't push him.

His eyes darted to the entrance.

My own followed as I sunk down to the floor with the rest of the residents, following the words of the song. My eyes locked with Berk's, the smile on his face just as big as Greg's. My heart swelled, hoping he'd found some kind of peace while he'd been away. I knew my decision not to press him about his appointment had been a good one.

"Come on, join us!" I shouted.

"Berk!" Sam and Justin yelled in unison.

The group collectively turned and stared at Berk.

He shook his head no.

"That's her baby daddy!" Tanya yelled as we all jumped in the air with the beat of the song.

"Tanya!" I shouted in reprimand. As my feet hit the floor, a sharp pain hit my right side and I crumpled over in pain.

The music stopped and the room fell silent as everyone descended upon me.

"Move!" a deep voice growled, parting the group.

I looked up, expecting to see Berk. Instead, Greg's green eyes bore into mine, his filled with concern.

"I'm okay," I reassured him as I pushed up to my hands and knees. I drew in a breath trying to ease the pain in my side. It seemed to be working.

Strong hands wrapped around my waist but I pushed them away. I was surprised Greg was touching me, but I couldn't allow him to. When the hands didn't move, I looked up and was once again surprised at the face staring back at me. Berk.

His eyes were wide with worry as he scanned my face.

"Why the hell were you jumping around like that?" Berk's voice rang with reprimand. I felt like a small child who'd misbehaved.

"Oooo, you said hell," one of the residents said.

Berk and I both gazed up at the crowd.

"Das not nice, Berk." Sam's face was stern as he stared at Berk.

"I'm sorry." Berk lifted me to my feet. "Are you all right?" He stared at me, this time his tone much softer. He was really concerned.

I pulled out of his grip, my right hand still firmly planted on my side as I continued to breathe deeply. The pain was slowly subsiding. "I just overdid it," I reassured the residents.

"Geneva?"

I recognized Greg's voice even though I'd only heard it a handful of times. "Really, Greg," I said, turning to face him.

He reached out and gently touched my arm.

I gazed down at our connection, completely blown away that he was actually touching me.

"I promise, Greg." I laid my hand on top of his as I gazed up at him.

He snatched his hand away as if I were a scalding pan, casting his gaze to the floor.

"Let's clean up, guys." I was so tired, my words were hollow, but we couldn't leave the rec room in such disarray.

"Geneva, we'll get it."

My eyes followed the voice and I saw Willow, my supervisor, standing in the doorway with Justin behind her. He'd obviously gone to get her.

"I'm fine, really, Willow." She was a product of the 1970's hippy parents, her brother named River and her sister Sunflower. Seriously, those were their names.

"Go home, Geneva. We'll pick this up." Willow walked into the room, setting chairs up right. "Everyone, say good night to Geneva."

"Good night, Geneva!" they shouted in unison.

"Night guys. Sorry about ruining the song." I laughed, but no one joined in. Their eyes were filled with concern. Their worry made my heart ache. "I'll be fine. I'll see you guys in the morning."

"No, you won't," Willow corrected.

"What?" I pulled out of Berk's hold and stalked toward her. "Willow, what are you talking about? I have a full schedule tomorrow."

"Next week is spring break, the campus will be closed," she said, as if I'd forgotten.

"I know."

"Consider your break starting early."

"But—"

She held up her hand to stop me. "You've already put in a full forty hours this week, and it's only Thursday. Go. Home. Geneva."

Her words were forceful but kind. She was worried, and that was the last thing I wanted.

"Are you sure?" I whispered.

"Positive." She glanced over my shoulder and I followed her gaze and noticed Berk was behind me.

"Oh, um, Willow, this is my friend, Berk." I nodded.

"That's her baby daddy." Tanya giggled.

"Tanya!" Willow and I shouted in unison.

"What?" She furrowed her brows and shrugged her shoulders. "He is."

"It's nice to meet you, Berk." Willow smiled as she cut a menacing glare at Tanya, just daring her to say another word.

"Likewise." Berk gave a half-smile and a single nod toward Willow. He turned toward me, wrapping his arm around my waist and drawing me close. "Let's get you home." He gave me a slight squeeze and quickly guided me out of the room.

I gazed over my shoulder as we left. The faces of the residents looked tentative and concerned, and I hated that.

"You guys have a great spring break. And don't worry about me, I'm fine!" I shouted over my shoulder.

"Bye, Geneva!" they all shouted in unison. Their well wishes warmed my heart and eased my concern. As Berk led me down the hall and out of the building, the enormity of how tired I was suddenly hit me. I leaned against Berk for support as we walked together.

He tucked me in further, and I breathed in deep as his strength infused me. His familiar scent held my next breath hostage. I'd missed him.

"Let's get you home," he said, kissing the top of my head.

"I have to drop you off first."

"I'm staying with you tonight."

I pulled out of his hold and looked up at his eyes. I wanted that, more than anything, but I would never ask him. "Berk, you don't have to do that. I just overdid it and—"

His long finger pushed against my lips. "Are you always this obstinate?"

I smiled under his finger and nodded my head.

He laughed, rolling his eyes up toward the sky. "Lord, help me."

CHAPTER 21

GENEVA

"THE BABY SOUNDS FINE," Dr. Rusk said, pulling away from my bare stomach then swinging the stethoscope over her neck. She mashed and poked on my abdomen so hard I thought I might pee on the examining table.

Peanut kicked.

"Owe!" I shouted.

Berk bolted from his chair and took my hand, rubbing it frantically as he glared at Dr. Rusk.

"Apparently, he does *not* want to be moved." Dr. Rusk laughed.

"I think he drop-kicked my bladder."

She and I laughed, and I thought I'd *really* pee. I looked up at Berk, not surprised to see him staring at me with a distant, distraught look.

"He's fine," I whispered.

"It's you I'm worried about," he replied.

I stared at him in wide-eyed bewilderment. I knew he cared about me, but I had no idea he worried about me.

"Your blood pressure today is higher than last time," Dr. Rusk said, breaking the tension. "I'd like for you to take it easy for the next few days, keep your feet up and rest if you can. Then come back next week and let's re-check it."

"What are you saying?" Berk's hold on my hand tightened.

"Have you been working harder, are you more stressed than usual?" Dr. Rusk looked down at me, completely ignoring Berk.

His nose flared and his grip became painful. It was clear he did not like being disregarded.

I shook my hand, trying to pry it loose before he cut off circulation.

"Sorry," he whispered, releasing his hold and letting it fall to my side.

I hated the dejected look on his face.

"You're off for spring break, aren't you?" Berk asked, gazing down at me.

"Oh, that's right." I nodded my head. "I'm off all next week."

"Great." Dr. Rusk patted my stomach.

"Are you concerned?" Berk asked.

"I just want to be thorough," she answered. "If Geneva does have preeclampsia we can monitor her, have her come in more frequently. You still have," she looked down at my chart, "seventeen weeks to go."

"Uggh," I sighed. My hands flopped over my head.

"Is there someone living with you now, someone who can take care of your day-to-day tasks for a few days?"

There was Tori, but she'd been spending most of her time at Peter and Dana's with the kids.

"I'll stay with her." Berk's tone was decisive.

I was about to interrupt and correct him, but his firm stare and raised brow seriously frightened me. A tingle sparked between my legs. Shit.

Dr. Rusk's eyes darted between Berk and me. "Well, just make sure you have someone who can help out so you can rest and take it easy until next week." She gave Berk a wink.

Fuck. He would be with me for a week. I pushed up on the table, clutching at the stupid paper gown.

Berk lifted me the rest of the way, his hold gentle, as if I might shatter if he squeezed too hard.

"I'm not helpless," I whispered as I pulled out of his hold. The last thing I wanted was Berk staying with me out of sympathy or obligation.

His eyes narrowed and he held me tighter.

"Just schedule something for next week before you leave." Dr. Rusk closed the folder as she opened the door.

"We will," Berk answered before I could.

"I can do this." I jerked out of his hold and stalked toward the side chair where my clothes hung. From the corner of my eye, I saw Dr. Rusk smile and shake her head. It pissed me off even more.

"Bye, Berk. Bye, Geneva," she said just as the door clicked behind her.

"I don't need you to move in with me." My tone was curt. I wanted to look more menacing, but the fact I was only covered in a thin paper gown with nothing but fuzzy socks assured me that I just looked like an idiot.

"Obstinate." Berk laughed.

"Will you *please* leave so I can change?"

Berk stalked toward me, his body so close I could feel the heat radiating off his chest. "I'm moving in with you until this baby is born, and there isn't a damn thing you or anyone else is going to do about it."

His eyes were dark but I could see the fear. An electric charge spiraled through my body as I shuddered from the tone of his voice. This was dominant Berk.

His hands skimmed over my bare arms. "I'm going to take care of you, Geneva."

There was no missing the innuendo of what his *taking care of you* meant. At least I hoped there wasn't. These pregnancy hormones had left me hornier than hell, and I was tired of my vibrator and re-runs of *Grey's Anatomy*.

I wasn't convinced Berk wouldn't run if I let him into my heart, though. I couldn't bear that. If he was going to leave in the end, then I didn't want to get attached now and have my heart ripped out of my chest when he did.

"What's wrong?" He took a step back.

I shook my head, studying my fuzzy socks.

Berk's hand slid under my chin as he raised my head. His eyes were a mixture of honey and chocolate syrup, a myriad of feelings and thoughts racing across them.

"We can talk at home," I answered.

A smirk tugged at his lips.

"*My* home." I narrowed my gaze. "You're not moving in with me, Berk."

He turned his back and nonchalantly strolled toward the door, never saying a word.

"Berk," I warned.

"Geneva." He laughed, mocking me.

I stared at his back. It was a magnificent back, as backsides go. The T-shirt he wore was snugly molded to his broad shoulders and hung loose around his tapered waist. His plump ass filled out every seam and edge of his form-fitting jeans. The tingle between my legs was back, zipping up to my nipples, making them rock hard.

He pulled open the door and gazed back at me over his shoulder. His face was a blend of emotions—sadness, concern, worry—but the overriding one was desire.

"Get dressed," he whispered, his eyes grazing over my barely covered body. "Then we'll go get something to eat."

As if on cue, my stomach growled like a grizzly bear.

"My boy likes to eat," he laughed, "and so do I." Berk's full lips split wide into a sexy smile, the dual meaning not lost on me.

I was pretty sure I came right there in the middle of Dr. Rusk's examining room. How the hell was I *ever* going to keep my distance from Berk Rigby for seventeen more weeks?

CHAPTER 22

GENEVA

WE WERE on day three of Berk trying to do *everything* for me, and he was driving me fucking insane. This was ridiculous. I wasn't an invalid. Sitting down all day with my feet propped up was getting boring as hell.

Checking behind me to make sure Berk was still gone, I snuck down the hall to the washer and dryer. Surely, I could fold my own clothes. I did *not* want Berk putting away my bras and panties.

"Dammit, Geneva, what does 'Stay on the couch until I get back,' mean to you?"

I jumped, dropping all the clothes at the sound of his voice. I thought I'd have a good ten more minutes before he came back from the store.

He plopped the bags onto the kitchen table with a thud as he stalked toward me.

I recognized that look. It was his, "Don't fuck with me," stare. Unfortunately, it had the opposite effect on me, making my insides prickle with desire.

He scooped me up easily into his arms.

I yelped in surprise. "Berk, stop. I can walk, dammit!"

"The doctor said take it easy. How the hell do you think *doing laundry* is taking it easy?"

His eyes roamed over my face. The warmth of his breath caressing my skin made my stomach do a flip-flop.

"I'm bored," I pouted like a spoiled child.

"I know." He curled his lip and actually snarled.

That was when I noticed we were heading in the opposite direction of the living room. "Where are we going?"

He remained silent. This wasn't a good sign. Berk wasn't happy.

"I thought you were taking me back to the couch."

He scooted us through the doorway of my bedroom then made a beeline to my en suite bathroom.

"It's late. It's probably best you get ready for bed." He set me on the counter.

I gazed out of the window high above the tub and noted it was dark outside. "I must have dozed off on the couch while you were gone," I said to myself.

"You're tired, Geneva." His tone was different now, worried and anxious. He leaned over the tub and turned on the water.

He was drawing me a bath. It seemed romantic, but I reminded myself that Berk and I weren't involved. Yes, we shared a child, but that was all.

"May I ask you something?" My words were tentative.

He peered over his shoulder. "Yes."

I drew in a deep breath. I hadn't asked him about his therapy session and didn't want to pry. But I had to know if he was committed to getting better, to settling the ghosts of his past.

"What's wrong?" he asked, standing in front of me, his hands on either side of me as he pushed me against the mirror.

I gazed down at his chest, covered with another snug-fitting T-shirt. I wanted to rub underneath the material to feel his warm skin against mine. Dragging in a deep breath, I sighed heavily.

"What is it?" His furrowed brow and narrowed eyes told me he was worried. I was worrying him.

"I was just wondering." My eyes rolled up to his. They were darting between mine in question. "We never talked about your therapy session."

Without a word, he pushed off the counter and fell against the opposite wall as if I'd shoved him.

"I don't want to pry or anything, but—"

"But what?" Berk growled.

"Look, Berk, I don't know what's going on between us." I motioned my finger back and forth. "I can't have an on-again off-again relationship with you. Our son deserves something better."

"What are you saying?"

"I'm saying, if you're not going to deal with the issues from your past, then we can't do this."

"Do what?"

Oh, shit. Maybe I'd read this wrong. Maybe he wasn't physically attracted to me any more.

"Look, Geneva, I don't know what to tell you." His hands raked through his short hair as his eyes cut to the floor.

I loved that this shorter cut showed off his strong features, but part of me missed the longer strands of his raven hair. "I just want you to say you're working on it."

His eyes remained downcast. "What did Dr. Elsher tell you?" he asked.

"She hasn't said anything. I've never asked her. And I never will. She's required—morally, ethically, and professionally—to keep her sessions confidential."

His head lifted, his eyes growing darker by the minute.

"If you want to talk about it, I'm here, Berk. But if you don't, that's okay, too."

"I walked out," he finally said.

"Of your session?"

"Yeah." His head fell back against the wall with a thud.

"Are you going to go back?"

"I don't know." His eyes remained closed but his chest rose and fell in quick succession. He was scared.

"I'm not asking you to do this for me, Berk. You need to do this for yourself, and for your son." I paused. "But if you can't, if you can't work through whatever this is going on with you, then you need to leave. I won't let you be one of *those* kind of dads."

"What kind of dad are you talking about?" His eyes snapped wide.

"The kind of dad that wanders in and out of his son's life when it's convenient for him. The kind of dad a kid can't rely on."

"What if I hurt him, Gen?"

My breath caught at his use of my nickname. He was becoming familiar with me. "Berk, how could you hurt him?"

He shook his head as if trying to erase the words he'd already spoken.

I knew he fought so many demons, ghosts that I couldn't help him with. "Camille understands what you're going through."

"Who's Camille?" he asked.

"Camille Elsher. Dr. Elsher, your therapist."

"What do you mean, she understands?"

"Her son committed suicide ten years ago."

Berk's eyes grew wide, like a wild animal about to be shot.

I pushed off the counter and took a step closer to him, placing my hand on his chest.

His eyes darted around the small room, looking anywhere but at me.

"Berk," I called out softly.

His gaze finally landed on me. He was so vulnerable in that moment. All I wanted to do was take his pain away.

"I have no idea what you've been through or what you're going through."

My hand slid across his chest and up to his shoulder, squeezing it gently. I wanted to infuse him with the unconditional love I knew he needed but wouldn't let himself receive.

"But I'm here if you ever want to talk. If it's not me, I think it needs to be someone, someone who understands, like Camille does."

His hand covered mine, stopping its motion.

"It's just hard, Geneva."

I nodded my head, understanding a little of his grief and guilt. "I felt guilty about my mom's death, too."

He stepped away, staring down at me in confusion.

"She died of cancer just before I turned eight, but I couldn't help but blame myself. I never got over it, and I shut myself off. From everyone. Even my father." I shuddered, remembering all the terrible things I'd done to my family and friends.

"Why would you blame yourself?" His question was genuine.

"I don't know. Same reason I guess you blame yourself for your family's death."

"It's not the same, Geneva." He pulled away from my touch.

I'd said too much. Gone too far. "I'm sorry, you're right." I lifted my hand to stroke his cheek, surprised when he leaned into my touch. "I've dealt with my own demons, though. I had to because it was destroying not only my life, but the lives of the people I loved."

He lifted his hand and placed it on top of mine. His eyes fluttered closed and he drew in a ragged breath.

"I'll be here for you, Berk, to help you pick up the pieces of your broken soul, if that's what you want. But *you* have to want it, for you and for our son."

He nodded as tears fell from his closed lids.

Oh, God. Had I done this to him? I slid my other arm around his waist and tucked him in tight to my body. I hadn't meant to upset him. "I'm sorry."

He shook his head. "No, you're right. I'll go back," he whispered into my hair.

"For you, Berk. Go back for you. Okay?" I squeezed him tight.

His chest heaved in and out with short breaths but he nodded. "Okay," he sighed, kissing the top of my head. "I'll do it. For me. And for Peanut."

I couldn't see it, but I felt it, a small smile emanating from within him. He had hope.

"I'm tired of just existing," he exhaled.

"Then let's live."

"Okay." He pulled me in tight, stroking my back.

I drew in a deep breath, inhaling the familiar scent of Berk Rigby, memories of our time in Hawaii flooding my senses. "Ho'oponopono," I said. It was the Hawaiian expression Berk taught me on the cliff in Hawaii just before we jumped. It meant absolution, to make things right, a fresh start, a cleansing of sorts.

He pushed me away, staring into my eyes. "How did you remember?"

I shrugged my shoulders. How could I tell him I remembered every single minute detail of my time with him? That I'd never gotten over what I thought had been his betrayal.

He leaned down and brushed his lips over mine, pulling away too soon. "Ho'oponopono, Geneva."

"Gen!" Berk shouted down the hallway.

"I'm in here." I splashed the bubbles around my body as I sunk deeper in the tub, my belly nearly poking through the water. I couldn't believe how much Peanut had grown inside me in the last few weeks.

We'd been to my follow-up doctor's appointment earlier that day, and my blood pressure had dropped minimally, enough for

Berk to at least give me some breathing room and leave me alone for more than ten minutes.

Under Berk's care over the last few weeks, he'd insisted on nightly baths for me, to help me relax and lower my blood pressure. It was the one indulgence I'd decided to keep, even though the doctor had cleared me for normal activity. Berk always insisted on a foot massage afterward. The doctor said it would help with the swelling. Who was I to argue with doctor's orders?

Berk had been to two more therapy sessions with Camille in the last week, and I could tell a difference in his physical being. It was as if he was able to breathe again for the first time probably since his wife and daughter had passed away. I was happy that Camille was finally breaking through some of his walls.

We never talked about his sessions, I didn't want to intrude or impose. And it seemed as if things were going well enough that I didn't need to ask or pry.

"Are you in there?" He knocked on the bathroom door.

"Yeah, I just got in."

"Okay, I'm going to start on dinner. Is chicken parmesan okay?"

Was he serious? I was lounging in a bathtub, and the man had grocery shopped, done my laundry, *and* was now going to cook dinner. Yeah, I was totally okay.

"That sounds perfect," I sighed and reclined further in the tub, my eyes rolling up to the ceiling. There was a dark spot in the corner that I focused on. Suddenly, it moved. A spider.

The sound that erupted from my mouth could only be described as a murderous scream. I was petrified of spiders. Everyone knew it. And Rory delighted in putting those fucking plastic ones everywhere just to scare me.

I bolted straight up, water sloshing all over the floor as I tried to jump from the tub but failed.

"Geneva!" Berk yelled. The door flew open and he caught me in his arms just as I was about to fall onto the side of the tub. "What's wrong?"

"Spider!" I shrieked.

"What?" I heard his muffled laughs.

"A spider, goddammit! It's not funny." I swung at his chest.

"Where?" He righted me on my legs and leaned me against the counter.

"There." I pointed to the corner of the ceiling. My eyes drilled shut so I wouldn't have to see it. When I heard no movement to indicate he was trying to kill the eight-legged beast, my eyes fluttered open.

He was staring at me.

"The spider, Berk!" I screamed, pointing to the ceiling.

His eyes roamed over my body, and I realized that I was completely naked. I moved to cover my body but he sprung forward, capturing my wrists with his hands and bringing them down to my sides, leaving my body on display for his perusal. And peruse he did.

My core heated and my nipples puckered as his eyes drank in every inch of my body. There was a time when I relished in a man's predatory gaze, but therapy had taught me I didn't need anyone else's approval to feel good about myself. It sure as hell didn't mean that I didn't love it, though. Especially when it was from Berk.

"My God," he breathed out. His face was mere inches from mine. His eyes were still fixated on my body, specifically my breasts.

I watched in apprehension as he lowered his body, his lips a breath away from my over-sensitized nipples. The pregnancy had made them responsive to the slightest touch. They throbbed and pulsated, begging for his kiss. As if hearing my pleas, his mouth covered one of my breasts, his tongue feasting on me.

"Oh, God, Berk." My head fell back and my eyes rolled up in my head. Sparks of desire shot straight to my core.

He lapped and licked, his own moans vibrating against my skin.

I felt an orgasm building between my legs, and he wasn't even touching me. Was that possible?

His fingers worked on my other breast, kneading it and rolling the nipple, tugging on it with perfect pressure, in sync with his mouth.

I rubbed my thighs together, trying to create the friction I needed for a release that threatened to destroy me.

His teeth scraped along the sensitive skin of my nipple, pulling it taut with his mouth as his fingers played with the other, twisting it just this side of pain.

Without warning, my orgasm ripped through me, heating me from the inside out. I screamed out garbled words as my hips rocked forward trying to touch anything.

Berk's thick thigh parted my legs and rubbed against me as I rode out my orgasm on his leg. The tremors rippled through my body as I continued to grind against him. The thick material of his denim jeans was setting me up for another explosion.

My chest heaved as my breathing grew ragged. My climax rolled on, threatening to last for all eternity. I'd never had an orgasm go on like this.

Berk's tongue moved up my neck as his thigh continued to rub against me. Heat shot through my legs as another more intense orgasm rocked me to my core. I wasn't sure where the first one ended and the second started. My voice grew hoarse from moaning.

As I finally came down from my high, my body fell limp against him. The embers of desire were still burning deep in my belly. How was that even possible?

Berk pulled away from me, his eyes so full of desire I nearly came again just from his lusty stare.

He released my other hand and I brought both up to his shoulders as my hips rubbed against his erection.

"God, that was fucking awesome." His smile was lethal, and I actually felt a swelling in my core as another orgasm built just from the vibrations of his voice.

"What?" I panted, still out of breath from my post orgasmic bliss.

"You, coming." He slid his hands under my arms and lifted me in the air, setting me on the bathroom counter as he spread my legs wider.

Oh, fuck.

Before I could draw in another breath, he was on his knees, his lips skimming across the skin of my inner thighs. I ventured a gaze down and saw his eyes fixated on me, his lips curled into a delicious smile as his long, deft tongue trailed its way up my leg.

My midsection spasmed and my hips jerked.

Berk's hand spread me wider as he worked higher up my thigh. His other hand skimmed over my rounded belly and over to my breast, his fingers working over my nipple again.

Another zing of electricity shot from my breast straight to my sweet spot, setting me on fire. Was it possible to have three orgasms in a row? Before I could think of an answer, Berk's tongue was on me, circling me, stroking me, licking me. I fell over the edge again.

"Fuck!" I shouted, thrashing on the counter, my legs spasming and engulfing him. "Berk," I begged as he continued to lick and suck, his other hand tugging on my nipple. The room exploded into bright lights that blinded me. I closed my eyes, trying to shield myself from the burning rays of my ecstasy.

I gasped, and my eyes flew open as something suddenly entered me.

Berk was standing tall in front of me, his hips aligned with mine as his dick pulsated deep inside me. He thrust hard against me, his rhythm unrelenting.

I came again, so quick and so fast I thought I might actually die.

I knew I'd been really horny since the pregnancy. All the books said it happened. But this? This many orgasms in a row was insane and totally unbelievable.

"Oh, fuck," he growled against my neck as he pumped into me. "Lean back."

I braced my arms behind me and fell back, supporting myself with my hands as he pushed me toward the mirror. This new angle put his cock square on my g-spot. I gasped as my feet and hands went numb, the tingling almost painful.

"No way," I whispered. There was no way I could have *another* orgasm, was there? This stuff only happened in my romance novels. Even then, I thought they were full of shit.

Berk's hips gyrated against me and within seconds I had an answer. Yes, yes, you could have multiple-multiple orgasms.

My world exploded and my center contracted around Berk, drawing his dick further inside me as I screamed out his name.

He continued grinding into me until his release exploded deep inside me. He grunted several times as he stilled against me, shock-waves of my own orgasm still pulsating against him.

"Fuck," he sighed against my neck.

I trembled as his breath washed over my skin.

"God, Geneva, that was…" he panted, unable to catch his breath.

Neither could I.

He pulled out of me and moved to the linen cabinet, pulling out a towel and cleaning me.

Finally, he looked at me and I feared what I might see. Would he regret this? Would he hate me?

His whiskey-colored eyes were filled with something I hadn't seen in a long time. Love. Complete and utter love.

"You said something about a spider?" He smirked.

I sat in front of him, gloriously naked. "What spider?"

I yelped as he scooped me up, making his way into the bedroom. He tossed me on the bed and stripped himself of his clothes. A naked Berk Rigby was a sight to behold.

Yeah, what spider? Fuck that spider.

CHAPTER 23

GENEVA

"FIVE ORGASMS. NO FUCKING WAY." Dana sipped on her margarita as we sat in the rounded booth of our favorite Mexican restaurant.

"I don't know," I said, "it was like I didn't know where one ended and the next began. It was one long, monstrous orgasm, you know?"

"Oh, yeah." Hindley nodded. "Those pregnancy hormones make sex insane."

"You and Rory are fucking nuts about sex already so your opinion doesn't matter." Dana laughed.

"Speaking of crazy sex." Hindley turned her attention to me. "Has my chair been delivered yet?"

"What chair?" I asked.

She leaned in. Dana, Tori and I followed.

"It's a Tantra chair," she whispered as she wiggled her brow.

I probably didn't want to know more.

"You think that fucking sex swing you installed in your bedroom isn't kinky enough, Hindley?" Dana was going for contrite, but you could hear the jealousy in her voice.

"Hey, don't knock it till you try it." She smiled.

"Oh, I'd like to try it." Tori's lips curled into a salacious smile.

"So, what the fuck is a Tantra chair?" Dana finally asked the question we'd all wanted to but were secretly afraid of finding out the answer.

"Oh my God, it's like the best piece of furniture ever created." Hindley's eyes rolled back in her head as she moaned.

"I'm assuming it's sexual in nature since it has the word 'Tantra' it." Dana shook her head. "Well, that and the fact that your fucking eyes are glazed over more than a Krispy Kreme doughnut."

"Oh, please," Hindley jerked back, "you're a freak, too. It's not like you and Peter don't go at it all day and night."

"Yeah, but I don't screw my husband in a special swing that's bolted to the ceiling like you two fuck monkeys do," Dana answered.

"You don't need one, Dana, because you can bend like a pretzel." Hindley giggled. "I, on the other hand, am a friggin' whale. I need the help of a harness and furniture to bend me over."

We stared at her in disbelief and immediately burst into laughter.

"So, what about this chair?" Dana's elbows were glued to the table as her head rested in her upturned palms.

"It's a special chair that helps you get into all of the Tantra sex positions. For those of us not like Limber Lucy over here." Hindley pointed her thumb toward Dana.

"Where did you find it?" I asked, now mildly interested.

Hindley darted her head around the booth, surveying the restaurant before leaning in again.

"The Playboy channel."

"The what?" Dana jerked back as her face contorted.

"Oh my God, like you don't have a closet full of porn DVDs." Hindley shook her head.

"Not any more," Dana sighed as she fell back in the booth.

"Why?" I knew better than to ask, but I did anyway.

"Peter's not into that kind of stuff."

"Give them to me," Tori said. "Lord knows I'm not getting any action."

"Oh, girl, we've got to hook you up with someone. That's just un-American not to be fucking someone when you're as hot as you are." Dana laughed.

"Dana! That's your sister-in-law," Hindley scolded.

"So."

"I do need to get laid," Tori said.

"Oh my God, I can't believe we've come to this." I laughed.

"What?" Dana stared at me. "*You're* the one who had to rub it in our faces that you had *five* orgasms in five minutes. That's an orgasm a minute, you skank."

I caught movement from the corner of my eye and we all went still.

"I'll just come back for your order," the waiter said as he scurried off.

We erupted into a fit of laughter.

"Well, I'm jealous of both of you," Tori said, her gaze going from me to Hindley. "It sounds like you're having amazing sex."

"Yeah, with swollen ankles, heartburn and hemorrhoids to match." Hindley shook her head.

Dana and Tori laughed so hard I thought they'd fall out of their seats.

Hindley and I shared a knowing glance. She was right, on all accounts. "And don't forget constipation," I added.

Hindley reached across the table and gave me a fist bump. "Giving us super-sensitized genitalia and breasts for better sex is the *least* God could do for us."

"Stop, oh my God, stop, please." Dana wrapped her arm around her waist as she doubled over with laughter. "I'm gonna piss myself."

"Well, now you know how I feel," Hindley sighed. "I can't sleep through the night without waking up at least three times to pee."

"Amen to that," I added.

"Okay, enough talk about pissing, pooping, and other gross preggers shit," Dana said. "What happens now, Gen?"

"Now what?" I asked.

"Now that you and Berk are doing the deed," Dana said, "how's this whole thing gonna play out? Does this mean you're going to give this relationship thing a try?"

I shrugged my shoulders. "Berk and I really haven't talked about our future."

"Do you love him?" Tori asked.

My eyes darted around the table but I remained silent.

"Well, daylight is a burning, baby girl." Dana looked down at my stomach. "You don't have much time to figure this shit out. Either he's in or he's out."

"Sounds like he's in *and* out." Tori paused. "And then in again, and then out." She snorted.

"Shut up." I hit her arm as well.

She scooted next to my hip and started dry humping my leg. "And then he's in and out." Her words came in staccato as if she were about to have an orgasm herself. Hindley and Dana joined in, their words in perfect rhythm to Tori's dry humping. "Then in and out and in—"

Abruptly all three stopped, their eyes cutting behind me.

I turned and followed their gaze.

The waiter stood behind me, his face flushed with red and his eyes wide as he visibly swallowed. "I'll just give you ladies a few more minutes."

"You might want to try giving us the rest of the night, sweetheart!" Dana shouted after him. "Oh, shit, I think the dude just passed out." She laughed hysterically and we all joined in, nearly hyperventilating.

"Well, no matter what happens, you know you always have us." Hindley leaned over the table and grabbed my hand.

"I don't deserve you, Hindley." Tears stung the back of my eyes.

"I know." She winked. "But we're sisters, so you're stuck with me. Besides, Abbi is so frigging excited about having a cousin she can't see straight."

"Oh, fuck, are you crying now?" Dana's lip snarled as she stared at me.

"Fuck you, Dana." I laughed, dabbing at my eyes. "It's called hormones."

"Leave her alone, Dana." Hindley nudged her arm.

"I'm just fucking with you, Gen." Dana smiled. "You know I love ya. And I got your back, too."

"Me three," Tori added.

"Yes." I laughed. "You definitely took care of me in Colorado."

"Well, he was a major fuckwad." Tori pursed her lips. "I had to drop kick him in the nutsack. And I'll do it again if he screws with you. Be sure to tell him that."

I fell back in my seat, my cheeks sore from laughing. I'd waited my entire life to have *real* girlfriends, women who would not only stand up *with* me but stand up *for* me. Their strength gave me confidence.

I'd made many strides over the last few years and none made me prouder than rebuilding the bridges I'd burned with Hindley and my family. It had taken a lot of hard work, but I'd done it.

Maybe with enough time and enough love, Berk could find his way back, too. To me, and to Peanut.

When it is dark enough, you can see the stars.
-Ralph Waldo Emerson

CHAPTER 24
BERK

I'D BEEN LIVING with Geneva for almost two weeks…and I loved it. I'd forgotten what it was like to cohabitate with a person of the opposite sex. Yeah, I'd been sleeping in her guest bedroom, and we'd only had sex twice—once in her bathroom after the spider incident and again in her bedroom that same night. Thank God for spiders, was all I had to say. But I was still sharing space with her, doing things that couples did.

Making love to Geneva filled me with hope. Hope of a future that I'd given up on having a long time ago when I buried my wife and daughter.

I'd returned to see Dr. Elsher and, with her help, I was making real progress, or so she said. I wasn't sure if it was true, but I definitely felt better, not as nervous and anxious. And the nightmares I'd had for years didn't seem as real any more. They still came, but thankfully I wasn't screaming out loud like I did the first night in Geneva's guest room.

It had been horrific and embarrassing. I'd woken up in a pool of sweat with Geneva shaking me violently. The look of horror on her face was almost as frightening as the screams in my dreams.

My nightmare was always the same. Jaime and Alana were

calling my name, quietly at first, then building to screams that chilled my bones even now. I would run through the woods, searching for them, but their voices eluded me. I'd shout after them in a sick game of Marco-Polo, but they would disappear as soon as I got close.

Always, right before I awoke, I would be standing next to the lake where they both had drowned. I would walk out on to the ice, praying that it would break so I could fall through and join them. I could see their faces just under the sheet of frozen water and would jump up and down, trying to break the thick layer of ice. Try as I might, it would never crack. Then slowly their faces would sink into the dark blue water.

I would wake up screaming their names, clawing at my sheets like it was the ice, trying to dig my way to them, to pull them to safety.

My body broke out in chills and I trembled just from the memory of the nightmare. I would have to remember to share them with Dr. Elsher at my next session.

I laughed inwardly. *Next session.*

When I left after the first one, I never anticipated returning. Her words rang through my head for days after I left. *You must deal with it or it will eat you alive.*

My guilt and shame surrounding Jaime's death *had* been eating me alive, from the inside out. It was hard to push away the people I loved the most—my parents, brother and sister, my in-laws. They were my last link to Jaime and Alana, and I had banished them, forbidden them from speaking their names. In doing so, I lost the good parts of my life, the memories that I now allowed myself to remember. Bringing Jaime and Alana to the forefront of my mind *had* helped me.

As I tugged on my shorts and threw on a T-shirt, I heard the doorbell ring.

"Berk!" Geneva's voice echoed down the hall. "Will you get that please?"

Not wanting her to get up from the couch, I sprinted down the hall toward the door, surprised when I didn't see her on the sofa where I'd left her.

I knew I was being overprotective. I'd given her tons of grief about going out with her girlfriends the night before. The truth was, I had no hold on her, no stake, other than my son she was carrying. In the end I knew she needed a break, from me and from the house, so I'd conceded—not that I truly had any say in the matter.

I was glad that at least Geneva wanted to have my "approval." She didn't want to worry me, and that gave me hope. Of what, I had no idea. But it was nice to have the word whirling around in my mind again.

"Where are you?" I called from the living room.

"In here, making us dinner."

I peered around the corner of the kitchen and saw her stirring several pots. "The doctor said you should take it easy, keep your feet up."

She rolled her eyes. "I was hungry, and you were busy."

"I was in the shower for two minutes, Geneva."

We stared at one another, neither blinking. God, she was as hard-headed as—

The doorbell chimed again, saving me from finishing my thought.

"My hands are messy. Will you get it? Please." Her lips curled into a smile that made her entire face shine. She was gorgeous, beyond compare. Carrying my son gave her another level of beauty that took my breath away.

"Fine. But after dinner, you're taking it easy," I warned.

She grinned, batting her eyes.

Not only was this girl obstinate, she was a genius at getting her way.

I peered through the peephole and saw a man dressed in a brown uniform. "I think it's a delivery man." I swung open the door to find the man holding a clipboard.

"Delivery for Hindley Gregor," he said.

"Oh, yes, I'll sign." Geneva scooted me out of the way.

How the hell had she shown up so quickly?

"Will you go turn off the burners?" She glanced over at me. Her eyes darted from me to the delivery man. She was nervous. And now I was, too.

My gut told me Geneva was hiding something.

"I'll take you next door and you can put it inside." Her instructions indicated that she was expecting the delivery. Geneva fished around on the hooks next to the door and pulled down a set of keys. "I'll be right back." She pushed me back and scooted across the threshold, closing the door in my face.

I walked to the kitchen and switched off all the burners, then ran out the front door, making my way around the bushes to the other side of the duplex in time to see Geneva opening the door.

"What's going on?" I asked.

She jumped. "Oh my God, Berk, you scared me." She clutched the key ring to her chest, pushing back the hair that had fallen in her face.

We stood silent again, staring at one another in a battle of wills. This time I wouldn't back down.

"What's in the truck, Geneva?" I nodded toward the street where the huge delivery truck was parked.

"It's just a piece of furniture Hindley bought. A chair."

"Why is she having it delivered to the duplex and not her house?"

"Well…" Geneva stammered.

I stepped in closer.

Geneva's eyes widened as she stared at my chest.

"Geneva," I growled.

"Where do you want it, ma'am?" The delivery man interrupted me as he and his partner hoisted a huge box that was at least three feet high and six feet long.

"Anywhere in the living room is fine," Geneva answered.

I'd never seen furniture come in a box before. As they walked past us both, I noted the large 'TC2' written on the side of the box.

"That's a chair?" I scratched my head. I'd never seen a chair that big.

"Um…" Geneva stumbled again. "I think it's like a chaise lounge or something." Her eyes darted around, looking at anything but me.

I stepped forward to follow the men inside the duplex.

"I can get it from here." Geneva grabbed my arm and pulled me back. "Why don't you go check on dinner?"

"Yeah, right, like I'm leaving you alone in a house with two strange men. Are you insane?" I gazed down at her, my face washed with worry.

Her eyes lit up as a smile tugged at her mouth.

"What?" I asked.

"You're protecting me."

I slid my hand across her cheek and let my fingers wrap around the nape of her neck, dragging her closer to me. "I'll always protect you, Geneva." And I meant it. I hadn't done it with my wife and daughter, but I would protect Geneva and Peanut. *Peanut.* The name was growing on me.

I dropped my head, our lips nearly touching as I stared into her blue eyes. I hoped our son would have every feature that made Geneva so beautiful to me—her eyes, her face, her hair, her smile.

Her eyes fluttered closed as I pulled her in the final few inches for our lips to meet.

"Sign here," the delivery man said.

We both jerked back, nearly stumbling on ourselves as one of the delivery men shoved the clipboard between us.

Geneva took the form from him, scrawling out her name quickly, her eyes never leaving mine.

The guy looked down at the form. "Um, not really on the line, but okay." He shrugged. "We left it against the wall. It's not really heavy so if you and your husband want to move it, it shouldn't be too hard."

Husband?

A bucket of ice-cold water hit my throbbing dick.

"He's not my husband." Geneva's words were punched out almost as quickly as my dick shriveled up.

I stared at her, her eyes wide with fear. It was more than obvious she didn't want me to be her husband any more than I wanted to be. I never planned to marry again. Ever. I didn't want that responsibility. I didn't want to give myself over to someone like that again.

"Well, it's inside," he said. "You can tear off the packaging."

"Thanks." Geneva waved him off.

I watched as the delivery men loaded up their dolly and made their way out the door.

Husband.

"Hey, it's here. What do you want me to do?" Geneva's voice sounded from inside the duplex.

I followed her voice inside and closed the door.

She was on the phone, standing in the middle of the living room, staring at the box as if it held kryptonite and she was Superman, or Superwoman in this case.

"No, it's in a cardboard box." She stared at the piece of furniture a second longer before her head turned to me. "You can go back home." She stared at me. "The delivery men are gone." Her gaze returned to the box. "No, it's Berk," she spoke into the phone.

There was no *way* I was leaving now, not until I found out what was in that box.

"Seriously, Hindley, you want me to open it?"

I was all smiles. This mystery would be revealed soon.

"But Berk's here," she mumbled into the phone, trying to hide her words.

I was *really* intrigued now.

"I don't have a knife or anything to cut it."

I walked into the kitchen, pulling open drawer after drawer. This was Rory and Hindley's home-away-from-home so the entire house was fully furnished. I pulled out a pair of scissors and walked back into the living room.

"Here." I held up the scissors in victory.

"Thanks." Geneva grabbed for them. "You can go."

"No way are you cutting this thing open without me." I smirked. I split the blades of the scissors wide and placed one point on the upper corner of the box.

"Berk!" Geneva shouted.

I jumped, nearly dropping the scissors, and turned to look over my shoulder. Geneva was white as a ghost. "What the hell is *in* this thing, Geneva?"

"Just cut a small part. Hindley wants to make sure the color is right."

Fuck that. I was opening this entire box. I slid the blade down the first seam then went to work on the other side.

"Berk, that's enough." Geneva moved next to me, reaching for my arm to stop me.

I pulled away and moved on to the other side, stripping the massive box of its tape. Finally, after cutting three sides, the cardboard covering fell away, revealing the contents.

"What the fuck is that?" I stared at the "chair" then looked at Geneva. "This isn't a chair. It's a roller coaster lounger."

"Oh my God," Geneva said, covering her mouth.

"What is it?"

"It's yellow." Geneva spoke into the phone. "Definitely not plum."

I moved around the "chair" to the other side of the box, slicing open the side.

"No, Berk!"

I stopped mid-swipe and peered up at her.

"Hindley needs to send it back. It's the wrong color."

I watched as Geneva's eyes grew wide. "No way, Hindley!" she shrieked into the phone.

"What?" I scooted next to her, eavesdropping on her conversation.

She twisted around, her back now facing me as she walked away. "I'm not keeping this fucked-up shit, Hindley."

I studied the box again. 'TC2.' It looked more like the shape of an "S" not a "T." What the hell *was* this thing? I didn't have my phone on me so I couldn't do a Google search.

"Just call the company. I'll have Berk tape the box back together and they can come pick it up." There was a pause. "No fucking way." Her eyes cut to mine as they traveled the length of my body.

Shit. My dick was growing again at her sultry gaze.

"I'm doing just fine on a mattress thank you very much."

Mattress? Was this contraption something to sleep on? I studied the chair. It looked like a leather roller coaster, high on one end, sloping down low, then rising back up into another smaller curve on the other end. I imagined it might be fun to ride it if you were a kid. Maybe they'd purchased it for their daughter.

"Fine, whatever, but I'm not using it," Geneva said to Hindley. "Hell, I couldn't even afford the thing."

Now I was seriously out of my mind, wondering what the hell it was. It obviously wasn't for a kid. And whatever it was, it wasn't cheap.

"Bye." She punched the phone as if she was squashing a bug, her face wrinkled with disgust.

"What the hell is this, Geneva?"

She drew in a deep breath as her eyes surveyed the monstrosity. "It's called a Tantra chair." She exhaled.

"What's a Tantra chair?"

She raised her brow. "Think about it."

I thought about it, but still had no idea.

"You've never heard of Tantric sex?" she asked.

Oh. Shit.

"Yeah, now you're getting the idea." She walked over to the box, her hand skimming over the sofa that was wrapped in plastic.

Tantric sex. Now my dick was really throbbing. I didn't know a lot about it, but I knew you could do some funky-ass shit.

"The chair is supposed to make it easier to get into all the positions of Tantra sex."

That did it. I was full-on sporting major wood now, so hard I was afraid I might split through my zipper. Just the thought of getting Geneva in those positions had me throbbing.

"So, Hindley wants to send it back?" I tried to keep the disappointment from my voice.

Geneva glanced over at me, her brow raised. "It's the wrong color."

"Why did she have it delivered here?"

"Supposedly it's a surprise for Rory. They're kind of kinky in the sex department."

"Judging from this roller coaster looking couch, yeah, I'd say so." I laughed as I followed Geneva. "This doesn't look like a chair, though." God, I wished I had my phone so I could Google this shit.

"I know."

"So, I need to box it back up?" *Please say no, please say no.*

Geneva's eyes cut to mine. "She wants me to keep it."

Yes!

"But you don't?" My voice cracked like a pubescent boy.

She shrugged her shoulders.

I studied the sofa and saw a separate package taped to the plastic covering. "What's this?"

She came around and took the item from my hand, quickly ripping it open. She wanted to keep this sofa thing, too, I could tell. But she was fighting a battle of the wills.

"Oh my God," she said.

"What?" I butted up next to her.

"It's a DVD. A 'How-To' DVD."

"Well, all right." The words were out of my mouth before I could stop them.

"You want to watch it?" Geneva was going for Sunday School teacher shock, but the glimmer of excitement in her eyes was hard to miss.

"Hell yeah, I do. I want to see how this bad boy works." I patted the chair.

She bit her bottom lip and I thought I was gonna come inside my shorts.

"Okay." She powered up the TV and DVD player.

Oh, shit. I plopped down on the couch, breathing deeply, trying to think of anything to decrease the swelling in my pants. *Old lady swimming naked, tits hanging to her knees, wrinkly skin...* I gazed up and saw Geneva bent over in front of the television, her plump ass suspended in the air for my perusal. Fuck! There went that idea.

I was about to jump up and yank down her shorts and fuck here right here in front of the TV when she finally turned around and plopped down on the sofa next to me.

God, please don't let her look at my dick.

"I hope this isn't like a porno," she said.

I hope it is.

The video started up innocently enough, but quickly moved to the how-tos of using the chair. Holy fucking shit! It was *real* people having sex on this thing. And the positions they were in were unbelievable. The video was put to music, but it wasn't cheesy music like you find in those low-budget, drive-in porn movies. Not that I would know.

Their bodies moved to the music in a type of dance that was completely mesmerizing.

"That's the Tantra part, the way they're totally in sync with one another." Geneva's voice was breathy as she leaned forward.

Or I think that was what she said. I couldn't hear anything because the pounding in my dick was so loud it took over every sensory organ in my body.

I jumped off the couch and ripped off the rest of the packaging, revealing the "chair" underneath. My eyes found Geneva's, hers half-lidded and glazed with desire.

"Take your clothes off and get on," I growled.

CHAPTER 25

BERK

"But ..." Geneva stammered, swallowing hard.

I walked toward the television and hit the pause button. The couple on the screen was suspended mid-action. I studied their position.

"What about my stomach?" I watched as she lovingly but self-consciously rubbed over her abdomen.

Stalking toward her, I extended my hand.

Her blue eyes stared at my upturned palm before they rolled up to meet mine.

I gave her a slow smile that I hoped spoke of my desire for her.

She slid her hand into mine and I lifted her to her feet.

"You are beautiful, Geneva." I breathed against her neck, watching as goose bumps erupted across her skin. I ran my hands along her waist, snaking underneath the material of her shirt as I lifted it high. "Raise your arms."

She obeyed and I quickly stripped her of her shirt. "Don't laugh," she said, covering her chest.

I took both wrists in my hands and unwound her arms. "Why would I laugh?" I gazed down at her skin. It was lighter than my native tan, but still flawless and warm, like melted caramel.

"I'm trying out nursing bras." She shifted nervously from foot to foot.

I stared at her bra, my thoughts going back to Jaime and her pregnancy.

"Berk." Geneva's voice brought me back from my thoughts. "Are you all right?"

I nodded my head, trying to push old memories from my mind.

"It unhooks here," she pointed to one of the straps, "so you can nurse without having to take off the entire bra."

"And you're trying them out now? Before the baby is born?"

"Well, my boobs are pretty big already."

I smirked and nodded my head. "I love your boobs."

She smiled. "Well, you may love them, but they're hard to carry around."

"Maybe I should help you." I stepped closer, my hands running along the straps until I found the hook. I released the latch and tugged at the material until both sides fell free, exposing Geneva's breasts. Instantly her nipples hardened into caramel nubs. I lowered my head to her chest and brought one of the puckered tips into my mouth.

"Oh, Berk," she moaned. Her fingers dug into my hair, pulling me toward her.

I wrapped my arms around her waist as I continued sucking, pushing her toward the chair until her calves were butted up next to it. "Sit down," I mumbled.

"Berk." She pushed me off her chest, my lips making a popping noise as I pulled away.

"What?" God, if she stopped this now, I was pretty sure I'd have blue balls for the rest of my life.

"This isn't our chair. Hindley wants to send it back."

I raised a brow? "Oh, really? It kind of sounded like she wanted you to keep the chair to me."

Geneva's eyes darted down to the floor, avoiding my gaze.

"According to the video, the leather is cleanable," I said.

She cut her eyes to mine. "That's gross."

"Well then, I guess we'll just have to keep it."

"Berk, it's like fifteen hundred dollars!"

"I'll make payments." I unbuttoned her shorts and pulled down the zipper as I tugged them and her underwear down her toned legs. My hands skimmed over her calves as I tapped them.

She understood and stepped out of her clothing.

As I rose, I took every opportunity to study her body. It was amazing, just the right amount of curves and lusciousness to make you remember why you should thank God for women.

"Sit." I pushed on her hips.

She stared up at me, her long lashes fanning her lids, but I could see the marked sense of want in her eyes. Slowly she descended on to the sofa.

Before I could even make another move, her hands were on the waistband of my shorts, her fingers making quick work of my fly. My dick sprung free, jutting out in front of her face. She wrapped one arm around my hips and drew me in further, my cock nearly touching the soft skin of her lips.

Her eyes rolled up to meet mine, her lashes feathered out across her lids. She was exotic and erotic.

My dick twitched.

With her eyes still glued to mine, she parted her full lips and leaned in the few inches needed to touch me.

As my cock slid into her warm mouth, my body shuddered and my hips automatically rolled forward.

Her tongue swirled around the tip and pressed against my underside, nearly sending me over the edge.

I was torn. I wanted to be inside her, but this felt so good, I didn't want it to end. I slid my hand into the silken mass of hair that swung around her shoulders.

Her head inched further down my shaft then pulled back with

just enough suction I thought I'd die. With every push and pull, her tongue coiled around me, pressing against every spot that had me moaning. "Fuck," I breathed out.

Before I could stop myself, my hips gyrated against her, fucking her sweet mouth. This was wrong. She was pregnant, carrying my child. I gazed down at her, her eyes now closed, her cheeks hollowed as she sucked me hard. The sight tortured me. My mind lost all reason and I pumped into her, glad that she didn't stop me.

Both of her hands wrapped around and grabbed my bare ass, drawing me in further. She wanted this. I wanted it. Hell, I couldn't stop this even if I tried.

Her hand slipped lower between my legs, her fingers pressing against the skin at the base of my balls. Fuck! She massaged it back and forth.

My hold on her head tightened and I reached out to secure myself on the chair. This was the best fucking blow job of my life. I tried to hold off, but it was all too much—her mouth, her hands, her tongue. God, that tongue.

I rolled up on my toes as I pumped into her, my release so violent I feared I might actually blow her head off. I pushed on her shoulders to pull away but she drew me in even further. How the hell could she take more? I didn't question. Instead, I fucked her beautiful mouth until my body stilled.

She slowly pulled away, licking her lips.

I scrubbed my face with my large hands. "Fuck," I muttered as I shook my head, trying to gather my bearings without completely falling over. Finally, my eyes opened. The sight before me was breathtaking.

Geneva was straddling the chair, reclining back on the foot of the sofa, everything God gave her on display for my perusal. "Here," she said, handing me a brochure.

"What's this?" I looked at the cover.

"It's a booklet of all the Kama Sutra positions that this chair was designed for."

What the fuck? I thumbed through the booklet and found she wasn't lying. These models were in every kind of sexual position known to man.

"I'm pretty limber." She smiled.

I peered over the brochure and found Geneva had completely removed her bra and was rubbing herself, one hand on her nipple, the other between her legs.

Holy hell. I'd meant to be in charge, direct our positioning on this "chair," but Geneva was slowly taking control. Looking at her body splayed out before me, I was totally okay with that.

"Pick one," she whispered.

My dick pulsated with each beat of my heart. *Pick a fucking position before you explode on her face, man.* My eyes fell on the title of one and I burst into laughter.

"What?" She sat up, stopping her ministrations.

I dropped the booklet on the floor. "Lay back, Geneva. It's time to go for a ride."

She giggled, laying back all the way on the end of the chair, her back arched, her breasts pushed high.

I straddled the chair and stood over her, looking down into her blue eyes, her hair fanned out on the leather of the sofa.

Her hands rubbed up and down my thighs as best she could from her position.

"What do you want, Geneva?"

"You, Berk. Just you. Inside me."

I leaned down and scooped my arms underneath her upper thighs, lifting her high enough for me to sit underneath. My dick dragged along her midsection as I eased my way down.

"Oh," she moaned.

I pushed her further up and watched as her body slid effortlessly up the chair. Reclining back fully, I lowered her down, the tip of my dick grazing against her several times before impaling her.

"Ah, God!" she shouted as I pushed inside her. Her eyes locked on mine.

"You okay?" I asked.

"Very," she said, smiling. "God, that feels amazing."

"Lay back down and straighten your legs."

She followed my instructions, her nipples now jutting out. God, I wanted to jump up and take them in my mouth, but this position would bring her maximum pleasure and that was what I wanted tonight. *Her* pleasure.

"Grab under my knees," I instructed. My legs were nestled next to her.

She slid her hands over my thighs and gripped me under my knees like I'd asked.

"Pull on me. Use my legs to move."

"Berk," she moaned as she brought herself against me.

With my arms still secured under her thighs, I pushed her away, my dick pulling out.

"Pull," I said. We both pulled at the same time and I drove so far inside her I thought I could actually reach the baby. "Fuck," I breathed out.

My head fell back as I slipped my hands under her ass and lifted her body. She slid over the arch of the chair with ease then tugged on my knees and slid back down my shaft. The friction was unbelievable, the angle hitting every spot that sent us both out of our minds. I was in her, balls deep.

"I need more," Geneva said between pants.

I pushed up on my knees, driving myself further into her, then pulled my hips away, doing a tug of war against her.

"Right there, Berk, oh my God, that..." she trailed off. "Yes, right there."

My legs were burning, my arms on fire as I pushed harder,

faster, trying to take her past the release she needed while staving off my own.

She tightened around my dick as her hips bucked under me. A few more strokes and I knew I'd be done for.

"Geneva," I panted.

"Ah, ah!" she shouted. "Ah, oh, God, Berk." Her voice was at a fevered pitch. "Ahhh!" she screamed as she convulsed around me, her legs wrapping around my waist and drawing me in.

I gave her three more quick pumps then shouted out my own release, my dick convulsing inside her. My eyes were drilled shut and stars exploded in bright colors behind my lids. As I came down from the high of my intense orgasm, my head fell back onto the chair and I gasped for air. "Oh my God," I panted.

My breathing finally slowed to a normal rhythm. I opened my eyes.

Geneva was still sprawled out on the chair, her arms hanging loosely off the side as if she was comatose.

"Are you all right?" I asked.

"Uh," she grunted.

I moved up slightly.

"No, don't." She raised up on her elbows and stared at me. "Don't pull out yet." She clamped down on me with her internal muscles.

"If you keep that up, we'll just start this all over again." I smirked.

"That's okay with me." She smiled, her face lighting up the now darkened room. "What was that position called?"

"You really want to know?"

She tilted her head, her hair spilling to one side. God, she was gorgeous. "Yes."

"It's called the spider."

She gripped the chair with her hands, trying to push off me, but

I held her hips in place. Just the mere mention of spiders had her freaking out.

Her eyes narrowed and her lips pressed into a thin line. "You're lying."

"Wish I was, sweetheart." I laughed. "Seems old Mr. Kama Sutra there likes insects."

"Stop." She swatted at my leg. "You're serious?"

I nodded my head. "You can look for yourself when we get up." I eyeballed the brochure sitting on the floor.

"My turn." She pulled off of me and scampered over to the floor, her bare ass on display as she bent over and picked up the pamphlet.

"Shouldn't we clean up here first?" I looked down at my dick and the spot she'd just vacated.

"I thought you said you were going to buy it." She sat down on the bottom of the chair as she thumbed through the booklet. "Oooh, this one looks like fun." She pointed to a picture in the booklet and smiled up at me. Her eyes were still glazed and needy. She'd been thoroughly fucked and was ready for more.

"I'll buy it," I said as my dick popped back to life.

She wrinkled her nose and rubbed her chin on one shoulder. She meant to be coy, but instead she looked hot as fuck.

"You'll have to make daily payments to me, though," I said. I stood and scooped her around the waist, bringing her down to sit on top of me, our eyes level.

She squealed in surprise. "So, what, you're like the mob, holding furniture ransom and blackmailing me?"

"I prefer to call myself the *middle* man." I bucked against her hips.

She giggled, wrapping her arms around my neck.

I liked this. I liked teasing with a woman, inserting myself into her life and into her routine. *And inserting yourself inside* her *isn't too bad either.* I laughed out loud.

"What?" she asked.

"I like this." I nuzzled up to her chest.

"My boobs?" She slid her hands into my hair.

"Yes, those, too. But it's more than that."

She tilted her head, and her brow furrowed.

"I like being here with you, Geneva."

Her face broke into a velvety smooth smile.

"Can I stay?" I asked. "With you and Peanut, I mean?"

Her eyes roamed over my face as she scrutinized me.

"I mean, I know I don't have a good track record, and God knows—"

Her lips were on mine before I could finish my argument, her mouth stealing my breath as her tongue washed away my words. She was cleansing me, absolving me, and for that I would always be grateful.

Our kiss lasted forever and I couldn't tell which way was up when she finally pulled away from me. My eyes darted between hers. I didn't want to fuck up this moment by saying something stupid that I might regret later.

"Did you find a position?" I asked, hoping I looked and sounded sexy.

She stroked my hair, her hand gliding down my face and cupping my cheek. "Any position with you, Berk, is what I want."

Her words had a deeper meaning as did mine tonight, but I didn't want to ruin the moment with trite words. Tonight, I wanted to *show* her what she meant to me.

I pushed her up on the sofa, her body once again gliding along the leather fabric until her back was arched perfectly with the frame of the chair. This had to be the most amazing invention ever. I made a mental note to thank Hindley the next time I saw her.

I clasped behind Geneva's knees and brought them up, thankful she really was as limber as she said.

Without saying a word, she lifted her legs higher and draped them over my shoulder, her lips curling into a deviant smirk.

Spreading her hips wider, I positioned myself at her entrance, staring down at not just Geneva Barton, the mother of my son, but the woman who was bringing me back to life again.

"I want you," she mouthed just before her head fell back, her hands running down her protruding abdomen, stopping where our bodies were joined.

I pushed in and she gasped. I held my position until she opened her eyes, staring up at me as I leaned over her. There was no judgment, no remorse, no anything in her eyes except love. Unconditional love. For me.

I thrust into her and watched as her face washed over in ecstasy, pretty sure mine was the same.

Her hand worked on herself as I bent over her distended belly to take one puckered nipple in my mouth. God, she tasted good, like sweet wine and fresh sunshine.

My mind tried to tell me that I didn't deserve a second chance, that I'd destroyed my wife and I would likely do the same thing to Geneva if given enough time.

Geneva's hands grabbed my face, pushing me off her breast.

I stared down at her, slowing my pace.

She looked at me as if I were the most precious treasure she'd ever found. "I love you, Berk," she whispered.

My heart stopped, along with my body.

"I'll love you until you find a way to love yourself again," she whispered.

Her words were both a dagger and a salve to my heart.

"And then," she continued, "I'll love you just for me." The tears in her eyes spilled out of the corners as I felt my own tears burn my eyes. The smile that enveloped her face was majestic, ethereal, like an angel.

It was the first time in over three years that I actually did feel worthy of another person's love.

"I'd like to make my first payment for the chair now though," she said, laughing. "If that's all right with you." She moved her hips against me.

And just like that, the moment was gone. But not forgotten. In my heart I knew I loved this woman, but my mouth wouldn't let me speak it out loud. I still wasn't convinced I wouldn't hurt her if I did.

CHAPTER 26

BERK

"How goes it?" Dr. Elsher asked.

I reached out and snagged a bottle of water from her small refrigerator and plopped down onto the green sofa. "It goes, Doc."

"Sofa today?"

"I knew it." I laughed, stretching out my legs and twisting off the top to the bottle.

"Knew what?"

"You *were* psychoanalyzing which seat I took."

She shook her head as she sipped on her own bottle. "Tell me what's going on this week."

"Well…" I didn't know how much detail I should give her about my new sexual relationship with Geneva, especially since she worked with her.

"You seem nervous." She leaned back in her chair.

"What I say stays here, right?"

She nodded. "If I feel like you're a threat to yourself, a threat to others, or I receive a court order, then I'm obligated to discuss your case. Otherwise, things stay between us."

I let out a heavy breath.

"Why?"

"Well, Geneva works here and I just don't want what I say in here to affect her." I nodded toward the window. "Out there at work, you know?"

"Yes." She smiled, and instantly I was set at ease.

"Geneva said she loves me." I pushed the words out as if they were pained.

Dr. Elsher's bottle stilled as she brought it to her mouth.

"I didn't say it back," I added.

"But…"

"But, I felt it, in my heart."

Dr. Elsher studied me as she drank more of her water.

A wave of vulnerability threatened to take me under.

"How did she respond when you didn't reciprocate?" she asked.

"She said she would love me until I could love myself."

Dr. Elsher's eyes roamed around the room as she tilted her head.

I knew better than to interrupt her when she was forming her next sentence. Instead, I gazed outside her window. The freshly cut grass was green and vibrant, and the blooming flowers under the gazebo next to her office hinted at new life.

"You've been living with her for several weeks now, is that correct?" she asked.

"Yes."

"And I'm assuming you haven't lived with anyone since Jaime."

I smiled inwardly, realizing I didn't flinch when she said Jaime's name any more.

"That's nice," she said.

"What?"

"You're smiling at the mention of Jaime's name rather than clutching at the chair as if it were your life preserver."

"Yeah, it's nice not to grimace when I hear her name, or Alana's. And sometimes I share memories of them with Geneva. Good memories."

"That's wonderful, Berk."

"I still have dreams, but they're not all nightmares like before. Sometimes I dream about happier times with them. But it's still hard."

"What is?" She scooted up on the edge of her chair.

"The guilt. It hits me hard, especially at night when the house is quiet and Geneva's already asleep." I closed my eyes and felt a pang of disgust wash over me.

"It's not wrong to feel your emotions, Berk. We've discussed that. Grief will come, sometimes in waves that overwhelm us and nearly drown—"

My eyes popped open at Dr. Elsher's abrupt stop. It was the first time she'd ever censored herself for me.

"It's all right, you can say it," I said. And I meant it. For one of the first times since I'd lost my family, I wasn't going to stop someone from saying the word "drown."

"I'm sorry, Berk. I meant no disrespect. It was just an analogy gone horribly wrong."

I nodded my head, wanting to absolve her of any guilt. "May I ask you something?"

"Yes."

"How did your son die?"

She didn't bristle or go taut. Her eyes cut to the rug on her floor and she twirled the bottle between her hands.

"He hung himself," she said quietly.

I gasped. I didn't mean to, but her revelation was just so unexpected. I stared at her for a long moment. She was bereaved but not broken, haunted but not paralyzed with guilt.

"That's him." She pointed to a frame on her desk.

I scooted toward the edge of the sofa and studied the picture. It was obviously a school picture. He looked like your typical awkward male teen caught somewhere between boyhood and man. He had dark hair and dark eyes like Dr. Elsher. To most he would probably be considered average. I knew he was anything but.

"How old is he there in that picture?" I asked.

"He was sixteen."

I remembered Geneva had said he'd died at sixteen.

She lifted the frame from her desk and stared down at her son, the raw emotions on her face seemed like a private moment between mother and child.

I cast my gaze down to the bottle in my hand. "Will it always be hard?" I didn't even look up. She would understand my question. "Will it always feel like a sucker punch anytime someone asks me about Jaime or Alana?"

"It's like anything else, Berk. You'll have good days and bad. Some questions will catch you off guard. Like today."

I peeked up and saw she'd returned the photo to its original position on her desk.

"I'm sorry," I said.

"Don't be, Berk." Her eyes were filled with compassion and empathy, a look only parents who'd lost their own child could fully comprehend. Only Dr. Elsher was doubly saddened. She'd lost a child to suicide. I couldn't imagine her grief.

"Is it something I need to prepare myself for?"

"You can't prepare yourself for the grief that engulfs you some days. You just have to ride it out. Like I said, some days are better than others, but for me, they don't last for hours and days and weeks any more."

"That's good to know."

"Have you contacted any of the support groups I suggested?"

"I went to one, but it felt awkward."

"That's okay." She nodded. "It works for some, but not for everyone." She took another sip of her water bottle.

"Did they work for you?"

"Yes."

Her short answer warned me this was the end of our conversation about Dr. Elsher's grief.

"How do you like living with someone again?" she asked.

"It's hard to say. I still feel like a guest."

"But you're sleeping with her, I assume."

I audibly gulped. Did I want to go there? My voice left me. I nodded.

"Why do you feel like a guest then?"

"She and I haven't talked long-term."

"Do you want long-term?"

I shrugged. Did I?

"It's okay not to know, Berk. We don't have to have all the answers right away."

I took another sip of my water, my anxiety beginning to slip away.

"I just need to make sure you're still working through the steps of grieving and not putting off the process by focusing on Geneva instead," she explained.

I wrinkled my brow, completely baffled by what she was saying.

"You've experienced what we call *complicated* survivor's grief."

"How is that different than regular survivor's grief?" I asked.

"Yours was prolonged by your own choosing. You delayed your grief, denied it, and that can make your anguish worse when it finally hits you."

I remembered the unbearable grief I'd experienced when I'd first arrived back to Colorado and decided to compete again. I'd tried to put all my mental fortitude into training. But as soon as my feet hit the snow, the grief hit me hard, literally dropping me to my knees.

"You've come a long way since you first came back from Hawaii."

I'd left Hawaii shortly after Geneva had, my need to rebuild my life fueled by my anger at her sudden departure. I returned to

Colorado, fortified and ready to do battle with the ghosts from my past...or so I thought.

"Yes," I finally answered.

"And in that time, you've done a great deal of grieving, but not much moving on."

"If you mean crying and throwing shit, then yeah, I've done a lot of that."

"But never with anyone, never getting your emotions out with someone there to help?"

"I'm pretty sure I was a blabbering mess when I told Geneva about Jaime and Alana."

"And you shared with her that you believe Jaime committed suicide?"

I flinched. This time the mention of suicide and Jaime together did hit me, hard.

"Yes." That was all I could muster.

"I think you're making tremendous strides in the month since I've seen you, Berk. Please don't get me wrong. I mean, a month ago, just the mention of Jaime or Alana would have you ready to snatch me bald."

I gazed up and saw the small smile on her face. It gave me reprieve, and hope. She was a survivor. If she had trudged back from the death of her son, maybe I could, too.

"May I share something with you about my son Shawn?" she asked.

"Of course."

"Shawn suffered from mental illness."

My body stiffened, paralyzed, unable to even breathe.

"Did Jaime?"

The tears burned my eyes and I willed them away, but like the ghosts from my past, they refused to leave.

"We've talked about this before, Berk. You're not all-powerful, you're not in charge of another human being's decisions."

My heart beat so fast I thought it would explode from my chest. Adrenaline coursed through my veins and burned me like a raging wildfire.

My fist clenched and I ground my teeth together. I hadn't felt rage like this in a long time. "Is that what you tell yourself at night, hoping for a reprieve from the guilt that suffocates you when you think about all the things you *could* have done to save your son, Dr. Elsher? That you were powerless."

My words were daggers aimed directly at her. I did *not* want to talk about Jaime's possible mental illness. To anyone. Ever.

"You're a goddamn therapist and you couldn't even save your own son for fuck's sake." I jumped to my feet, my body trembling and my chest heaving with labored breaths.

"You're absolutely right, Berk. I couldn't." Her words were void of any emotion. I turned and found her head dropped to her chest as she stared down at her fumbling hands now perched in her lap.

Shit!

"So, I should just absolve myself, say I played no role in her death because Jaime was fucked up in the head. Is that what you're saying?"

"There is no absolution. For anyone, Berk. Ever." Her last word was a whisper.

I had to get the fuck out of here. The walls in her office were closing in, threatening to crush me.

"Berk," she called after me just as I was about to slam the door.

I turned and glared at her.

Her eyes were dark and brimmed with tears, but still she kept them at bay, unlike me.

"I'll see you next week?"

What the fuck? See her next week? Was she serious? I drew in a deep breath, trying to suppress my need to kick something. "Sure, see ya next week." I sighed, slamming the door behind me.

CHAPTER 27
BERK

"THIS WAS AN AWESOME IDEA!" Dana shouted from the other side of the table as the band on stage continued to play. "Thanks for inviting us, Berk." Her huge eyes danced with brilliant hues of blue in the hypno-tronic lights overhead.

"What time does your brother go on?" Tori asked. Her own eyes sparkled, but for a very different reason. She liked Rhen. She was a cool chick or seemed to be in the short amount of time we'd spent together.

I gazed down at my watch. "In about twenty minutes. He'll probably stop by before he goes on."

"Oh, good." Tori clapped.

Rhen had joined Geneva and me at Dana and Peter's house for a swimming party a few days before. He hadn't paid much attention to Tori. But then again, he didn't pay attention to any woman since his fiancée had totally fucked him over several years ago.

Tori seemed like a nice girl and I wanted to warn her not to get tangled up with him.

My gaze fell to Geneva. The dark circles under her eyes and her sagging body told me she was tired. "We don't have to stay long!" I yelled in her ear over the obnoxious noise of the band.

"I'm having fun." She stroked my forearm and immediately I pulled back. "What's wrong?" she asked.

My last appointment with Dr. Elsher had spooked me and I hadn't been back. My suffocating guilt over Jaime's death had returned, heavier than ever. I didn't want to bring Geneva into that. The only way to do that was to pull away from her.

I gazed into her blue eyes now filled with regret and sorrow. I hated being the one to fill her with doubt.

"Hey, dude." Someone hit me square on the back. "What's up, big brother?"

I turned and found my brother Rhen standing behind me. "Rhen, you remember everyone," I said, waving my hand across the table at Gen's friends. "Rory, Hindley, Dana, and Peter." My hand stopped when I hit Tori. "And you remember Tori?"

Tori's smile lit up the room.

Rhen nodded once.

Tori's smile fell.

I wondered if that was how I made Geneva feel. Did I disappoint her, make her lose hope? My attention turned to her.

She was perched high on the bar stool, her head moving with the beat of the song, her lips silently singing along.

I was transported back to the bar in Hawaii, back when she had been sitting on a similar stool, a teakwood bar separating us. Geneva had been vulnerable that night, putting herself on display and singing her heart out even though she was scared shitless. I hadn't realized it at the time, but even then, she was teaching me how to be brave.

I butted my stool up next to hers and draped my arm around the back of her chair. She stayed still, her attention completely transfixed on the band. I needed to be vulnerable. I needed to let her in. I needed...her.

"Hey." I leaned in next to her ear, putting my chin on her shoulder.

She tilted her head, her hair tickling my nose.

"After Rhen sings, let's get out of here, okay?"

She turned to stare at me.

I'd barely touched her in the last week. We hadn't even made love, and I knew she was hurt and confused, probably thinking it had something to do with her declaration of love for me.

"Let's go home." I smiled.

She grinned and her head fell against mine. "Okay."

"How long is your set?" I asked Rhen. The sooner he was done, the sooner I could get Geneva home and talk to her, and touch her, and hold her. *And have sex with her?* Yeah, that, too.

"Forty-five minutes. Why?"

I shook my head and drew Geneva in closer.

Her head fell on to my shoulder. She was weak, I could tell. I hadn't done a good job taking care of her. It seemed to be a selfish pattern of mine. But that would change. She needed me.

My hand caressed her arm, giving her shoulder a slight squeeze.

She let out a deep sigh and I thought she might fall asleep in my arms. I relished the idea of carrying her home.

"Well, I gotta go!" Rhen downed the rest of his water then slapped me on the back before skirting through the growing crowd.

Tori's face fell as her blue eyes followed him.

"Don't try, Tori," I said, leaning over toward her. "He's as messed up as I am."

"Yeah, you're pretty fucked up!" Dana yelled just as the music from the band went silent.

All eyes fell on her. Her normal bronze skin blushed red. I never thought this chick got embarrassed. About anything.

Her words were true, though. I was fucked up. But I was trying now. For Geneva. And for Peanut.

"Yeah, I'm totally fucked up," I said. Everyone's attention turned to me to gauge my reaction. My mouth fell open as I laughed out loud, a good belly laugh, hard laughing that made my eyes water.

The entire table joined in.

I peered across the table at Dana. Her eyes were forlorn and distant. It was clear she thought she'd wounded me with her words.

"Totally fucked up." I nodded, trying to ease her guilt.

"Totally." She laughed.

"Ladies and gentlemen, welcome to Metal Mike's Pub." My brother's familiar voice rang through the speakers. "I'm Rhen Rigby."

"I love you, Rhen!" a pubescent female screamed from the back.

My brother having groupies was just wrong.

"I love you, too!" he yelled into the microphone. "We're Nineteen Seconds Down, and we'll be rocking you with some originals and some covers tonight."

The crowd burst into screams of anticipation, including all the girls at our table. Rhen having chicks throw their panties at him was about as comfortable for me as a prostate examine.

Rhen and his band formed shortly after his fiancée dumped him almost seven years ago. She'd left him at the altar. Literally.

It had been me who'd had the unfortunate task of telling him she wouldn't be showing up at her own wedding. Why she'd waited until the day of the blessed event was beyond me.

I remembered Rhen's face went ashen just before his knees buckled, and he tumbled to the ground, passed out cold in front of two hundred friends, family and guests.

When he came to, he said his life was forever changed. For the better. He said it only took him nineteen seconds down on the ground, passed out cold to realize what a mistake he'd almost made in marrying his long-time girlfriend.

There was no denying Rhen was a star. His voice had the right mix of smooth and raspy, grain and grit. He'd been approached by a record label early on in his career to make a solo album, but he was committed to his band. It was a dream he'd given up once for a woman who'd shattered his heart. He said he'd never leave them again.

True to his word, forty-five minutes later, their set was over and Rhen was saying his thank yous to the crowd.

I wrapped Geneva in my arms, preparing to head home.

Her shoulders were drooping and her eyelids were heavy. I feared she might pass out at any second.

"Before we leave, we'd like to perform one more song." Rhen's voice rang through the speakers.

Great, an encore. The chicks went crazy, screaming like they were at a fucking *NSYNC reunion concert.

"We'll need some help with this one, though."

Hands went flying in the air as girls who looked no older than middle schoolers jumped up and down like they were in a Jazzercise class.

Rhen covered his eyes and peered out into the audience.

A sick feeling rolled through my gut.

"Geneva," Rhen called out, "I hear you're an amazing singer."

Geneva's face went ashen and her eyes grew wide with fear as her body stiffened in my arms.

I remembered the look. It was the exact one she'd had in Hawaii just as she was about to sing Karaoke. I was going to kill my brother.

Her eyes pleaded with me as they darted back and forth like a wild cat.

"Come on!" Dana shouted.

"Do it!" Hindley encouraged.

"I hear Evanescence is one of your favorite bands." Rhen continued to coax her.

Geneva's head lowered, her lips pressed firm as she clung to me.

My fucking brother. He'd asked me days ago who Geneva liked.

I always heard her singing along to Evanescence so I'd told him. I had no fucking clue he'd embarrass her like this.

"I'm sorry," I whispered. "Fuck him, we can just go."

The girls latched on to her arm. "Come on, Geneva. Just one song," Tori pleaded.

Geneva looked like she was about to pass out or throw up, or both.

"One song?" Rhen pleaded.

The crowd began to cheer.

"Only if you want to, sweetheart." I kissed her head. She had the voice of an angel, and the body of a temptress. Seeing her on stage singing would be heaven for me. But I wouldn't push her.

"One song," she finally exhaled.

All the women at our table screamed in delight, which set off the entire bar. They began chanting her name just like they had in Hawaii.

I led her up toward the stage as the crowd parted.

Rhen held out his hand and together we lifted her onto the stage.

"As you can see, ladies and gentlemen, Geneva here is with child," Rhen said, pointing to her stomach.

The crowd let out a collective "Awwwww."

"And it's a very special child. This is my baby nephew. They're naming him Rhen, after me."

Everyone laughed, except Geneva.

"Kidding, Geneva." He bumped her arm. "Have you guys come up with a name yet?"

She stared down at me, her eyes wide as if she'd been caught red handed. I knew her nickname for our son was Peanut, but other than that, we'd never talked about a name. Her expression told a different story. She had a name, but she was scared to share it.

Rhen cast his gaze over to me as if seeking approval for a question I didn't know.

I shrugged my shoulders.

"I've been thinking of one, but I haven't talked to Berk about it."

Her voice was barely above a whisper. She looked so vulnerable and scared.

My heart ached for her but swelled at the same time. I used to see vulnerability as a weakness. I was slowly learning that it was just a stepping stone to healing. I was ready to heal.

"What?" I mouthed to Geneva.

"Can you share it?" Rhen asked, looking from Geneva down to me.

I nodded my head. Now *I* was curious.

"It's a combination of our families," she said quietly, her eyes never leaving mine.

"What? Are you going to name him Rhen Jr.?" Rhen laughed, along with the crowd.

Geneva shook her head, her blonde hair whipping around her shoulders. She was glowing and not from the lights on the stage.

Carrying my baby, being vulnerable in front of me and this crowd, gave her an ethereal glow that I wanted to bask in for days, maybe weeks…maybe for the rest of my life.

"John Paul," she spoke into the microphone. "It's a combination of Berk's father and mine."

My breath caught. John Rigby was my father. Paul Barton was hers. Two strong men. One strong name. My son's name. I loved it. And I loved Geneva.

~

It takes courage to grow up and turn out to be who you really are.
- E.E. Cummings

~

CHAPTER 28

GENEVA

WHAT THE HELL was I doing? I hated singing in front of crowds. All of my friends knew that. Surely Rhen knew, too. He'd been in Hawaii working at the resort when I was there.

I shielded my eyes from the stage lights and looked at the table littered with my friends and family. Any one of them could have let it slip. But they were all looking at me so expectantly, like I was about to offer them the gift of a lifetime. I couldn't say no. Besides, I knew the exact song I wanted to sing. Just for me.

I looked over at Rhen. "Do you really know Evanescence?"

"Yep. Name your poison, princess." He smiled.

God, he was almost as adorable as Berk, with his lopsided grin and sparkling light brown eyes.

"Do you know 'My Immortal'?" I asked.

Rhen walked around his keyboard and punched on an electronic tablet propped up like sheet music.

"Got it." He nodded toward the screen.

"I thought you played guitar."

"I do." He interlaced his fingers and pushed them away, cracking his knuckles like they do on *The Three Stooges*. His eyes surveyed the keyboard then darted up to mine. "You ready, toots?"

Toots? Shit, was I really going to do this?

Rhen leaned over the keyboard, pushing the microphone away. "You don't have to do this, Geneva."

I drew in a ragged breath, covering my chest trying to calm my racing heart as I shook out my other hand by my side.

"God, you're scared shitless." Rhen reached out to touch my arm. "Hell, I didn't know. Tori made it seem like you love to sing. Oh, hell." He walked around the keyboard. The compassion in his eyes was overwhelming.

I held up my hand. "No. I want to sing. Just give me a minute." I stared at Rhen. "I *need* to do this," I said under my breath.

Berk had come such a long way on his recovery, working hard with Camille to bridge the gap from his past, heal the guilt that had shattered his heart.

I'd done soul searching over the years, trying to break free from the chains of my guilt that surrounded my mother's death. Neither of us were responsible for our loved ones' deaths, and it was time I let the demons free. This song spoke the words of my heart. Maybe the lyrics would touch Berk, too.

I gave Rhen a single nod. "I'm okay."

He took his seat behind the keyboard and punched at his tablet.

I studied the stage and noticed Rhen's bandmates were sitting off to the side. "No band?"

"Just me and you, toots." He smiled.

Panic flooded my veins, robbing me of my next breath. I needed more instruments to hide behind. Shit. I raised my head, blinded by the stage lights. I could do this. I had to. "Here goes nothing," I sighed as I inched closer to the mic.

"Go, girl!" Dana's rough voice rang through the silent bar.

Calls and claps followed, and it infused me with strength. I closed my eyes, willing my mother's soul to give me strength. "This one's for you, Mom," I whispered.

Rhen began playing the intro to the song. Evanescence was a

hardcore rock and roll band like Rhen's. Hearing only the piano play was eerie but fitting for the mood I wanted to set.

I started the song quietly, feeling every word as it filled the room. I was tired, tired of hiding behind the guilt and shame of my past. The dark cloud of my mother's death had rolled in on me at a young age and built into a turbulent storm over the years, leaving behind a bitter young woman who was obsessed with wielding her vengeance on innocent victims.

My journey back to redemption had been long and painful, filled with love and forgiveness that I didn't deserve. But at least it wasn't a journey I'd traveled alone, not like Berk had.

The lyrics to the song were hauntingly true, not just for me, but for Berk, too. We had both gotten stuck in a maze of pain that haunted us, leaving us with only the memories of our loved ones. They'd never meant to hurt us. But their early departure from this earth had totally destroyed us.

I missed my mother every day. She *had* wiped away every tear, fought every fear that filled me as a child—until the day she couldn't any more.

Even though she died almost twenty years ago, she still held me captive, just like Berk's wife and daughter still had a stronghold on him. Together though, I knew we could find the strength to break away from the ghosts that haunted us. Maybe build a better life for each other and our son.

As the song drew to a close, I changed the lyrics and hoped that Amy Lee and the rest of Evanescence would forgive me. It was *my* mother who'd held on to *me*, who'd wiped away *my* pain and tears. I wanted to hold on to Berk, help heal his wounds that had festered for years.

My head bowed and I held the mic stand to brace my wobbly legs. I stared at the stage floor as Rhen played out the rest of the song. I was lost, transported to a world beyond this life.

My mother's face flashed before me, her eyes full of life and love, for me. Her spirit swept through me and I felt a calm like I'd never known before. It was surreal. I wanted to give that feeling to Berk, bring him the peace he deserved.

The cheers and whistles from the audience shocked me back to the present. I stared out blankly into the crowd that was just beyond the stage lights, only silhouettes to me. One shadow was missing. The one I craved the most.

I covered my eyes and leaned lower to escape the glare of the harsh stage lights, not surprised to find Berk's seat empty. Rhen offered his hand to help me off the stage as others gathered to assist me. I rushed to our table, out of breath, my eyes darting around to each person surrounding me.

"Where is he?" I panted.

"He said he needed some air," Peter answered.

"Front or back?" I stared at him. Something had happened during the song, their forlorn faces told me without saying a word. "Front or back!" I shouted.

Warm hands enveloped my shoulders. "Come with me, Geneva." I turned and found a face that resembled Berk's so much, I nearly cried.

Rhen motioned toward the front door, dragging me with him.

"Where is he, Rhen? Is he okay?" I was nearly shouting to be heard above the noise of the DJ now mixing music.

"We'll be back," Rhen said to the bouncer at the door.

The beast of a man nodded once as he held the door.

The Texas heat was still thick in the air even though it was late spring. I prayed for a gust of wind to take me away, or at least dry the sweat that was now covering my body.

Rhen walked beside me on the sidewalk, his hand gently splayed on my back to steady me. "What has he told you, Geneva?"

"What do you mean?" I played coy, not wanting to break Berk's trust. I wasn't sure how much even Berk's own family knew about Jaime and Alana.

"What has Berk told you about Jaime?" Rhen cut his light brown eyes to me.

I froze.

"So, you know." Rhen's words were a statement, not a question.

I nodded once. There was no need to re-hash the fact that Berk's wife had chosen to end her own life.

"Berk was a mess after Alana's death," he said, pinning me with his eyes.

"I'm sure. Losing a child has to be unbearable."

"It was. For all of us." The pained expression on his face confirmed how much Alana was loved by everyone in Berk's family. "Jaime took Alana's death the hardest, blaming herself. She went off the deep end."

I nodded, not sure how to respond. The despair in Rhen's voice was hard to ignore. The death of his sister-in-law and niece tormented him as well.

"And Berk wasn't there to catch her." He paused. "But I couldn't blame him."

I blew out a breath I didn't realize I'd been holding.

"He was as lost as Jaime was after Alana died," he continued. "They just handled their grief in different ways."

I stood on the busy street, watching as strangers walked past us, unaware of how turbulent our conversation was.

"I mean, fighting a mental illness is hard enough even in the best of circumstances," he said. "You add losing your child to the mix, along with guilt because you felt responsible, and it's just a recipe for suicide."

"A what?" I fell back against the brick wall. "A mental illness? Jaime had a mental illness?"

Rhen's eyes went wide. "I just assumed," he stammered, "I mean, I thought you knew about her suicide."

One hand clutched my heart as the other covered my mouth in shock. I shook my head. I assumed it had been suicide, Berk and I never talked about it, but mental illness, too?

"I'm sorry, Geneva." Rhen reached out to touch my arm, his eyes going soft. "I shouldn't have said anything. It's Berk's story to tell."

"It's all right," I said through my hand. It wasn't all right. No wonder Berk's grief was so real. "I knew about the supposed suicide, but not about the mental illness," I confessed. "How long?"

"How long what?" Rhen asked.

"How long had she been diagnosed?"

"Look, Geneva, it's really not my story to tell."

"No, it's not." Berk's deep voice vibrated beside me.

Rhen and I startled and turned toward his voice.

Berk was a giant of a man, towering over most, yet in that moment, he seemed so small, beaten down by the ghosts that still haunted him.

"Berk," I walked toward him, "you're right. It's your story to tell." My eyes searched his. His normally light brown ones were gone, replaced with dark shadows reflected in the nighttime sky. "If you want to," I added.

"Gen!" Tori shouted. "Gen!"

I peeked over Berk's shoulder and saw Tori frantically searching up and down the street.

"Here, Tori." I waved my hand to get her attention.

She rushed toward me, stopping just before she ran into Berk. "Are you all right? This asshole hasn't berated you again, has he?" She nodded toward Berk.

Berk's body tensed and his hands clenched.

"I'm fine," I said, leaning into her.

"What about him?" Her lips curled up into a snarl as she glared at Rhen.

"What the hell did I do?" Rhen stood his ground, his head tilted as his long, dark hair fell to the side.

Tori's eyes scanned Rhen's body. She was trying to intimidate him, but the desire in her eyes was hard to mistake.

"Why don't we give these two some space." Rhen looked from Berk to me. His face transformed with a compassionate smile as the streetlights shining overhead illuminated his face. Rhen was the one with the heart.

"No." Tori's tone was hard and unyielding as she stared Rhen down. I loved how much she was protecting me. "Not until I hear from Geneva that she's okay."

"I'm okay, Tori," I reassured her as I stroked her arm. "Really."

Her eyes darted between the two brothers. "If you're sure."

I nodded several times.

"Come on." Rhen stepped between Berk and me, taking Tori's hand and looping it through his arm as he led her away.

Tori gazed over her shoulder, a small smile chipping away at her supposed hardened exterior.

"Can we talk?" Berk asked.

I was startled by his voice and afraid to look at his face, fearful of what condition I would find him in. Was he mad, disappointed, angry?

As my gaze met his, a band tightened around my heart. His expression was so pained. His eyes shined glassy with unshed tears. "Of course. You can always talk to me, Berk." I offered a small smile.

He took my hand in his, interlacing our fingers. Searching up and down the street, his brow furrowed as if he were lost.

"There's a park around the corner," I said.

He grinned down at me. It was so slight I almost missed it, but it was there.

I blew out a sigh of relief as he led me down the street.

After several blocks, we turned a corner and walked toward a large park littered with playground equipment. Berk led me through the large patch of land, walking toward a massive swing set. He stopped behind one and pulled on the chains, silently asking me to sit.

I did. I watched with trepidation as he walked around me and took a seat in the swing next to me. His head fell and his feet kicked at the stones underneath.

I wanted to reach over and touch him, tell him it would all be okay, but I wasn't sure it would be.

"Alana loved to swing."

His words hit me like a poisoned arrow. Just thinking of him pushing his sweet baby girl in a swing had my eyes pooling with tears.

"She'd always yell, 'Higher, Daddy, higher!'" He laughed, raising his head and staring off into the night.

I held my breath.

"She was my world. My *whole* world," he confessed.

A boulder lodged in my throat, choking my tears. I hadn't even met Peanut yet, and I couldn't imagine losing him.

"I know Jaime should have been my world, and she was. It's just, with Alana, it was different, you know?" He twisted in the swing to look at me.

I tried to hold back my tears, I didn't want to upset him, but I was losing the battle. "The two loves are different, I'm sure," I said.

"When I lost Alana, my heart stopped beating. It was severed in two when I saw her lifeless body in the tiny casket." His words were choked.

I heard the hiccup of a stifled sob come from his chest. My own heart broke listening to his unimaginable pain.

"I lost a part of my soul, a part of myself the day Alana died, and I don't know if I will ever be whole again."

I looked up at him but remained silent, having no words to comfort him. Tears were streaming down his face as his hands gripped the chains holding his swing.

"I don't know if I'll ever be the same again, Geneva. I'm not sure I can give you all of me, but that's what you deserve, a whole person."

I reached out and stroked his arm. "I want you, Berk, in whatever way you come, broken or whole."

His eyes bore into me and I could tell he was trying to decide whether or not to believe me.

"They call it a 'new normal,'" I tried to explain.

"It doesn't feel like normal. It still feels like shit, even three years later."

I quickly swiped at my face, brushing away my own tears before Berk noticed. I didn't want to interrupt his story. If he saw it was upsetting me, I knew he wouldn't continue.

"When I met Jaime, I instantly knew that I wanted to be with her," he said. "She had a zest for life, a vibrant spirit that was so bright you couldn't help but follow her." His face broke with a smile that lit up the night sky. It was the first time I'd seen him mention her name and actually smile.

I drew in a deep, steadying breath as if I were the one about to divulge a heartbreaking story. I knew soon I would have to tell Berk about my past, but it wouldn't be tonight. Tonight, was about *his* story.

"She was always so upbeat and positive, making friends wherever she went. I was shy and introverted so I was drawn to that part of her, at first."

At first? What did that mean?

"Then came the storms." Berk white-knuckled the chains of his swing.

He was talking about her mental illness.

"She would run hot and cold all the time. One minute she'd be loving and kind, the next she'd blow off the handle at any little thing." His chin fell to his chest. "It was like living with Dr. Jekyll and Mrs. Hyde. That's the only way I know how to explain it." His head turned toward me.

I offered a weak smile.

"I learned to live with it. We all did—her family and friends I mean. I just assumed that was Jaime, you took the good with the bad like anyone else you loved. I saw enough good in her that the bad didn't matter. Until Alana."

Oh, shit. What did Alana have to do with this story?

"Alana was just a few months old and I noticed Jaime's mood swings were more frequent and more intense. She never harmed Alana, but she was enraged at times, throwing things, knocking things over when the slightest thing went wrong. Then she'd fall into a deep depression when she realized how awful she'd been to everyone, including me.

"I called her mom and her sister Jackie one day. They explained they thought it might be post-partum depression. I didn't know what the hell that was so I took Jaime to a doctor. He prescribed her some medication, but all it did was make her loopy. She hated it, and honestly so did I. Finally, her mood swings were becoming so volatile that I had no choice."

"What did you do?"

"I took her to the emergency room."

Oh, God.

"Luckily the doctor on call was familiar with postpartum psychosis. That's what he called it. Just the word 'psychosis' had me flipping out."

I nodded my head. I could only imagine. "What did they do, for Jaime I mean?"

Berk's eyes studied me. It was clear he was trying to decide if he could reveal all his demons to me tonight.

"The doctor suggested inpatient treatment for med management and psychotherapy but Jaime flipped her shit. She didn't want to leave Alana. And honestly, I didn't want to lose her. I didn't have any experience with mental illness or mental hospitals, only what I'd seen on television. And those all looked fucking insane.

"Not to mention the fact that Jaime was still skiing competitively. Well, she was on leave, but it had been her goal to return one day. If news of this got out, she feared it would stigmatize her and me both."

My mouth went dry and my head pounded, wondering if perhaps Berk had refused treatment for his wife because of his own reputation.

"I couldn't give a shit less what anyone thought of Jaime, Alana, *or* me," he said. "Let them say whatever the fuck they wanted. Jaime was different, though. She always worried about what others thought of her. So, for her, I refused treatment and we went home with orders from the doctor to find a psychiatrist as soon as possible."

"Did Jaime's family know?"

"No. She didn't want to share it with anyone. She was a perfectionist and this so-called diagnosis by an ER doctor had her completely rattled. We'd moved to Utah a year before Alana was born."

"I thought you lived in Colorado."

"We were both from Colorado and lived there during our off season," Berk answered. "But we trained with the U.S. pro team in Utah during the competitive season."

I nodded once in understanding.

Berk drew in a heavy breath, kicking at the rocks under his feet before continuing.

"Jaime had a lot of friends from the ski team and within the town of Park City where we trained, but none were as close to her as her mom and sister. The distance from them didn't help. I knew she needed them. And so did I. Caring for a newborn baby *and* Jaime, all while trying to train, was becoming too much for me."

"So, you moved back to Colorado?" I asked.

"I felt like I didn't have a choice. The move was only supposed to be temporary, until we got Jaime stabilized, then we could all move back to Utah so I could continue to train."

His hesitancy scared me. "But?"

"But," he paused, "mental illness doesn't work that way."

"What do you mean?"

Berk's eyes cut to mine. It was dark outside but I could still see the regret and sorrow that lived inside him.

"We went back to Colorado and shared Jaime's diagnosis with her mom and sister. They helped us find a doctor and get her on meds. They helped me with Alana." His head fell back and he looked up at the sky. "They saved our lives." He released a heavy sigh.

The streetlights flickered on and I could see the stream of tears running down the sides of his face as his eyes slammed shut. I wanted to go to him, wrap my arms around him, and infuse him with my love. But I couldn't. He was purging, cleaning the wound, and I had to sit by and watch his agony unfold.

"What happened next?" I asked.

Berk wiped at his eyes and sat up straight.

"The ski team was giving me shit for being gone so long. It was the middle of competition season. Fortunately, Jaime understood the pressure. She'd been competing professionally since she was sixteen so she didn't give me shit when I had to make the decision to return to Utah, without her."

Berk shook his head as if wiping away all the painful memories that haunted him before continuing.

"I would come home as often as I could to see Jaime and Alana. Jaime was doing so much better on the meds. Her doctor in

Colorado felt like she was stable enough to move back to Utah full-time as long as we found a well-qualified psychiatrist.

"I knew Jaime was scared to leave her mom and sister, but it was time. She had a new outlook on life. It was the first time Jaime had been stable since I'd met her. She was a different person. Not so manic, but not so depressed either.

"We existed like that for a long time. Jaime fell into a routine that we all seemed satisfied with. She was healthy and happy."

Berk stopped and so did my heart. He was preparing for the worst part of the story.

"When Alana was two, Jaime decided to start skiing competitively again. I encouraged her. She always said her dream was for *me* to win the gold. I loved her for that. But I knew she craved a medal just as much as I did."

Berk's entire continuance changed and I could see a blanket of pure love envelope him as his eyes lit up, remembering his late wife.

"Jaime wanted another baby, but I was against it, knowing what all she'd been through after Alana's birth. Instead, she threw herself into training. She would be at the slopes for hours, then work out religiously after Alana went to bed. Jaime was like that. She'd obsess about one thing, become fixated on it to the point of exhaustion. For the last two years that obsession had been Alana. Now it was switching. Her obsession was changing and I could see the warning signs but I couldn't stop her."

"Was she still seeing a doctor?"

"Oh, yes," Berk answered immediately. "There was no way I would let her miss. And she didn't want to, either. She understood how important her meds were. She'd tried to go off them when Alana was one, claiming that she missed the manic parts of her illness. It only took a few weeks for her symptoms to come back, only ten times worse. We'd nearly had to put her into a hospital, but thankfully her mom came and lived with us for a month while we straightened out Jaime's meds."

"So how long can the postpartum psychosis last?"

"Jaime's new doctor wasn't completely convinced that's what she had. He believed that she'd had bipolar disorder much of her life based on the information that her family and I provided."

"So, her family was involved in her care?"

"Yes." His answer was flat and I knew there was a story there, but I wouldn't pry.

Berk pushed out of the swing, tucking his hands in his pockets. "I'm sorry I left the club before you finished. It's just that…" He kicked the rocks under his feet, shuffling around. "The lyrics rattled me. It sounded just like how I feel with Jaime. Even though I'm working with Dr. Elsher and trying to sort all this shit out in my head, it's like Jaime still has me in her hold. All of me. And I can't get *me* back."

"I understand, Berk."

His eyes cut to mine.

I purposely stayed in the swing. He needed space, I could sense that. But he also needed an explanation. "I blamed myself when my mom died."

"Didn't she die of cancer?"

"Yes." I nodded.

"Then how could you blame yourself?"

"It's complicated." My head fell to my chest as I studied the pebbles at my feet.

Something slid under my chin and raised my head. Berk was kneeling in front of me.

"You weren't responsible for your mom's death, Geneva." His words were full of love and compassion—exactly what I needed.

"And you weren't responsible for Jaime's death either, Berk," I whispered.

He dropped my face like it was a hot coal and jumped to his feet, turning his back on me.

I'd poked the tiger and he was about to run. I stood from the swing and slid in behind Berk, wrapping my arms around his taut waist, pushing my extended belly against his back.

His body tensed under my touch. "I'm not good for you, Geneva." He spoke softly.

"Berk, I've fucked up in my life. A lot. Things you don't even know about. Things that might make you run from me. I'm not good for you either."

He turned in my arms and stared down at me. "What kind of things, Geneva?"

"You've already told me a lot of things tonight, Berk. I'm really tired. Can we just take a few days to process all of this before I dump all my stuff on you?"

"No. I want to know now."

"Why?"

"I just need to know everything. I've opened up to you. More than anyone else since Alana and Jaime died."

I let out a heavy sigh. "Can we at least do it at home?" I looked down at my feet. "I've got pebbles in my shoes, and my feet are so swollen they're about to split apart."

He gazed down at my feet.

Before I could say another word, he scooped me up in the air. "Berk!" I screamed.

"Be quiet," he whispered. "People are going to think I'm hurting you."

"We're parked like five blocks away. There's no *way* you can carry me that far."

He gazed down at me, his face twisted in offense. I'd questioned his manhood.

"Sorry, babe," he smirked, "but your ankles look like they were swallowed by your calves."

I swung at his shoulders, connecting with the mass of muscle.

He squeezed me tight against his body. "There's no way you're taking another step tonight. It's bath and bed for you."

Oh, my. That was something I could get used to. My head fell onto his shoulder and I nestled into his hold as I breathed in his scent. "A girl could get used to this," I sighed.

"A girl *should* get used to this." He kissed my head.

I wanted to believe him. In the recesses of my mind though, I knew once he learned all of *my* secrets, met all of *my* demons, he would leave me. Which meant he would leave Peanut, too.

CHAPTER 29
GENEVA

"CAN I ASK YOU SOMETHING?" I sat on the couch in my fluffy robe as Berk massaged my feet and ankles.

"Is it about Jaime?" His fingers stopped moving.

"Yes."

"Only if I can ask you some questions, too."

I dragged in a heavy breath. "Okay."

He nodded once, giving his approval to ask.

"How can you blame yourself for Jaime's actions if she suffered from mental illness?"

His eyes focused on my feet, his hands continuing to work their magic. "I wasn't there for her when she needed me. I was a selfish prick."

"You're still seeing Camille?"

He nodded.

"May I ask what happened?" I drew my feet away from his hands and sat up on my knees.

"I was just as big of a shit to her as I was to you and to Jaime." He rose from the couch, scrubbing his face with both hands.

"What did you say?"

"I don't want to talk about it, Geneva."

"But you need to, Berk. You're going to have to deal with all of this before—"

"Don't lecture me about working on my shit. Not when you haven't told me *anything* about *your* past."

I sat back on my heels and fumbled with the loose ends of the belt of my robe. He was right.

"Promise you won't leave?" I asked quietly.

He tilted his head, his lips pursing into a thin line as he narrowed his eyes. "Why would I leave?"

I shrugged my shoulders. "I mean, you can leave me, just not Peanut."

"Why the hell do you keep calling him Peanut? I really don't like it."

Okay, I could take that. I'd pushed him to his limit tonight. He was aggravated and acting out.

"I'm sorry," he said, sitting beside me. "I didn't mean it."

"When it was just me and—" My eyes went wide. Even though Berk was being a dick, I understood why, and I didn't want to push him further away.

"*Peanut?*" he grumbled, but smiled, taking my hand in his.

"When I went to the doctor and she gave me the first ultrasound picture of him, he looked like a peanut. He was so tiny on that big, black screen. It was just me and him." I sat back on the couch, crossing my legs in front of me and tucking my robe over my legs.

"It didn't have to be that way, Geneva. You could have called me."

I stared at his beautiful eyes, the color of honey swirled with dark chocolate.

"When I was in Hawaii, I overheard you and Jackie talking." I drew in a deep breath and exhaled before continuing. "I didn't know she was your sister-in-law, I thought she was an old girlfriend or something. She was talking about missing you and bringing you home and how everyone loved you, including her. She actually said she loved you." I pressed my eyes closed, trying to calm my breathing. "And then you told her that we weren't serious, that you weren't seeing me. I assumed that I really was just a vacation fuck to you, so I left."

"Gen," Berk whispered, his hand sliding up my leg and squeezing my knee.

I opened my eyes.

He was staring at me like I was a fragile doll and he didn't want me to break. "I'm sorry. For everything," he said.

"What do you mean?"

"I'm not sure. I just feel like I've fucked up this situation and I don't want to do that, to you or to *Peanut*." He shook his head as he said our son's nickname. I could tell the name was beginning to crack his hardened exterior.

"I'm sorry, too, Berk. When I got home from Hawaii, I didn't know I was pregnant. I'm not even sure how it happened. I mean," I raised my brow, "I know *how*, it's just, I was on the pill."

"I was furious when I saw you," he admitted. "I thought you'd lied to me, about being on the pill, and maybe you did this on purpose."

I shook my head. "It was as big a shock to me as it was to you."

"So how *did* it happen?"

"I'd been sick for almost a week right before we left for Hawaii. It was some kind of stomach virus or food poisoning. The OB doctor said I probably threw up most of the pill that week and it never made it into my system. She said that's probably how I got pregnant."

He nodded.

"I don't want you to think I did this on purpose or anything. I didn't even know who you were in Hawaii, that you were a professional athlete, I mean."

"I know." He scooted closer, staring down at my lap. "God, Geneva, even your hands are swollen."

I gazed down at my fingers and sighed. "I look like the Pillsbury dough boy. And I still have like ten weeks to go."

He shook his head.

"What?"

"Jaime was so swollen when she was pregnant with Alana, I thought her feet were going to split open." He laughed.

My heart swelled. "It's nice to hear you laugh when you talk about them."

"I guess Dr. Elsher is helping. I need to apologize to her. Maybe go back. For you. And for Peanut." He placed his hand on my stomach. "Maybe we could go together."

"I think that would be a good idea." I stroked his face.

He leaned into my touch and smiled.

God, he was beautiful. My breath caught, and my panties melted. *But wait, you're not wearing any panties.*

"Let's go to bed," Berk said.

Better words had never been spoken. But I knew I needed to get my story out.

"Can I talk to you before we go? You may not want to sleep with me after you hear *my* story."

"No. You're tired. I'm tired. Let's sleep tonight and then we'll talk tomorrow." He reached over me and kissed my cheek.

I felt like a revered princess.

"Come on." He stood and stretched out his arms.

I took his hands in mine as he gently lifted me off the couch.

"Please don't carry me." I palmed his chest, keeping my distance.

"Why?"

"I feel like a fat turd. I don't want you to hurt your back. You can't afford injuries in your profession."

Suddenly, the room shrunk and I felt claustrophobic as all the air was sucked out. Would he go back to Colorado to ski? Would he try to take Peanut with him? I hadn't thought about any of that since he'd been back.

"Are you going back to Colorado?" My voice was an octave higher and riddled with fear.

"I train in Utah," he corrected.

"Whatever."

"I want to ski again if that's what you're asking."

"How will all this work?" I pointed from my stomach to him.

"I don't know. We'll figure it out, Geneva." His words were gentle and calm. "But not tonight. Tonight, you need to rest. We can talk about all this tomorrow."

"Okay," I sighed, the weight of the last few weeks finally crushing me. I yelped as Berk scooped me up in his arms. I hit his chest. "I told you not to do that."

"I don't follow orders well." His eyes sparkled as he carried me down the hall, kicking my door open. "Here." He pulled back the comforter, waiting for me to get in.

Suddenly I became nervous. I wasn't wearing anything underneath my robe. We'd had sex several times but now I was shy.

"Is this the same book we read in Hawaii?" He leaned down and picked up my BDSM novel.

Oh, crap. I darted in front of him, trying to block him, but I was too slow.

"Still reading your smutty books, huh?" He was trying to sound judgmental but I heard the hope and desire in his voice.

"Well, I was all alone. I had to have *something* to keep me warm at night."

He set the book down on the nightstand and reached for the drawer. "Are there more in here?"

Shit!

"No, Berk!"

He held his arm out, blocking me.

"Oh, wow." He laughed as he pulled out the drawer. "Damn, there's like an assortment in here."

Fuck.

"How many vibrators does a girl need?" He held up my 'silver bullet' in one hand and my full-on, cock-sized dildo in the other. "What the fuck is this thing?" He nudged the rubbery butterfly with his thumb.

Oh, God, kill me. Kill me now.

"Um, you might not want to do that," I said.

"Why?"

"It's been…" I looked down between my legs.

"Where I've already been." He smiled with a devilish sparkle in his eyes. "And where I intend to be again." He tossed both vibrators on the bed as he moved closer to me. "Very soon."

Oh, shit. "Berk," I stuttered.

He pulled on my belt.

I watched as the strap dangled by my side and my robe fell open, exposing my distended belly.

His hands rubbed around my abdomen, reaching up and over my breasts as he pinched both nipples.

"Ahh," I moaned.

His hands moved higher over my shoulders, pushing the robe completely off my body. I stood in front of him, naked, vulnerable, and scared shitless for some reason. He was seeing more than just my physical body.

"You're beautiful, Geneva." His hands skimmed up and down my arms. Goose bumps erupted across my skin. His fingers slid around my neck and tugged my hair, bringing my face even with his. "God, I want you so bad."

Before I could answer, his lips crashed down on mine. His tongue was forceful, his actions primitive as he yanked me in closer.

"Berk," I tried to speak against the crushing pressure of his lips.

"No talking, Geneva." He pushed me back against the mattress.

I fell down on top of the bed with a bounce.

"Oh my God." Berk's eyes combed over my body like a seductive predator.

"What?" I wrinkled my brow, self-conscious of my nakedness. I moved to cover my body.

Berk bent down over me, pinning my wrists next to my head. "Don't cover yourself. Your body is amazing. And knowing that you're carrying my child inside you makes my dick so hard I'm about to explode in my shorts."

Crude? Kind of. Hot? Oh, hell, yeah.

His honey-colored eyes searched mine, desire pooling in his gaze.

"I don't know what the future holds, Geneva. I have issues. You have issues. We're both fucked up, and I get that. Maybe that's what makes us perfect for each other."

"What are you saying?" I panted as his hard-on pressed against my thigh.

"I'm saying, give me time. I want this. I want you and Peanut. I just don't want to fuck up again."

"Again?" I tilted my head in confusion.

Suddenly, grief and guilt overtook his expression.

"Berk, we're gonna fuck up. It's inevitable."

"I don't want to destroy you, Geneva." His hold on my wrists loosened.

"I'm way tougher than you give me credit for." I smiled, wiggling my hands out of his grip. I ran my fingers over his shoulders, coming to rest around his neck as my legs circled his hips, drawing him into me. I pulled his face as close to mine as I could, given the fact we had a huge basketball belly between us.

"That's what I'm counting on," he said. His face lowered and his lips were a breath away from mine. "I'm counting on your strength. For all of us."

Before I could respond, his lips brushed against mine, but this time he was gentle, loving, not as frantic as before.

His tongue slid across my lips and I opened mine, inviting in more than just his physical body. I wanted to give Berk hope, help him break free of the chains that held him captive. The same ones that held me.

His lips suddenly broke free from mine, leaving me breathless, panting as I tried to force more air in my lungs. He reached toward the nightstand and grabbed my book, flipping through the pages to the spot I had marked.

"Berk," I pleaded, reaching for the book.

He jerked back, thumbing across the page as he began to read.

West kicks her feet wider apart. "I said spread your legs, Priscilla. Don't make me say it again."

CC sits stark still, laid out in front of her master, completely nude as she slowly widens her legs. Wanting to please him has become second nature to her, but she still fears the unknown.

"Put your ankle in my hand."

Priscilla hesitates.

His palm slaps hard against her thigh, the noise of the contact echoing through his playroom.

She jumps from the shock, holding her breath so she won't make a sound. It doesn't hurt, but it stings enough to make her squirm.

"Do not hesitate when I tell you to do something for me, Priscilla, or there will be consequences."

West's voice is a low growl that vibrates against her clit like the toy in his hand.

He leans down and rubs where he'd inflicted the blow. His tongue slides out from his supple lips and slowly caresses her thigh.

CC shivers from the thrill of his body touching hers. She craves him.

"I will punish you when you disobey me. But there will always

be rewards for you, Priscilla. Never doubt that. I will always plea-sure you, even in the midst of your punishment."

His tongue slides over her leg, working tiny circles as he progresses higher, stopping just before he reaches her wet pussy.

"I knew you'd like the punishment." His voice is dark and brooding as his fingers slip inside her wet folds. "Pleasure and pain. Two sides to a coin, and you crave them both, don't you?" His thumb rubs against her swollen clit.

CC's eyes go wide, the sparks from his caress feeding a need inside her she didn't know she had.

"Tell me what you crave, Priscilla."

"You," she whispers, her walls spasming against his fingers.

"Me, or this?" West holds up a purple vibrator.

"You," CC whispers, breathlessly.

"I think you deserve both, don't you?"

"Yes, Master."

"Shit, Geneva." Berk's voice was a breathy pant.

I rolled over to my side, hiding my reddened face with the comforter. "Oh, God, this is so embarrassing," I said through muffled moans.

"This stuff is seriously hot."

I flipped over and stared at him.

Berk perused the vibrators lying next to me then looked at the book before his light brown eyes locked on mine.

"What?" I asked, completely baffled by his look.

"Me or those?" He nodded toward my sex toys.

I shrugged.

He grabbed my ankle and yanked me to the end of the bed. My body slid across with ease.

I yelped in surprise. "Berk!"

He knelt down in front of me. "Spread your legs wide, Geneva."

"You can't spank me, I'm pregnant. That's a felony." I stifled a laugh, but the look of desire on Berk's face made my entire body shudder.

He slid his hands up my calves and over my knees, his thumbs rubbing slow circles on my inner thighs, moving closer to my center.

"Pick one," he said, his eyes staring straight at the juncture between my legs.

Right now, he was seeing more of me than my gynecologist did. "What?" I panted.

"The silver one or the one that looks like a fucking donkey's dick?"

I giggled but jumped when his tongue hit high on my thigh, licking toward my aching center. I rubbed my fingers through his hair. "I just want you, Berk." Unable to see him over my ever-expanding belly, I pushed up on my elbows.

His ministrations stopped as he pulled back from me. He reached across the mattress and grabbed the purple dildo. He stared at me, brows raised. "Both it is." He smiled as his head slipped below my stomach.

I gasped when the vibrator slid inside me. One click and the thing came to life. I bucked my hips, unable to remain still. Before I could catch my breath, his tongue circled around me, pressing against my clit.

"Oh, fuck," I moaned. "God, Berk." I gasped for breath.

He sucked and licked, pushing me to the edge.

My legs stiffened as my hands clutched the comforter and fell over the cliff. I screamed out, my release exploding from deep within me. The tingling sensations shot out to every extremity and rebounded back between my legs, leaving me a throbbing mess.

The vibrator slid out and Berk stood over me.

"Me now?" He smirked, holding his cock in his hand. He was completely nude. When had that happened?

His eyes connected with mine. He was so vulnerable. I could see inside his soul, see all the pain he'd endured, all the demons that haunted him in his dreams. But there was also an endless pool of love spilling over from his heart. Love he didn't even know he possessed.

I nodded once.

He gripped under my hips, lifting me off the bed as he nestled at my entrance, slowly pushing in.

He filled me in a way no vibrator or sex toy ever could. His reverence for me was so overwhelming, tears burned my eyes.

"What's wrong?" he asked, stopping his movements.

"I wish you could see what I see, Berk." I smiled, trying to reassure him.

"What do you see?" He slowly slid into me, filling me completely.

I gasped.

I wanted to tell him. Tell him that I saw the two men fighting within him. Two sides to the coin. He'd beaten himself up for years, carried around the weight of guilt and shame that threatened to destroy him. That burden had nearly blinded him, making it impossible for him to see the loving man lying in wait.

But I couldn't tell him that. Not today. Instead of answering, I wrapped my legs around him, digging my heels into the back of his thighs, pulling him further inside me.

Slowly his hips began to move again, hitting every spot that lit me on fire.

"God, Berk," I sighed.

"No pain for you, Geneva." His face tightened as he worked for his release. "Only pleasure."

I reached out for him.

Sensing what I needed, he bent over my belly, bringing his face close enough for me to touch.

"No pain for you either, Berk."

He closed his eyes and leaned into my hand. With one final thrust he filled me, his body going rigid as I spasmed around him, calling out his name.

Berk and I had lived a lifetime of loss and pain. Now it was time for *me* to bring out the man inside of *him*, the one that yearned to love again. The one he didn't even know existed any more.

CHAPTER 30

GENEVA

"WELL, I'm glad you're back, Berk." Dr. Elsher closed the door behind us as she ushered Berk and me into her office. "And, Geneva, it's nice to see you here as well."

I smiled. "Nice to see you, Camille."

She nodded once. "Please, both of you, have a seat."

I moved toward the sofa and literally fell into it. I was as big as a whale now and had no control over my body when it came to gravity. I looked up and found Berk still standing above me, his eyes downcast. I wondered if I'd done something wrong.

He turned to face Camille. "First, I want to apologize, Dr. Elsher. For the way I behaved last time." Berk's tone was deep and gravelly.

Dr. Elsher moved to speak but Berk held up his hand.

"I also want to thank you for seeing me again after my outburst. I hope you know I didn't mean anything against you. I was just lashing out. The way I always seem to do with those I care about." Berk gazed over his shoulder at me and gave me a half smile.

"Thank you for the apology," she said. "It means a lot. To both of us I think."

Berk remained standing as he watched Camille in disbelief.

"Sit, sit." She motioned toward me on the couch.

Reluctantly, Berk sat beside me.

"It's actually a good thing, believe it or not," Camille said.

"What?" Berk asked.

"That you lashed out. It's a feeling. They're beginning to come to the surface. Good, bad, or ugly, you're at least feeling *something* again." She smiled, that warm motherly expression that all kids crave.

Berk sank further into me, and with that, he seemed pacified.

"So, you're here together. I'm assuming you're trying to make things work. As a couple, going forward?"

I flinched. Did we want to be a couple? Berk had invited me to this session, but we'd never talked about committing to one another.

"Well, I told Geneva about Jaime's mental illness."

My eyes traveled from Berk to Camille. She was nodding her head, holding back her words.

"And, I just thought maybe it might be good for her to hear from you exactly where I am with all of this." Berk waved his hand in the air.

"And where are you, Berk? With all of *this,* I mean?" She mimicked Berk's movement.

"Well, I'm able to say their names out loud again. And I'm talking about them, with Geneva."

"He's able to laugh at his memories of Jaime and Alana," I added.

"That's wonderful." Camille smiled.

There was deafening silence. Oh, crap. Had I fucked up by using his wife's and daughter's name?

"What do you want going forward, Berk?" Camille turned toward him.

He drew in a deep breath, reaching out for my hand before expelling it.

I gave him a small squeeze.

"I don't want to hurt Geneva and the baby. The way I did Jaime and Alana." He released my hand.

I gazed over at him, not surprised to see his eyes were drilled shut as he jabbed his thumbs into each eye socket.

"Berk." I rubbed on his leg.

He shook his head.

"How do you think you'll hurt Geneva and the baby?" Camille asked.

Berk removed his thumbs and scrubbed his face with his palms as if trying to cleanse it. "I don't know. I just…" He leaned forward, resting his elbows on his thighs.

I needed to touch him, infuse him with my own love. I reached out and gently rubbed on his back. My eyes connected with Camille and she gave me a small smile.

"I feel like I didn't do enough for Jaime, like I failed her. And it cost me both of them."

I withdrew my hand as Berk fell back against the couch, his gaze staring up at the ceiling.

"May I speak openly with Geneva here?" Camille stared at Berk.

He sat up straight, his eyes darting from me to Camille before nodding.

"Berk, you know Jaime had a mental illness."

"I know that," Berk answered. "I know, and that means I should have done more."

"No." Camille corrected him. "It means there are so many more variables that went into Jaime's actions that there was no possible *way* for you to know *what* to do for her."

Berk sat silently, staring into space.

I studied him, not knowing what to say, if anything.

"Berk, Geneva is not Jaime. I'm not saying Jaime was weak, but she came with a host of medical issues that you had no control over. Geneva doesn't."

I cringed at Camille's words. I *did* have a shit ton of issues, none of which I'd ever shared with Berk yet, though. They weren't mental illness, but I was definitely fucked up.

Camille glanced at me. "You don't agree, Geneva?"

"Well," I stuttered, "I definitely have issues."

"We all do," she said. "But you're working on yours, processing them, taking responsibility for them."

Berk turned toward me, his brows creased as he stared at me. "What issues?"

Shit. I knew I'd need to talk about them eventually, but I didn't think it would be here in a therapist's office. Maybe this was better. Camille knew my history. Maybe she would be able to help me explain my actions.

"It's up to you, Geneva," Camille said.

I scooted back from Berk, twisting around on the couch to look at him fully. "I told you yesterday there are things from my past, things I'm not proud of. Things that may actually make you want to leave."

Berk's eyes darted between me and Camille. "What things?"

I glanced over at Camille. She had a small smile on her face that gave me the confidence to open up.

I stared down at my lap, mindlessly rubbing on my belly. I silently asked Peanut for strength before I began to tell *my* story. "When my mom died, I became really bitter. Then my dad married my stepmom, Caroline. I loved Caroline, but she brought my stepsister Hindley into our family, too."

Berk nodded once in understanding. He knew my family members well by now.

"I hated Hindley."

"Why?" Berk tilted his head.

I gazed up and found him staring at me. "She was everything I wasn't, everything I always thought my dad wanted *me* to be but never could." I sunk deeper into the sofa, my walls building up around myself.

"What do you mean?" Berk asked.

"I blamed myself for my mother's death. I guess somewhere in the back of my seven-year-old mind, I thought maybe my dad blamed me, too. Then he met Caroline, and he seemed to just magically move on while I was stuck in the past. I watched my father laugh and love again, with Caroline and with Hindley. He hadn't done that since my mother's death. I mean, the two of us would have fun together some-times, but not like after Caroline and Hindley came along. He was in love, and it changed everything. I felt…," I stumbled.

"Alone?" Berk touched my knee.

I gazed down at his huge hand spread out over my leg and nodded my head, willing away the tears. This was Berk's session, not mine.

"You weren't responsible for your mom's death, Geneva. We've already talked about that," Berk said.

I lifted my head and saw Berk staring at me with such compas-sion. "I wish you could give yourself the same kind of forgiveness you're showing me right now, Berk."

His hand slipped away and the moment was gone.

Pressing on seemed like the only option. I knew Berk had to rip the bandage off his own wounds. It was time I did the same. I gazed up at Camille.

Her brows were raised and her head slightly angled.

"So anyway," I continued, "I grew up in a house full of love, but it wasn't the kind of love I shared. I was jealous of Hindley. Jealous of the love my father seemed to dole out to her effortlessly. As I aged, it became my subconscious mission to make her suffer. Not only Hindley, but others, too. I became a complete and total bitch."

My eyes cut to Berk's and I saw his face was flat. He was trying to absorb my words without judging me.

"The pinnacle of my hatred came a few years ago. I wanted to crush Hindley. I was married at the time and Hindley and Rory were falling in love. I didn't want her to be happy. I never did. I wanted her as miserable as I'd been growing up with her around. I blamed her for everything—especially for coming between me and my father, for breaking our special bond. I thought if I could break Rory and Hindley apart, maybe it would crush her. So, it became my mission to seduce Rory."

"Seriously?" Berk scooted away from me, his lips turned up in a snarl.

Shit.

"And you were married?" His voice dripped with disgust. I couldn't blame him. My actions had been deplorable.

"Yes," I squeaked out, my head hanging in shame.

"Man," he sighed.

"There's more." I didn't dare look at Berk for fear his expression may keep my secrets locked inside for all time. "Rory and Hindley were in Miami for a skating event. Caroline and I flew to Florida to join them. She wanted to cheer on Rory. I just wanted to screw Hindley over."

I shook my head, not even believing the person I'd been back then.

"I tried to seduce him, but Rory totally blew off my advances. He was in love with Hindley, all in, and it pissed me off even more. I was used to getting any guy I wanted."

"But you were *married*," Berk said, his tone filled with anger and judgment.

"Yes," I whispered.

"What happened? What did you do, Geneva?" The way Berk said my name sent chills down my spine, and not in a good way.

Rip the bandage off.

"I paid a guy to put drugs in Rory's food. That night I went to

Rory's room, knowing he'd be doped up, assuming I would be able to sleep with him."

"Oh my God, Geneva, are you serious?" Berk scooted to the other side of the couch.

I gazed up at Berk and saw his eyes wide with shock.

He angled himself in the corner of the couch, fully facing me. "Did you have sex with him? Did you fuck your own brother-in-law?"

"No!" I shouted, waving my hand. "But it wasn't because I didn't try." I touched my cheeks as the warmth of my tears rolled down my face. I looked up at Camille.

She sat quietly. None of my story was a surprise to her. She'd worked with me over the years to bring me back to the point where I was today—able to take responsibility for my actions.

"Hindley found us in his hotel room. I tried to make her think that I'd slept with Rory. It destroyed her. I'd accomplished my mission."

My head fell into my hands as I sobbed uncontrollably. "How could I have been so horrible? How could I have grown to hate someone so much that my only mission in life was to utterly destroy her? My own sister." My words were muffled, but I didn't care. They'd been spoken for my benefit, not Berk's.

"Yeah, how could you?" Berk's question hit me like a brick to the chest.

I raised my head, wiping at my tears. "I wanted to hurt her, Berk, because I thought she'd hurt me." My words came in hiccupped sobs. "Just like you wanted to hurt Jaime, because you thought she hurt you."

Berk's head jerked back as if I'd slapped him.

"I'm sorry, I know it's not the same thing at all." I reached for him, trying to eat my words.

He pulled back as if I were a contaminant. "Hell no, it's not the same. My wife killed herself because I wasn't a compassionate husband, because I couldn't console her, not because I fucked her sister!"

"Berk," Camille interrupted us.

I sat stark-still, like a wounded animal about to be devoured, praying that if I didn't move, perhaps he wouldn't see me.

"Why don't you let Geneva finish? I think you'll understand where she's coming from and what she's trying to tell you when you hear the rest of her story."

My eyes focused on Camille, trying to steal some of the strength and resolve she had. Drawing in a ragged breath to steady my words, I continued.

"I confessed to everyone, to Hindley, my husband and my parents, what I'd done. My husband divorced me, and my parents completely disowned me for a period of time. Hindley was the only one who even remotely gave me a chance to make amends. The one person I'd sought to destroy was the *only* person who gave me the opportunity to make amends." I shook my head, completely in awe of my stepsister.

"I served a lot of community service to avoid jail time for distributing a controlled substance." The words were punched out like someone else was telling the story, like someone else had committed these offenses. My stomach roiled and I thought I might vomit. "I did a lot of therapy to get to the heart of why I'd acted out the way I had. It took me a long time, but I was blessed that my family and friends saw the changes inside me and gave me another chance.

"I'd let hatred and guilt fester inside me. It grew to the point where it made me a different person, a human being who couldn't love anyone, least of all myself. When I denied that love from entering my heart, I became the shell of a human being, devoid of real feelings, for anyone. It calloused me and made me act out in ways I never thought possible."

I looked up at Berk, now feeling a bit more resolved.

His eyes were boring through me. He was judging me in the harshest of ways. I couldn't blame him, though. My story was difficult to hear, even for me. What I'd done, the lengths I'd gone to destroy people, was awful.

"I fucked up, Berk. A lot." I stared at him. "I hit rock bottom. But I didn't stay there."

"What are you saying?" he asked.

"I'm saying that it's taken me a long time to get where I am today, and yet I'm still scared shitless that I'm going to fuck up again. Or worse yet, fuck up our baby. I have no *idea* what it takes to be a mother. I've hurt people beyond repair. I'm paralyzed with fear that I'll do the same to this baby."

He moved closer to me, the first positive response to me since I'd started.

"But I don't have a choice," I continued. "I have to get better. For me and for Peanut." I gazed down at my belly as I instinctively caressed my rounded abdomen.

"You're not going to fuck him up, Geneva," Berk spoke softly.

"And neither will you, Berk." I caressed his hand and placed it on my belly, not surprised when Peanut kicked.

Berk squeezed my hand. "But what if I fuck *you* up?" His eyes were darker now, filled with fear and guilt.

"I'm already so fucked up, Berk, trust me, you couldn't possibly do more damage." I laughed under my breath.

"I could, Gen. I could cause a lot more damage."

"I'm stronger now, Berk. I'm not asking for forever. I'm just asking for a chance. A chance to show you I'm not afraid. A chance to help you learn to love yourself again. Because the man I see sitting in front of me deserves to be happy, he deserves forgiveness, he deserves a chance at a happily ever after."

"You read too many novels," he said. "I don't think those things exist in me." His words were so desolate, like the hollow expression on his face.

"Well, you at least deserve a second chance to find out." I smiled at him.

His amber colored eyes searched my face. He was in the same spot as I had been several years ago, at a crossroads—forgive himself and move on, or drown in the quicksand of guilt and shame that surrounded him.

"I don't know what the fuck I'm doing, Geneva."

"Neither do I." I laughed.

"Blind leading the blind?" He smiled.

"I'll be here, too, don't forget," Camille spoke.

Berk and I turned to face her. I'd completely forgotten she was there.

I pressed my hand against Berk's chest. "There's still a man inside you that has a lot of love to give, Berk. You'll have to work through some serious shit to get there. But I promise, if that's where you want to go, if you want to find that man inside you who deserves to be happy, I'll muck through the shit with you to get there."

Berk's lips pressed into a thin line as his brows wrinkled. "Why, Geneva?"

"Because my family gave me a second chance. I'd be lost without them. I want our baby to know his father."

"What kind of father will I be, though?"

"The same kind you were to Alana, the kind that loved her unconditionally. The kind of father who loves her even *beyond* death."

His eyes glistened with unshed tears.

"You're suffocating under a blanket of guilt," I continued. "It served you for a time, kept you warm, I know. I used to wrap myself up in one every night after my mother died. But at some point, you have to let go and try to live again, the best you can. I'm willing to hold your hand and take that chance with you. For Peanut."

He stared at me as if I were crazy—which I was—but I saw the hope in his eyes.

"We'll fuck up, Berk. It's inevitable. But we won't *give* up. *I* won't give up."

Berk turned to look at Camille who sat quietly. "Will you help us, Dr. Elsher?"

"Of course, Berk. I'll be here every step of the way if that's what you want."

"I'll definitely fuck up," he laughed, "but I'll try, Geneva." Berk slid closer to me, his hand gently stroking my face. "For Peanut. And for you. I'll try."

Efforts and courage are not enough without purpose and direction.
- John F. Kennedy

CHAPTER 31

BERK

"Here you go." I handed a drink to Hindley as she reclined in the chair next to Dana's pool.

"Thanks, Berk." Hindley smiled as she took the cup from my hands. Her stomach was so big, I feared she might actually give birth here at Dana's house.

"You're welcome. When are you due?"

"Ugh, any day now. I'm actually almost a week overdue." Her face dropped with disappointment. Everyone could see that her body was worn out and ready to have her baby.

I turned and gave Geneva her drink. "Here's yours."

"I could have gotten my own drink." She smiled up at me.

My stomach fluttered like a pubescent boy in middle school when the cutest girl in school says 'Hi' to him in the hallway.

"Doctor's orders," I said.

She rolled her eyes.

"What doctor's orders?" Dana asked.

It shouldn't have surprised me that Geneva hadn't shared our last doctor's appointment with her friends. As selfish as Geneva said she'd once been, that wasn't the Geneva of present day. I knew more than most how little she wanted her friends to worry.

"The doctor wants her to stay off her feet as much as possible."

"Why?" Tori leaned over her lounger.

"Because of my sausage toes." Geneva wiggled her feet.

"Those things look like they should be dipped in barbeque sauce and served on a cracker." Dana laughed.

The other girls joined in, but I didn't. Geneva had tried to play off the doctor's warning of her increased blood pressure, but I knew better. This could be a serious problem for her and the baby.

"I'm just kidding, Poseidon." Dana nudged my side with her elbow.

I stared down at her petite body. She didn't need to say the words, her blue eyes spoke for her. She was just as worried but didn't want to show it in front of Geneva and her friends.

"Berk." Someone tugged on my swim trunks.

I gazed down and saw Dana's son Levi staring up at me. "Hey, little man." I knelt down so we were eye level.

"Do you have your life savey thingy today?" He spread his arms wide as if I would understand what he was talking about.

I gazed over at Dana for help.

"He saw you in Hawaii, doing your lifeguard thing at the pool," she explained.

"That red thing you rescue people with," Levi said.

"Oh, my can," I answered, realizing he was talking about my floatation device.

"A can?" He wrinkled his eyes.

"Yeah, it's called a rescue can."

"Oh." He tilted his head and puckered his lips as if pondering the meaning of life.

I couldn't help but laugh. He was the most adorable kid I knew. Besides Alana.

"So, do you have it? Here with you?"

"Nope. Sorry, guy, it's back in Hawaii. Why?"

"Well." He kicked at the stone walkway. His eyes gazed over at the pool, staring at all the other kids and adults swimming around.

"You know, I only use the can if someone is drowning." *Drowning.* My stomach clenched. *Push it back, man.*

"I don't want to drown." His eyes went wide like I'd poked him with a hot coal.

Shit! I'd completely forgotten that Levi was terrified of the water.

"I would never let you drown, Levi," I said vehemently.

His eyes darted between mine, worry and fear pouring out from within him. I hated that any child would be this petrified of an activity that could bring so much joy.

"Why don't I teach you how to swim? I'm a certified lifeguard."

"Mommy! Mommy!" Levi bounced on the balls of his feet.

I turned toward Dana and saw her face washed ashen.

Geneva had shared with me some of Dana and Peter's story. Since Dana couldn't carry children because of cancer they'd adopted Levi, Lucas and Lilly, despite her special needs—or actually *because* of them.

"Can Berk show me how to swim?" Levi's excitement was contagious.

Dana's eyes went wide with fear.

"What's wrong?" I stood and moved next to her. "I mean, I don't want to—"

"He's never wanted to learn before. He's completely petrified of the water," she whispered under her breath. "How did you talk him into it?" Her blue eyes held mine captive, interrogating me.

"He asked me," I answered quietly.

Levi walked toward us. "Maybe Berk can show you, too, Mommy."

Dana swallowed hard, her eyes darting toward the pool.

"You don't know how to swim either?" I stared at her in shock.

She shook her head. "We tried to take lessons but Levi was petrified."

"Tell you what." My gaze fell from Dana down to Levi. "Why don't you and I start first, little man? Then together we can show your mom how to swim."

"Oh, Mommy, I can show you!" Levi shouted as he jumped up and down.

Dana's eyes brimmed with tears. I feared maybe I'd overstepped my bounds. She was the parent and knew what was best for her son. Perhaps she didn't want him near the water either.

"I promise not to let anything happen to him, Dana," I whispered, leaning in for only her to hear.

"It's not that." She peered up at me.

I tilted my head in confusion.

"He's been *petrified* of the water. I just don't understand what changed." She shook her head, truly baffled by her son's announcement that suddenly he wanted to learn to swim.

"I think you should just go with it," I whispered.

Her blue eyes cut up to mine. Slowly, she nodded her head. "Just please, be careful. If something—" Her eyes went wide, and I understood her abrupt halt. People did it all the time. No one wanted to remind me that my own daughter had drowned.

"It's all right, Dana. I promise I'll take good care of him."

Dana gazed down at her son as she ruffled his hair. "Well, okay. But you have to do *everything* Berk tells you, Levi. Do you understand?"

His face lit up like the sun overhead as he nodded his head, trying to contain his excitement.

"Let's go then." I held out my hand and he slid his tiny palm into mine. A pang of guilt hit my heart. I hadn't held a child's hand since Alana died, and I didn't realize how much I missed it.

I took a step into the pool and noticed that Levi stopped at the edge. Turning back, I saw that he was frozen, held captive by some invisible wall.

"You okay?" I asked.

He squeezed my hand. "It's deep," he whispered.

"We can take it step by step, okay?"

His eyes cut to the children on the other side, their squeals of delight muting my words.

"Levi," I said. I needed his undivided attention. Maybe today wasn't the best day to teach him, not at a pool party.

Slowly, his attention turned back to me.

"Just one step," I encouraged.

He held my hand tighter as he scooted to the edge, his foot hovering just over the water.

"I'm right here, Levi. I won't let anything happen to you. I can catch you."

The words sounded familiar, similar to what Geneva had said to me after we left Dr. Elsher's office the day she'd disclosed everything. We'd solidified our relationship, committing to be there for Peanut, for the long haul. We would take our own relationship one day at a time, one step at a time.

Levi's hand held tight around mine as he descended the first step into the pool. He stared at the water surrounding him.

"You did it, little man." A proud smile spread across my face, as if Levi had accomplished the greatest task known to man. For Levi and his family, he really had. From the corner of my eye, I noticed Dana walk toward us. I turned slightly and shook my head, glad to see she understood and retreated. She was afraid of the water, too, so I didn't need her subconsciously scaring Levi.

I backed down two steps but still held Levi's hand. He was holding it so tight, even the *real* Poseidon wouldn't have been able to pry it away.

"Why don't you sit down on the step first? That way you can have more of your body in the water without going deeper."

He nodded once, not even hesitating as he sunk his little body down into the water. His dark brown eyes went wide but I could see a spark of excitement within them.

"It's cold, right?" Even though it was late spring in Texas, the water still hadn't warmed.

"It's *very* cold." His teeth chattered as he continued to grip my hand. Maybe the temperature would be a distraction.

"Have you ever put your face in the water?" A lot of people who were frightened of the water actually were just afraid to get their face wet.

"No." His voice was barely above a whisper.

"Not even in the bath?"

He shook his head. "Mommy just gives me a cloth." His eyes were wide and his breathing grew shallow. This was not the way to start a lesson.

"It's all right, Levi," I assured him. "We won't do anything that you don't want to do today. Okay?"

He nodded once.

"Why don't we start with putting your face in the water?"

His head jerked up. His normally dark complexion went a shade lighter.

I ignored his fear, choosing not to play into it. "Like this." I put my head face down in the water and I stayed under for a few seconds. I stood straight up, wiping the water from my eyes. "Do you want to try?"

He squeezed my hand tighter, his eyes boring through me as if I'd asked him to eat a bug. Eating a bug probably would have been easier than what I was asking him to do.

Slowly he spread his legs and lowered his head until his face was almost touching the surface.

"It's okay." I squeezed his hand. "I'm right here, Levi."

His face sank below the water.

My breath caught. I understood how monumental this was for

him. My eyes cut to Dana and I saw her hand slap over her now gaping mouth. The sound of bubbles floating to the surface caught my attention. I looked down and saw that they were coming from Levi.

His head popped up, water dripping down his face as a smile spread wide.

"I did it!" he shouted. "I blew bubbles like Lucas does!"

"That's awesome, bud." Peter walked up next to the edge and squatted down, holding out the palm of his hand.

Levi released mine and slapped Peter's hand with a high-five.

I didn't want to lose momentum. "Want to move down another step?" I asked Levi.

He turned to face me and nodded his head, although a small amount of apprehension still lingered in his expression. He scooted to the edge of the first step and extended his leg until he felt the security of the step below. Then slowly, he slid off his perch and sat on the next step.

The enormity of his action was not wasted on me. He was taking the next step. In the big scheme of my own life, I needed to as well.

"Oh my God!" I heard someone shout.

Levi flew into my arms. With him safely tucked around me, I turned toward the commotion and noticed Hindley doubled over in her chair, clutching her abdomen. Oh, no. I bolted from the steps, still carrying Levi.

"What's wrong?" Rory shouted as he rushed to her side.

Hindley gazed up at her husband, pain littering every square inch of her face. "It's the baby," she pushed out through gritted teeth.

"Is she okay? Is Renee okay?" He was panicked as he frantically scanned her body from head to toe.

Hindley's body went lax as she fell back into the lounger, taking in a deep breath. "Oh my God, that hurt."

"What's going on, Hindley? You're scaring the shit out of me."

Rory's eyes darted up and down his wife, fear radiating from his body.

She reached out and stroked his face, the love in her eyes for her husband nearly choking me. "It's time." She smiled.

"Time?" Rory asked, his voice an octave higher. "As in now, she's coming now?"

Hindley nodded her head as a smile spread across her face.

Everyone in attendance suddenly swarmed her.

"Let me get up before the next contraction hits me," she said, pushing off the lounger.

Rory scooped her up.

Hindley yelped. "Rory, I can walk."

"The hell you can." His words were frantic and I completely understood his fear.

"Paul, grab the keys from inside and help me get Hindley into the car." Rory punched out the instruction.

"Rory, I'm all right." Before she could get the words out, her body doubled over in pain.

"Shit, Hindley, they're coming fast. Oh my God." Rory's eyes darted around the mass of people.

"Daddy say 'shit,'" Abbi said, pulling on Rory's shorts.

Rory completely ignored her, all his attention focused on his wife.

Hindley's mother scooped the little girl into her arms. "It's okay, Abbi." She pressed a kiss to the girl's temple. It was an act I'd done to Alana a million times. "Daddy is just worried."

"Is Momma tick?" Abbi asked, her blue eyes wide with concern.

"It's time to meet your sister." Caroline comforted her.

"Sissy, sissy." Abbi bounced in Caroline's arms as she clapped her hands.

Someone squeezed my arm. "Rory doesn't do well when Hindley's in pain," Geneva said. "We should probably go with them to the hospital." She stood, staring at me like I was an alien. "But you can stay, you don't have to go."

"I want to go with you." I smiled.

"What about you, squirt?" She poked Levi in the stomach. "You want to come see Aunt Hindley have her baby and meet your new cousin?"

I smiled at the familiarity with this group. Even though Hindley, Geneva and Dana weren't related by blood, they were family.

Levi wiggled from my arms and I released my hold. "Mommy, can we go see Auntie Hindley and the baby inside her?"

Dana held out her hand. "Why don't you stay here with Aunt Tori right now, and I'll come get you after Renee gets here. It could take a while. Okay?"

"Renee is my cousin," Levi announced proudly to no one in particular.

"We better go," Dana said, looking over at Geneva. "You know Rory is no good for her now." Dana turned to me. "He's worthless when Hindley's in pain."

I gazed over at Geneva, her face so beautiful in the afternoon sun. I completely understood Rory's plight. When a man loved a woman, her pain was his.

"You ready for this, Poseidon?" Dana laughed as her eyes lit up and she scanned the pool area.

People worked frantically, gathering up their belongings and making their way inside.

I almost asked 'Ready for what?' but I saw it in her expression. Her question was global. She was asking if I was ready to mix myself with the craziness of Geneva's life, her family and friends.

I wasn't sure if I was ready to commit to everything, but I knew I wanted to take the first step.

"Yeah." I smiled, taking Geneva's hand in mine as my eyes connected with hers. "I'm ready."

CHAPTER 32

BERK

I WATCHED ANXIOUSLY as Hindley's dad paced the waiting room like a nervous cat. We'd all been cramped in this tiny room for nearly three hours and it was grating on everyone.

I'd put Geneva in the corner with a chair in front of her to prop up her feet. Her head was tilted back and her eyes closed as she slept. Her hands rested on her stomach in a protective pose. She loved Peanut and would do anything for him, of that, I was sure.

"Is there a Mr. or Mrs. Barton here?" Someone called out from the doorway.

We all turned toward the voice. My eyes went wide at the familiar face. Dr. Rusk, Geneva's OB doctor, stood in the doorway.

"I'm Paul Barton. I'm Hindley's father." He flew toward the doctor.

"Well, I'm happy to announce that you are a proud grandpa." She smiled.

"Oh, God." Paul covered his mouth as tears welled in his eyes. "What about Hindley? Is she all right?" His voice was riddled with worry.

"She and the baby are both fine. The baby is a big one."

"How big?" Hindley's mother, Caroline, scooted in next to her husband.

Paul wrapped a possessive arm around her waist. "Yes, how big?"

"Eight pounds, eleven ounces," she said, "and almost twenty-two inches long."

"Damn!" Dana exclaimed. "I bet that felt like a frigging watermelon coming out her—"

Peter wrapped his hand over her mouth.

Her eyes rolled up to meet his as her hand pulled his away. "Sorry." She shrugged her shoulders as if to say "That's me."

"Geneva," Dr. Rusk called, casting her gaze over the crowd that now filled the waiting room.

"She's asleep," I answered.

"Oh, hello…" She fumbled with my name.

I could only imagine how many women she saw in a week. Keeping up with her patients was hard enough. Remembering their partner's name would have to be impossible.

"Berk," she said with surprise, as if my name had just popped into her mind.

I extended my hand and she took it in hers.

"How long has she been asleep?" Dr. Rusk's eyes narrowed as she stared at Geneva.

Her worried expression had the hair on my neck standing on end. "I don't know, maybe thirty minutes."

"Geneva," Dr. Rusk called to her as she tapped her hand.

Geneva's eyes fluttered open as she blinked in rapid succession. She gazed around the room, her face clouded with worry as she pushed herself up on her chair and lowered her legs to the floor.

"Dr. Rusk?" she said, focusing on the doctor as she stretched. "What are you doing here?"

"How long have your feet been this swollen?" she asked, completely ignoring Geneva's question.

Geneva's eyes cut to mine. Shit. Dr. Rusk was seriously worried.

My stomach knotted in fear.

"Um," she stuttered, "I don't know."

I looked down and saw Dr. Rusk pressing on Geneva's feet.

"What are you doing?" I asked.

Dr. Rusk completely ignored me. "I'd like to take you to a room and check your blood pressure."

Geneva's eyes went wide. "Why?"

Suddenly the entire room hovered around Geneva.

"What's wrong, Doctor?" Paul asked before I could.

"How do you know Geneva?" Dr. Rusk's tone was clipped.

"She's my daughter," Paul answered with vehemence.

"Wait, so both your daughters were pregnant at the same time?"

"Yes," Paul answered, his stern face never faltering.

"Dr. Rusk, what's wrong with Geneva?" I asked.

She turned her attention toward me. "Her legs are markedly more swollen, along with her fingers and face."

I gazed down at Geneva and noticed what Dr. Rusk was saying. I hadn't noticed until now, but I could see the puffy bags under Geneva's eyes and the way her face had filled out, seemingly overnight. The spot on her foot where Dr. Rusk had pressed still showed a little of the indention of her finger.

"I want to check her blood pressure."

"Why?" Caroline asked, butting up next to me.

"She's my mom," Geneva answered with a smile. "It's okay."

"Well, Geneva has been suffering from some preeclampsia symptoms. I've been monitoring her blood pressure with each visit and have asked her to take it easy."

All eyes swooped down to Geneva, each one with an accusatory glare. She hadn't shared any of this with them and now they weren't happy.

"Why didn't you tell us this?" Paul asked.

"She didn't want to worry you," I answered for Geneva, knowing it was best not to get her upset. Inwardly I was shaking, fearing for not only Geneva, but for the baby, too. "Come on." I reached down for her hand.

"If you try to carry me, Berk Rigby, so help me—"

I scooped her up in my arms, not surprised when she yelped. "Where to, Doc?"

"Berk!" she shrieked, hitting my chest.

"Calm down, Geneva," I whispered in her ear, "or I'll tell your father about your special drawer."

She went stiff in my arms, her eyes wide.

Perhaps that hadn't been the best approach. "I'm kidding." I smiled down at her.

"Let's get her inside room four fifty." Dr. Rusk pointed down the hallway. "I'll be there in just a moment."

"Is she going to be all right?" I heard Paul's voice waver behind me.

"She's fine," Dr. Rusk said. "I just need to hook her up to a fetal monitor and check her blood pressure. Trust me," she said, her gaze traveling over everyone standing in front of her, "this is the best place for Geneva to be right now."

"Wait!" Geneva shouted, her movements nearly causing me to drop her. "What about Hindley? What about Renee?"

"They're both doing fine," I comforted her. "We'll get you checked out and then you can go see her, okay?"

Geneva's eyes traveled to Dr. Rusk.

"Yes." She nodded once. "Let's just check you out while you're here, and then you can go see your niece."

"I have another niece." Geneva smiled up at me, her blue eyes dancing with delight.

My breath caught. She was beautiful. I tried to calm my racing heart, assuring myself that this was just precautionary.

"I'm fine, Berk." She lifted her hand to my cheek. "But you need to get me to the room before you have a hernia. I'm like a bazillion pounds." She laughed.

I tried to smile, but it was useless. I was scared shitless. If anything happened to her or to Peanut—

Geneva jerked my head so that I had no choice but to stare directly into her eyes. "Don't go there, Berk."

I nodded once, knowing I needed to keep my shit together. For Geneva.

"Right in there." A nurse pointed to a room.

I turned sideways so Geneva and I could fit through the doorway.

"Just place her on the bed."

"What are you going to do?" Geneva asked.

"We're going to put an external monitor on your belly so we can listen to your baby's heart rate and check your blood pressure."

I laid Geneva on the bed.

"Why? What's going on with Peanut?" Geneva's eyes darted between us.

"It's okay, babe." I stroked her arm, trying to reassure her. "They just want to make sure everything is okay with you and the baby."

The nurse gave a small smile that did nothing to reassure either of us.

"But first, why don't you change into a gown." She turned and reached into a cabinet. "While you're changing, just try to give us a urine sample as well."

"Why?" Geneva's face went ashen.

"We need to check your protein levels."

"Why?" Geneva was starting to sound like a broken record.

"It will help us determine if you truly have preeclampsia."

"And what if I do?"

"The doctor will talk to you more about it when she comes in."

The way she said it left no doubt in my mind. This was serious, and she didn't want to divulge any more information.

My heart raced, nearly beating out of my chest. I drew in deep breaths, trying to calm myself.

"Berk," Geneva pleaded, looking up at me with doe eyes, "will you help me change?"

"Of course." I forced a smile, knowing I needed to keep her calm.

"It will be all right," the nurse said. "The most you'll have to do is be confined to bed for the remainder of your pregnancy." She skimmed over Geneva's body. "How far along are you?"

"Just over thirty-two weeks."

"You'll be fine, sweetie." She patted Geneva's leg and gave her a wink that seemed to pacify her. The nurse held up a cotton gown covered in cartoon animals. "Just change into this attractive gown," she laughed, "opening to the back. But be sure to pee in this delightful cup first." She shook a plastic jar in the air as if it held magical powers.

I looked down at Geneva, relieved to see her face relax a bit.

"I'll be back in just a sec, hon," the nurse said, leaving us alone.

I supported Geneva's arm as we walked into the bathroom.

"No." She pushed me away.

"What?"

"You're *not* helping me pee in this friggin' cup. I'll change and do it myself."

"I'm going to help you," I stormed.

She pressed her palm against my chest. "No. You're not," she corrected me. Her face was furrowed and her lips pressed into a thin line.

I didn't want to cause her any more stress or anxiety, so I backed up and watched helplessly as she closed the door.

I searched around the room. It was larger, larger than the one

Jaime had been in when Alana was born. I pushed down the thoughts of their deaths, trying to block out the images that floated around in my head thanks to years of tortured nightmares.

Sitting down on the bed I drew in a deep sigh. *Don't go there.* Geneva had told me. I tried to repeat the mantra.

"Is she in the bathroom?" the nurse asked as she wheeled in a cart with a machine on top.

"Yes."

"She'll be fine, sweetie, don't worry."

Her southern accent comforted me.

"Have you seen this before? Preeclampsia, I mean?"

"Oh, yeah, it's nothing new. We'll check the baby's heart rate and Geneva's blood pressure."

"What if it's too high?"

"Then she'll have to be put on bed rest." Dr. Rusk's voice boomed from behind me.

"What!" Geneva shrieked as the bathroom door swung open with a bang. "But I still have six weeks until the school year is over. And I haven't even seen my niece yet. And…" Tears pooled in her eyes.

"It's all right, baby." I rushed to her side and led her over to the bed. "I'll be here to take care of you. It's for Peanut, okay?"

Her eyes were frantic, but with the mention of our son, she visibly relaxed.

As soon as Geneva was settled into the bed, the nurse started moving quickly, placing things on Geneva.

"What are you doing?" Geneva asked.

"I'm placing this monitor on your belly so we can check your baby's heart rate." She strapped a plastic circle on Geneva's stomach. "And this will monitor your blood pressure." The nurse wrapped a blood pressure cuff on Geneva's arm.

"Let's get this monitor turned on." Dr. Rusk returned, moving around the bed to flip on a switch. "We'll be able to see the baby's heart rate and your blood pressure."

"Okay." Geneva's voice wavered.

I was thankful for the diversion, but scared shitless at what the readings would show. There was a whooshing noise followed by what sounded like galloping horses.

"It's checking her blood pressure," the nurse answered my silent question.

"And that's the baby's heart beat," the doctor added.

"You'll be fine." I smiled down at her, not sure if my words were meant to reassure her or me.

Geneva held out her hand and I took it in mine.

"Mary, why don't you start an IV and draw some blood," Dr. Rusk instructed the nurse.

"Why?" Geneva and I asked in unison.

Geneva squeezed my hand.

"We need to check your blood to see how bad the preeclampsia is," the nurse answered.

My gaze fell to hers and she gave me a weak smile before turning to look at the monitor. Every sensory organ was on high alert for me.

"What does this mean, Doctor?" Geneva's words broke my heart. She was so worried, and I hated that I couldn't take that away from her.

"It means that for now, you'll need to be on bed rest."

Geneva winced as the nurse stuck a needle into her arm and pulled back two tubes of dark blood. She hooked up an IV bag filled with clear fluid and set it to a slow drip.

"For how long?" I asked.

"Indefinitely," Dr. Rusk answered, giving the nurse a knowing glance.

Geneva's head dropped to her chest in disappointment.

"What can we do?" I asked.

"Rest, try to take it easy, and avoid any stressors."

I nodded my head. Geneva's comfort would now be my utmost concern. I turned to look at her. Her face was so swollen it broke my heart. "It's only a few weeks, babe." I tried to console her.

"It's eight weeks, Berk. Two months, in bed."

"Bed could be fun." I wiggled my brows, hoping to lighten her mood.

"Um, no sex," Dr. Rusk said, adjusting the monitor.

Well, shit.

"There's always your drawer." I laughed.

"Berk!" Geneva's face went red as she swatted at my arm.

Suddenly the monitor blared with a hideous sound, like that of an alarm clock, its noise echoing throughout the room. The numbers flashed in quick succession on the display.

"Owe!" Geneva yelled, clutching her stomach.

"What is it?" I shouted.

"Geneva, are you all right?" Dr. Rusk looked over her shoulder, her brows knitted together. The worried tone in her voice did nothing to settle my already queasy stomach.

Geneva's face was nearly white and her jaw clenched as her hands fisted her gown.

"Geneva, what's wrong?" I asked.

"Ahh," Geneva moaned louder. "Oh, God, it hurts."

I watched helplessly as she bent over in pain.

"Geneva?" Dr. Rusk asked again.

A scream like I'd never heard burst my ear drums. It sounded like an animal being gutted alive. My body burned as if a thousand needles were stabbing my skin. The sound coming from Geneva.

"Geneva!" I shouted, grabbing her shoulders.

Her body went rigid under my hands as she fell back onto the bed, her eyes rolling back.

"Oh my God!" I yelled, shaking her shoulders.

"Mary!" Dr. Rusk shouted at the nurse. "Call the OR, tell them to clear a room. She's having a seizure."

Seizure?

Mary stood in stunned silence.

"Now!" Dr. Rusk yelled.

Geneva's body began to shake uncontrollably.

My periphery vision faded as my legs wobbled.

More nurses piled into the room, surrounding Geneva's bed. One injected a clear liquid through a syringe into her IV and fiddled with the bag, making the drips go so fast it was almost a steady stream of fluid into her body.

"What's wrong?" I shouted. "Dr. Rusk!" I clutched at her coat but she ignored me.

She grabbed the wall phone and banged at the numbers. "She's seizing. We're on our way." There was a pause. "I don't give a shit, clear it now!" She slammed down the phone.

I watched in stunned silence as the nurses kicked at the wheels on the bed. They yanked the wires from the monitor and began to wheel the entire bed toward the door.

That was when I saw it. On the sheets. A pool of blood so large and so dark I thought I would vomit.

"Dr. Rusk." I grasped her arm as she rushed to the door.

"Go to the waiting room, Berk. I'll come find you when we're done."

"What is it? What happened?"

"I won't know for sure. Right now, we need to get your son out of Geneva as quickly as possible so we can work on her."

"But you know something."

She tugged out of my hold.

"Is she going to die?"

Her eyes cut to mine, the look in them similar to the ones I'd seen on two occasions in my life. Both preceded words of death. First my daughter. Then my wife.

"We'll do everything we can, Berk."

I almost didn't hear Dr. Rusk's last words as she ran down the hallway after Geneva's bed. They were surrounded by a swarm of hospital personnel.

What if they can't do enough?

Geneva was wheeled around the corner and I lost sight of her as I sunk to my knees. What if they can't do enough?

CHAPTER 33

BERK

My head rested on the cold porcelain of the toilet as my body slumped on the floor. I'd expelled all the contents of my stomach twice already but still felt the rumbling deep in my bowels.

Death.

It was a ghost that haunted me.

"Berk!" Someone pounded on the door.

My head stayed glued to the toilet, the cold press of its rim taming the maddening heat of my rage.

"Berk!" the familiar voice called again.

It was Rhen. What the hell was he doing at the hospital? And why was he in Geneva's room?

"Open the door, man. The doctor is here and she wants to talk to you."

I leapt to my feet and yanked open the door.

Everyone sat around the large room, their eyes bloodshot and cheeks stained with tears, like mine. I had no idea how long I'd been in the bathroom. I didn't even remember collapsing when they wheeled Geneva down the hall, her body flip-flopping on the bed like a fish out of water. I shook my head to clear the image.

"Berk." Dr. Rusk moved toward me.

Paul butted up next to me.

"Is she all right?" he asked before I could.

"I'm here to talk about the baby," she said quietly. "The surgeon will be in shortly to talk to you about Geneva."

"Is she alive?" My throat constricted, my voice sounding gravelly and desperate, reminiscent of the words I'd asked of Jackie several years before. I couldn't believe I was in the same spot again, fearing for the life of the woman who bore my child.

"She's alive." Dr. Rusk's words were monotone and I knew we'd get no more information.

At least she was alive. It was something to hold on to.

"What about the baby?" I asked.

"He's doing well." She smiled, finally showing *some* emotion. "He's small, just under four pounds. But he's a fighter."

You could hear the audible sigh of everyone in the room. Everyone but me. I still held my breath. I wouldn't be able to exhale again until I saw Geneva *and* our son, alive and well.

"Can we see him?" Paul asked.

"Not quite yet. He's in the neonatal intensive care unit undergoing evaluations. You'll need this to see him." She held out a white band. "Let me put this on your wrist, Berk. It will allow you access to see your son."

I stood still, holding out my arm with a blank stare as she secured the band around my wrist. *My son.*

"But he's going to make it?" Caroline asked, her own words as desperate as mine.

"His prognosis is good. They have an amazing NICU at this hospital," Dr. Rusk said.

Prognosis is good. Prognosis is good.

I repeated the words over and over in my head, trying to rid myself of the torrid images burning through my mind. Geneva and Peanut in a casket, being lowered into the ground, dirt covering their—

"Stop." Rhen slid in beside me. "It's not the same, bro. They're both alive."

I turned to face him. "For now," I whispered.

"When can we see Geneva?" Paul's voice broke my heart. I knew what it was like to lose a daughter. No matter her age.

"Like I said, the doctor will be in shortly."

"Just fucking tell us!" I shouted.

Dr. Rusk winced.

I glared at her.

"Geneva had what we call placental abruption. Her placenta broke away from the wall of the uterus due to her seizure. This can cause a lot of blood loss."

I gasped, along with everyone else in the room.

"How much blood did she lose?" Paul asked.

Her eyes darted between me and Paul, trying to keep her expression calm. "She lost a lot." She punched out the words as if they pained her. "Her type of abruption is the most severe."

"What the hell does that mean?" My face wrinkled in confusion. "Is she going to be okay or not?"

"We were able to stop the bleeding, but not before Geneva went into shock."

"Oh my God," Caroline whispered.

My head darted from hers to the doctor. "So, what does that mean?"

"The surgeon will be in—"

"I don't give a fuck about the surgeon!" I shouted.

Large hands wrapped around my arms pulling me back. "Calm down, man." Rhen spoke in my ear.

"Berk," Paul called to me.

I glared at Dr. Rusk, piercing her with my eyes. "Please," I whispered.

"It could mean many things for her. We have her in ICU right now. We'll be monitoring her very closely."

"For what?" My stomach lurched.

"For heart or kidney damage. She's also at high risk for cardiac arrest."

Caroline broke down into hysterics and the room erupted into sobs.

"Could she die?" Paul's voice was broken, just like my heart.

My body slumped as I awaited Dr. Rusk's answer.

She paused, drawing in a deep breath. No answer was needed.

My body burned like it was on fire, my gut twisted in knots by Dr. Rusk's silence.

"I gotta get the fuck out of here." I frantically scanned the room, looking for the exit. Pushing past Paul and the doctor, I all but ran to the door.

"Berk!" Paul called after me.

I ignored him.

"Come on," Rhen said beside me, his arm wrapped around my shoulders.

We remained silent as he led me to the elevators.

"Do you want to see him?"

"Who?"

"John Paul," he said as we waited by the bank of elevators. "Your son."

The elevator dinged, announcing its arrival. My feet felt like lead bricks as I dragged them over the threshold of the elevator. "No," I said quietly.

"Berk," Rhen scolded.

"Just get me to your car."

"Why?"

"Just fucking do it, Rhen."

I stood in the elevator, my mind racing with dark images. I could see Jaime's face just below the ice, her hands clawing at the frozen barrier that kept her below the water's surface. Her muffled screams pierced my ears.

"Come on." Rhen tugged on my arm as he rushed me through the lobby.

I walked blindly toward the parking lot, thankful that my brother could lead me. I had no sense of time or direction. I was lost in a bubble of uncertainty. But one thing was clear.

"Here," he said, opening the car door and all but pushing me inside.

I reached for the glove box as he slid into the driver's side seat.

"It's probably good for you to get some fresh air," he said. "We can sit out here while you catch your breath."

I dug through the paperwork until I found the familiar envelope. My hand tugged on the papers inside, unfolding them as tears rolled down my face.

"What are you doing?" Rhen asked.

"Do you have a pen?"

"Why?"

I stared at the papers. The title glaring back at me was my only way out. "Petition for Termination of Parental Rights."

"It's all my fault. Death follows me everywhere," I said to no one in particular.

"What the fuck are you talking about?" Rhen gazed over my lap at the papers.

I dug through the glove box again until I secured a pen. With a shaking hand, I flipped through the pages until I found the sticker marked "Sign here." I gripped the pen as hard as I could, trying not to drop it as I scribbled my name across the line.

I couldn't save Jaime and Alana, but I would save Geneva and my son. I knew Geneva would never give up on us. She'd said as much in our counseling session. So, I would. Even if it broke my heart into a million pieces to walk away, I would. I had to. To save them from myself.

Where there is love there is life.
- Mahatma Gandhi

CHAPTER 34

GENEVA

I LICKED AT MY LIPS. Well, I tried, but my tongue was stuck to the roof of my mouth. My eyes felt like they were sealed shut with Super Glue, but I pried them open anyway.

The room was quiet and dark, very cozy. The smells around me were distinct, but I couldn't place them in my befuddled mind.

Where the hell am I?

The incessant beeping around me made my already throbbing head hurt even worse. I raised my hand to rub on my head. Maybe I hit it and blacked out. I reached for my head but pain shot through my inner elbow. I peered down, my eyes adjusting to the light just beyond the glass door in front of me.

I drew in a deep breath—tubes, IVs, wires. They seemed to be everywhere. I turned to look at my other arm and found a white cuff wrapped around the upper portion, with more tubing. I moved my hands but they were trapped, more IVs attached there. And my pointer finger had something clamped to it like a white clothes pin, only this one glowed.

My gaze fell to a form in the corner, its body curled up on a chair.

"Berk," I whispered, my throat burning like it was on fire.

The body stirred.

"Geneva?" The person jumped from the chair.

"Daddy?"

"Oh, God, baby." He rushed to my side, taking my hand in his as he brought it to his mouth, smattering it with kisses.

I winced at the pain in the crook of my elbow.

"What's wrong? Where does it hurt?"

I nodded to my arm since my voice seemed to have disappeared.

"Oh, I'm sorry, sweetheart." He gently placed my arm next to me on the bed.

"Let me go get the nurse."

Nurse?

Shit, I was in a hospital. But why? I watched as my father slid open the glass door and stepped out to the counter in front of my room. The entire setup seemed odd.

I noticed a pink cup sitting on a tray next to my bed. Reaching over my body, I struggled to pick it up. That was when I realized there was no stomach for me to rest my arm.

My hand slid down my abdomen. There was no gentle swell any more, and no life kicked within me.

"Peanut!" I screamed, scooting up in the bed. "Peanut!" Searing pain shot through my abdomen.

Several people rushed in my room, lights flickered on and blinded me.

"Where's my baby?" I screamed through my tears. "Oh, God, someone—"

"He's fine, Geneva. Please calm down." My father butted up to my side.

"Is he…"

"He was born two days ago."

"Two days?" I shook my head. "Daddy, what happened?"

My father looked cautiously at the nurse.

She shrugged her shoulders but continued checking all the

equipment I was attached to. "Vitals still look good," she said to no one in particular.

"Daddy," I pleaded, reaching out for his hand.

"They had to perform an emergency C-section to deliver him."

"Why?"

Again, my father and the nurse shared a glance.

"Is my baby all right?"

"He's small," my dad smiled, "but he's really strong. A good grip."

"That's a good thing, right?"

"That's a great thing, Geneva," the nurse said, patting my leg.

"When can I see him?" I sat up in the bed but grabbed my stomach with the pain. My head started to spin and I flopped back down.

"Easy, baby girl." My father rubbed my shoulder.

"What's wrong with me?"

"You lost a lot of blood, Geneva." The nurse's words were matter of fact. In her profession she probably couldn't afford to show much emotion.

"How much?"

My father hesitated as he rubbed the edge of my bed's blanket.

"Daddy?" I whispered.

"It was a lot, baby girl."

Something in his tone warned me not to ask more. "You said Peanut was born two days ago. Have I been out that long?"

My father nodded his head.

"When can I see him?"

"Let me get the doctor," the nurse said. "As soon as he gives you the go ahead, I'm sure we can put you in a wheelchair and take you down to the NICU."

NICU. I knew the abbreviation. *Neonatal Intensive Care Unit.* My Peanut was in trouble.

"How long will that take?" I asked the nurse.

"He should be here any minute. I paged him as soon as your father told me you woke up."

I gazed up at my father. Stubble littered his face and his eyes were rimmed with red edges. Bags hung low underneath. I hadn't seen him look this lost since my mother died.

"I'm okay, Daddy." I smiled up at him.

One lone tear rolled down his cheek, and I knew in that moment, whatever had happened to me, my own life had been in danger.

I reached up and wiped away his tear, forgetting about the pain in my arm.

Before I could pull away, he took my hand in his, bringing it to his lips and gently kissing my palm before placing it on his heart. His chin quivered and I feared he might completely break down.

"Have you seen him yet?" I asked, deciding a diversion was the best tactic.

His brow furrowed.

"Peanut, your grandson?" I laughed.

Immediately his expression changed, his eyes lit up and his mouth morphed into a smile only a grandfather could express. "Oh, Geneva," he sighed. "He's amazing. He has your long legs, and your tenacity for life."

I smiled, thinking about my son. *Son.*

Images of our visit to the hospital days before resurfaced. We'd been here to see Hindley and the baby.

"How are Hindley and the baby?"

My father smiled, his face beaming with pride. "She and Renee are doing well. They were released this morning."

I sunk back in my bed with a sigh of relief. "That's wonderful." I was so grateful for the news of my sister's well-being, but still feared for my son's.

"Wait!" I frantically scanned the room. "Where's Berk?"

My father stood still, his silence saying it all.

"Did he think I was going to die? That the baby and I were going to die?"

My father scooted closer, his breathing coming in short spurts. "We all did, sweetheart."

"Oh, no." My hand covered my now gaping mouth. "He thinks he hurt us. Or that he's going to hurt us. Where did he go? Have you seen him?"

My father shook his head. "He left this, though." He walked to the drawer by my bed and pulled out an envelope that I recognized.

"No!" I held my hand up and pushed my father away. "He's not running away."

"What's in here, Geneva?"

"Worthless papers," I hissed. "Papers I never should have drafted."

"Well, hello, Geneva." A tall, thin man wearing a white coat and carrying a chart walked through the sliding glass door. "I hear you finally woke up and joined the land of the living." He chuckled.

Land of the living. Yes, that was where I was now. And I would bring Berk back with me, kicking and screaming if I had to. I would drag him out of the valley of death if it were the last thing on earth I did.

"You ready to go see your baby boy?"

I had a son. We had a son.

I knew without a doubt that Berk had left us, thinking he would save us. It was up to me and Peanut to prove him wrong. We were *all* in the land of the living now, even Berk. Especially Berk.

"I'm ready." I smiled, knowing truer words had never been spoken.

CHAPTER 35

GENEVA

My heart beat out of my chest as my father wheeled me down the long corridor. We slipped through the double doors marked maternity.

"I wasn't in the maternity ward?" I asked, looking up at my father.

He shook his head.

"Where was I?"

"ICU."

And that was it. My father was not going to talk about what had happened to me. If I ever wanted to find out the details, it would have to come from someone else.

I saw a placard hanging from the ceiling that read 'NICU' with the words "Neonatal Intensive Care Unit" written in smaller letters underneath.

My father stopped the chair just before he reached the door. He walked around my chair, squatting down in front of me. "He's small, Gen. Really small. I just want to tell you."

"How small?" Suddenly my heart was in my throat as I squeaked out the words.

"He weighed three pounds thirteen ounces when he was born."

I gasped as my hand covered my mouth. Doing the math, I quickly realized that Peanut was eight weeks premature. What did that mean for his future?

"Is he okay, Daddy?" Tears burned my eyes.

"He's doing really well, baby girl. He's a fighter. Like his mother." My father's deep laugh brought a respite of relief.

"I'm a mother," I whispered.

"Yep, you are." He stood and walked behind my wheelchair. "Now let's go meet your son, little momma." He pushed through the doors and I held my breath.

The large room was packed with machines tucked away in varying nooks. No one even looked up as we made our way inside.

"He's in room 3. But we need to wash our hands first."

He wheeled me to a large sink and helped me lean over, then lathered my hands and dried them.

"You've been here before?" I asked.

"Everyday. As much as they'll let me. They're probably tired of seeing me." He smiled proudly.

I looked at my father. He was tired, rumpled and weathered. It occurred to me that he'd probably split his time between being with me and being with his grandson.

"He's just down here." My dad nodded down a small walkway.

I looked high above my head and found the same signs from outside marking each little cubby. As we passed nooks one and two, my hands tightened around the handles of my wheelchair. The air in the room became thick. It was difficult for me to breathe as I anticipated seeing my son for the first time.

"Here he is," my father announced proudly as he pushed my wheelchair in between tons of equipment.

I feared I might actually roll over something and jeopardize Peanut's well-being.

My father made his way to the front of my chair, locking my

brakes as if hearing my silent concerns. He kissed my head before stepping back.

Lying before me was a clear, plastic container with tubing jutting out from the top. A soft cushion covered in cartoon animals lined the bed.

"It's an incubator, to keep him warm," someone spoke behind me. "Here, let me open it." The woman walked to the other side of the container and swung the lid open.

From my vantage point in the wheelchair, I still couldn't see him so I pushed up on the arms and stood, despite the discomfort in my abdomen.

"Be careful," my father warned as he came up next to me and secured his arm around my waist.

All throughout my pregnancy I'd wondered what it would be like to see my baby for the first time, but nothing could have prepared me for what I saw.

He was so tiny, lying on his back, his legs spread wide like a frog. They were thin and translucent, his veins prominent. Wires jutted out from nearly every inch of his body. What looked like an IV was wrapped around his arm and several electrodes were stuck to his chest and abdomen.

He was small.

He was weak.

And he was perfect.

"What are those?" I pointed to the tubes protruding out of his nose.

"One is called a CPAP."

I furrowed my brow.

She smiled at my confusion. "It stands for continuous positive airway pressure."

"It's oxygen?"

"No, it's a pump that gives him tiny puffs of air to help him breathe on his own."

"What's the other?" I asked, rubbing my hand along the tubing.

"That one is a feeding tube."

"He can't eat?" I glanced up at the nurse and noted her badge said her name was "Danielle."

"Not yet. Sucking wears out preemies. We'll have you start pumping breast milk soon though and feed it through his tube."

"May I touch him?"

"Oh, of course. Have you washed your hands?"

"Yes, I did when we came in."

"He'll love to hear from his mommy." She leaned closer to his bed. "Won't you, Peanut."

"How do you know his name?"

Her eyes cut to mine, her face dropping as if she'd offended me.

"Oh, I'm sorry. The name placard hasn't been filled in yet." She looked up at a light blue card attached to what looked like a heating lamp. "But that's what his father calls him."

"Father?" I drew back from the incubator.

Her eyes darted between me and my dad, fear etched across her face. "I'm sorry, I just assumed that Berk was the baby's father. He has the band on his wrist allowing him access."

I turned to look at my father. "Has Berk been here?"

My dad shrugged his shoulders. "I haven't seen him, sweetie."

A small smile tugged on my lips. Maybe bringing Berk back to life wouldn't be so hard after all.

I slipped my hand down toward Peanut, his own so small. Rubbing lightly on his fingers I pulled back when he twitched.

"It's all right, you won't hurt him," Danielle reassured me. "He's just super sensitive right now. But they love touch, babies thrive on it actually."

I rubbed Peanut's palm with my finger, marveling at how tiny he was. His fingers suddenly wrapped around mine. "Oh my God, look, Daddy."

"He knows his momma," my father said, saddling up next to me.

"He's beautiful," I whispered.

"Beyond beautiful. Like his mother." My father kissed my temple.

I brought my other hand over the railing of the incubator and lightly rubbed his stomach around the tubes and wiring surrounding him.

"He's already gained half an ounce in only two days," Danielle boasted.

"That's good, right?" I asked.

"That's amazing. I think he's going to be a brute like his—"

I gazed up at Danielle and her eyes were wide. "How often has he been here?" I asked.

She stared at me unable, or unwilling, to speak.

"It's okay." I smiled. "Berk and I are somewhat estranged. But not for long."

Her brow furrowed.

My dad squeezed me tight.

"He comes every day, stays around the clock," Danielle said.

"And you've never seen him here?" I asked my father.

"When I tell Berk that the baby's grandfather is here, he always leaves," Danielle said. Her eyes darted between me and my dad. "I'm so sorry, I just thought…"

"No, it's fine. I'm glad he's here for the baby." I smiled, trying to reassure her that everything was all right, that I wasn't upset.

My gaze fell back on my son. *Son.* I couldn't believe I was a mother. My heart fell instantly in love with this tiny creature lying before me. I leaned down close to his body. "Momma loves you, John Paul."

"Is that his name?" Danielle asked.

"We haven't decided for sure," I answered.

"My vote was for Paul Barton, Jr." My dad laughed.

Danielle smiled, her emerald green eyes warm and inviting. You had to have a special soul to work with preemies.

My finger traced over Peanut's body, marveling at how something so small could capture my heart in the blink of an eye. I brushed through his dark hair that looked so much like his father's.

The baby startled but soon nestled into a new position, squeezing my other finger.

I began to hum.

"Your mom used to sing that to you when you were a little girl."

"What?" I looked over my shoulder at my father.

"'You Are My Sunshine.'"

"Is that what I was humming?"

He nodded.

"It's really weird," Danielle spoke.

"What?" I asked, turning my attention back to my son.

"His uncle sings that same song to him," she said.

My hand stopped mid-motion. "Rhen's been here, too?" I looked up at the nurse.

"Who's Rhen?" my father asked.

"Berk's brother," I answered. "So Rhen has seen the baby, too?" I asked Danielle again.

"Oh, yes," she swooned. "He has an amazing voice."

I sat silently, trying to sort out this new detail. Rhen had been here as well. Berk was planting roots.

"Well," Danielle cleared her throat, obviously thinking she'd said too much, "I'll just leave you all alone with—"

"John Paul," I answered. I glanced over my shoulder and stared at my father.

"John Paul." He nodded his head in approval.

"Oh, um, I'm sorry to disturb you." Another nurse stood at the entrance to our tiny cubby. "The baby's father is here to see him. I'm afraid there can only be two people here at a time." Her eyes darted between me and my father.

"It's all right," I said. "I'm feeling kind of tired right now anyway." I stared down at JP, blissfully unaware of the turbulent storm surrounding him. "May I kiss him?"

"It's probably best that you not," Danielle said.

I gazed up at her face. She had nothing but remorse and compassion.

"I'm sorry," she said. "I know how hard it must be. But it's what's best for John Paul. Right now, anyway."

I nodded once, pushing back the tears that threatened to fall from my eyes.

"As soon as he's stabilized, you should be able to hold him," Danielle offered in concession.

A smile split my face in two at the thought of holding my son.

"Come on, sweetie," my dad said. "You're probably worn out. You need your rest, too."

I reached over the plastic encasement. "I love you, JP. More than you know," I whispered against his ear. "And your daddy loves you, too. I'm going to go now, so he can see you. But I'll be back later, I promise."

I scooted away, biting my cheek to keep from sobbing. Leaving my son felt like someone was ripping my insides out. But I knew I needed to stay strong, for him. I could feel myself fading and that wasn't good for JP

"Will you do me a favor?" I asked both nurses as my dad turned me toward the exit.

"Anything," Danielle said. Her copper-colored ponytail swung in her face as her bright green eyes stared at me with apprehension.

"Please don't tell Berk, JP's father," I nodded toward the cubby, "that I know he's been coming. He wouldn't want that."

The two nurses exchanged a glance, contemplating my words.

"Um, okay, I guess," the other said.

"Thank you." I gave a smile, hoping to show my gratitude. "Daddy, don't let him see me when we leave."

"Why, Geneva?"

"It's a long story, but I have a plan."

"You can go through the nurses' exit if that helps," Danielle said.

"Thank you." I reached out and squeezed her hand.

"And don't worry about John Paul." She smiled down at me. "We'll take really good care of him."

Tears welled in my eyes as I took one last look at the bassinet that held my JP. "Bye, baby. I'll be back soon," I called softly.

Berk may think he would destroy John Paul and me if he stayed, but his actions proved he felt differently. He wanted to be a part of his son's life. Whether he wanted to be part of mine or not was still a mystery. But I was patient. For once in my life, I could wait.

I gazed down at my baby, resting peacefully in my arms. JP was off the feeding tube and I'd been breastfeeding him for almost a week.

His face was fuller now, his skin not as red and transparent. He looked so much like Berk it hurt my heart.

"Wow, look how big he's getting," Danielle said as she walked into our NICU room. "He's going to be ready for our step-down unit soon."

I gazed up at Danielle with a questioning gaze.

"The doctor hasn't talked to you about it?"

I shook my head.

"Don't be worried, Geneva. It's a good thing. It means that JP is doing better and doesn't need as much care. And it will give you more time to spend with him, one-on-one."

"But you'll still watch him?"

"Well, I won't directly, but Elizabeth, our head of NICU nursing, oversees the staff there. You'll get the same specialized treatment as well."

I smiled thinking of JP getting stronger and maybe one day soon coming home with me.

"Has Berk been here today?" Berk and I were still in the ritual of seeing JP on opposite schedules. To my knowledge he still had no idea that I knew he was seeing his son. That fit perfectly into my plan.

"No, not yet. It's unusual. Most days he's here before the morning staff changes." She shrugged her shoulders.

I held JP closer to my chest. This wasn't a good sign. What if Berk had finally given up, had enough with this and really decided to absolve himself of his parental duties?

JP let out a small whimper as he readjusted in my arms. I combed my fingers through his head full of hair. Thick and black, just like his father's. "You're right, Peanut. He would never give up on you, no matter what."

"Did you say something?" Danielle turned to look at me.

"No." I laughed. "Just talking to JP."

"Geneva," someone called my name.

I gazed up and saw Elizabeth, the head nurse. "What's wrong?" My stomach twisted in knots, fearing one of JP's daily tests had come back with horrible results.

"He's fine." She smiled, rubbing my shoulder. "You have a visitor."

"Berk?"

She shook her head. "Not Berk, but someone who looks a lot like him."

"It's probably his brother Rhen. He's staying in town now to work on his music with his bandmates."

"This is a female," Elizabeth said.

"Female?" Then I remembered Berk's sister Palla.

"She says she's JP's grandmother."

Holy shit! Berk's mother. Oh my God.

"I'm judging by the look on your face that maybe the NICU

isn't the best place for your meeting." Elizabeth's words were so true. But I wanted Berk's mom to see JP, maybe even hold him.

"After I talk to her, can I bring her back to see JP?"

"Of course, dear," Elizabeth said. "He's getting so strong." Elizabeth reached over my shoulder and rubbed the back of JP's hand.

He grabbed her finger and squeezed so tight, his small knuckles turned white.

"Look at that, a regular power house." Elizabeth laughed, and Danielle and I joined in.

"Let me put him down and then, if all goes well, I'll bring her back," I said.

Elizabeth gave me a wink and a nod. Every person in the NICU had been so gracious and understanding of the unique relationship Berk and I had, or actually *didn't* have. And their care of my son had been amazing. Mere words would never be able to express my gratitude for each of them.

I stood and lowered JP into the isolet, covering his legs with the blanket Caroline made him. "I'll be back, Peanut," I whispered as I gently kissed his head.

"Wish me luck." I waggled my brows at Danielle.

"No luck needed, Geneva. JP's amazing, you and Berk are amazing. I'm sure his mother will be amazing, too."

"God, I hope you're right."

"She's in the day lounge down the hall," Elizabeth said. "I put a sign up so no one else will enter. It should give you some privacy for a bit."

"Thank you." I reached out and squeezed her arm.

"It will all work out, Geneva."

I nodded once, giving her a weak smile. Berk hadn't been to see JP yet today and the staff said that was unusual. And now his mom was here. A rock sat in the pit of my stomach. What if JP and I had lost Berk for good?

I pushed through the exit doors of the NICU and walked down

the hall toward the lounge. The butterflies in my stomach were quickly turning into a swarm of bees, stinging me relentlessly.

For better or for worse, Berk's mom would always be a part of JP's life. Maybe she could give me more insight into Berk's past.

Standing outside the door of the lounge, I drew in a deep breath. I needed to do this, for me and for JP. I blew out my breath as I twisted the handle and pushed it open.

As I entered the room, a pang of sorrow hit me when I suddenly realized this woman had already lost a grandchild and a daughter-in-law. She, like Berk, may still be in mourning.

Berk's mother sat in the corner of the room, her hands on the table, fingers knotted together as she nervously twisted them. When the door shut, she looked up and I wasn't surprised to see her resemblance to my son. I vaguely remembered her from our interaction at the restaurant in Colorado.

Her dark brown eyes bore through me, but maternal love shone through. Her jet-black hair hung straight and long, well past her shoulders. The powder blue sweater she wore coupled beautifully with her naturally dark skin. The string of pearls around her neck gave her an air of sophistication. Her face lit up with a huge smile, but apprehension was also evident in her eyes. She was just as nervous as I was.

Pushing out of her chair, she walked around the table, making her way toward me. She was petite, much shorter than my five-nine stature. She held out her tiny hand, fingers well-manicured, bracelets littering her arm. She was regal and refined.

"Hi," she said with a wavering voice. "I'm Kalani Rigby. Berk's mother," she added.

"What a beautiful name," I said, taking her hand in mine. Her shake was firm, but I could feel the tremble reverberating through her body.

"Thank you," she said shyly, lowering her head.

It was obvious that Berk did not get his hard-headedness from his mom. Her demeanor told me she wasn't meek, she wasn't fragile, she was conciliatory.

"Shall we?" She dropped my hand and waved it toward the table.

I took a seat at the round structure and was shocked when she sat directly beside me, leaving nothing between us. This was a good sign.

"First, I want to say thank you for meeting me. Especially since you were spending time with your son."

Her dark eyes were shining like marbles. I was completely transfixed by her beauty.

"I understand from my son Rhen that Berk is trying to forfeit his rights to JP."

My eyes went wide.

"I'm sorry, that is his name, isn't it?"

She thought I was surprised by her use of JP's given name. "Yes." I nodded with a smile. "It's a mix of our fathers, John and Paul."

Her hand went to her chest as she let out a sigh. "That is...." She couldn't go on, choked with unshed tears. "Thank you, Geneva." She placed her hand on my arm. "You don't know how much that means to me, and to Berk's father." Her smile was genuine and I saw the relief in her eyes.

I stared down at her hand. Her touch emanated a nurturing kindness.

She quickly withdrew it. "Well, I wanted to come to explain a little about Berk and his past, maybe give you some explanation as to why he's acting this way."

"You really don't need to. I understand the hurt and the guilt he lives with."

"Yes, Rhen told me that Berk has spoken to you at length about Jaime and Alana, about Jaime's illness. I just want to tell my story, from a mother's perspective. Maybe it will make a difference."

"Make a difference in what?" I tilted my head in confusion.

"I want Berk to be a part of his son's life. He needs closure. Our entire family would like to know JP." She drew in a deep, steadying breath. "I'm afraid that Berk's departure after JP's birth may have jeopardized that with you. As I understand it, you have a signed document that could absolve Berk of his parental rights."

She was scared, worried that I would take JP and never share him with Berk's side of the family. "Kalani, I would never do that. I know Berk signed it because he thinks he's going to hurt us. It's his distorted way of thinking."

"So, you haven't filed the papers?"

"The only place I filed them was in the trash." I laughed.

She slumped back in her chair, her face washing with relief. "Oh, thank you, Geneva. My Berk can be hot-headed and stubborn as a mule, like his father. I just want you to know that his heart is as big as the sun though, and when it's alive, it shines brighter than any star in the galaxy."

Warm tears burned my eyes.

"I'm sorry, I didn't mean to upset you." She reached for my hand and gave it a squeeze.

"Did it shine bright with Jaime and Alana?"

"Oh, yes." She beamed with pride. "He loved Jaime and Alana with all his heart. It broke him when they died." She looked up at me with a pleading expression. "It completely destroyed him, Geneva. I can't tell you as a mother what that was like to watch him suffer."

She didn't have to. In the short amount of time that I'd been a mother, I understood that bond. "When your child hurts, you hurt," I said.

"No matter how old they are, Geneva." Her eyes rolled up to the ceiling as she drew in a ragged breath. I could tell she was trying to keep her tears at bay.

Her head finally fell and her eyes landed on mine. "Berk has taken on the weight of Jaime's and Alana's death and it has crushed him. It's kept him from living. I don't want that for him, Geneva."

"Neither do I."

"There's more to Jaime's story that I think Berk hasn't shared with you."

"He told me Jaime had a mental illness and that she had a break-down shortly after Alana was born. But once she went on meds she stabilized."

She nodded her head.

"But there's more?"

"Yes," she said quietly. "Berk never speaks of it. I only know because of Jaime's sister, Jackie. She was the one who told Berk. To this day, I don't think he even knows that I know it."

My stomach cramped with fear. What the hell could this be?

"Jaime wanted another baby more than anything. She'd discussed it with Berk, but he was vehemently opposed."

"Why?"

"She would have to go off her meds."

"Oh, no," I whispered.

"Going off of medicine for bipolar disorder can make the symp-toms even worse than the onset. Berk wasn't willing to go through that again. Not only had Jaime been manic during her acute episodes, but she'd also been suicidal as well."

"Oh my God." I sucked in a sharp breath as my hand slapped over my mouth. I sat in stunned silence. Slowly my hand slipped away. "So, this accident of Jaime's wasn't her first attempt at suicide?"

Berk's mother shook her head.

"Then why does Berk blame himself?"

"Jackie told us that Jaime took herself off the meds without Berk knowing. She wanted to get pregnant so badly that she was willing to deceive him and risk her own mental and physical well-being."

"Oh, God, Kalani, that's awful."

"What makes it more than awful is that no one knew. No one knew the struggles that Jaime was going through mentally." Kalani took a breath, obviously distraught over the situation. "No one knew she was off her meds except her sister."

"Why didn't her sister tell anyone?"

"I think deep down, Jaime's family had a hard time really relating to her illness. I don't think Jackie was deceitful in keeping the secret, I just think she was naive."

I reached my hand out and squeezed Kalani's arm.

She covered mine with her own.

"Berk carries around so much guilt and anguish, blaming himself for Jaime's death, for Alana's, too, in some strange way."

"But he didn't know she was off her meds, did he?"

"No, not at the time of her death."

"Then how could he have helped her?"

"I'll admit, Berk wasn't the nicest person to be around after Alana's death. It was understandable. Who would be after losing their child to such a horrific accident?" Tears pooled in her eyes.

I scooted closer.

"It wasn't that he came out and blamed Jaime, but he didn't support her either. He was stuck in a sort of limbo, and he couldn't process anything."

My hand found hers and I squeezed, willing her to continue.

"Days later," she said, "when Jackie explained the situation, that Jaime had been off her meds, Berk was furious. Jackie called me, fearful of what Berk might do, scared for her own safety. I knew Berk would never hurt her, but I was disappointed in her as well. I could understand Berk's rage."

"But Berk doesn't know that you know Jaime was off her medication?"

"No. I asked Jackie not to tell him."

"Why?"

"I'm really not sure, Geneva. I just felt like Berk had so much to process, and he hated any signs of sympathy. I just didn't want him to have any more reason to go over the edge himself."

Kalani's eyes darted around the room as she pondered her next words.

"Shortly after the funeral, Berk left for Hawaii. He made it clear that he didn't want to talk about Jaime or Alana. At the time, I thought giving him space to process it all was what he needed. But as the weeks turned to months and the months into years, I knew this wasn't good. He'd closed off his feelings which would only make it harder if he ever returned."

"Is that why Jackie went to Hawaii?"

"Yes."

"Did you send her?"

"I didn't send her. She told me she wanted to go and I didn't stop her."

I laughed.

"What is it, dear?"

"I'm sure you've heard about the misunderstanding."

She shook her head.

"You know I met Berk in Hawaii."

"Yes. And I'm so glad." She smiled, patting my hand.

"Well, while I was there, I overheard Jackie and Berk talking. The conversation sounded like she was his girlfriend and that she wanted him to come home. Like they'd been involved before."

"Oh, no," Kalani said.

"Yeah, I'm that dumb." I laughed. "I took off shortly afterward without a word to Berk. A few weeks later I found out I was pregnant. I thought Berk was in a relationship, so that's why I never told him."

"I can understand." She smiled.

"You can?"

"Geneva, I would never judge you for doing *anything*. It's your life and you know what's best for you. After Berk's outburst at the restaurant that evening in Colorado, I'm surprised you even spoke to him again, let alone that you're allowing me to be here talking to you in the hospital where my grandson is." She choked on a sob and covered her mouth.

"Would you like to see him?"

"Oh, Geneva," she cried as tears rolled down her cheeks. "Would you let me?"

"Of course. You're his grandmother. Isn't it *tutu* in Hawaiian?"

She laughed, a belly laugh that rang through the room. "Yes, *tutu*. *Kuku wahine* is the formal name, but *tutu* is what we say."

"It's such a beautiful language. I'd love to learn it and teach JP one day."

The sadness in her eyes was palpable. She'd been a grandmother once before. Her losses were devastating as well.

"Well, come on, Tutu Kalani." I stood, extending my hand. "You have a grandson to meet."

"Thank you, Geneva." She flung herself at me and wrapped her arms around my waist. "I'm so sorry for everything my hard-headed son has said and done. But I promise I'm here to kick some sense into him."

I put my hands on her shoulders and pushed her away, peering down at her face. "I'm glad to hear you say that, because I have a plan."

"I like plans." She smiled.

Rhen was already on my side, calling Berk every name in the book for leaving me and JP. Now Berk's mom was committed to my team, too. My plan may not work in the end, but I had to try. For the first time in my life, I would take a chance at love.

I'm trying to find myself. Sometimes that's not easy.
- Marilyn Monroe

CHAPTER 36

BERK

I FLOPPED down on Rhen's couch, my body limp with exhaustion and my spirit falling fast. I stared at the ceiling, wondering what the fuck I was going to do.

"What's up, big bro?" Rhen asked as something nudged my shoulder.

I turned to look and saw a beer bottle shoved in my face. I yanked it from his hand and drank half the bottle in one gulp. I wasn't much of a drinker, but today I needed something to calm my nerves.

"JP gets released in two days," I sighed.

"Yeah, I know."

Of course, Rhen knew. He'd been going to the hospital with me to visit his nephew.

"You're a fucking idiot, you know that, right?"

I sat in silence as I gulped down the rest of my beer.

"When are you going to give up this stupid-ass charade you're putting on and just tell the girl straight up that you love her?" he asked.

"I did that once, remember? Didn't turn out so good."

"I don't know what the fuck you're talking about. You had an amazing family, a wife who loved you and a daughter who absolutely adored you. She thought you hung the moon."

"And they died!" I shouted.

"Not because of *you,* Berk!"

"What do you know?" I yelled, jumping to my feet. "You've never even been married or had a kid. Ever!"

Rhen's head jerked back as if I'd slapped him.

"It's not because I didn't want those things once, Berk." He readjusted in his chair and I sat back down.

It wasn't unusual for Rhen and me to get into heated debates and arguments. When we were young, we'd physically fight it out. Now, we hit one another with words. We were brothers first and foremost, so our arguments never lasted long. Rhen and I had a bond that ran deep and could never be broken. Not even by foolish words said in the heat of the moment.

When Alana and Jaime died, it had been Rhen who followed me to Hawaii to make sure I was okay. It had been Rhen who took care of all the shit at home that I couldn't or wouldn't. He was my best friend, and I hated that my words had hurt him.

"Look, man, I get that you think you're 'saving' Geneva and JP." He used air quotes. "But I've seen her, I've seen JP. Trust me, dude, you're not saving them by leaving them, you're destroying her."

"You've seen Geneva?" My tone was accusatory.

Rhen rolled his eyes. "Whatever, you're missing the point, Berk."

I scrubbed my face with my hand, the stubble littering my jaw scratching over my palm.

"Do you love her?" Rhen asked quietly.

I drilled my eyes shut. If I admitted it now, if I said the words out loud, I'd never be able to leave Geneva and John Paul.

"So, what?" Rhen asked. "You're just going to walk away from them, leave your own son? You don't think *that* won't fuck him up?

That's a slow form of death, my brother." Rhen stood and made his way into the kitchen, reappearing with another beer for me.

I snatched the bottle from his hand and chugged down the contents, trying to drown out his words.

"Just talk to her, man."

"And say what? Sorry I fucking walked out on you for the last two months?"

"It's a start."

"She'll punch me in the nut sack."

"Well, she should." Rhen laughed. "This has been a total dick maneuver on your part."

"I don't know, man." I raked my fingers through my short hair. "I've fucked this up *really* bad, Rhen. I'm not sure I'll ever be able to make it right with her."

"Why don't you come to my show tonight?"

"No offense but listening to your band scream their lungs out with your psychotic music isn't my idea of a pleasant evening."

"Whatever. It will clear your head."

"No, it will give me a damn headache."

"Maybe it will knock some sense into that thick skull of yours."

"Did you invite the nurse?"

"What nurse?" His eyes cut to the fireplace.

"What nurse?" I laughed. "The cute redhead that you make goo-goo eyes at every time we go see JP."

He snorted.

"I swear, I don't think you're there to see your nephew, you're there to look at her ass."

"It is a fine ass." He waggled his brow.

"Whatever." I chuckled and threw a pillow at him.

He ducked and it hit the grate of the fireplace, which fell to the floor with a bang.

"I hope you paid your security deposit." I glanced around Rhen's new apartment. His band was having a lot of success in the

Austin music scene. He and his bandmates decided to migrate here and make Texas their central hub for all things band related.

"I can't believe you're moving to Texas," I said with a moan.

"Why?"

"It's hot, people talk weird…"

"And it's where your son will be."

I shook my head. No fucking way I was moving to Texas. "There's no snow here. How the hell am I supposed to ski?"

"Where there's a will—"

"Don't say it." I held up my hand.

"Why? You don't want to hear Mom's golden nuggets of wisdom?"

"Not from a dumbass like you." I laughed.

We sat in silence for several moments. It was never awkward with Rhen. He was giving me time to process without filling my mind with endless chatter like my mother had several weeks ago when she'd come to town.

"The bottom line is this, Berk. Regardless of how you feel about Geneva now, do you want to know your son? Do you want a relationship with your son?"

"Yeah," I whispered. "Yeah, I do."

Peanut and I had bonded over the last eight weeks. I visited him every day at the hospital. But now, with the news that he would be released in two days, Geneva would have full-time custody. I couldn't see him anytime I wanted. Now I would be forced to talk to her if I wanted to spend time with my son.

"Then you've got to figure out a way to deal with your baby momma drama."

I shook my head. "You watch too much daytime television."

"Hey," he laughed, "it makes me feel better about myself." Rhen stared at me, his eyes boring into me, eyes that looked exactly like mine. Physically we'd inherited most of the dominant Hawaiian genes of our mother, but there were a few things about us that resembled our dad, like our height and our eyes.

"Maybe I should try watching a few because right now I feel like shit about my life." I leaned back on the sofa with a sigh.

"You know you can get yourself out of the shit hole you dug for yourself, don't you?"

"How?" I perked up.

"Gen's a cool chick."

"How would you know?" A jealous spark ran up my spine.

"Chill, Kahuna. I'm not making a play on your woman. I see her from time to time at the hospital."

"Do you go to see my son, or the hot nurse?"

His hands flew up in the air in innocence as he shook his head. "I refuse to answer that question on the grounds that it may incriminate me."

I laughed at his playful antics. Rhen's solution to any problem was to throw a joke at it.

"So come tonight," he said.

"Fine," I sighed. "I need to clear my head and figure out a new game plan. What better way to do that than for your suck-ass music to grate through my brain."

I always gave Rhen shit about his music, but the truth was, he was an amazing singer. But more than that, he was a hugely talented songwriter. I knew if he could make it anywhere, make his dreams come true, it would be here in Austin.

Maybe I could, too.

CHAPTER 37

BERK

I SAT at the back of the club at a high, wooden table, taking in my surroundings as people of varying ages and dress walked by.

Austin was an eclectic town. Their motto of "Keep Austin Weird" was definitely holding true tonight.

Rhen's band was playing at a club called Einstein's Brewhouse, known for its locally brewed beer. As I downed my second mugful, I had to admit the shit was good. Maybe there was more to Texas than I'd initially thought.

I combed the crowd, watching as the small venue filled with people. The opening band had just finished their last set and I was waiting for my brother's band to go on.

It still floored me every time he performed, watching the chicks go fucking nuts for him. If they only knew that the guy still slept with a stuffed animal and had pissed his bed until he was ten, they'd keep their panties on and ask for their cover charge back.

I stared down at my watch. It was a little after ten. Still early in band hours.

"Is this seat taken?" someone asked behind me.

I turned on my stool and saw familiar green eyes staring back at me. "Hey, Danielle." I stood and gave her a hug. It was amazing how close you could get to the medical staff who cared for your son. They'd all become like family to me, and I assumed to Geneva, too.

"So, getting out for a night on the town?" She smiled, and I could see why Rhen was smitten. Small dimples that I'd never noticed before appeared. Her long red hair that was usually pulled back in a ponytail was flowing down past her shoulders in loose curls. She scanned the bar. "Has Rhen been on yet?" The way she said his name, all breathy and sultry, made it clear she was a goner for my rocker brother.

"Nope, not yet. Have you heard him play before?"

She shook her head, her thick copper-colored hair brushing across her shoulders. "I don't get out much." She laughed as she sucked on the straw of her fruity drink.

"You work a lot, don't you?"

She nodded her head. "But I love what I do, so it's not really work to me."

"Well, you guys are amazing. I can't believe how much my son has changed while in the NICU."

"And he's going home soon." She bounced with joy that I couldn't match. "What's wrong?" Her brow creased.

"Long story."

"Oh, right, you and Geneva don't see each other, I forgot." She rolled her eyes.

"What?"

"It's not my place to say."

"Well, if you can't say it at a bar over drinks, where can you say it?"

She nodded once. "True."

I could tell she was wavering, wondering if she should talk to me about what was on her mind. "Just say it," I said.

"Okay," she sighed. "Working in the NICU has been an amazing time for me. I see the joy of parents walking out with a child they thought was not going to make it." She drew in a deep breath.

I didn't need to hear the words that were coming. A rock landed square in my stomach and worked its way back up my throat, nearly choking me.

"You've seen death, too, though," I continued for her.

She nodded her head. "Our NICU is one of the best in the country. But we can't save every child."

The troubled frown and the dullness of her eyes told me she'd experienced this personally.

"Have you ever lost a child?"

Her eyes cut to mine, now wide with fear.

"I'm sorry, you don't have to answer that, it was rude of me to ask," I said.

She rolled the straw around in her fingers. "No, it's okay," she sighed, her shoulders going limp.

"Fuck, I'm sorry. This is your night off and here I am bringing you down."

"You're fine, Berk, really." She reached her hand over the table and patted my arm. "I've never lost a child, but I came close," she said.

"You have a child of your own?"

Her eyes caught mine and I could see the pain and the joy emanating from within her. "Yeah, I have a son." She paused as if caught up in memories that haunted her. I recognized the blank stare. "I never thought I'd have a second chance, you know," she finally spoke.

I sat still.

"But when you get one, you take it. You don't ask questions, you don't wonder 'Why me,' you just…take it."

"I get it," I whispered.

She looked over my shoulder and her eyes lit up like the stage lights in front of us. "Hey, Rhen." Danielle smiled.

"Hey, guys." Rhen butted up to our table. "Glad you could make it." He meant the words for both of us, but his eyes were squarely on Danielle.

That fucker did *not* go to the hospital to see my son, he went for Danielle. She was beautiful though, with a heart of pure gold, so I couldn't blame him.

"We're about to go on," Rhen said, looking over at me.

"Great, now my head can *really* start banging. Like that first band didn't already suck ass." I laughed.

"Well, we have a special treat for you, big brother. Maybe something that won't give you such a headache." He punched my arm. "Although you deserve the pain with the way you've been acting like such a dumbass for the past two months."

I looked at my brother, raising my brow in warning. I panned over to Danielle.

She was staring at me, nodding her head.

"You think I'm a dumbass, too?"

"Pretty much." She smirked. "The woman is in love with you. Your son is thriving. I'd say Rhen is right. You're a *certified* dumbass."

Rhen's head fell back as his laughter echoed through the crowded area.

The rock in my throat was choking me. "But what if—"

"There are no *what-ifs* in life," Danielle said. "There's only today, this very moment. That's all we're guaranteed, Berk. *You* of all people should know that."

I looked over at Rhen, his face filled with sympathy as he brought his hand to my shoulder and gave it a squeeze.

"Gen and this baby *are* your second chance, bro."

"You can't hold yourself accountable for things that were out of your control, Berk." Danielle leaned in, her words covering me like a blanket. "I don't know your whole story but trust me when I say this. If you want to be the kind of father that your son deserves, you can't live in the past. You can't let the weight of the *what-ifs* drag you down."

I fell back into my chair, my eyes darting from Danielle to my brother. They shared a glance with one another before looking at me with inquisitive eyes.

"You gonna be okay, man?" Rhen asked.

"I need to find Geneva," I said. My heart pounded in my ears.

"Dude, it's almost ten-thirty. I'm sure she's already asleep. Just take it easy tonight. We'll go see her tomorrow."

My palms were sweating and my skin felt like it was on fire. Would she forgive me? Would she give me a second chance?

"I've been such a fucking idiot," I said to myself.

Rhen and Danielle nodded.

Yeah, not so much to myself, I guess.

"Sit back, enjoy the show, calm the fuck down," Rhen said, patting me on the back. "We'll go see Geneva and JP tomorrow, I promise. We'll even stop at the store and buy you a pillow?"

"Why?" I asked.

"Because you're going to need it while you're down on the floor on your knees, begging her to forgive you."

"Has she filed the papers?"

"What papers?" Rhen asked.

"No," Danielle answered. "She threw them away as soon as she woke up in the ICU." Her smile said it all.

I had a second chance. And this time I wasn't going to fuck it up.

"Hey, everyone. Welcome to Einstein's," Rhen announced, standing in front of the mic stand, a guitar strapped across his chest. "My name is Rhen Rigby and this is our band, Nineteen Seconds Down."

The crowd cheered for my brother and his band, jumping up and down in anticipation.

"What does the name of his band mean?" Danielle asked, leaning over the table.

"Long story." I rolled my eyes.

"I want to thank you guys for coming tonight," Rhen said. "And please welcome my dumbass big brother, Berk Rigby." Rhen extended a hand in my direction.

The crowd parted and a spotlight fell on me as they all clapped. My lips snarled as I gave Rhen a menacing stare, assuring him that I would kick his ass tonight when we got home.

"We've got a great show for you tonight. We'll be performing some covers you know well, plus some original songs."

The crowd applauded and the chicks went crazy. I shook my head. Didn't they know my brother was a certified bone-head?

I turned to make fun of him with Danielle but found the same starry-eyed look on her face as well. God, strap a guitar over your shoulder and suddenly chicks throw themselves at you. I understood the attraction from the girls in the crowd, but Danielle was an astute, well-educated woman. What could she possibly see in my dipshit brother? I rolled my eyes in disgust.

"But first, to start the show off, we've got a special guest coming to the stage to perform with us."

I scanned the small stage, looking for the "special guest." My eyes stopped and my body stiffened when I saw her. My jaw dropped and my heart slammed into my chest, my blood roaring in my ears.

Her red dress floated as she walked across the stage, the hem grazing the floor.

My eyes migrated up her body. I recognized the familiar flowers that littered the material of her dress. I'd seen this girl before, seen her in the same strapless red dress, listened to her as her siren voice had called to me in a place four thousand miles away, in a time that seemed like a lifetime ago.

The pounding in my ears deafened me. My breathing became shallow and labored. My body tingled from head to toe as if needles pierced every inch of skin.

"Are you all right?" Danielle asked, reaching over to touch my arm.

I shook my head, fearing the action may cause me to vomit right here on the table.

"Hello, everyone." Geneva's voice was shaky. She was visibly trembling as she tucked away a stray piece of blonde hair behind her ear. Her familiar diamond stud earrings sparkled in the stage lights. "My name is Geneva. Thank you for letting me start off the show." She turned back and smiled at my brother and nodded once.

His returning grin had the green-eyed monster in me coming to life.

"This one is for Berk," she said softly into the microphone.

Everyone in the bar turned to stare at me. Shit! This was a setup of the worst kind, planned by my brother and Geneva, and possibly Danielle.

Rhen strummed his guitar.

I didn't recognize the notes and wondered if it was an original song.

Geneva's voice traveled through the room like a gentle ocean breeze. The controlled vibrato in her tone caused a hush to wash over the crowd. She had an amazing voice. *She* was amazing.

I sat still, paralyzed by her performance, captivated by her blue eyes that now bore into me.

Her voice, mixed with the acoustic guitar solo, created a melody that warmed my soul. I heard the lyrics, but still didn't recognize the song. She sang about not wanting to be alone any more, and that we didn't have to have our future figured out.

Suddenly, her robust voice rang out with the chorus.

"Taking Chances" by Celine Dion. That was the song. Taking chances, second chances.

I'd said the same thing to her in Hawaii as we went on adventures together. She'd been scared, overwhelmed at times, but I promised her even back then I would take care of her if she trusted me.

The other instruments joined in, backing her, turning the once acoustic song into a full-on rock and roll performance.

Geneva's hand slapped her thigh to the beat of the music. She was alive. She became part of the song. Whether she knew it or not, Geneva was born to perform.

"Oh my God, she's amazing," Danielle whispered.

She was. Not just in singing, but in every aspect. I'd been a dumb fuck for not knowing sooner, for thinking that leaving her would ever be what she needed.

She was asking me to start over, to take a chance—on her—on us. On a future that we couldn't predict, nor did we want to.

Geneva pulled the mic from its stand and held out her hand as she continued to sing the song. Several people lifted her down from the stage. The crowd parted and she stared directly at me, the spotlight never leaving her.

Her voice echoed through the small club as she walked toward me. The words of taking chances and starting over rang clearly through the club, and my mind.

I gazed up at my brother who was now strumming away on his guitar. The smile on his face was enormous, and contagious. He had planned this. And for once in my life, I wasn't going to beat the shit out of him for thinking he knew what was best for me. This time he did.

Geneva stood a few feet away from me as she sang the final notes. The words to the song hit me square in the chest.

Could I take a chance? Could I jump off the ledge with her? The truth was I already had, months ago and thousands of miles away.

The song slowed and the accompanying instruments died out, leaving only Rhen on the acoustic guitar. Geneva sang the final few words then her voice died away, but not the love in her eyes.

Rhen slowed to a finish.

The crowd was silent, all eyes staring at us.

"What do you say?" Geneva whispered, staring at me as the microphone dangled by her side.

My hands slid around her neck, my thumbs caressing her cheeks now littered with tears.

"I say I'm a dumb fuck, a dip shit, a man who doesn't deserve you."

"But what if I give you a second chance?" She smiled. "What if we give *us* a second chance? What would you say then?" Her blue eyes sparkled with adoration, and it was all for me. In that moment I felt like her hero.

"I'd say I'd be a fool not to say yes."

She came closer, pressing against me. "Then I'd say, don't be a fool," she whispered against my lips.

I tugged her in the mere inches necessary for our lips to connect.

The room erupted in cheers and whistles, but all of it faded away as I lost myself in the arms of this woman, a woman who had brought me back from the dark recesses of my mind.

She pulled away from my embrace, staring up at my eyes, oblivious to the crowd surrounding us. "Welcome back to the land of the living, Berk Rigby." She grinned.

"What?"

"Nothing." She laughed. "Let's go get our son."

"*Our* son," I repeated.

"Yeah, *our* son. Let's bring him home."

CHAPTER 38

BERK

"GOD, HE LOOKS SO SMALL," I said, looking over the railing of JP's crib.

Geneva pulled a blanket over our son's sleeping body.

"He's already over five pounds." She smiled with motherly affection, rubbing on his arm.

"I can't believe it. Who would have thought five pounds for a baby would seem like so much." I laughed nervously.

Geneva and I both knew how fragile JP still was. Neither one of us took the doctor's orders lightly. Our son would still be prone to a host of problems, infection being the biggest. She and I had opted to stay at home for the past two weeks while we settled in to our new roles as parents.

I kissed my fingertips and rubbed them lightly on JP's head.

Geneva stretched with a wide yawn.

"Let's get you to bed," I said as I slid my arm around her waist, pulling her from the nursery. She would stay in here and stare at him to ensure his safety all night if I let her. I couldn't fault her though, so would I. "The monitor's on." I nodded to the camera in the corner that would simulcast JP's every move to a monitor in our bedroom.

She hesitated at the door, peering back over her shoulder at the crib.

"And we've got the backup monitor there on the changing table next to his bed."

Her blue eyes rolled up to meet mine. Nothing but motherly love and concern reflected in them.

"He'll be fine, babe. I'll get up with him so you can rest."

She laid her head on my chest as she drew in a deep breath. "I am tired," she sighed.

"Come on." I dragged her out of the room, leading her down the hall to our room. *Our* room. Making my way to the bed, I pulled back the sheet and comforter and motioned for her to crawl in.

She reached for the book laying on the nightstand. "I just want to read for a bit. It's so good."

"Another smutty book?" I laughed, making my way around the bed to the other side.

Geneva and I had fallen into a routine of sorts. Neither one of us talked about the future. We didn't have to. We were both content with living in the moment with each other and our son.

"I love VM Wilson," she said, as if telling me the author's name would justify her addiction to soft porn.

"Whatever." I laughed. "Mind if I pull out a *Playboy* while you're reading that shit?"

"Berk," she scolded, hitting me on the chest. "If I remember correctly, reading one of VM's books is what helped us conceive our little boy in there." She nodded toward JP's bedroom.

"Ah, yes, the BDSM book. Who could forget?" I fell back onto the pillow, a smirk spreading wide across my face as I remembered our sexual escapades. "So, is that one kinky, too?" I asked, pushing up onto my elbow and rolling over to look at the cover.

"No, this one is just a simple love story like her other ones."

"It's a shame." I smiled up at her.

"Why?"

"I thought maybe you could read it out loud to me." I waggled my brows.

"I didn't say there wasn't sex in it." She grinned.

Hot damn.

"But I think we'd better leave the sex scenes to VM."

"Ah, man," I pouted.

She placed the book back on the nightstand, rolling over to face me, her hand rubbing up and down my shoulder. "I didn't say we couldn't write our own sexy book." She cocked one eyebrow and lifted her lips in a devilish smile.

"What did you have in mind?" I pulled her toward me, my hard-on pushing into her thigh.

"Oh, my." She tried to sound shocked, but Geneva knew the effect she had on me.

"So, what would this book of ours be about?" I asked.

"Well," she trailed a finger down my chest, "it would be about a sexy man who lived in Hawaii." Her finger traveled lower to the elastic waistband of my boxers.

I sucked in air through my gritted teeth as her fingers slipped below my underwear. "And what else?" I gulped, my voice cracking.

"He is a very stubborn, very naughty boy." Her hand worked lower as she wrapped it around my throbbing dick.

Oh, God. "So, he's going to be punished?" I croaked out.

"Yes. Most definitely. He needs to learn a lesson." She slid down the bed.

I clenched my fist, along with every other appendage, including my dick. We hadn't had sex since before JP was born. I didn't want to hurt her. I had no idea how long her recovery would take given the fact that she'd had a C-section and had slipped into a coma after the delivery.

Coma.

My hands trembled as sweat broke out on my forehead.

Don't go there, man. One day at a time, no past, no future.

"Berk?" Geneva lifted her head, her hand releasing me. "What's wrong?"

Her face was glowing with desire, her eyes bright with a hunger that I'd only dreamed of seeing in a woman's eyes again.

"Nothing," I answered, grabbing her shoulders and lifting her on top of me. "Everything is perfect." I wrapped my hand around her neck and pulled her face down to meet mine, my lips engulfing hers as our tongues intertwined in an erotic dance.

She wiggled her hips on top of mine, her hands skimming across my arms as they moved toward my waist.

"Are you sure?" I leaned her back from me. "I mean, are you okay to do this? Physically?"

She nodded her head, biting her bottom lip in anticipation.

Who was I to deny her?

I flipped her over and spread her legs with mine. "So, tell me more about this handsome, sexy Hawaiian fellow from your book." I smiled down at her.

Her fingers dug into my hair, her eyes darting between mine. She drew in a deep breath, holding it for an eternity, before blowing it out, her chest heaving from the exertion.

"Well." She hitched one side of her mouth up in a knowing smirk. "He becomes a real shit, a dumbass some would say."

"Oh, really." I grimaced.

"Um hmm." Her hands fell from my head as she slid them down my shoulders. "But it's okay. Because eventually the hot chick wins him over, kicks his ass and makes him fly straight."

"Well, thank God." I lowered myself and placed light kisses along her neck. "It sounds like a best seller." I licked at her throat, making my way down to her collarbone. I remembered her erogenous zones well.

She moaned, bucking her hips up against mine.

"So how does this book end?"

"I'm not sure," she said.

I pushed off her, staring at her face in confusion.

"This guy only lives for the here and now," she whispered.

"And how about the *now* part?" I ground my erection between her thighs. "How is it going to end tonight?"

Her eyes went wide as her face lit up like the sun. She was more than beautiful. She transcended the word.

"I think it's safe to say the book will have a very happy ending." She giggled.

"Sounds like a book worth reading." I placed a light kiss on her lips, pulling back to stare down at her. "I love you, Geneva." I'd never said the words out loud to her. Hadn't said them since before my daughter had died.

"I know." She smiled. "You're the only one who didn't."

I laughed at her answer. She was right.

"I love you, too, Berk." She lifted her head and touched her mouth to mine.

I pulled her in for a deeper embrace, trying to show her my love as I ground my dick between her legs.

She moaned in anticipation.

I gave her a small peck on the lips and sunk my fingers into her hair, gazing at her flawless face. "Now, about that happy ending...." I smirked.

Her lips crushed mine.

Oh, yeah, this was definitely going to be a novel-worthy night that would make even VM Wilson blush.

～

I still miss those I loved who are no longer with me, but I find I am grateful for having loved them.
The gratitude has finally conquered the loss.
- Rita Mae Brown

～

EPILOGUE

GENEVA

-NINE MONTHS LATER-

I watched through the windshield of the warm car as Berk knelt at the headstone, his hand brushing away the fallen snow from the cold granite slab.

Today was the second time we'd visited the cemetery where Jaime and Alana were buried. Up until a month ago, four years had passed without him visiting their gravesites.

A dark blue sedan pulled up next to us, the driver waving at me. I recognized the man from the first time we'd met—and from the countless number of family photos Berk now had in his possession.

Jaime's parents.

I opened the car door and a blast of cold Colorado air hit my face. I feared it might take me forever to get used to this type of weather, thankful that at least during the off-season, Berk had agreed to live in Texas.

"Geneva," the man called out with an excited expression on his face. "It's so wonderful to see you."

"You, too, Mr. Fuller."

"I've told you before, please call me William." He smiled. "Is that precious baby boy with you?"

"Yes. I just kept him inside the car because he fell asleep on the way over here. And it's *freezing* out here." I pulled my silver coat tight around my neck.

William neared our car and peeked inside the back seat. "Yes, I'm sure it never gets this cold in Texas."

I'd checked the temperature in the car as we'd driven to the cemetery. I wasn't sure I would ever get used to readings in the single digits. But Berk wanted to ski, and I wanted to support him. This was my life now. And I loved it.

"Here, I'll get him out now that you're here." I opened the back door to our SUV.

"Oh, don't wake him," Mrs. Fuller said as she came from the other side of the car.

"Hello, Mrs. Fuller."

She raised a perfectly manicured brow.

"Sorry." I smiled. "Janet."

She winked and leaned in for a hug which I gladly reciprocated. "I imagine it's too cold out here for JP." I could hear the anticipation in her voice.

"We were out earlier with Berk, but the wind picked up and he thought it best to get JP back into the car."

"He's probably right," she said. "You don't want to take a chance with babies getting a cold." She wanted to see him, and I didn't want to deny her such a simple pleasure. I knew she missed her only granddaughter as much as Berk did.

"Here let me get him." I reached for the door handle.

"Oh, no, that's okay. I don't want him to get sick."

"He'll be fine," I reassured her.

"Looks like he's itching to get out anyway." William laughed.

I turned my attention and found JP waving frantically with a huge smile on his face. Even though he'd only met the Fullers twice before, he seemed to have a special bond with them. That, and the fact that JP didn't know a stranger. The boy would go to anyone that showed him the slightest bit of attention.

I opened the back door, listening to his squeals of delight.

JP was like his father. He hated being tied down, he preferred being outdoors, playing in the snow. Berk said he couldn't wait to get JP on a snowboard. I could.

"Oh my goodness, look how much he's grown!" Janet squealed. "Come here, baby boy." She held out her hands and he fell into them, playing with her short auburn hair.

I teased that JP was going to be a hair stylist someday because he was fascinated by hair.

"Dee-bah," JP mumbled.

Janet looked at me, her face wrinkled in confusion.

"Beats me." I shrugged my shoulders with a chuckle. "He babbles all the time and I have *no* idea what he's saying."

We all burst into laughter.

"What's so funny?" Berk asked, sliding in next to me and wrapping an arm around my waist.

"Your little boy here and his gibberish," William answered.

"It's a language all his own." Berk shook his head.

"I remember Alana used to do that, too," Janet said.

I gazed up at Berk, wondering what the mention of his daughter might do.

He smiled at Janet, his eyes lighting up with memories that no longer haunted him. "I'd completely forgotten about that, but you're right, Janet, she did."

"Hey there, Berk." William extended his hand and Berk took it in his, shaking in a familiar way. "How are my girls today?" William nodded toward the headstones Berk was leaning in front of earlier.

I still couldn't imagine the loss of a child like the Fullers and Berk had endured.

"Good, I think." Berk cast his gaze back at the plot of land now covered with snow. The only indication that it was a cemetery was the mass of headstones littering the grounds.

JP clapped his hands and held them out to William.

"Well, hello, fella." William smiled wide, grabbing JP from his wife and hoisting him high into the air.

JP squealed with delight, his face glowing with joy.

"Sometimes he looks so much like Alana, it steals my breath," Janet whispered, her hand clutching her chest.

"He really does," Berk answered, his eyes stuck on JP.

"Thank you for sending the photo albums of Jaime and Alana," I said to Janet.

"Oh, I'm just glad to pass them on. And so glad you called to ask for them." She took my gloved hand in hers and gave it a light squeeze.

Berk had banned any pictures of Alana and Jaime in his home for years after their death. I'd explained that JP needed to know his sister, and he needed to make peace with Jaime. In the end he'd agreed.

"Would you kids like to meet us for lunch after we visit Alana and Jaime?" William asked.

I looked at Janet and saw her eyes were focused on the headstones that marked where her daughter and granddaughter lay. Even years after her daughter's death, I'm sure the hole in her heart never fully healed. And losing her granddaughter as well had to have crushed her.

"I'd like to," Berk said, "but we have someplace we have to be this afternoon."

"We do?" I looked up at him in question.

"That's all right, dear." Janet put her hand on my arm. "But we're still on for dinner this Sunday at our house, right?"

I nodded my head, excited about formally meeting Jaime's sister Jackie and her brother Jason.

"The kids will be so happy to finally meet JP." Janet poked at JP's belly and he laughed. She reached up and ran her hand through his dark hair. "Same color as Alana's," she said.

JP bounced in William's arms, his own arms flailing about in glee.

"You kids get going." Janet leaned in to hug me. "It's cold and your baby boy doesn't need to freeze out here."

"Thank you, Janet," I whispered in her ear.

She pulled back and stared at me, her eyes so much like the ones I'd seen in the photos of Jaime.

"For giving Berk this," I whispered.

She furrowed her brow.

"Closure," I answered. "Forgiveness. A new start."

Janet's eyes traveled to Berk's, his glued to us.

I'd hoped my words would be for Janet's ears only, but judging by the soured expression on Berk's face, I assumed they hadn't.

Janet walked up to Berk, her hand reaching up to his face, rubbing his cheek like an adoring mother. "It's like I've told you before, sweetheart. There's *nothing* to forgive, Berk." She smiled up at him, her own broken heart I'm sure littered with regret.

"I know." He placed his large hand over hers. "Thank you."

As if sensing Berk wouldn't want this meeting to turn emotional, Janet pulled her hand away then clapped both of them together. "Dinner. Sunday. Six sharp," she instructed, giving each word a slap of her hands.

JP clapped and shouted wildly. "Yah yah yah!"

"Looks like someone's excited about Sunday." William laughed.

"We'll see you then." Berk leaned down and hugged Janet, giving her a quick peck on the cheek.

"What can we bring?" I asked.

"This little one." William held JP high in the air, shaking him again.

JP's arms and legs flailed about as his laughter rang through the cemetery. What a wonderful way to end our visit, with laughter instead of tears. It was a new beginning for Jaime's parents.

We said our final good-byes and Berk strapped JP into his car seat as I took my seat in the front. I watched William and Janet hold hands as they traipsed through the snow on the way to their daughter and granddaughter's gravesite.

Tears stung my eyes, thinking of the tragedy that had hit this family. They seemed to be coping well, but as with any parent who'd lost a child, I knew their heart would never fully heal. They were just finding a new normal. Like Berk.

"Thanks for coming," Berk squeezed my thigh as he slid into the already running car.

"You know I never mind coming here." I looked into his caramel-colored eyes, the same ones as our son. "I want JP to know his sister and extended family."

He gave me small smile, leaning over the center console and stealing a kiss. "I love you, Geneva. For a multitude of reasons."

"I bet it's my butt you love the most, right?"

"You do have a sweet—"

I held up my hand to silence him. "Little ears have big mouths." I nodded back to JP.

"He's not even talking yet," Berk scowled.

"Well, I don't want his first word to be a curse word. His Aunt Dana is already having a hard time censoring herself as it is."

"That woman will *never* be able to tame that mouth of hers." He laughed as he reached around my seat into the back. "Here." He extended a present wrapped in Christmas paper.

"Christmas was two weeks ago," I said.

"Santa left this one behind."

I gazed up at his face, his eyes alight with mischief.

"Berk Rigby, what is this?"

"Open it." He put the car in reverse, turning to look behind us.

I stared at the gift in my lap. What could it be?

"You'll never know unless you open it."

"Fine," I huffed. I ripped off the paper. "Oh my gosh, Berk, it's VM Wilson's latest book. I thought it wasn't going to be ready for several more weeks!" I squealed. I stared down at the cover, the words "Uncorrected Proof Not for Resale" glaring back at me.

"I have connections." He wiggled his brow as we made our way onto the interstate.

"Wait." I looked out the window. "Where are we going? Our house is that way." I pointed behind me.

"Look inside the book." His smile was so wide, his excitement infectious.

Cautiously, I opened the book and saw two tickets inside. Pulling them out slowly, I read over the description. "'Authors in the Snow?'" I said, reading the description. "Is this?"

"It's a book signing."

"No way!" I shouted.

"Way." He laughed.

I stared down at the ticket. "In Denver?"

"Yep." He nodded once.

"But the ticket says it's today."

"I know." He grinned at me.

"We're headed to Denver?"

He nodded.

"Today?"

"That's the plan."

"As in right now?"

"Yes, Geneva." He shook his head. "Read the rest of the ticket."

I scanned the ticket. "Oh my God!" I screamed, my voice nearly shattering the windshield.

JP shouted.

Berk swerved. "God, Geneva, you scared the shit out of me." He righted the car on the road. "You act like it's front row seats to Justin Timberlake."

"This is soooo much better." My heart raced with such excitement I feared it might explode. "Is it true?" I held up the tickets. "Is VM Wilson *really* going to be at this signing, Berk? And don't screw with me. It would be just like you to make fake tickets and get me all excited."

He laughed. "No, they're real. She's really going to be there."

"Oh my God, oh my God, oh my God." I held the tickets to my chest as if they were gold. "I'm so excited." I bounced up and down in my seat.

"You're welcome?" he said with a lift of his eyebrow.

"Oh, thank you so much, baby." I leaned over the console, stretching my seat belt as I pecked him on the cheek.

"That's it?"

"You're driving, silly."

"So?" He waggled his brow.

"And your son is in the back seat."

"Crap," he sighed.

"Do you think she'll sign my book?"

"She said she would."

My head jerked to his. "What do you mean, she said she would?"

His eyes went wide as he gripped the steering wheel. "I mean, on the website, it said you could bring in your own books and she would sign them."

"Oh, okay." I sagged back in my seat, staring at the new book and the tickets. "This is like the best gift you've ever given me. Besides your son."

"Well, I thought since he was conceived while you were reading her books, it would be good for him to meet her."

We laughed together. It was nice to have these moments with Berk.

I gazed back at my son whose eyes were growing heavy.

"How long is it to Denver?" I asked.

"From Winter Park, less than two hours. That will give JP enough time to take a nap."

I glanced at the back seat, not surprised to find JP completely zonked out.

"What about you?" Berk cut his eyes at me.

"Are you kidding?" I held the tickets in my hand. "I'm too nervous to sleep. I can't believe I'm going to meet VM Wilson. Today!"

"You know there are other things you could do while your son sleeps."

I glanced up at Berk, not surprised to see a wanting look in his eyes.

"Berk!" I swatted him with the book.

"What?" He rubbed his shoulder. "You can't blame a guy for trying."

I shook my head, knowing full well if JP weren't in the back seat, I'd be buried in his lap to thank him for such an amazing gift.

"Later." I smiled.

"Why don't you read me the book?" He nodded to my lap.

"No way. You think you have blue balls now."

We both laughed.

"The beginning can't be that bad, can it?"

"Um, hello, have you *not* been reading her books with me? This is the last one in her BDSM trilogy."

"So, we finally find out what happens to West and CC?"

My eyes darted to his. "God, you sound like a girl."

"What? Can't a man appreciate a literary piece of work?"

I laughed. "I guess. As long as that literary work includes chicks tied up by a dominant man as he smacks her ass with a riding crop, right?"

He cut his eyes to mine. "Why don't you just take a nap?" He squeezed my thigh. "We can read tonight."

I shook my head. I was too excited to sleep. "Why don't I get a head start? That way we can just skip to the good parts tonight since our time is limited thanks to that little guy back there."

Berk took my hand in his and kissed the back and held it to his heart.

"Thank you," I said.

"For what?"

"For the book and the tickets."

"You're welcome." He gave me a wink and a half smile before releasing my hand.

"And for introducing me to Jaime's parents. I know it wasn't easy for you, but I hope they brought you closure."

He nodded.

"You know," I said, looking back at JP in his car seat, "he looks like he's down for the count." I slid my hand up Berk's thigh.

He jumped.

"Maybe we could write our own novel."

"Uh, not in the car. I'm pretty sure I'd swerve off the side of the road if your hand wrapped around anything south of my waistband."

"But you just said," I pouted.

His eyes grew wide in surprise. "Seriously?"

I bit my lip as I tilted my head in a wanton look.

His deep laughter rang through the car. "Better leave that until tonight, baby." He slid my hand off his thigh and placed it back in my lap.

I sank back with a sigh.

"Read." He smiled.

"Okay." I opened VM's book and turned to the dedication page. I gasped as I read it. "Holy shit, Berk."

"What?"

"Her dedication. Did you read it?"

My eyes cut to his, but his remained on the road. I could see the half curve of a smirk.

"You knew about this?"

"I may have."

I looked down at the words staring back at me, my heart filling with joy.

Dedication
To anyone who has had a second chance and took it.
And to JP Rigby. By far, my best work to date.

"She *knows* about us?" I sat dumbfounded, struck speechless. "You actually *talked* to her?"

"Yeah," he said casually. "I reached out to her last year after JP was born. Told her what a huge fan you were and how JP was conceived."

"You *did not* tell her." I swatted at his arm, my voice a deep grumble.

"She thought it was amazing."

"So, you *actually* talked to *the* VM Wilson."

"She told me her name is Virginia, but her friends call her Virgie. And yes, I actually talked to her."

"Like voice to voice?"

"God, Geneva, you act like she's the president or something. She's just a chick who writes books."

"Bite your *tongue*, Berk Rigby. She's a woman who writes incredible love stories. So amazing that you and I were able to conceive a baby."

"Well, you got me there. Her shit is pretty amazing. But it was weird."

"What?"

"She sounded really innocent and shy on the phone."

"And?" I asked.

"Well, I mean she writes some fucked-up shit. I expected her to sound more…"

"Sexy?"

"Yeah, kind of, I guess."

"Oh my God, I can't believe you did this. I can't believe you actually talked to VM Wilson." I squeezed the book in my hand.

"That copy she gave me is what she called an ark, or something like that."

I squealed.

"You know what that is?"

"It's A-R-C," I spelled out. "It stands for advance reader's copy. And, hell yes I do. It means I'm one of the first people to read a new novel by a best-selling author who's sold a *gazillion* books. Oh. My. God!" I fell back in my seat, letting out a huge sigh. I couldn't believe I was holding on to something so coveted.

"Well, anyway, she said not to pass it around or let anyone else see it."

"Hell, no, I won't. I'm guarding it with my life." I clutched it tighter to my chest.

"She said that she named a few supporting characters after us."

"Shut! Up!" I hit his arm again.

"Quit hitting me, dammit."

"Sorry," I whispered, thumbing through the book. "Holy shit, Berk, we're actually in here. In one of VM Wilson's books."

"Her name is Virgie."

"Whatever." I read through the book. "It looks like you're a pilot."

"Pilot? Cool. Are you a hot sexy flight attendant who gives me blowies in the *cock* pit?"

I sat in silence, blown away by what I was reading.

"What is it? Are you some strung out whore in the book?" He laughed.

"She also named one of the characters Alana," I whispered.

"Are you shitting me?" He reached over for the book.

I spread it open and pointed to the passage.

"Who is she? Who is Alana in the book?" he asked.

"She's the daughter of one of the supporting characters."

"Wow," he sighed.

I glanced over at him. "Are you mad?"

"Why would I be mad?"

"I don't know." I shrugged my shoulders.

"Gen, it's like you and Dr. Elsher said. Just because Alana and Jaime are part of my past doesn't mean they can't be part of my future. It doesn't mean I have to always associate bad things with them. And being able to connect with Jaime's parents again has really helped me, knowing they don't blame me." He gave me a reassuring smile. "I think Virgie naming a character after Alana is amazing."

"Really?"

"Yeah, really, babe." He squeezed my leg. "It's like Virgie said in the dedication."

"What is?"

"Life is about taking second chances."

"Yeah, it is." I sat back in my seat, memories of my past racing through my mind. I'd been devastated by the loss of my mother. Instead of dealing with it, I let my pain fester, spending years taking out my anger on my stepsister, nearly destroying her and my entire family.

I let out a heavy sigh.

"What?" Berk asked.

"I'm just thankful that Hindley and my family gave me a second chance."

"I'm glad you took a second chance on me."

I turned to face Berk.

His eyes glanced at me for the briefest of seconds.

"I love you, Berk."

"I love you, too, Gen." His smile was reassuring with a hint of promise in his gleaming eyes. "Read the book." He nodded toward my lap.

I turned to the beginning. "Prologue," I read.

"You're going to read it out loud, even *before* the sexy parts?"

"Yeah, I am. You deserve to hear CC's story from the beginning."

"Okay, lay it on me. We've got a little over an hour before we get to Denver."

I cleared my throat and began to read.

My name is Priscilla Carter. I died once.

No, this isn't a ghost or some spirit hovering over my dying body. This is me, in the here and now.

I'm a fucked-up mess, and some days I wish they would have just let me die on that fateful day.

I've spent the last ten years of my life trying to figure out why I lived and why he *didn't. Why I was saved and* he *wasn't.*

He was the good one, the smart one, the one everyone flocked to. I was the bitch, the bully, the one who made everyone else's life a living hell. Everyone probably wished that I had died instead of him. *I know I did.*

But here I am, because he *isn't. Because* he *made a choice in a split second that saved me instead of* himself.

After ten years of only existing, I've finally decided to join the land of the living. And it's all because of him. A new him. He's given me a second chance to try again. Life is too precious to squander. I know that now thanks to him.

He gave me life.

But it would be him who showed me how to live it.

I refused to waste this second chance at a new life...and a new love.

Berk gazed over at me. "I won't waste my second chance either, baby." He gently squeezed my leg.

I smiled up at my husband, covering his hand with mine. "Neither will I, Berk."

Thank you for reading
Extreme Courage

If you or someone you know suffers from mental illness, or if you are the caregiver of someone who does, please turn to the **Resources** section to find help.

You don't have to suffer alone.

~

Be sure to turn the page for a sneak peek at

Extreme Promise
X-Treme Love Series, Book 7
Between *The Epilogue* and *The End*
comes the promise of forever.

Available now

BONUS CHAPTER

Can't get enough of Geneva and Berk? Me neither. So I wrote a bonus chapter. Visit my website to read it.

Link to the bonus chapter
www.kaymanis.com/pages/extreme-courage-bonus-chapter

WANT TO RECEIVE A FREE EBOOK?

Join my email list and I'll send you *Extreme Beginning*, the X-Treme Love Prequel for free. It's the story of Caroline Hagen and Paul Barton. Just visit the website below and join today.

I also give away free things all the time, including ebooks and signed paperbacks (my own and from best-selling authors) and more.

You'll also receive exclusive sneak peeks and teasers of upcoming books in my series.

Visit my website to join my email list now and receive your free ebook today!

www.kaymanis.com

IF YOU ENJOYED THIS BOOK

Please:

1. Write a review. It's so important to my work.

2. Tell your family and friends about my books.

3. Visit my website and sign up for my newsletter. You can also send me an email. I love to hear from my readers.

www.kaymanis.com

4. Follow me on social media.

Facebook: www.facebook.com/kaymanisauthor2

Twitter: www.twitter.com/kaymanis

Instagram: www.instagram.com/kaymanis

EXTREME PROMISE

RORY AND HINDLEY'S WEDDING

When prominent Austin attorney Hindley Hagen puked all over her prospective new client outside a trendy downtown nightclub, little did she know she'd met the man of her dreams. Pro athlete Rory Gregor made a promise that night to keep Hindley safe. A year later, he's keeping his word.

As Hindley prepares for their wedding day, a different man stands in the way of her happily ever after. With the news of her assailant's pending prison release, Hindley must do the unthinkable and face her attacker once again. Can she find the strength to stand on her own, or will the threat of a new trial destroy her?

Memories of his childhood and the sister he couldn't save torment Rory Gregor. With his fiancée's ultimatum to make peace with his past before they marry, he must expel the ghosts that haunt him or risk losing her. As Rory travels back to his home in Colorado to unearth the truth behind his sister's death, he discovers more haunting details about his own life that threaten to push him over the edge...again.

With the countdown to their wedding looming, can Rory and Hindley find the strength they need to overcome the obstacles that stand in their way to a happily ever after? Or will the demons from their past prevent them from making the ultimate promise...til death do us part?

Available now

Also available now

Extreme Gift

Trapped in Paris

X-Treme Love Series, Novelette

Only two weeks away from delivering her first child, Hindley Hagen goes against her doctor's orders (and her overbearing husband's) and travels five hours away to the small Texas town of Paris. She and her best friend, Dana Di Grazio, want to experience one last girls' only weekend. But this year Paris, Texas, is experiencing epic floods and Hindley is trapped.

Against his better judgment, Rory Gregor has traveled to Paris, France, to participate in a charity pro-am, even though his wife is days away from giving birth. His sponsors assure him he'll make it home in time to welcome their new baby girl. But one day before his expected return, Paris is hit with an unexpected blizzard and the threat of record-breaking snowfall halts all travel.

Will Hindley and Rory be able to reach one another in time to welcome their new daughter together? Or will Hindley give birth to their first child alone in the confines of a small Texas hospital where the doctor-on-call has gone MIA?

Join the cast of the X-Treme Love Series in this funny, touching, heartwarming novelette that proves true love can weather any storm.

Available now

EXTREME PROMISE EXCERPT
X-TREME LOVE SERIES, BOOK 7

– HINDLEY –

I bolted toward the exit of the dress shop, jaw clenched as I shoved the glass door so hard, the frame bounced back and nearly smashed me in the face. Their exasperating jeers echoed behind me.

The cool winter air hit my skin but didn't temper the heat coursing through my body. I jammed my hands deep into my coat pockets and scanned the city sidewalks right and left. Should I scream? Should I run? Maybe both.

Suddenly, my phone vibrated. Again. Shit.

I didn't need to see the phone to know who was calling. The man had been blowing up my phone for days. He'd left several messages, none of which I'd listened to for fear his words would send me spiraling out of control.

Run, definitely run.

My heels set a blistering pace as I raced down the street toward Dana's car.

"Hindley!" Rory shouted behind me.

I sprinted down the street and never looked back. I refused to acknowledge my fiancé's presence. He'd humiliated me.

"Hindley, wait!" My best friend's voice joined in.

Their cries didn't faze me. I was on a mission. Get home, vomit, crawl into bed, and hide from the world. I'd developed the pattern years ago.

I searched up and down the street. Bustling cars jammed the busy thoroughfares of downtown Austin. In my periphery I spotted Rory and Dana gaining on me. I darted out into traffic, narrowly missing a car and two bicycles.

"Fucking cyclists," I mumbled.

"Hindley!" Rory's frantic cries drifted down the street.

Good. Be worried. Served him right.

I leaped onto the sidewalk across the street just as strong, beefy hands grabbed my shoulders.

I squirmed out of his hold and prepared for an all-out sprint to Dana's car. I positioned my feet like a runner on the starter block but one massive arm grabbed my waist and lifted me off the ground before I could dash away.

My body trembled. Oh, God, not again.

He's back. Back for you. Run!

"Hindley, what the fuck?" Rory grumbled in my ear. His voice wavered with fear and annoyance.

I beat his hands that were clasped across my stomach and kicked my legs as they dangled in mid-air. "Put me down!" My voice resounded across the street and caught the attention of a few passersby.

"Not until you tell me what the fuck is going on with you." He gripped me tighter.

His deep voice brought me back to the present. It was Rory. My Skater Boy. But I was still pissed at him.

"What the fuck is going on with *me*?" I mocked. "What the fuck is wrong with *you*?"

Rory's hold loosened.

I slid down his chest and whipped around, my eyes darting between his.

"Hindley, what's wrong?" Dana scooted up beside Rory and dropped her hands to her knees as she gasped for air. "You nearly got waxed by three cars crossing the road."

"Like you care." I rolled my eyes and folded my arms across my chest.

Dana straightened and her head jerked back as if I'd taken a swing at her. In reality, my words had. If anyone cared about me, my best friend, Dana Di Grazio, did.

I scanned both their faces. Their expressions mirrored my own. Anger, resentment, but most of all fear.

"You both told the dress designer that her material looked like baby shit yellow," I huffed as my fists pounded my hips.

Rory and Dana glanced at each other but had the decency to stifle a laugh.

"I'm sorry, baby, but it did." Rory's smirk slid up one side of his face.

His mischievous expression normally warmed my heart, along with other parts of my anatomy, but not today.

The sting of unshed tears burned my eyes. I refused to cry. Not here. Not now. Not over such a lame excuse.

"It's three months before the wedding." I held up three fingers and shoved them in his face. "Three!" My eyes narrowed and my chest heaved with frustration. "I lost one dress designer already. The other has a wait list well into next year."

I gazed along Rory's lean body, at his legs encased in denim, showing off his muscular form. Not now. I shook my head to clear the sordid thoughts. Sometimes I hated how much he affected me.

"This woman was my last chance," I choked out, "my last chance." My words broke with my statement. But my emotions had nothing to do with a fucking dressmaker.

The countless voicemails and phone calls barraging me had created the real fear and anxiety coursing through my mind. The anticipation of listening to the caller's voice scared the shit out of me. What could he possibly want?

"Baby, I'm sorry." Rory scooted closer.

I backed up.

"Hindley?" His brow furrowed.

Rory was scared and he understood my mood had nothing to do with a dressmaker. I both loved and hated the fact he could read me so well.

Dana darted between Rory and me. "Hey, why don't you and I stop at one more store? Regan told me about some awesome chick on the East Side."

Regan was a mutual friend who owned a sex shop in Dallas. I'd designed sexy stripper clothes and lingerie for her when I was in college and law school.

I stared at Dana, furrowing my brows. I didn't want to wear crotch-less panties with my nipples showcased through teaser holes in my wedding dress when I walked down the aisle.

"She doesn't specialize in wedding shit, but her designs are amazing." Dana shrugged her shoulders. "It's worth a try." Sensing I needed distance, Dana grabbed my hand and pulled me further away from Rory.

"Hindley?" Rory's usual husky voice broke in a whisper.

I wanted to reassure him everything was all right, that three months from now we'd be joined in wedded bliss. But the vibration of the phone in my pocket stole my confidence.

Could Rory endure the inevitable pain with me? For me? Could I even ask him to?

I gazed at him for answers to my silent questions as one lone tear rolled down my face.

Rory moved to wipe the moisture from my cheek.

I didn't stop him. I needed to feel his touch, even if the connection was fleeting.

"Can we go to dinner tonight? Just the two of us?" He slid closer.

His scent enveloped me like a warm blanket. I needed time and Rory understood. He was willing to give me the space I needed. But for how long? Long enough for me to sort out my shit and make things right?

"She'll call you." Dana jerked on my hand and pulled me away from my fiancé, the man who'd had my heart for almost a year.

I stumbled as Dana dragged me down the sidewalk with her not-so-unusual display of strength.

"Please call me, Hindley." I heard him call out.

I glanced over my shoulder.

Rory's once bright blue eyes grew darker as he beseeched me.

He needed reassurance that I wouldn't run away for good. I nodded once. I would call him. I just didn't know if he'd ever want to see me again after I told him about the calls.

Was he strong enough to endure this battle with me, possibly for the rest of our lives?

Dana shoved me into the passenger seat and raced to her side then cranked the engine. As we drove away, I glanced back at Rory.

One hand was shoved deep in his jeans pocket and the other gripped the nape of his neck. He released his hold and gave me a single wave.

"Mind telling me what the fuck is going on?" Dana asked as she maneuvered through the busy streets.

I twisted around in my seat and let out a sigh. I hated scaring Rory, but I needed time to think.

"This." I held up my phone. The screen illuminated the familiar name along with his title.

Dana stopped at a red light and glanced at my phone. Her gaze darted from the screen to mine, her eyes growing wide. "Shit," she whispered.

"Yeah. Shit," I repeated.

～

To find out the conclusion to Rory and Hindley's love story, and the finale to the X-Treme Love series, purchase
Extreme Promise

Available now

JOIN MY PRIVATE FACEBOOK GROUP
THE MANIS MOB SQUAD

We support and enable those diagnosed with **MOB Disease (Mania of Books)** - a rare and debilitating disease that causes sufferers to become unable and/or unwilling to stop reading and obsessing over all things book related.

Are you a book-aholic? Do you have a One-Click addiction? Then come join this support group. We're all about fun in here, no judgment.

ALSO AVAILABLE BY KAY MANIS

X-Treme Love Series

Extreme Risk (Hindley and Rory)

Extreme Devotion (Hindley and Rory)

Extreme Sacrifice (Dana and Peter)

Extreme Trust (Dana and Peter)

Extreme Attraction (Geneva and Berk)

Extreme Courage (Geneva and Berk)

Extreme Promise (Hindley and Rory)

Extreme Gift: The New Arrival (Hindley and Rory)

Extreme Beginning: The Prequel (Caroline and Paul)

Baxter Bay

You Could Be Mine (Aiden and Olivia)

Sumner Brothers Series

Born to Be My Baby (Ben and Maggie)

Never Say Goodbye (Emmett and Elle)

Thank You for Loving Me (Max and Devlin)

With These Two Hands (Aaron and Kayleigh)

I'll Be There for You (Jake and Lina)

If That's What It Takes (Grant and Sophie)

Now and Forever (Max and Devlin)

Season of Love Short Story Series

Second Chance Heart

Dance with Me

Fall for Me

RESOURCES

Mental illness and postpartum depression/psychosis are very serious diseases that destroy thousands of lives and families every year. Going undiagnosed and untreated, the condition may be fatal. The devastation of suicide is endless, not only to the person suffering but for those who are left behind.

Mental illness knows no boundaries of race, religion, gender, or citizenship. Most of us either know someone who has dealt with mental illness, or we ourselves have dealt with it at some point in our lives.

I did not want to end this series, and this book in particular, without giving you a list of resources if you or someone you know is in crisis, whether victim or caregiver. Please do not isolate yourself. Reach out, no matter how hard it may seem. *There is hope.*

SUICIDE PREVENTION/HOTLINE
National Suicide Prevention Lifeline
www.suicidepreventionlifeline.org
1-800-273-TALK (8255)
1-800-SUICIDE (1-800-784-2433)
International Suicide Hotlines

www.suicide.org/international-suicide-hotlines.html

American Foundation for Suicide Prevention

www.afsp.org

Kristin Brooks Hope Center

www.hopeline.com/gethelpnow.html

1-800-442-HOPE (4673)

I'm Alive (Online Crisis Chat)

www.imalive.org

Suicide Prevention Resource Center

www.sprc.org

MENTAL ILLNESS

National Alliance on Mental Illness

www.nami.org

1-800-950-6264

National Institute of Mental Health

www.nimh.nih.gov

1-866-615-6464

POSTPARTUM DEPRESSION

PPD Moms

www.1800ppdmoms.org

1-800-PPD-MOMS (1-800-773-6667)

Postpartum Support International

www.postpartum.net

1-800-944-4773

DEPRESSION

Depression and Bipolar Support Alliance

www.dbsalliance.org

1-800-826-3632

Depression Connection

www.depressionconnection.org

1-817-810-9599
Anxiety and Depression Association of America
www.adaa.org

GRIEF AND LOSS

Open to Hope
www.opentohope.com
The Grief Recovery Method
www.griefrecoverymethod.com
1-800-334-7606
Grief.com
www.grief.com
Journey of Hearts
www.journeyofhearts.org

ACKNOWLEDGMENTS

I've said it before and I'll say it always—writing a book takes lots of help. I want to thank those people who have helped me make Geneva and Berk's story special.

Elizabeth Theeck, MSN, CRNP, my medical expert – You have been my go-to girl for everything medical in all of my books. Without your help, I could not have made Geneva and Berk's story as authentic as it should be. JP's arrival and survival is all thanks to you.

Connie Humphreys, MS, LSSP, LPC, my mental health expert – You're an amazing therapist, and I'm lucky to call you my sister-in-law *and* friend. Without your advice and feedback, Berk never could have made it back to the land of the living. Thank you for reading through his therapy sessions and making sure I got it right. To the real Dr. Elsher.

Julie Deaton, my proofer – Once again you stepped in at the last minute and saved the day. You're my hero, and I'm lucky to call you friend.

Jaime Conklin, my first "fan" – You're my muse. Thank you for reaching out to me after the release of *Extreme Risk*. You and your family will always be special to me. I'm sorry I had to kill you off. I like you much better alive, #deadjaime.

Billie Jo Humphreys, my mom – I lost you during the writing of this book, and for that I will always be sad. But I know you live on with Jaime and Alana. You will be in every book I write because of the creative gene you gave me. Hopefully, wherever you are, you're drinking a margarita, smoking a cigarette and reading my books. I hope you like them.

ABOUT KAY MANIS

Kay Manis is a funny chick who's sprinkled with a little crazy on top. Okay, let's be honest...there's ALOTTA crazy up there.

She writes books filled with passion, promise and purpose (with laughter and a few tears, but always an HEA).

She is a native Texan and lives with her family in Central Florida. When not reading or writing, you'll find Kay eating out with friends or napping with her favorite pillow (stolen from an Inn in Vermont—true story).

Please feel free to contact Kay at:
www.kaymanis.com